The Six Train to Wisconsin

To Friends of Betsi,
Enjoy !

The Six Train to Wisconsin

The Six Train to Wisconsin Series

xoxo,

KOURTNEY HEINTZ

Aurea Blue Press

THE SIX TRAIN TO WISCONSIN
The Six Train to Wisconsin Series Book 1
Trade Paperback Second Edition/September 2016
Aurea Blue Press

By Kourtney Heintz

Cover Design by Creative Paramita
Internal Design by Nick DeSimone
Author Photograph by Brett D. Helgren

Copyright © 2013 **Kourtney Heintz**
ISBN Paperback: **978-0-9891326-6-4**
ISBN Ebook: **978-0-9891326-0-2**

Printed in the United States of America

Dedication

To Dr. Fabien Bitan, for giving me back my life and proving that dreams can become actualities. This book and I are here because of you and your miracle disc replacement surgery.

CHAPTER 1

Oliver

Like any man, I loved my wife; but these 3 a.m. suicidal thoughts were killing me. Her thoughts seeped into my dreams and tugged me toward consciousness. Without opening my eyes to look at her side of the bed, I knew she was in the kitchen stirring her tea because the image filled my mind. The spoon clanged against the sides of the mug and the steam rose from the cup to tickle my nose.

I wasn't fully awake when the tsunami of her misery slammed into me. Images flooded my mind. Our lifeless shih-tzu puppy limp in the street, her grandmother's eyes dimmed with death, a six-year-old girl bruised and beaten into silence.

The blood pounded "Your fault, your fault, your fault" against my temple. Sorrow pinched my nostrils and grief crushed my trachea.

I sputtered against the onslaught, blindly lashing out at the darkness coalescing around me. *These are not my feelings, these are not my thoughts, this is not my pain, this is not me.* The mantra became a way to survive my wife's inadvertent attacks.

I kicked away the sheets, pushed myself upright, and pressed my

1

back against the cold certainty of the headboard's wrought iron bars. I gobbled up air. My jackrabbit pulse began to tortoise.

I imagined slabs of granite entombing me. Re-establishing the boundary of me. Creating a psychic shield from my wife. Her emotions had eviscerated my last chance at sleep. Why?

Because my wife was a suicidal telepath.

Lately, it had become my job, nah, my sworn duty, to anchor her sanity.

Wonder if old Mrs. Thompson next door felt it. Last time it got this bad, the entire building fell into a funk for a week. No one realized it was my wife's feelings broadcast over a special bandwidth that screwed with their heads.

She couldn't help it. Hell, I didn't know how she did it. Imagine standing in Times Square 24-7, then multiply the noise by 10,000. The thoughts and feelings of everyone within a half-mile radius beat around in her head all day, while she kept hers under wraps.

Her emotional attacks always came at night. They were a complicated calculus equation derived from emotional intimacy and physical proximity. Being her husband rendered me ground zero. She probably didn't even realize her feelings had poured into me and were trickling out to the neighbors. I couldn't be mad at her. Annoyed, yes, but not mad.

By the time I padded down the hall to the kitchen, she'd already whisked the Jacques Torres cocoa mix into the warmed milk—the one perk of a telepath. Maybe tonight wouldn't be so bad. She still heard my thoughts. Shit, not all of them. Please not all of them.

She looked up, plastering a smile on her tired face. Amusement lurked in her dark blue eyes. "Some of them. And I'm not gonna do that, so stop dreaming about it."

I laughed as I made my way to the side of the kitchen counter that jutted into our living room. I pulled out my stool and sat down. The kitchen light blazed above my wife as she measured a shot of Grand Marnier and poured it into my mug. Her trembling hands worried me.

2

The living room behind me remained blanketed in semi-darkness. No matter how late my wife was up, she didn't turn on the lights in the living room. She didn't venture in there. Crossing that threshold was tantamount to admitting she'd never fall back to sleep. And my wife preferred to pretend this was going to pass. That it was just a little summer storm. Not the blizzard of her existence.

She glided around the counter, her feet never straying from the sections of the hardwood floor lit by the kitchen. It was how she demarcated the dining area from the living room. She pushed the warm mug of hot chocolate into my hand and perched on the stool beside me. Her fiery red hair fell over her face as she blew into her teacup.

"Rough night?" I rested my palm against the granite countertop.

"The usual." Her voice lost its warmth.

"Work?"

She stared into her tea.

"One of your cases?"

Her voice quivered. "They're not cases, they're kids."

"What happened?"

She shook her head and hunched her shoulders. "Bad day."

It was her seventh bad day in a week. "Let's go back to California." I'd spent the entire year begging her to relocate. "Somewhere near Death Valley." Desolate enough to allow her mind to recover from the city's constant bombardment.

"No," she said.

"Once things calm down, you can do your work in a smaller city or a town." There were children in need all over the country.

"I'm not leaving Manhattan." Her fingers flexed around her mug. "I won't abandon them."

"You can't save them all."

She shook her head. "I'm just having a bad spell. It'll pass. This is our home."

It's where we'd started our adult life together. The place we returned

3

to after we got married. Leaving meant accepting defeat. Admitting that she wasn't the same person.

Sadness clipped my chin. On nights like these, sitting this close, the psychic shield she'd taught me to build was almost useless.

"Sorry," she mumbled. I reached out and she scooted away from me. "I can't protect you if you touch me."

"I can handle the depression." I dug into my memory of the first time she kissed me. Her fingernails tickled my forehead as she swept my hair back from my face. I couldn't stop staring into her eyes. They were darker than the night sky and warmer than a Wisconsin Indian summer. They reminded me of home. Her mouth tasted of powdered-sugar munchkins and creamy coffee.

I pulled her into my arms, let her hopelessness fill me, extracted some of her pain.

She tensed, but I didn't release her. We'd been through this before.

Minutes ticked by. Finally, she relaxed and whispered, "I miss munchkins."

I pressed my lips against her hair.

The next morning, I sipped my third cup of office coffee and wished I'd gotten more sleep. I bit into the powdered donut I grabbed from the cart in front of my building. Sugar and caffeine were the only things that kept me running lately. Sleep was a Rolex beyond my reach. Sometimes, I booked a conference room for a 20-minute snooze to remain functional. If a meeting lasted over 30 minutes, my boss, Mr. Gong, wanted to attend. Naps were the least negotiable item on his list of office infractions.

Unless of course you were Jameson, trained by me and promoted over me. He sat in the office beside Gong's. All that privacy didn't help him turn a report in on time. He took two-hour lunches. He was known to open a beer at his desk after 5 p.m.

I bet he never worried about his wife killing herself because of a five-alarm fire on the news. Shaneeka in front of me was good for a crazy story about her boyfriend, but she never had to hold him while he shook for hours after someone died within a 10-block radius.

They say people are only given what they can handle. That pain is a personal and private experience. They've never met my wife. She experienced everyone's emotions as her own. People telegraphed their most painful thoughts. Emotions, the rawest form of thought, lanced through her. Death reverberated inside her head like a continual scream over the din of ten thousand voices. She couldn't block it out. Emotional pain wore down her shield, but death shredded it.

What about happy people? They saved up all their joy for themselves. Selfish bastards.

In the cube adjacent to mine, Murray's voice dipped low. "I'm sorry, baby."

Only a hip-high partition separated us. I could reach over and yank away the phone he cradled to his ear.

Another late night out with the guys—poker night my ass. We all knew where he went with that wad of dollar bills. But he'd send roses, and his wife would forgive him again. Then I'd get to hear about the makeup sex.

In my emails, a meeting invite from Gong popped up. I didn't want to click ok and let him capture an hour of my afternoon, but his invites were never optional. The littlest Napoleon on Wall Street could only intimidate via email.

A text from Murray popped up on my screen. *Another Gongathon.*

Gong didn't allow us to talk at our cubes. The racket interfered with his concentration when he was shopping online in his office.

Get ready for a demotivational speaker, I typed.

Hello hump day.

Gong probably wanted to lecture us on how we had to focus and be more ambitious. If only he had a pint of my ambition. It was simple. I wanted to make life better for my wife. To take away the telepathy. But I couldn't.

Next best thing? I had a plan. A plan I'd carefully laid out while I sat in my cube, 3.3 miles from our apartment and 4.5 miles from her office. Way outside the perimeter of my wife's telepathy. The plan necessitated going places I never wanted to return to. To save my wife from her own best intentions.

I looked up from my computer as the new admin sashayed toward me. She paused when she caught my eye. Her lips curved into a kitten's saucer. "Is that a new tie?"

I glanced at it. "My wife bought it for me."

She leaned over my cubicle wall so that her breasts strained against the edge of her top. "It brings out the amber in your eyes."

"They're brown." She needed to stop flirting with me and put her boobs back in her shirt. Hell, buy a shirt. When she didn't leave, I added, "I have to get an email out."

"Stop by anytime." She sauntered away.

I didn't have time for distractions. This was my wife's life we were talking about here. The report due tomorrow, I didn't start writing it. I worked best under pressure—they'd never know how much.

CHAPTER 2

Oliver

It wasn't always like this. In the beginning, she saved me. Nine Novembers ago. I'd screwed up my midterms, caught my best friend in bed with my supposed girlfriend, and my father died making it impossible to get over what he'd done—all in a 12-hour period.

Those events forced me out of my dorm room and onto the paved pathways writhing across campus. But Friday night at 11 p.m. was prime time for people movement. I didn't want to see them. I didn't want them to see me. I swerved off the path and hugged the trees. Woodchips crunched beneath my sneakers until I got beyond the landscaping. Then my sneakers chewed up dirt and rocks.

Her betrayal itched like a mosquito bite, but his stung like a hornet attack. Tim hadn't just been my drinking buddy and my roommate. He'd been my best friend since freshman orientation. Now he was another person I thought I knew but didn't. That list was getting disturbingly long for the nineteen years I'd been on this planet.

I emerged from the trees and made my way down the hill. I skirted the pathways, barely avoiding another group of people. I kept my head down and plowed through the night with one destination in mind—the library. It was the only place I might find some quiet. Peace wasn't something I looked for anymore.

Movement propelled my mind to the next issue. My dad and I. We hadn't spoken much since I left his house last year. I found jobs to keep me on campus over breaks. If I went back to Butternut, I'd have to pretend he was the same person who raised me. Trying to bury the past, I didn't realize I'd bury him so soon. The image of him in a coffin sliced through my skin, exposing muscle and damaging nerves I thought were long dead.

I didn't run unless I was late for an exam or someone was chasing me. Tonight, I ran to the library. Inside the concrete and glass building, relief didn't come. The walls swelled toward me. The air tasted stale. The quiet rang in my ears. My feet took me to the back stairwell.

By the time I reached the fourth flight, the sound of my breathing echoed around me. If I stopped, I'd calculate the losses of this night. My thighs burned and my calves screamed, but I forced myself up the sixth flight. To that door marked *Do Not Open*. I shoved it away. Fresh air. Solitude. Time to find perspective.

My lungs begged for air. I stood there, sucking it down. My mind started calculating. I couldn't help it. I had to tally the balance sheet of my life. My liabilities were racking up. No Mom. No Dad. Not even a bad dad. No best friend. No girl to lose a few moments inside.

No ties to bind me to who I had been.

No anchors in the world.

I walked to the edge of the roof and looked down at the ground below. The tiny figures moving across the pavement could cause significant damage. If I let them. And I hadn't let them. Not since I left Butternut.

A thought flitted across my brain like a lone snowflake batted around in the wind. *A six-story drop could do a person in.* I took one, two, three steps backwards and sat down. I didn't want the end of me. Over a girl like her. Or a friend like him. Or even a father like mine.

8

I leaned back on my elbows and stared up at the night sky. The moon was still the moon. Tonight she was almost full.

I'll admit it. I let myself fall for the lore about college being the place where we form lifelong bonds. I wanted that college bond shit to be true. But it was all shit.

"Not always." A girl's voice resonated in the shadows.

"What the hell?" I scrambled to my feet.

She moved closer, copper hair and moonbright skin unfurling from the darkness. She was dressed in shoulder-to-toe black. "Who actually."

Then she smiled at me with the most perfect…

"Dick-sucking lips?" she said.

Shit. How'd she do that?

She rolled her eyes. "What brought you up here?"

"The lip thing, how'd you know?" I stuffed my hands in my pockets.

"I get it a lot," she tossed back at me.

She was creepy. Hot but creepy.

"Ditto," she said.

"What?" I asked the total stranger who had trespassed on my private time.

Her voice softened like butter in the sun. "You don't really want to be alone."

"Which is why I came to the library rooftop. I expected a raging kegger."

"Being alone and wanting to be alone aren't the same thing."

"Are we talking about you or me?"

She shrugged. "Maybe both."

"I just wanted…"

"Solitude, perspective, and fresh air." She ticked the items off on her fingers.

Somehow the crazy girl had read my thoughts. I was so out of here.

Then she smiled, the kind of smile that reached all the way to her eyes, and offered, "Millie and Al's?"

9

I fought the urge to smile back. I should be mourning my dad and drinking my way past Tim's betrayal. Not chatting up some chick who might be a mind reader. "I came here to clear my head."

She sighed. "I'll tell you how I do it, if you tell me what happened. Deal?"

"Are you seriously asking me out for coffee right now?"

"Dinner. And dessert. Your treat." Her stomach growled. "Make that two desserts."

Something told me there was steel in the tips of her black Doc Martins.

"There's only one way to find out." She threw the words over her shoulder as she headed toward the stairs.

She had a valid point, so I followed her. Best decision of my life.

CHAPTER 3

Kai

Everyone has daily rituals. Mine are a little different.

Before I left the apartment, I set my iPod to repeat the Great Performances from Leonard Bernstein and the NY Phil. No words or voices. Just instruments producing sounds that distracted and soothed. Sounds I surrendered to in order to survive my commute.

I closed my eyes. Breathed in for a count of four, held it for seven, and exhaled for eight. I repeated this 4-7-8 breathing until I felt lightheaded. The closest I came to calm lately. I pictured quartz crystals breaking free of a chandelier and dancing around me. They sparkled and dispersed light in all directions. Pairing up to waltz around me until they encased me in a crystal Fabergé egg. My shield in place, I headed for the subway.

As soon as I got inside the subway car, bodies pressed in on me from all sides, radiating thoughts and emotions. I took a shallow breath of air. Air that I shared with hundreds of people packed into one tiny train car. Air that carried the stench of a pedophile, the decay of insanity, and the moldiness of desperation.

I couldn't separate the individual trains of thought. Couldn't keep them on tracks destined away from me.

Sweat dripped into my eyes. I wiped the back of my hand across my face and took a 4-7-8 breath. I buried my thoughts in the music. Nothing but the instruments and me.

The train spasmed and the brakes cried out. Fear rippled through everyone around me and slammed into my shield. A tiny fissure appeared in my crystal egg. I breathed my 4-7-8s all the way to my stop.

Emerging from the subway at City Hall Park, I greeted the Brooklyn Bridge on my left and gave an imaginary high-five to the ginkgo trees on my right. They had become constants in my existence. Milestones to my day.

Music blared in my ears, muffling the street noise around me. I still heard the din of people's thoughts. Still felt the puffs of emotion that pushed through the tiniest crack in my crystal shield. I would hold everything at bay until the bay became a tsunami.

While I waited for the walk signal, my eyes trailed up to the double turrets of a former newspaper building. To be above it all. They couldn't build a tall enough building for me.

A few blocks later, the Children's Administrative Services building loomed. I showed my badge and made my way to the 4th floor. The outer walls housed offices, and cubicles crowded the middle of the room. Mine was toward the back.

I sat down at my desk and tugged out my headphones. Dropped my purse under my desk. Pressed my fingers to the picture of Grandma, my brother Caleb, and me in her backyard. Caleb sprawled across the rock. He was so confident, even at 11. I cuddled into Grandma.

I smiled at the photo of my husband and me at Torrey Pines Beach. He hated his legs in board shorts, but they reminded me of a gazelle— full of graceful movement and sweet strength.

Daily rituals to remind me why I was still here.

With enough concentration, sometimes I lost myself in my work. Not blocking out the telepathy, but existing around it. Co-workers piled into the building. The massive offices around me awakened. Hailstones of thought clinked against my crystal egg, chipping away at my shield.

Just finish this task. I bargained with myself to make it a little longer. To not buckle under. Each task took more time, more concentration, more rechecking. My focus wavered. My shield warped under the strain. Thinking became a monumental undertaking.

Laura sped past my cube and headed toward the ladies' room. Ribbons of purple trailed behind her. Guilt that only I could see. No one heard her screaming inside her mind. She'd just gotten the call. One less case to work. Not because the child was out of danger, but because the danger got the child.

Her pain lanced through my shield. It was an eclipsing realization: *Nothing I do matters.* That kind of helplessness washes over us. But hers deluged her mind, threatening to carry me along with her.

Sara. Sara. Sara, she cried. *Dead on her 12th birthday. Couldn't get away from her parents' drugs. Didn't want to become her mother. Sliced her arms from wrists to elbow and bled out instead.*

Guilt found the fissure in my shield. It licked and bit and pressed its way through the crack and tore a fist-sized hole in my shield.

I tried to take a deep breath, but the air refused to cooperate. It wouldn't stay in my lungs. It wanted to escape me. I should go to her, but I'd only make it worse. Two mortally wounded people can't heal each other.

I reached for the phone, praying my boss Angela would be there. I dialed her extension. "Laura, bathroom, code 4."

"I'm on it." Angela hung up.

Angela was the only one who could make Laura believe it would get better. Until then, I had to hold it together. Thousands of voices

13

speaking in my head. All about themselves. Their pain. Their needs. Their frustrations. My fingers curled around my pen. I barely saw the paper. I had to write the words. The ones they were speaking to me. Some in languages I didn't know. Impossible to isolate a thought. I wrote ten thousand thoughts at once. Words upon words upon words. The pad was black by the time Laura emerged from the bathroom.

The thin file at the bottom of my stack shouldn't have caught my attention. She wasn't due for a home visit. She wasn't even on my schedule for this week. But something made me open Jenny's file again. My failure to save her glared back at me in perfect black serif font.

I couldn't prove neglect. I couldn't prove abuse. I couldn't prove what he was. A father who preyed on his daughter. I shuddered. My anonymous tips to the police never brought her any justice. He was too clever. She was too afraid.

I'd searched for a living relative who might intercede. Someone with the power to pull her away from him. There was no one.

Sometimes I hated my job.

I tried to put her file aside and work on the cases that required my attention today. But her thoughts from my last visit filled my head. She sat with her hair tied up in a blue ribbon. She looked at her hands. Never into my eyes.

I miss Mama. She braided my hair. She kept me safe. Papa does bad things. Things that hurt me inside. He says he has to. Because Mama died.

I dropped my pen. The blood beat against my temple. No matter how many times I tried to get her to talk, she wouldn't. She was more afraid of being alone than of being with him.

I stared down at my case file on Zach. He needed my help too. But Jenny. Something about Jenny wouldn't let me go. The thudding in my temple grew louder. I tried to massage it away.

"Hey." Angela stood beside my cubicle. She leaned in. "Thanks for the tip on Laura."

"I figured she needed you."

"How about you?"

I tightened my cheeks and tugged a smile from my lips. "I'm pretty okay."

"Migraine?" she asked.

I nodded. Debilitating migraines were how I rationalized my bad days. Out-of-control telepathy wasn't something a doctor could diagnose.

"You got in before me," she said.

"How's Laura doing?"

Angela shrugged. "I told her to go home. Take a personal day or two."

"It's hard."

"Harder than a doctor losing a patient. We invest so much time in these kids. We can't keep that emotional distance doctors have mastered."

"I know." Jenny still weighed on my mind. She lived six blocks from my apartment. I could see her building from my living room window.

"You look tired. Why don't you cut out a little early?"

I rubbed my temple. Pain pulsed against my fingertips. Not a medical migraine, but an emotional one. "I'll take some files home with me."

"Try to get some rest." She patted my arm.

As soon as I exited the subway car on Bleeker Street, I heard it inside my mind. A death scream. The kind someone makes when death is moments away. It obliterated my shield. Tens of thousands of voices tumbled into my mind. Above them all, she wailed for help that wouldn't come in time. I tripped and caught myself against a wall.

An aneurism of fear burst in my brain. Her fear. Her pain. Her panic. I tried to focus on it. Figure out where it came from. But without my shield, I couldn't trace her location. I could only experience her last moments with her.

Something tightened around her throat. She begged for him to stop. For it to stop. He was too big. Too strong. Too powerful.

Daddy, stop.

Jenny. Not Jenny. Please not Jenny.

I tried to move faster but my body wouldn't listen to me. I dragged myself toward Avenue C and Jenny.

Her scream cut off. The echo reverberated in my head, but the original scream died. I was only three blocks away when death came for her. I should have pulled away from her mind. I should have let her go. I should have done so many things differently.

CHAPTER 4

Kai

Darkness blinded me. No perception. No depth. No light to cast shadows. Just the oblivion of blackness. Dampness clung to my skin. My teeth chattered. Dank underbelly of the earth smells infiltrated my nose. I remembered this place. I hated this place. I feared what came after this place.

"Jenny, I'm so sorry," I said.

"He hurt me," she whispered. Brightness coalesced around her, giving her form. Her dark hair hung around her too pale face. The bruises around her neck faded as she spoke. "Where are we?"

How could I tell her? "You're going to go be with your mommy now."

Her eyes brightened. For the first time, I saw a spark of hope there. "Really?"

"She's on the other side of that light," I said.

"Is Daddy going to be in trouble?" Her brows twisted up in fear.

"He can't hurt you any more. You're safe."

"Are you an angel?" she whispered. "Am I in trouble for lying?"

I shook my head. "You didn't do anything wrong. He scared you

17

into lying. He hurt you."

"Can you feel the light?" She raised her right hand, touched it and smiled.

It stung my skin. "It's meant for you."

She edged toward it. The brightness enveloped her. The blackness closed in on me.

I woke up on the sidewalk to a crowd of people hovering over me, hissing and coiling around me.

"Drugs. It must be drugs."

"Someone hit her?"

"No, she's got her purse."

"Could she have slipped?"

"Drunk at this time of day. Really, some people."

My tongue was a popsicle stick—flat and inflexible. My head throbbed, but I tried to sit up. I must have fainted. I always did if I didn't let go before someone died. I lost consciousness and followed them. If I let them go, I woke up. If not, well, I couldn't think about that right now.

Someone pushed a bottle of soda into my hands. It slid through my grasp and bounced on the sidewalk.

"Could it be a seizure?" a hushed voice asked.

A man picked up the bottle. He knelt in front of me and opened it. "Should we call an ambulance?" He had teddy bear eyes.

"No. It's nothing. I skipped a meal today." Blessed numbness. Even my telepathy was off-line. It was the calm before the cyclone. "I need to get home."

"Give the girl room." Mrs. Thompson's voice reached me before she did. Her cart full of shopping bags plowed through the crowd and stopped in front of me. "What happened, dear?"

"You know her?" Teddy Bear Eyes asked.

"Lived next door to her for four years." Mrs. Thompson gestured at him. "Help her up."

The crowd sighed and dispersed.

Once I was on my feet, she told Teddy Bear Eyes, "We live three blocks from here. Keep her upright and we'll get her home."

"I'm fine." I stumbled and he caught me.

"My bones are too brittle to support anyone. Even a wisp of a girl like you," she said.

"I'm sorry," I said to him.

"Happy to help two damsels in distress." He smiled like this wasn't an annoyance to his afternoon.

Mrs. Thompson snickered. "I haven't been a damsel in decades."

My mind jumped through the moments. Mrs. Thompson griped about how girls don't eat enough. His strong arm encircled my waist. The entrance to our building. My apartment door. Mrs. Thompson fished my keys out of my purse. Someone turned on the living room light. I sank into the couch. A cup of juice and a bagel sat in front of me.

And then I was alone.

I didn't have much time. I gulped the juice and stumbled to the kitchen. Pulled out my pay-as-you-go phone and called the police.

"A little girl was screaming and gagging. Then she went silent. At 659 East 5th Street. It was coming from Apartment 407. I knocked on the door, but no one answered. I'm afraid something really bad happened." I hung up and turned the phone off.

I slumped against the counter and stared into the living room. I hated that room. It reminded me how close Jenny was and how little I could do for her.

Did for her.

I flicked off the lights and walked past the furniture and toward the windows to watch for the police cruiser. The siren echoed in my mind, slashing through the numbness. The rumbling inside my head came moments before my telepathy returned. I didn't try to raise my

19

shield. I witnessed the aftermath of her death as I'd witnessed the brevity of her life. Never close enough to make a difference.

Like a tidal wave breaking on land, thousands of thoughts broke against me. Ten thousand emotions assaulted me.

Repulsion. Rage. Regret. They came for me.

Burnt sugar stung my nose. Salted caramel choked me.

My world disintegrated.

CHAPTER 5

Oliver

My boss trapped me in one of his two-hour meetings. A trader had gone all cowboy on us, exceeding his trading limits and restrictions. Maybe the multi-million dollar bonus went to his head. More likely he'd always had a Zeus complex. The trader wasn't in the meeting. Neither was the desk supervisor. We never pulled them off the desk until after trading hours and only with their consent.

There was just so much wild-west mentality any east coast financial institution could contain. According to my audit, his actions put us over the limit. He didn't even bother hiding what he'd done, making it easy for me to hand him over to my boss.

Unfortunately, Gong couldn't let it be that simple. He made me lay out all the evidence and piece it together for him in excruciating detail. Me educating my boss on his job.

Gong asked again, "Are you sure this isn't some sort of misunderstanding?" His eyes begged me to be more like Jameson.

He needed it to be a mistake. Because if I was right, he'd have to do some work. I said the three words he despised: "Potential rogue trader."

His lips thinned to a sheet of paper. "That's a serious accusation. Document it as trading above limits."

"I knew you'd know what to do." Or call it something less offensive and document it into oblivion.

He leaned back in his chair. "Why didn't you bring Jameson in on this one?"

"I figured the less people who knew about it, the better. You always said to bring the big things to you."

He rubbed his lips. "Next time punt it to Jameson. Otherwise you might be seen as going over his head."

I swallowed my "God Forbid" and nodded.

Meeting adjourned.

Two more hours of my life wasted, I sat down in my cube for some email and web surfing—my version of a smoke break. I never made it to YouTube. When Explorer opened up, I automatically scanned the local news for car crashes and suicides. The kind of things that set off my wife. That was when I read about a six-year-old being choked to death by her father. The article mentioned sexual abuse. Didn't say what. No one says what when a kid is involved. Too horrific to contemplate.

They found the body in the East Village. Fifth Street between Avenue B and C. Six blocks from my apartment. The location set off a cacophony of firetrucks and ambulances and police cruisers inside my head.

I didn't log out or grab my coat in my rush to get to my wife. I tripped over my chair and kicked it aside.

Murray asked, "Everything okay?"

"I have to go." I sprinted through the glass security doors to the elevator banks.

The elevator ride was a series of thumb jabs to the door close button. I zigzagged through the lobby and broke into a run on the sidewalk. One block from the office, the sky opened up, compounding the chaos of rush hour.

I plunged into the heart of it, jostling pedestrians, dodging cyclists, darting between cars toward the Downtown 6 at 51st Street. Horns blared and bicycle tires screeched across slick pavement. A herd of people exited up the subway stairs. Momentum and adrenaline were on my side. Swears trailed my downward movement as I forced my way through the crowd and into the station.

The rain had just started, but the subways already had delays. Three layers of people crowded the platform. I excused my way down the platform, searching for a space on the yellow line, the one that warned about proximity to the tracks but guaranteed me a spot on the next train.

Eight minutes passed before the train showed up. I shoved my way into the car. No need to hold on. There was nowhere to fall in the crush of bodies.

At Grand Central, I held my own against the mass exodus that threatened to sweep me out onto the platform. When the doors opened at Union Square, I ignored the dirty looks and the pointed pushing as I maintained my position near the door, forcing everyone to move around me.

I had two more stops to Bleeker. I had to be first off when we got there. I had to make it to my wife in time.

CHAPTER 6

Oliver

I opened the apartment door, and grief slammed into my gut. I stumbled toward the light switch.

"Don't," my wife croaked from the corner of our living room.

Dusk painted the room in shadows of gray, punctuated by fading daylight and dawning streetlights. She'd wedged herself between the window and the bookcase. I edged toward her huddled figure.

"Stop." Aftershocks rocked her voice.

I kept inching toward her like I would any wounded animal— without fear or aggression.

She clutched a pill bottle in her left hand.

Sweat burst out across my forehead. I thought I'd flushed them all last time. I wiped my face on my sleeve. The cap was still on them. She hadn't done any harm yet. "Give me the pills."

She pressed the bottle to her breastbone.

Why didn't I bring my cell to the meeting? "Sweetie, what happened?"

Mascara-coated tears spilled down her cheeks. The slacks and blouse she wore meant she'd gone to work today. Maybe it wasn't the kid I read about.

"Work?" I asked.

A wail tore through her.

She hadn't been this bad in months. Not since the night I pried the razor blade from her grip. It clattered against the tiles of our bathroom floor. She melted into the tub.

Tonight, spasms jerked her body. She curled into herself.

This was going to hurt. I hoped for more of an oven burn and not a knife wound. "Can you show me?"

I fell forward onto the hardwood floor as images forced themselves into my consciousness. Memories that weren't mine. Jenny in a conference room at the Administration for Children's Services. Jenny's thin file lay on the table. The interviews where Jenny never spoke a word. But my wife saw it all. Jenny's father liked to hurt her. He made her do things. Things that made her feel bad. He liked to make her scream. He always did it until she screamed.

My wife spent months trying to build a case against him. But there wasn't enough evidence. The original accusation was recanted. Every time she did a home visit, he played the doting father. But he thought about what he was going to do to Jenny later. My wife saw it all. And she was absolutely powerless to stop him.

"My fault," she whispered.

"You did everything you could."

"Not enough." Bitterness twisted her face.

I reached for her and she shrieked. Touching didn't just transfer emotions when she was this far gone. I risked becoming as suicidal as she was.

I didn't care what happened to me as long as I saved her.

"My fault. All my fault." She rocked in place.

Shock had set in. I had to break through her misery, even if it was only for a second.

It wasn't about one memory. No. This kind of pain required the sum total of us. From the first rooftop meeting to our wedding. The memories cascaded through my mind. Best friend, lover, wife. Home. She was all of these to me.

I gathered her into my arms and let her depression swarm me, buzzing in my ears and stinging the lining of my heart.

I couldn't chant my way out of this suffering. I sunk deeper under its influence the way I'd let Vicodin take me away from the agony of a broken arm. Her pain depressed my breathing, floated my brain, pixilated my vision, and dismembered my sense of self.

I latched on to one image. The look of blissed-out sugar high on my wife's face as she devoured slices of lemon meringue pie and chocolate cake on our first date.

My lungs found a pocket of air. My head weighed 10 pounds again. My vision crystallized. I emerged inside a memory.

We stood together on a circle of red dust and pebbles. From Dante's View, Badwater Basin stretched out below for miles. It looked like marshmallows melted and swirled over the land below. Straight out of some crazy sci-fi landscape. Except it was sunset in Death Valley, California. We'd tricked her younger sister Naomi into coming along. She loved being the only member of the wedding party. I'd corralled a retired judge into officiating and his wife into witnessing. We had no guests.

My bride wore white. Sort of. If you counted my white tank, which she paired with jeans. She wrapped the blue-green silk scarf I gave her for her birthday around her neck and threw on her bright blue Nikes. The wind whipped her hair around her face like a California wildfire. She kept tucking it behind her ears, but it refused to stay there. She'd never looked more beautiful to me.

In our living room, she sighed in my arms. Such a tiny sound—I thought I'd imagined it.

I mentally recited every vow she made to me. "I promise not to laugh when you order your frou frou pineapple salad and not to tell anyone who really fixes things around the apartment." She winked.

I wiped my sweaty palms on my jeans.

Her eyes looked right into mine. No trace of fear. No doubt as she said, "I will love you until my last breath. Take your side no matter how wrong you are. Be there when you are ready to talk about your past. Celebrate each and every holiday, birthday, and anniversary with you."

When it came time to say my vows, the wind ripped the paper out of my hands and threw it off the summit. I didn't know how to continue.

But she did. She took my hands in hers and smiled like we shared the best secret in the world.

Back in our dark apartment, she burrowed deeper into my arms. I slid my fingers around the neck of the pill bottle, tugged it from her grasp, and laid it down beside us.

I returned to the memory. Gripping her hands, I said, "I promise to always wash my feet after a long summer day. I promise to not mention any weight gain and to hold your hair when you throw up."

Then I got to the serious stuff. "I promise to rebuild our life in New York. I'll stand beside you against the world. I will be there to catch you every time you fall."

I planned to keep that promise until my dying day.

CHAPTER 7

Kai

G rief pinned me to the bed. The sun crept through the blinds. Another day snuck into being without a care for what had been lost yesterday. The world continued as if nothing were amiss.

Inside my mind, Jenny's death scream still echoed. Reverberating off the walls of who I was and ripping through who I wanted to be. Thoughts roared in my head. All the people in our building. All the people in the surrounding buildings. All the people in the nearby subway. They were starting a new day. I closed my eyes and sighed against the avalanche of eventuality.

My husband whispered in my ear, "Please, come have some breakfast." He knelt in front of me. His coffee bean brown hair fell across his forehead. His eyes were sweeter than maple syrup. "You have to eat."

I didn't want to be the cause of his dark circles. I never wanted to suck him into my darkness. I shut my eyes and tried to find my way out of this world and back to the oblivion of dreams.

He kissed my forehead. "Sleep. I'll be here."

The blinds shushed and crackled up to let the day strike me.

"It's past three. We need to get some food in you," he said.

I rolled away from his words and back toward sleep, needing to forget myself for a little bit longer.

The mattress sank beside me. He tugged me toward him. "You have to get out of this bed."

"I never should have married you," I whispered.

He scooped me up, carried me to the bathroom, and sat me on the counter. His fingers worked the buttons on my blouse and tugged my arm free of the sleeve. After he undressed me, he put me in the tub.

I didn't care. No matter how much soap he used, Jenny's blood bathed my hands. I deserved this pain. This agony. For what I'd let happen to her.

The shower spritzed my face. I sputtered and lashed out.

"That's my girl," he said.

"Stop it," I panted.

"You stink and you need a bath," he said.

"Leave me alone."

"I will not let you go all Gollum on me. You aren't pulling away from me."

Tears crowded my throat. "I can't. I can't. I can't."

"You have to," he said.

I curled into myself and cried. For Jenny. For him. For me.

He let me have my sorrow. Then he washed me, dried me, dressed me and put me back to bed. I slept until darkness shadowed the city. To appease him, I sat up and ate crackers and swallowed some orange juice. I laid back down and surrendered to my exhaustion.

He slid into bed beside me. He wrapped his body around mine. His lips kept promising, "You'll be alright."

Eventually. But right now, I had to feel my way through the loss. Tomorrow, tomorrow, I'd pull myself back from the edge.

CHAPTER 8

Oliver

My wife was so far into the abyss, she didn't realize she'd passed the edge weeks ago. On the subway ride home, I imagined slabs of granite surrounding me. Added a huge slab below and another above me, encasing me in granite. No doors. No windows. No entrance. No exit. It was the only way to shield my thoughts from my wife.

She'd expect me to have my shield up. She'd expect me to be careful with her after what happened two nights ago. She'd expect me to protect her. And I would.

Maintaining this kind of focus wasn't easy. But I only needed to keep it up a couple hours. Just 180 minutes at most. And I could do that for her.

When I opened the apartment door, a romantic table for two greeted me. She had cleared away all the stuff we piled on our dining room table and transformed it from office area to intimate table for two in our living room. She even dug up candlestick holders. Our plates were filled with the chicken parmigiana and spaghetti she pretended to make but actually ordered from the Italian place three blocks away.

She darted out of the kitchen and kissed me. Not a light brushing of the lips, but a soft and powerful pressing of herself into me. I dropped my bag on the floor and followed her to the table.

I didn't know how she managed to put on this display of okayness, but no amount of makeup could hide the shadows in her eyes. Her soul sunk under the enormity of what she'd lost. I wouldn't let her go under.

Her hands shook as she filled my wine glass.

"This looks terrific," I said. She'd even remembered the cheese-covered garlic bread I loved. "Do we have any Parmesan?"

"How could I forget?" She went into the kitchen.

Granite all around me. Nothing could get through. Time to activate my plan. I stood up, blocking her view of the table. While she searched the fridge, I poured powdered pills into her wine glass, topped it off, and swirled it around until all the white dissolved into red.

"Not too much for me." She came back to the table and handed me the cheese.

I shook it over my pasta. "How are you feeling today?"

She stole a sip of wine. "Better."

"Thanks for all this." I gestured at the table.

The words rushed out of her mouth. "I'm really sorry about how I was."

"You scared me."

She pushed the food around on her plate. "I'm sorry."

I reached over and laced my fingers through hers. "I can't lose you."

Her lips tipped up. "You won't."

I wanted to believe her. But hope is a tricky thing. Too much and you don't see the catastrophe coming. Too little and you surrender to the inevitability.

After dinner, she cleared the plates. "I know what you're doing."

"What?" I stared down at the lemon-scented bubbles pooling in the sink. Dunked the sponge in the warm water until it became soft and bloated. Granite. Granite. Granite.

I glanced into the living room as she rounded the table. Her hip banged into the chair, nearly tipping it over. She didn't seem to notice as she stumbled toward the kitchen. It was working. Twenty more minutes was all I needed.

"You can't fix me." She slurred her "x" into a "sh."

"Who's trying?" My voice rose. The wine played with my concentration. My granite walls slithered away. I had to think puppy dogs and balloons, not about what I planned to do. No. Focus on clowns and circuses.

She laughed. "Seriously? You're going soft."

Machine guns and *Platoon*. Men being men. Blowing shit up.

"Not gonna work." She practically sang the words to me.

If she knew what I did, she'd....

"Think you were a wonderful husband." She left the empty wine glasses on the table to wiggle in between the counter and me. I let the plate slip back into the soapy water. Her lips tasted like cherries.

She looked up at me with her serious face. "I'm not leaving New York."

I needed to get her far away from everyone. Somewhere quiet and peaceful with lots of open space. The familiar white farmhouse flashed through my mind.

"A farm in the woods? We'll go crazy there." Her cheeks pinked up from the wine and medication.

Shit. I'd let my mind think about the one thing I never thought about around her—the plan. "We're going crazy here. New York is the worst place for a telepath."

She refused to see what it was doing to her. To us.

"Okay. We move to the country and what do we do? Shoot anyone that tries to get within half a mile of me?" Her laugh tasted like the perfect Pinot Noir. Creamy with a hint of cardamom.

"Better than losing you." A year of arguing hadn't helped. The depressions lengthened and deepened from crevasses to Grand Canyon. Pushed her closer to taking her own life. She still didn't get it. I needed her. Screw New York. Screw work. Screw everyone.

"I need you to be happy and farm living ain't gonna cut it. Face it, you're a city boy." Her fingers twined in the hair at the back of my neck.

"But you'd have time to write like you used to." And we can live a simple life together.

"We always promised our life would be remarkable and worth living." She swayed slightly.

"Key word: LIVING. You're barely surviving here."

"I don't want to go." She added six *O*s to *go*.

"You don't have a choice. I always repay my debts."

She lost her balance and clutched at my arm. "What did you do to me?" Her pupils had dilated.

"Muscle relaxants in your wine. You'll be out for a while." Long enough to get her far away from New York.

"You're so dead," she promised before she collapsed into my arms.

"But you won't be," I whispered into her hair.

CHAPTER 9

Kai

Whenever life got too big or too much, I hid inside my memories. Burrowing into the past, returning to the places of my childhood, conjuring up the spaces where I once fit. Tonight, I stood below the Ocean Beach Pier among my tidal pools. On the cratered, lava-colored rocks rounded by the sea. Bright green slipperiness coated them. My bare feet curved around the rocks, toes gripping where they could as I made my way to the nearest tidal pool. I knelt down and peered into the clear water, glimpsing a secret world that could only be visited at low tide. Under the water's surface lived sea anemones, tiny crabs, and a sea star. Things whose names I'd forgotten cluttered the bottom of the pool.

I shouldn't intrude, but I couldn't help it. I slid my finger into the cool water and gently prodded the sea anemone's center. It curled in on itself, changing shape to survive.

I giggled and looked over my shoulder, certain my older brother Caleb would be there. He'd been a dreamwalker as long as I'd been a telepath. He usually wandered into my dreams, especially the beach ones. He seemed to have a sixth sense for them. Or maybe he influenced me to have them. Either way, it had become our favorite place to meet.

But he wasn't there on the sand. He wasn't in the water. No one was.

The wind threw strands of hair across my face. Clouds scattered over the sky. Dulling the colors in the tidal pool.

"Caleb?" I called out.

His voice warbled back, sounds without meaning.

Maybe I needed to concentrate more. I stared into the tidal pool. Remembered all the hours we spent together here. How his tanned fingers would reach in and pick up a crab so I could touch it. I willed him to join me. To enter my dream like he had ten thousand times before. But he didn't appear.

My head felt like an overripe peach. Fuzzy, swollen, and about to burst. I couldn't keep it upright. I had to lay it down on the rocks. Remnants of wet sand scraped over my cheek. When I looked into the tidal pool from this angle, I swear I saw my brother's face emerging from the water.

"Can you hear me?" I raised my head. The water flattened back to water. I pushed myself to my knees. My palms slid over the slick rocks as I crawled closer to the tidal pool.

Gazing into it, I whispered, "I need you."

CHAPTER 10

Oliver

My headlights illuminated the sign, *Welcome to Ohio*. Goodbye Pennsylvania. The odometer clocked another mile. Another mile closer to the hometown I'd abandoned a decade ago. Swampy palms suctioned to the steering wheel. Ten years had to be enough time to relegate what happened to the recesses of everyone's minds. Well, most everyone.

My wife stirred beside me, hands fumbling for something in her dream. She should have been out a couple more hours. I wasn't ready to face her. Chicken shit? Nah, still preparing what I'd say. She mumbled something. I kept my eyes trained on the road, hoping she'd settle back to sleep.

She'd be pissed, especially when she realized I'd handcuffed her to the door. Purely a preventative measure. The first chance she got, she'd run. Christ, I'd handcuffed my wife to the car door for her own good. Never thought I'd be the kind of guy who said that.

Maybe she'd wake up and come to her senses. Maybe she'd see this was the only way. Maybe monkeys would fly out of my ass. If she came around, it wasn't going to be for a long time. Then we could use the handcuffs for something else. Right, like she'd ever let me touch her again. I'd make that sacrifice to keep her alive. Eventually, she'd understand.

Too late to turn back now. Already emailed my resignation to my boss and bcc'ed the cubemates. I'd miss Murray's jokes. The moving company should be packing up the apartment around eight this morning. We still had six months on the lease. I'd paid next month in full, and our landlord was thrilled to jack up the rent for the next tenant.

The hardest part? Crafting my wife's resignation letter. She loved that damned job more than herself. Didn't matter that for every kid she saved, five were lost. She kept trying to even the score.

When she woke up, I'd ease her into the transition with increments of the truth. Tell her it was a leave of absence. She needed this. Hell, we needed this. We'd be within 15 miles of the Turtle Flambeau Flowage, a water lover's paradise perfect for hiking and kayaking. She liked water, well, the East River, anyway. We'd finally have a house. Space we'd only imagined in our 600-square-foot apartment. Plenty of room for a study. She kept saying one day she'd get back to her writing. One day was finally arriving. We'd have time to think and talk, do all those things we never got around to in the city. She'd come around.

I dreamed big on that long ride to distract myself from what I would face when she woke up.

CHAPTER 11

Kai

I would have waited forever to see Caleb, but time moves differently in dreams. The tides shifted, forcing me off the rocks and back to the shore. As soon as my toes touched the sand, the beach disappeared. My consciousness returned to my body before I was fully awake. None of my senses worked. I figured I was in bed until my eyelids opened. Darkness lit by the dashboard of my husband's car.

"What the hell is going on?" I asked.

"We left New York." His gaze didn't stray from the road. "We're two hours into Ohio."

I tried to shift position, but my wrist was tethered to the door. I rattled the cuffs against the door. "What's this?"

"For your protection."

"I am not up for a round of naughty girl and horny cop. Take them off."

"It's only for a little while."

"Now."

"No," he said.

I tried to remember what had happened. Dinner. Dishwashing. Then my memories became plush, and I sank away from everything. "Did you drug me?"

"It was the only way," he said.

"To kidnap me?" I asked.

"To protect you."

"You're insane."

His voice was softer than a stingray's skin. "Just desperate and afraid."

I imagined my crystal egg shield. I hadn't been able to create a window in it for two years. I missed that kind of control. The ability to listen without being overwhelmed, to separate each stream of thought. Instead, I found a place where a chunk was ready to give way. I pushed on the broken area and the piece fell away. I peered out at him. He'd erected a granite tower around himself. No doors. No windows. No way inside. "Where are you taking me?"

"Somewhere safe," he said.

"I have kids depending on me. Do you understand what will happen to them?"

"Angela will take care of them," he said, "during your leave of absence."

"I won't do it."

"Angela helped me file the paperwork," he said.

"I didn't sign anything." I grasped at the details.

"I did."

He'd forged my signature. "You can't do this."

His eyes met mine for the briefest of seconds. They were crystallized amber. "I already did."

I blinked. My husband was kidnapping me. And he acted like it was for my own good. "You can't do this to me." My mouth caught up to my brain and unleashed a litany of swears on him. He blared the radio to drown out my cussing. Half an hour later, the rockets of profanity gave way to sparklers of mumbling.

He lowered the volume. "Ready to talk?"

"I have to pee," I said.

"Right."

"Someone drugged me for seven hours. Guess what? My bladder's full and I gotta unload. NOW." He didn't respond, so I added, "I'd hate to ruin your leather seats."

"They're beige." Horror flooded his voice.

I couldn't make out much along the highway. "There have to be a few 24-hour rest stops."

"Like I'd trust you there." He got off at the next exit, pulled to the side of the road and parked the car.

"You want me to pee in the woods?"

"Not at this time of night."

"So?" I asked.

"No one's around. Pee beside the car."

"You're kidding, right?"

"You've done worse." He levitated his eyebrow, daring me to refute it.

"Asshole."

"Be nice or no TP." He grabbed a roll of Charmin Ultra Soft from the back seat.

As soon as he unlocked those handcuffs, I was gone. Didn't care if I had no cell phone, no purse, no money. No one was dictating my life to me. Not even my husband.

He pulled another set of handcuffs from his pocket and handcuffed himself to me. "No escaping tonight."

"Screw you," I said.

"Whenever you like, my love."

"When pigs speak Chinese while making tamales."

"So it's in the realm of possibility?"

I bit the inside of my cheek to repress a smile. "Always the optimist. You must be feeling pretty smug, pulling this off on a telepath."

"Hardest thing I've ever done. Never letting myself think about it when you were around."

"I shouldn't have told you how my abilities worked."

He slid over me to unlock the cuff from the passenger door. His face was inches from mine. I could bite the hawk nose I loved so much. That would distract him. But it fit so perfectly on his face, anchored by his cheekbones and accented by his brows. I hesitated to mar that beautiful face. Before I had time to reconsider, the cuff snapped open and we wiggled out of the car together.

"Don't look," I snapped as I copped a squat.

"Wouldn't dream of it." His eyes wandered up to the evening sky. A window appeared in his tower and he shoved his thoughts out at me. *First stars I've seen in a while. Reminds me of the night sky in Death Valley on our honeymoon.*

"Stop it." I didn't want him softening my heart.

"Can't help it. You peeing outdoors gets to me," he said.

"Don't think this changes anything."

"I'm still the heartless villain. I can live with that."

"Not sure I can," I muttered.

CHAPTER 12

Oliver

My wife had a night's sleep on me. No amount of coffee can keep you going after a certain point. I knew it. She knew it. We had another seven hours ahead of us, when I almost hit the motorcycle in Illinois. Decision made—I headed to the town of Midlothian.

Back when I played wingman to my high school buddy Alex, we spent months hooking up with Midlothian chicks we'd met at a club in Chicago. The second half of senior year, I learned every back road from there to Wisconsin. Kids sniff those things out as they do their youth-in-revolt thing.

"Or in their desperate search for a private place to stick it in," my wife snapped.

Damn it. She'd focused all her attention on me, found the weakest part of my shield and slipped through. I imagined a wall of solid rock surrounding me. The rock was 10 feet thick and completely smooth. No crevasses. No cracks. Unbreakable.

Nothing could escape. Nothing could sneak in.

When it felt impenetrable, I tested it by mentally ticking off the reasons we had to leave New York. No reaction from my wife. Good. I'd just have to maintain this level of concentration the rest of the ride. And then I'd bench-press 1000 lbs.

She stared out the window, biding her time. She never gave up or in. Wasn't a part of her DNA. When I parked under some trees on the isolated dirt road, she glanced around, searching for an out. I left her handcuffed to the door and secured her other hand to mine with the second set of cuffs. Then I shoved the keys into my left back pocket and settled into a reclining position. She glared at me.

I nodded off pretty quick, only to be jerked awake by my wife's frantic cries of "He's kidnapping me! Please, help me."

I looked around, ready to take out the threat, until I saw the gangly teenager standing outside my window and realized I was the threat. He knocked on the glass pane and made that rushed gesture to roll it down.

I played along.

As soon as the window was out of the way, he leaned in. "What are you doing to her?"

I stretched and reached into my jacket pocket.

The kid shifted. Licked his lips.

I gave him a slow smile and flashed a police badge. "Transporting a prisoner back where she belongs, son."

The boy gulped. His gaze jumped from me to her and back again.

My wife shrieked, "He's lying."

"Don't be taken in. She's a real psycho." I mimicked my father's raspy, seen-too-much tone. "Killed her own kid. Took me months to track her down. She's going back to prison."

"I am not. He's crazy. Don't believe him." Panic lifted her voice a couple octaves. She must have heard his thoughts.

Me, I saw it in the kid's eyes. He was happy to believe my story; otherwise, he'd be dragged further into this mess.

"Why aren't you in a squad car?" He chewed his bottom lip, needing

48

that final reassurance before he'd leave.

Smart kid. I crooked my finger and he leaned in. I lowered my voice. "Her friends broke her out of the last one. Had to travel under the radar, if you know what I mean."

The boy stuffed his hands in his pockets. "Sorry, sir. She was pretty convincing."

"Yeah, that's why we couldn't take a plane or train. She's too dangerous for the general public."

"I'll show you dangerous, you bastard," she said.

The boy hurried back to his pickup and tore out of there. He never glanced back at us.

Her eyes narrowed. "You are truly evil."

"Who tried to get me arrested?" I asked.

"An escaped prisoner? Really? Pretty ballsy of you to flash a fake badge."

"It's not fake."

"But..."

"It's my dad's," I said.

"I thought you got rid of everything when he died." Her voice hushed like she'd come to the end of a lullaby.

"Some things were worth holding onto."

"I'm not giving in."

I started the engine. "Neither am I."

We had miles to go before I slept again.

CHAPTER 13

Oliver

As we pulled into town, my wife read the sign aloud, "Butternut, Wisconsin. Population 407." It took her five seconds to make the connection. "This is where you're from?"

I glanced at her and continued driving.

"You said you'd never come back here."

"You're a powerful motivator." Your sanity. Your safety. I'd sacrifice my own to preserve them.

She pressed her forehead against her window.

There wasn't much to see. Not because it was a great town past its prime. No, folks here liked to say that it was a town waiting for its moment. More like a 60-year-old woman waiting for a prom date.

"They might as well say *and shrinking by the moment*," she said.

"Today's their lucky day." I made a right on Creamery Road.

"Why?"

The air thickened around me. Baked-bread warm. Buttery thick. Her power surged. Prodded my shield. Trying to slip into my head. Solid schist, Manhattan's bedrock, all around me. Impenetrable.

I let out my breath, said, "They get to add two more to the sign," and waited.

"We're staying here?" she asked.

"Give it a try."

"Is that a slaughterhouse?" She pointed to an old barn on the edge of the Wiesners' land.

"A cow and poultry farm actually."

She groaned. "Take me back to New York."

No.

She rubbed her temple. "Ouch! No need to yell."

"Sorry." I was worn out from visualizing a rock cave around me.

"How would you like it if I drugged you and carted you off to my parent's basement?"

"You know I'm Austrian. We like basements." I waggled my eyebrows at her.

Her cheek muscles twitched. Dimples appeared. And the smallest of smiles escaped her control. "How long?"

"A little while." We passed a couple pickup trucks and an old sedan. This was the most traffic she'd see for some time.

"HOW LONG?"

I swallowed. "Until your abilities are under control."

Her jaw dropped. "That could take our entire lives."

I flexed my fingers around the steering wheel. "Sounds good to me."

"I am not spending the rest of my life here, hiding from the world. I'd rather be dead."

I winced. That statement cut too close to our reality this year. "You always wanted to see my hometown."

"V-I-S-I-T."

"Exactly. A nice long visit."

She muttered something that sounded like log duck, though on second thought probably pig fuck.

Several excruciating miles of silence stretched between us. I turned onto Cherry Lane and took a left onto the dirt road that ran two miles into the farm. No chance she'd find her way back to civilization from here.

"Are we camping?" she asked in bewilderment.

"Nope." Guess she didn't remember what she'd seen in my head before the pills kicked in and she passed out.

"A cabin?" She sounded almost optimistic.

"Just wait." I wanted to see her reaction to the place. But two miles of rutted dirt road took longer than I remembered.

She coughed. "Dusty ass road."

I rolled the windows up. "It didn't used to be." When I lived here, Grandpa kept it well fed with gravel.

A little while later, I came to a stop and threw the car in park. The headlights gave us a first glance at the house.

"Your grandfather's house," she murmured.

In my mind, my grandparent's farmhouse had remained the pristine white building with Grandma's well-tended garden, several acres of farmland worked by a few hands, and the untamed woods that lay beyond the fields.

Nine months ago, when Grandpa passed on, I inherited it.

From the looks of it, the old codger couldn't maintain the place his last few years. Why hadn't Aunt Ines done something? She was the only family left in town. The paint had blistered off, exposing raw wood underneath. The roof looked solid enough, but the bushes invaded the porch and had clearly set their sights on taking the living room next. The windows were boarded up. Please, let there be glass underneath.

My wife reached over with her unshackled hand and gripped mine. "It's got potential."

I laughed. A bitter, burnt toast kind of laugh. "Not the homecoming I'd planned."

She rubbed my hand. "When has anything gone according to plan?"

"What are you up to?" I asked.

She blinked. "Can't a wife be sympathetic?"

"To the guy who kidnapped her?"

She took her hand away. "I can feel what this place meant to you."

It was a sanctuary from my father. The only place where I belonged in Butternut. "So you don't mind being here?"

She laughed. "I'm not staying long."

"We'll see."

"Game on, asshole." She sounded more like the wife I knew and loved.

"Stop. You're turning me on."

"Not a chance until you take these off." She rattled the handcuffs against the door.

"Promise you won't run away?"

"Not tonight." The corners of her lips tipped upward.

I reached over and unlocked the handcuffs.

CHAPTER 14

Oliver

She had been great while I struggled to get the front door open. When we saw the state of the inside of the house, she said, "It just needs some TLC." Her nose, however, twitched against the smells of mold, dust, mildew, and air long passed its expiration date.

My grandmother would have wept if she saw the torn wallpaper and dingy gray crown molding. "The hardwood floors look solid."

My wife rolled her lips outward. "A good sweeping and oiling will help."

"They're part of the original farmhouse. See how wide they are? Best wood his father could afford, Grandpa said." I rubbed my forehead. Aunt Ines said the place needed work, not years of hard labor. "You should have heard the pride in his voice when he talked about adding the top floor in '61."

Now, using the fireplace in the living room risked setting the house on fire. I added hiring a chimney cleaner to my to-do list. Fall nights in northern Wisconsin demanded a fire.

She helped me unload all the supplies from the car. I had everything you needed to camp for a week because that was the only vacation her telepathy allowed. The glow of the kerosene lanterns softened the living room. I swept the floor and ceiling before I set up the air mattress. Didn't want any surprises dropping down on us while we slept. She didn't complain about anything until she needed to use the toilet.

"Where am I supposed to go?" Her face cramped up. She had a kerosene lantern in one hand and a roll of Charmin in the other. "The campsites always had toilets," she reminded me.

No electricity or water rendered the downstairs toilet non-functional. "Why don't you go outside?"

"Peeing is one thing. I'm not doing this outside," she said.

I looked at what we had in the house. A plastic storage container with a lid would have to become a makeshift portable toilet. I pulled out a hunting knife and carved a circle in the top of the lid. I used duct tape to cover over the rough edges and to reinforce the lid.

I stepped back to admire my work. "Here you go."

"Seriously?"

"Or you can go outside."

"Fine, but I'm not emptying it."

My contraption. My responsibility. "I'll do it."

"Can you bring it into the bathroom?"

I picked up the container. "Just don't put too much weight on it or you might end up sitting in poo."

"This is so much better than New York," she muttered.

While she was in the bathroom, I imagined granite entombing me. Then I slipped outside, disabled my Cherokee's motor and hid the keys. By the time she finished in the bathroom, I was sitting on the air mattress. We swapped the clothes we'd worn the past 34 hours for new ones and laid down on the makeshift bed. I stared up at the peeling ceiling, inventorying everything that needed work. What we had to do to get the place safely inhabitable versus pleasantly livable.

Exhaustion claimed me before I knew it. I woke up alone at 3:32 a.m. A car door slammed. She was outside, trying to get the car started. I stretched and contemplated going back to sleep. She couldn't go anywhere. Still, alone in the dark, she could hurt herself.

Or my Jeep Cherokee.

She bolted when I opened the front door.

I was not up for a predawn chase. "Honey, there are wolves and snakes in these parts, the likes of which you don't want to meet. Come back inside before you get hurt."

She gasped. "Liar."

"We're in the Northwoods of Wisconsin."

She backed away from me.

"Bear country. Please, come back in the house." I wanted to high-five the coyote who picked that exact moment to bay at the moon.

My wife flew at me like a banshee. I caught her in my arms, savoring the feel of her body against mine. She stiffened and started to pull away. I guided her back into the house.

"I'm not giving up," she said.

I shut the door behind us, slipped the handcuffs from my pocket, slapped them around our wrists. "Neither am I."

The next morning, breakfast consisted of Pop-Tarts and bottled water and angry glances at my wife.

She scarfed down the last bite of her breakfast. "What?"

"You lied to me." She never lied to me.

"I promised to stay the night."

"And?" I asked.

"I didn't try to escape until the next morning."

I snorted. "If we should be sleeping, it's still night."

"By all standards of time measurement, it was the next day. Do you really want to determine who has told the most lies lately?"

She had a point. One I didn't want to acknowledge so I assembled the cleaning supplies.

She waved her arms at the piles of stuff in the living room. "You thought to pack all this, but not to turn on the electricity and water?"

"I had planned to leave New York in November, not September."

"How long were you planning this?" she asked.

A cave-in of schist blanketed my mind in darkness. "I always have a backup plan."

"Not a good one," she muttered.

"I was afraid to turn things on when I wasn't around." What if there was a flood or an electrical fire?

"Doesn't your aunt still live in Butternut?" Her forehead crinkled like a Chinese fan.

"She's on a cruise right now." Aunt Ines planned to be here in November.

I lugged garbage bags, a pack of paper towels, rags, Murphy's Oil Soap, Windex, and Clorox toward the stairs. "Please, help me clean this house up."

"Why?" she asked.

"Because I can't stand seeing it this way," I said. "I'll do the kitchen, if you take the master bedroom and bath. Then we can tackle the living room together."

My wife picked up the broom, dustpan, and lantern. "When we're done cleaning, we talk about how long I'm staying here."

Schist boulders enclosed me. "Today we clean, tomorrow we talk."

We got to the top of the landing and turned left. At the end of the hall, a window allowed light to sneak in. I opened the first door. Light filtered through four grimy windows.

The master bedroom was stripped of all its possessions. Grandma's bed covered in white crocheted lace was gone. The comfy brown armchair Grandpa read in wasn't by the window anymore. Grandma's vanity had disappeared from the corner of the room along with her hairpins and creams. Like they never existed.

"It used to smell like baby powder and lilacs in here." Just like Grandma. Now the air tasted sour, dust caked the floor, and spider webs kitty-cornered in every nook.

She cleared her throat. "I'd better get to work."

I handed her all the supplies, trying to remember it was a room. Just a room. "I'm going to work on removing the boards from the downstairs windows." I handed over her iPod. She loved cleaning to music.

"I'll open the windows to air everything out," she said.

"Yell if you have any problems."

"With the house or you?"

"Just the house. I don't want you straining your vocal chords."

CHAPTER 15

Kai

A guided tour of his grandfather's property did not distract me from being kidnapped. I barely listened to him as I checked my shield. No sections ready to give way. Not a fissure anywhere. I dropped it, allowing his thoughts to reach me.

"Why'd you bring me here?" I asked.

Shards of schist sprouted out of the ground around him, forming a pyramid of secrecy. "You wanted to see it."

I stomped my foot. "Not *here* here, but Butternut?"

"You needed a vacation."

I dug the tip of my sneaker into the dirt. Working the dent into a hole. Burrowing into the earth, the way I wanted to burrow into his shield. "How long do you think you can keep me here?"

He adjusted the straps of his backpack. "I'm not the enemy."

"Could've fooled me." I squinted at the sun.

He fished around in his backpack. "Give me one month."

"To do what?" I peered up at him, hating how he towered over me in my sneakers.

He held out my sunglasses. "Fix up Grandpa's house."

I snatched them away and slid them on my face. "Then what?"

"If you absolutely hate it here and don't feel any better, you can leave."

"One month?" I asked.

"You owe me that."

"I hate when you play the guilt card."

A doorway appeared in his pyramid of schist. It creaked open. His thoughts rushed out and echoed in my head. *I rarely do, but your life is at stake. And I am not going to lose you again. This time I'll make sure you don't slip away. I'll hold on until my raw palms ooze pus.*

"Ew. Gross imagery." This was the place he grew up. In a family I'd never met. Maybe some time here was what he needed. I stuck out my hand to seal our bargain. "One month. And then I can leave."

I tried to listen for his thoughts, but I couldn't hear them. A rock waterfall poured over him, shielding his mind from me.

We shook hands.

We arrived home to pockets of congestion in the kitchen and living room. Over one hundred boxes piled between clumps of our furniture.

"This is our stuff," I said. "ALL of our stuff. From New York." Packed up by strangers and delivered here without my consent.

He put several feet and a few boxes between us. "One month."

"All our stuff is here. How am I going to leave?" He never planned to leave this place. To go home with me. My stomach plummeted to my heels. "I don't have an apartment or a job to go back to, do I?"

He shrugged. "You always said your home was with me."

Angela thought I'd abandoned her and the kids. My kids. "You lied to me." I lunged around the boxes.

A granite tower formed around his mind, protecting his thoughts from me.

"Angela understood. She said there will always be a place for you there. When you're better."

Tears burned my eyes. "I can't believe you lied to me. About my job. About how long we'd stay here. About everything that matters to me."

"I had to get you away from everything that was harming you." His voice shimmied toward logic. "One month and I'll give you the movers' number. You can do whatever you want."

"Bullshit." I stabbed my finger into his chest with each word. "You. Aren't. Getting. Away. With. This."

"You promised."

"So did you," I said.

"I'll hold up my end."

"Separate bedrooms." My fingernails bit into my hips to keep from grabbing him.

"No."

"I'm not sleeping with you."

"One month until you sleep alone," he said.

I grabbed my kerosene lamp and stomped up the stairs to the master bedroom.

Once I fell asleep, gold, tan, and black sand glinted beneath the cliffs at Torrey Pines. I stared into the sea, letting it edge me away from furious. The water stretched out for miles, shifting in color from sandstone to green fluorite to Navajo turquoise. A line of milky quartz cut across the sea before it settled to a dark blue topaz and met the edge of the afternoon sky.

Caleb appeared on the horizon, walking on the water. He strolled toward me in linen pants and a white V-neck T-shirt. All San Diego calm.

He stopped where the waves frothed against the sand and held his arms out.

I leapt into them. "Best entrance ever."

"I knew you'd appreciate it."

My brother smelled of sandalwood. Even in my dreams.

"Ringlets look better on you." Caleb stood beside me in all his 30-year-old grandeur minus the hair gel, which meant golden curls were framing his face in the sea air.

"My dream, my rules. Besides, you look so much better this way," I said.

"What did that husband of yours do now?"

"Besides drugging me, kidnapping me, and forcing me to live in Wisconsin?"

Caleb winced at Wisconsin. "Tell me all about it."

We had hours before he had to wake up to trade the U.S. markets in London. It put us on the same sleep schedule despite the time difference and gave me enough time to catch him up on the past few days of my existence.

"Why couldn't you come into my dream at the tidal pools?" I asked.

He shrugged. "I'm guessing the muscle relaxants and wine messed with your mind. Altered it just enough that I couldn't get a lock on it."

"Damn him." My fingers curled into fists. I picked up the nearest rock and threw it at the sea.

"I warned you not to marry him," he teased.

"I'll accept the *I told you so* after you help me."

"I'm guessing he took it a step further?" he asked.

"He sent in my resignation and lied about it."

"That would do it." He raised one of his perfect eyebrows. "So the kidnapping was okay with you?"

"I could understand it," I said. "But heaping my caseload on my co-workers. Making it look like I just abandoned the kids…"

Caleb looped his arm over my shoulder. "What can I do to help?"

"Anything?"

"The more amoral the better." The corners of his eyes crinkled in amusement.

"I just need you to help me get the keys and fix the car."

His eyes were like the ocean. Green and blue and calming. "I have your permission to use my abilities on him?"

Caleb had been a dreamwalker since we were kids. He could invade the dreams of anyone he was close to. "Whatever needs to be done," I said.

He chuckled. "I'll have to leave you then. Go see what your husband's up to. I'll report back soon."

I clutched his shirt. "Remember I love the idiot."

"He won't even notice I've tiptoed through his mind." He tapped my nose. "I'll fix this for you."

"Thanks." I wrapped my arms around him.

He held me, letting me steal some of his strength. Then he walked back out to sea, fading from sight.

CHAPTER 16

Oliver

After another breakfast of Pop-Tarts, I dragged my wife to Turtle Flambeau Flowage while the electrician and plumber came to work their magic without her interference. And by interference, I meant raising hell and demanding to be taken home. I'd suffered through her silent treatment all night, and didn't quite trust her commitment to the whole Butternut retreat.

On the ride over, I realized baby wipes only worked for so long. After nearly four days without a shower, we both reeked. I prayed I'd get the stink out of my Cherokee.

I avoided the popular trails. Cherokees were built for off-roading, tackling miles of unpaved roads to make my own parking space among the trees. Leaving the car behind, we dodged branches and leaves, weaving through a secluded section of woods along a path my father had carved into my memory years ago.

"Are we lost?" she asked. First words she'd spoken to me after receding into her own head last night.

"Nope."

"Are you sure?"

My wife saw no indication of a path, just shades of camouflage. Leafy greens, muddy browns, trunks of gray. I saw the fragile ferns my father trampled over on our way to his favorite fishing spot. The mushy ground that bore my father's boot print when he tried to track a deer. The scaly bark of a sugar maple that skinned my palm and tested my ability to pretend away pain.

"My dad used to bring me here," I said.

"When?"

"On Saturdays."

"With your mom?"

"No." She was dead then.

"When was the last time you came out here?"

"The weekend after my sixteenth birthday." It was right before my father fell from his Empire-State-Building-sized pedestal.

"You left for college at 18." She chewed on the corner her mouth. Trying to map out the timetable. To understand when the bad thing happened. The one I never recovered from. "What happened?"

"He wasn't the man everyone believed he was." Even after all this time, the truth still burned my throat and inflamed my bronchi and charred my lungs.

She stopped walking and swiveled to face me. "You can trust me, you know."

The sun pierced through the maple leaves above us, streaming down on her. Sparkling where it touched her red hair. Making her eyes lighter. Warmer. Safer.

"There are some things I can never talk about." Things I had boxed up and buried in the basement of my mind.

She looked away.

I rocked on my heels. "If I ever could, it would be with you."

"I'm here." Her mouth compressed, reaching the threshold of concern.

"Even when you're uber pissed at me?"

"Even when you go all caveman on my ass." She took a step closer and whispered, "I get why you did this."

The muscle knot in the back of my neck released a millimeter.

Her voice became petrified wood. "Doesn't make it right. Doesn't mean I'm happy about it."

"I tried everything." Exhausted every rational method of helping her. Not like there was a Suicidal Telepaths Anonymous to join. Her disease wasn't substance abuse or cancer. It was something we had to hide from the world. So we came up with coping mechanisms. But all of them had failed.

"I was dealing," she said.

"How do you feel?" I asked.

"In need of a shower."

"Any desire to take a razor to your wrist?"

She shook her head.

"Migraine?"

"Minor headache."

"How long since you burst into tears? Not since we left New York, I'm guessing."

Her expression tightened.

"How's your shield? Are you gaining more control over it?"

She pursed her lips.

"Suicidal became your normal. But you know that is never normal. It is always the outlier. It's the extreme you should stay away from, not gravitate toward."

She gazed at something just over my shoulder. "You've never been suicidal. You couldn't possibly understand it."

"Because it's the opposite of living. How can I possibly understand dying while I am alive?"

"You can't."

"You shouldn't," I said.

She quieted her voice as if the trees shouldn't hear what she was about to say. "I've seen death. I've been with people when they died. Not just beside their hospital bed. But in their head."

"And what has that done to you?"

Her nostrils flared. Her cheeks flushed with annoyance. We both knew the price she paid to escort someone into death. The price we paid for her to sacrifice herself.

"Tomorrow is not a given. Death can take us at any time." I rubbed my forehead. "Isn't our life worth fighting for?"

"I'm still here." Her arms folded up like a card table. "But I will not run from death."

"Death is a certainty. Why rush toward it?"

"Sometimes, I need to go there. To realize every day I stay here with you is a choice. My choice."

"I can't let you give up."

Her eyes glistened but she refused to let the tears fall. "Loving someone doesn't give you the right to take away their choices."

"Free will doesn't give you the right to harm yourself."

"There is no greater free will than choosing life every day." She'd espoused that point since our college ethics class.

"Do you want to end your life here?" I asked.

"I don't have much of a life here." She stretched her arms out to encompass the woods around us.

"Just me. And our future."

"You mean the future you've chosen for me?" she asked.

"I'm doing everything I can to save us."

"I swear to God, if you start talking about the greater good, I am going to call you Stalin." Her voice Linda-Blaired on me.

I pulled out a Dean & Deluca chocolate chip cookie from my backpack and offered it to my wife. It was her favorite.

Her face scrunched up. Finally, her fingers darted out and grabbed it.

"The discussion isn't finished," she said.

"I hope it never is."

CHAPTER 17

Oliver

Four days later, my wife still refused to nest. Instead, she submerged herself in *Wuthering Heights*. She sat at the two-seater table that had fit perfectly in our living room/dining room/office back in New York, but looked completely out of place in what she called my grandmother's "ginormous" kitchen.

Filling a four-bedroom farmhouse with furniture from a one-bedroom apartment skyrocketed past minimalism and headed straight to barebones. Maybe I could tempt her with picking out a new table?

We had more countertops and cabinets than a New Yorker dreamed possible, but I'd been the one who spent hours bleaching them back to white and laying the contact paper inside them.

At the stove, I prepared a dinner of macaroni and cheese with bratwurst. It tasted better than it sounded. Though my wife always wrinkled her nose when I added the mustard and sauerkraut to mine.

"How was your shower this morning?" I asked.

She didn't look up from her book. "Lukewarm."

"The boiler seems temperamental. I'll call someone to come look at it."

Her gaze wafted toward the curtainless windows.

I hated her silence more than the yelling.

She still refused to see how much good the days of solitude had done her. For the first time in five years, she looked almost relaxed. She didn't have to guard against everyone's thoughts. It was just mine. Most of the time, I was good at shielding. She finally had a chance to be alone with her own thoughts. How could she not see this as a blessing?

She slammed her hand on the table. "How many children are suffering for my peace of mind?"

Sheets of schist slammed around me. "You can't save them all."

"I'm not saving any of them now. Does that make you happy?" Her words ringed me with fire.

"We lost five years to your good intentions. We couldn't take much more." My explanation stamped at the flames.

"Don't tell me what I can handle. I'm stronger than you think."

The fire licked at my waist. "You don't have to be. Not all the time."

She took a deep breath and released it. As if speaking to me was a monumental undertaking. "You can't save me."

"I did. End of discussion."

"It's who I am." The plastic cup recoiled in her grip, crackling as the sides caved in and snapped back out.

"It's who you forced yourself to be when she died."

"Don't blame my grandmother."

"You never let yourself mourn her." I power-stirred the powdered cheese into the melted butter and milk.

Her chair skidded across the floor. "I mourn her every day of my life."

"No. You pay homage to her by sacrificing your sanity. That's screwed up."

"She saved me." Her cup flew across the room at me.

I ducked.

The plastic cup bounced off the cabinet, spewing water and ice cubes on me before it rolled to its resting place by the table.

My voice rose with my frustration. "You're barely here because of what you do in her memory."

"That's not true."

"You have an irrational, no scratch that, insane need to risk yourself to prove you deserve to be alive."

A tremor started at the roots of her hair and worked its way down to the tips of her toenails. "It's the only way I can keep going."

"That's my point. Life is more than enduring. It has to be."

Her eyes became the night sky. Distant. Inhuman. Untouchable. She walked out of the room. Out of the house. Out on me.

CHAPTER 18

Kai

I slammed the front door and stomped down the steps. The underbrush and weeds smushed beneath my shoes as I cut across the overgrown yard toward the distant cover of trees. How dare he blame my grandmother? I wouldn't be alive without her. She sheltered Caleb and me when our powers blew apart our childhood. She understood how it obliterated me. She taught me how to use it, accepting it as a part of me and living around it.

It had been almost five years since she died. But I never forgot her. How her auburn braid tumbled down her back. How she always smelled of roses. If I tried really really hard, I heard her voice. How she said my name when she disagreed with what I was doing—extending the vowels and rolling them around in her mouth.

All I wanted to do was repay her. If that was insanity, to hell with sanity. Each child I helped was a thank you to her. How did he rationalize taking me away from them? Sacrificing them for me.

I wished I could see her. Talk to her. She'd know what to do. She always did. But the only words in my head were my husband's. They imploded every time I replayed them.

I stumbled over a tree root and fell against a rock. Unsure where to go, I sat down. What I would have given for a cell phone. To be able to bounce all my thoughts off Caleb. To vent to someone about my husband and gain the perspective only a third point of view could provide.

Panic welled up inside me. It pushed against my lungs, needing an outlet. "I don't know what to do," I blurted out.

There was no one to hear me in the woods. The trees and the ferns and the undergrowth absorbed my voice. But sometimes it helped to say things out loud.

I babbled, "I always thought he got me. That he saw inside me and understood how my mind worked. Well, at least enough of it to mesh together."

Maybe it was the wind caressing the trees, but the leaves made sympathetic sounds. I'd swear the ferns nodded in agreement.

I whispered the truth that ate away at me. "He hates my telepathy. He wants me to bury it the way he buried his past." I couldn't slice off a limb and pretend it didn't matter. "That's not me," I confided to the ferns. "That's not who he fell in love with."

A bird cried out. Through the trees, I glimpsed the kitchen. The light cut across the yard. A beacon to a house that still didn't feel like my home.

CHAPTER 19

Oliver

An hour and nineteen minutes after my wife walked out, she stood in the kitchen doorway. "I'm sorry I threw the glass at you."

I remained seated at the kitchen table. "It was a plastic cup."

Her foot traced an imaginary half circle in front of her. "I know it's been hard to live with me."

"Every day, every couple hours, I scanned the headlines on CNN.com praying nothing would set you off."

She leaned against the doorframe. "I didn't know."

I wrapped my left hand around the fist of my right. "Everything that happens to you happens to me. Don't you get that?"

She chewed her lower lip.

"I want you to be happy and healthy."

"I can't turn off the telepathy." She tucked her hair behind her ear.

"I'm not asking you to."

"Aren't you?" She tilted her head.

"I want you to find a way to live well with it."

She shook her head.

Our chasm of misunderstanding couldn't be bridged tonight. "Can you set the table?" I walked over to the stove and turned the gas burner on to reheat our meal.

She frowned at the cabinets.

I cleared my throat and tried again. "Get the dishes."

"Don't know where you put them." She practically sang the words.

Right. Because she left me to unpack everything. Except her books and her clothes. Those she'd seen to immediately.

"In. The. Cabinet." I tossed my head toward the cabinet three doors down from me.

She opened and shut each one in rapid succession.

She hated it here. I got it.

She whispered, "Let's go home."

"We are home."

She slammed the cabinet so hard it bounced back open. "This is not my home."

I put the wooden spoon on the counter and twisted to face her. "Do you remember what it was like in New York?" I let the memories play through my mind. All the times I found her broken on the floor. Four times curled in a corner of the living room. Three times on the hardwood floor wedged between our dresser and bed. Twice on the tiles in the bathroom. Once in the bathtub. How much her depression dismembered me. How hard I worked to bring her back. How I feared that one day I wouldn't get there in time and she would be gone forever.

Her eyes went glossy. "You're not playing fair."

"We tried it your way the past few years. Can't you give me one month on my terms?"

"I don't want to be locked up." *Again* was the unspoken word that hung between us. She'd vowed to die before she'd let it happen again.

So would I. Couldn't she see I was trying to rescue her from a life that was unraveling?

She crossed her arms. "I was getting things under control."

"Bullshit."

"Being a stellar auditor doesn't make you an impartial judge," she said.

"I promised to love and protect you. Remember? It was right before the Until Death Do Us Part thing."

"I want to talk to my parents."

"You can call them after we finish dinner," I said.

Her top teeth snagged on her bottom lip. She toyed with her rope bracelet.

"Provided you ever get the plates on the table."

CHAPTER 20

Oliver

I'd never seen my wife shovel food in her mouth like that. As if a buzzer had gone off and her happiness hinged on winning an eating competition. I was halfway done with my food when she leapt up, grabbed both our plates, tossed them in the sink.

Another wonderful meal in our new home.

She drummed her fingers on the counter. I sipped my Coke until she swooped in again, claiming the glass for the sink.

Brushing her hands off, she said, "I'll do the dishes later. Time to call my parents."

"Give me ten minutes."

She gave me her no-substitutions look. The same one she used when she waitressed back in college.

"It'll be worth it. Trust me," I said.

"I bet you say that to all the girls you kidnap."

"I'm gonna need you to stay in the bedroom for 10 minutes."

"Don't you trust me?" She made the cutest pout, almost suckering me in.

"Not yet." I couldn't risk her seeing where everything was.

I followed her upstairs and left her sitting on our bed. I shut the door and used a skeleton key to lock her in. Before I descended the stairs, I visualized my granite tomb. No doors. No windows. Pure granite around me.

I made my way down the hall to what had been Grandpa's old office and was transitioning into my study. I guarded the telephone like the Holy Grail, hiding it in Grandpa's safe behind the bookcase he'd built into the wall. The old codger never trusted banks.

It only took a couple minutes to hook up. But this was my wife I was dealing with. She might not be able to get in my head, but she could still hear what I was doing. So I stomped around the entire downstairs and raced upstairs twice.

I unlocked the door to our bedroom and found her meditating on the floor.

Without opening her eyes, she asked, "Ready?"

"Yup."

She followed me to the study. The rotary dial phone sat on my desk. On the off chance she decided to dial 911. No way she could get all three rotations around that dial before I stopped her.

She threw herself into my leather chair and glared at me. "Do you have to think of everything?"

"With you? Yes." I handed her the receiver.

Three times she slid her finger into the wrong hole and had to redial the whole phone number. I sucked in my cheeks to prevent a smile. Someone answered on the fourth ring.

My wife burst out with "Mom, I need your help. Oliver's kidnapped me. I'm stuck in Butternut, Wisconsin. You have to talk some sense into him." Then she shoved the receiver at me.

I put the phone to my ear. "Hi, Mrs. Guhn. Don't worry, I'm taking good care of Kai."

"Is she being difficult?" Mrs. Guhn asked.

"No more than usual."

"Her father indulged her too much. She doesn't have a sense of self-preservation like Caleb. He got it from my side, you know."

Before I could ask about Caleb, Kai yelled, "He's holding me prisoner with handcuffs."

I hadn't used them since the first night.

"Oliver, dear, we don't like to intrude in your sex life," Mrs. Guhn said, "but you might want to try fur-lined wrist cuffs, they never chafe delicate skin."

Kai peered up at me. "What'd she say? Why are you turning red?"

"Mrs. Guhn, Kai wants to talk to you."

Kai hesitated to take the phone back, perplexed by the lack of her mother's wrath. "Mom, you have to do something."

Fissures of frustration rippled across her forehead during her mother's reply.

"I don't need saving from myself. You're being absurd," she said. "Put Dad on."

Her mom's reply was muffled.

"Now," Kai said. Her tone changed, wrapping me in ribbons and jelly bracelets. "Daddy, can you please come get me? I don't like it here. I want to go back to New York."

She twirled and untwirled the receiver's spiral cord around her finger while she listened to him. "My work is more important than my life."

Didn't she get how crazy she sounded?

She didn't look at me, but her voice shouted in my head, *I am NOT crazy.*

To her father, she said, "I can't believe you're doing this to me. I thought you loved me." She turned her back to me, cradling the phone with both hands. "Daddy, how about I come out to San Diego for a while? We can grab fish tacos at Rubio's."

They'd done that most weekends of her childhood.

"Caleb wouldn't let this happen to me," she said.

Silence stretched from California to Wisconsin.

"Daddy? Are you there? Hello?"

I'd won. We all understood what was good for Kai. Except Kai. And she was way too stubborn to admit we were right.

Suddenly, her mom screeched through the phone about the chickens getting loose again. What can I say? My wife's parents had been going green since the 1970s.

Her dad must have handed the receiver to her mom because Kai's next words were "Mom, please, put Dad back on." Her shoulders edged toward her ears. "Forget the chickens. I'm his daughter."

While her mom talked, she curled her body around the phone as if proximity could somehow sway them. "Is Naomi looking at colleges yet?"

Her mom's answer made Kai tighten her grip on the phone.

"Tell her to check out NYU. Awesome city. I'll be back there in time to show her around," Kai said.

I quirked an eyebrow. Someone was feeling pretty confident.

"Christmas? Here?!" Kai's voice heliumed. Her eyes slitted cobra-style. Shit. They weren't supposed to tell her.

"Sure, you can come visit for Christmas. But I won't be here." Her bravado cracked along with her voice. "I can't believe you're siding with Oliver over me."

She listened to her mom for a couple minutes, blinking back tears. "I love you too, Mom. Tell Dad I'm sorry."

She slammed the receiver down and punched me in the stomach. I doubled over.

"LIAR! Christmas?! Seriously? That's three months away. You promised one month."

Unable to speak, I thought at her. *I had to get you to agree to stay here.*

She hurled her chaotic thoughts back at me. *How dare you steal my parents? I don't deserve to be treated like a child!* And the worst one: *I HATE YOU.*

I struggled to catch my breath when something snaked around my neck. Everything slowed. My lips couldn't form the words. My mind fuzzed up. Darkness closed in.

CHAPTER 21

Oliver

The grooves in the wood floor bit into the side of my face. My Cherokee's engine revved outside. The dirt driveway crackled beneath spinning wheels. I'd taken away everything that mattered to my wife. Then I'd broken her trust. She'd left and she wasn't coming back. Ever.

I swallowed. Remembering the last time I felt this alone. I was seven when my mother died. The emptiness she left behind filled our home. Dad sent me to stay here with Grandma and Grandpa. I sat in Grandpa's office, waiting to go to Mama's funeral.

I pretended to understand what dead meant. Mama looked so pretty napping in the fancy box, I tried to wake her up and tell her. Daddy slapped my hand.

Grandma took me by the arm and explained, "Oliver, no one wakes up from death."

I stared at Mama in her casket the entire mass, willing her to wake up. To prove Grandma wrong. To stay with me.

But no one would ever call me Li'l Oli and kiss my forehead after making me hot cocoa with chocolate covered marshmallows again.

Mama's face slid out of focus and morphed into Kai's. I leaned in to kiss her. Cold, unyielding lips. Dead. Because I failed to protect her.

My head ached as I struggled to stand. How long had I been out? She'd had enough time to find my keys and reconnect all the wires in the engine. She couldn't manage it on her own.

Caleb.

Damn it, couldn't her brother see I was trying to save her?

I touched the back of my head, searching for a tender spot. A blow to the head to explain my unconsciousness. No bump forming, no painful area, no memory of contact, and no evidence of violence. Except for the phone on the floor. Had she hit me with it?

I didn't remember. I did remember becoming her personal dictator and not anticipating an uprising. It sounded so right in my head. But now. Shit. My head ached.

It wasn't just physical distance growing between us. I couldn't feel her thoughts brushing against mine. She'd withdrawn into herself where I couldn't follow. I don't know how long I lost it for. Might have been minutes or hours. It didn't matter. For the first time, I was completely alone in the world.

The night I became an orphan, Kai adopted me. The next day, she popped up outside my class to slip me a note that read: *I almost like you. Even with that haircut. Let's hang out tonight. Your room.* Two weeks later, she showed up at my orchestra performance with blue roses. "Because they were your mom's favorite" was all she said.

A couple months later, I started eating family dinners at her parent's house on Narragansett Street in Ocean Beach. She carved out a cabinet in her life for me and gave me something I'd lost the day my mom died. A place to call home.

I didn't want to be here without her. Problem was I didn't want to be anywhere without her.

CHAPTER 22

Kai

In the driver's seat again, I turned the key in the ignition. The engine roared to life. I imagined my Fabergé-egg shield. I concentrated on creating a window. It blurred and disappeared. I took a deep breath and put all my energy into it. A tiny window solidified in my crystal shield. I opened it a crack to control the stream of thoughts, so it wouldn't overwhelm me. Oliver wouldn't feel my presence, but I could leave without worrying about him.

When I felt his mind awaken, I revved the engine and threw the car into drive. I never wanted him hurt. Not by me or my abilities. But I had to leave. To get back to the kids whose lives depended on me.

His loneliness whistled through my window. The desolation only a child experiences. Absolute abandonment. Without a mother. At a funeral he never understood. Death stealing everything that mattered to him. An orphaned man. Unable to ever set things right with his father. A husband without a wife. Left by the only person he loved.

I gripped the steering wheel and pressed my foot down on the gas. It was the first time I saw what resided in the deepest recesses of his mind. He wasn't going to fight it. He was going to go darkly into his depression.

Oliver who had always been my anchor. Oliver who never let me drown in my sorrow. Oliver who fought for me when I wouldn't.

He wasn't going to fight for himself.

Tears fell harder and faster, like a blinding rain. Forcing me to pull over and wait them out. He never asked me to help him. Never expected me to heal him. Never put any of his pain on me.

Tonight, his agony branded my heart.

CHAPTER 23

Oliver

I couldn't do this alone. Thank God, Grandpa kept a stash of Jack Daniel's in his safe. Didn't matter how long it sat there. Whiskey was whiskey. I twisted the cap off and downed it. In the morning, I'd be sorry. But right now, I needed something, anything, to defer the sorry.

The burning liquor short-circuited my mind. I gulped it down, prolonging my temporary escape. Grandpa swore whatever ailed you, Jack could fix. I started to believe it. For the first time tonight, I felt nothing. Followed by a false sense that everything would be okay. I took a swig whenever it threatened to disappear.

Polished off the bottle so fast, I started hallucinating. Saw Kai standing there in the doorway, her eyes dead seas of sadness. Sadness I'd put there.

"Why'd you leave me?" I asked the mirage of Kai.

She leaned against the doorframe. My key ring dangled from her knuckle. "I wanted to go home."

"I think you made a wrong turn." My Kai was gone. This phantom was Jack's doing.

"You are my home."

I blinked a few times, trying to get rid of the mirage of Kai.

She came closer. "Six months here. Then we go back to New York. No questions. No fighting." The keys clanged on my desk.

I smelled her pear shampoo. I dragged her into my lap, held her face between my palms, and searched her eyes. Her skin was as soft as Kai's.

She whispered, "I am your Kai," and pressed her lips to mine. Her kiss tasted of cherries, Jack Daniel's, and hope all rolled up together.

She finger-brushed the hair off my forehead. "I'm so sorry about your mom."

I closed my eyes. Shoved the memory back into its marble box. Focused on the heat her body radiated into mine.

She dropped butterfly kisses on my eyelids. "I won't leave you, I promise."

This was my Kai. She'd come back to me. "I'm sorry I lied. I didn't know how to keep you here."

"I know." Her lips curved into a tentative smile. "Telepath, remember?"

"I didn't feel you."

She shrugged. "Who taught you how to shield?"

"You heard me?"

"Every single emotion. It's why I had to come back." She traced the planes of my face with the side of her palms, sculpting the tension away. "There's just one condition."

I tightened my hold on her.

"You get a job so we don't deplete our savings."

"Ten thousand dollars could last a while in Butternut."

She surveyed the room. "Not if we're going to make this place livable."

"Bank auditors aren't in demand here."

"Or we can go back to New York right now." She polished my collarbone with her fingertips.

"We stay in Butternut six months and I get a job."

"At the slaughterhouse?"

"It's a farm."

"I can try making preserves," she said.

The image of my wife wearing an apron splattered from mashing raspberries made me laugh. For the first time this year, we had a future to imagine.

Cotton mouth. Throbbing headache. Bright sun blazing through our bedroom windows. First coherent thought: Buy some goddamned blinds. Second coherent thought: Jack Daniel's was no man's friend. I pulled the covers over my head and reached for my wife. Her side of the bed came up empty-cold. My heart stuttered G-G-G-G-o-n-e.

I lay there trying to make sense of last night until she shuffled into the room careful not to spill two mugs of coffee. She wore her bunny slippers and Hello Kitty pjs.

"Kai?" Was she really here?

She put the mugs on our dresser and dive-bombed the bed, wrapping her arms and legs around me like a horny octopus. "Who else?"

My heart thumped hel-lo to hers. She loved snuggle time. Today so did I. "Are we good?"

"Almost." She rolled onto her stomach and looked up at me.

What else did she want?

She made swirlies with her pointer finger in the pit of my elbow, knowing how much it turned me on. "Groceries and sex."

"In that order?"

"Yup. Sad to say, we're out of eggs." She leapt off the bed before I could grab her and reverse the order.

Sometimes my wife was too practical for my own good.

I burrowed under the covers. With only 407 residents, Butternut barely commanded its own grocery store. When the town grocer died, everyone expected someone to fill the void. No one did. Now, the whole town trekked south to Park Falls for their major food needs. Last week, while my wife was tucked away in her bedroom, I made my first trip down Highway 13 to gather supplies.

"How about I make the grocery run in an hour?" I asked.

"We make a grocery run in twenty minutes."

Park Falls had a probable population of 3000 people and covered 4 square miles. "Are you really up for all those people?" She'd made so much progress out here. I didn't want to see it vaporized.

She brushed her hair into a ponytail. "There's less than 1000 people in a half-mile radius?"

"Pure math puts it at 589, but people from surrounding towns tend to congregate in Park Falls's shopping areas."

"Totally doable." She secured her hair with an elastic.

"Maybe we should wait." I wanted her shield completely intact before she ventured out.

"You really think I'm that fragile?" She lowered her chin and gave me her mischievous face. "And I was going to let you use the handcuffs tonight too."

I groaned and covered my face with her pillow, catching a whiff of her scent.

She gave me two whole minutes before grabbing the covers and ripping them off the bed, while chanting, "Grocery time. Grocery time."

I didn't move.

"Daddy wants ice cubes?"

"NO." I hated when she poured ice cubes onto my stomach. It painfully demolished my morning wood when they spilled onto my dick, or Herr Peoples as she nicknamed it one plastered night in her dorm room. Same evening she had named her lady parts Empress Qi Qi. Don't ask. No idea how we came up with them, but the names stuck.

I rolled out of bed and headed for a cold shower. The woman was merciless when it came to grocery shopping.

On the drive south to Super One Foods, Kai cranked up the radio, blaring her favorite angsty-folk music with a dash of sixties beatnik and singing along at the top of her lungs.

I let her have her way for two songs before I lowered the volume. "How'd you do it?"

"Do what?" Sugar powdered her words.

"Escape last night."

She chewed on her lower lip.

"Caleb." I gripped the steering wheel with both hands, pretending it was her brother's throat.

"He's been riding to my rescue since I was born."

"Uh-huh." My wife only needed one knight in semi-tarnished armor, and damn it, that was me.

She reached over and squeezed my hand. "I came back for you, didn't I?"

"How'd you get away?"

"Caleb doesn't just dreamwalk into family members' dreams." She crossed her legs. "He can walk into anyone's dreams. Well, provided he's spent time with them and formed an emotional connection."

"Since when?"

My wife shifted in her seat, trying to decide how much to tell me. "A while."

"Uh-huh." No wonder he took me out for drinks when Kai and I got serious. "So what emotional connection does he have with me?"

"It's more of a rivalry." She got quiet. Probably trying to construct an argument to rationalize her brother invading my mind.

Newsflash: Never Fucking Okay.

"He was very respectful."

"When he mind-raped me?" I slammed my palm against the steering wheel.

Kai touched my arm. "It's not like that."

I shook her off. "Right."

"He influenced your dreams to get the info he needed to help me escape."

"You planned to knock me out with the phone?"

"I didn't knock you out with the phone," she said.

"Then how'd I end up unconscious on the floor?"

She squirmed in her seat. "That was totally heat of the moment. And I'm really, really sorry."

"What did you do?"

"I'm not sure." She bit her fingertip. "I think…I put you in some sort of emotional chokehold."

"You think?"

"It happened so fast. I never touched you," she said. "I wanted to put you in a headlock and wrestle you to the ground. But I didn't. You dropped to the floor and dragged the phone along with you." Her voice collapsed under the guilt. "I never meant to do that."

"But you had a plan." Screw apologies, I wanted truth.

She stared at the floor mats. "It doesn't matter now."

"Does to me."

"Can't you let this go?" She flicked at her nails.

"No."

"Fine," she said. "It was going to be a hot night of sex. When you fell asleep, I'd make my escape. Happy now?"

Angry. Careening toward furious. "Were you going to drug me?"

She shook her head. "You always fall asleep after sex. Even when our minds are still intertwined."

I took a deep breath and blew it out. My nails dug in, trying to restrain my temper.

"And none of this would have happened if you didn't kidnap me," she said.

My temper tore the fingernails from their nail beds. The odometer climbed in speed. I stared at the road ahead, wondering if she understood her words hit me like a tree at 90 miles an hour.

"What are you angry about? My accidental attack or Caleb's invasion or Caleb and I teaming up against you?"

"Pretty much." I'd been dealing with her abilities for almost a decade. I couldn't deal with his too.

"I'm sorry for knocking you out. You know I didn't mean to do it."

"I'm supposed to trust you now?"

"I didn't start the lying game."

I clenched my jaw and concentrated on not ramming the car in front of me. "How do I keep him out of my mind when I'm dreaming?"

"Don't know. He's always popping into mine."

"AWESOME." All those times I'd played with her while she was sleeping, teasing her back to consciousness for sex. "What about Naomi? Any special powers she recently developed?"

"Nah, the freak gene skipped her."

"Is that supposed to be my silver lining?"

"I could be your silver lining." She used her deep, phone sex voice.

I didn't trust myself to speak.

"Does that mean you're going to punish me tonight?" Hope threaded through her words.

"I'll sleep on the couch for a while."

"Fine." She licked the tip of her pointer finger and sucked on it gently. Sliding it between her pink lips, partway into her mouth. Slowly, she pulled it back out again.

I cranked the stereo back up, blaring my old school drum and bass. Out of the corner of my eye, I watched her trace the moist pad of her finger over her bottom lip until it glistened. It had been too long. Herr Peoples missed her. I wasn't sure how long my conviction would last.

Punishing her was the appropriate response, but punishing myself verged on overkill.

CHAPTER 24

Oliver

I searched the entire seasonings section for the one spice Aunt Ines swore by when making wiener schnitzel. I only remembered the label was red and the lettering was yellow. Maybe white. Snippets of people's conversation circled around me, but the old crow cawing on the next aisle caught my attention.

With a voice that could shred steel, I recognized Mrs. Kohler without seeing her. The town's self-appointed matriarch hadn't mellowed in the ten years I'd been gone. She clucked to her friend to get her attention. "I can't believe Oliver moved his boyfriend into the Richter farmhouse."

I stiffened, hating when people talked about my sex life even if they had it all wrong.

"But he dated Michaela in high school." Mrs. Wiesner's high-pitched voice was almost as annoying as Mrs. Kohler's.

Michaela Fuchs. Mickey to me. First girl I ever loved.

"Such a weird child. Remember when he ran over my dahlias with his bicycle? I knew he was a bad seed," Mrs. Kohler said.

"Do you really think he is, well, you know?" Mrs. Wiesner asked.

Mrs. Kohler must have given her a definitive nod because Mrs. Wiesner said, "Heinrich must be spinning in his grave."

Heinrich, my grandfather, wouldn't be surprised to hear Mrs. Wiesner still lapping up every word Mrs. Kohler said.

"Why would Oliver bring that into our town?" Mrs. Kohler happily judged, sentenced, and carried out the execution when it came to people's personal lives.

On my first grocery run, everyone stared at me. I chalked it up to curiosity over my not-as-familiar mug. Nope. Rumor mill said I was gay and ashamed of my "abnormal" lifestyle, so I stashed my boyfriend away.

I let the story stand. It kept people away from Kai.

"He blows back into town driving a big expensive car and takes over his grandfather's house. Doesn't invite anyone over. Doesn't pay his respects to his elders." Mrs. Kohler sniffed.

"All the kids are living together these days." Mrs. Wiesner was the one who snuck me cookies after Mrs. Kohler threatened me with damnation for ruining her dahlias. Mrs. Kohler's face must have flashed disapproval because Mrs. Wiesner rushed to add, "And it's a crying shame."

"A pity he's gone and ruined the Richter name."

Mrs. Wiesner tutted before asking, "How's the church raffle ticket sale?"

Mrs. Kohler kept to my sex life with renewed condemnation. "Do you know what the boyfriend's name is?" Mrs. Wiesner probably shook her head because Mrs. Kohler announced, "Kai Guhn."

Everyone knew Kai was a boy's name. Well, everyone that spoke German, which included most of my small town and excluded my wife's parents, who'd given her a Hawaiian name that meant ocean.

"German or Oriental?" Mrs. Wiesner whispered.

"Neither is appropriate."

"Oh dear, what next?"

I peeked around the corner to see how the old biddies had aged. In a word: badly. Mrs. Wiesner shrank into herself. Her eyes dominated her face like an emaciated owl. Mrs. Kohler clearly enjoyed one thing more than gossiping: eating. Boy, did she enjoy it.

"He came from such a nice family…" Mrs. Wiesner bit her tongue when her friend began shaking her head.

I caught a flash of red hair before Kai grabbed me and yanked me right into the sights of Mrs. Kohler and Mrs. Wiesner. From the gleam in her eye, she was about to throw down Kai style. She laid a kiss on me that woke Herr Peoples right up.

Gasps encircled our PDA. Kai pulled away and turned to face them.

Mrs. Kohler pressed her palm to her chest. "Well, I never. You should be ashamed of yourself!"

"For kissing my husband?" Kai asked. "It's not like I'm gossiping."

Mrs. Wiesner scurried to Mrs. Kohler's side.

Mrs. Kohler liked to throw her weight around. The 300-pound, seventy-something-year-old woman said, "Just who do you think you are, barging in on a private conversation?"

"I'm the Oriental/German houseboy you were so interested in," Kai paused. "It must be difficult preaching about decency, while spreading lies about my husband."

Mrs. Kohler stared at Kai.

"But you're a girl." Mrs. Wiesner's palm crept up the side of her face.

Kai laughed.

Grandpa used to say Mrs. Kohler came out of the womb fighting and never stopped. She stepped forward. "As a prominent member of this community, I must voice my concerns."

"If you were concerned, you'd have talked to Oliver, not behind his back. And his sexuality is his business, no one else's."

"It's God's business," Mrs. Kohler thrust her chin up and out and looked down at my wife.

"Oh, my mistake. Are you God?" Kai crossed her arms and raised both eyebrows.

Having Kai defend my honor was too much. I'd never wanted her more in my entire life. "Honey, we should get going." I put my arm around her and tried to steer her away.

She wrapped both arms around my waist and pressed against me. "I was so enjoying the welcoming committee."

I imagined dead kittens in the road. Blood all over the pavement. Anything to keep Herr Peoples in check. I smiled at the old biddies. "Nice to see you again." I nodded in their direction. "Mrs. Kohler. Mrs. Wiesner."

Mrs. Kohler sniffed. "Oliver, you should stop by soon to pay your respects." It wasn't an invitation, but an edict. All in town paid tribute to the Kohlers.

Kai rested her head on my chest. "I'm sure you can remember way back when you were young. We have so much to do to get the house in order and Oliver can be so demanding."

The sound of a finch being strangled came out of Mrs. Wiesner's throat.

"Hey, stranger." Mickey winked at me as she started scanning our items at the checkout counter.

"Hi, gorgeous," I said on auto-reply.

Kai cleared her throat and gave me her *clarify now* stare.

I rushed to explain, "It's how we'd greeted each other since we were eleven."

Mickey smiled. "Though we've known each other since three."

"Mickey, this is my wife, Kai. Kai, this is Mickey, my..." Ex girlfriend? First lover? "...old friend."

Kai's eyes flashed right before she forced a smile and extended her hand. "I didn't think Oliver had any friends here."

Mickey shook her hand. "He definitely does."

Same old Mickey.

"It's a shame we're so wrapped up with the house. Leaves us little time for friends." Kai went back to unloading the front of the cart.

"Oliver's always made time for me," Mickey said.

Kai slammed the olive oil on the counter.

"How's it feel to have water and electricity again?" Mickey asked as she scanned our items.

"Almost livable." Item 4 and 5 of 500 had been crossed off my to-do list.

Kai snorted.

"My brothers would be glad to help out. I'll even whip us up some gulaschsuppe," Mickey said.

"I may take you up on that." Mickey made the best beef goulash soup in town and her brothers were all around fix-it guys.

The wheels of the cart hit my toes.

"Ow."

"It slid out of my grasp," Kai said.

"Did your aunt know you were coming?" Mickey asked.

"We moved the date up. She planned her cruise last year, I wouldn't let her miss it."

"We should have her over when she gets back," Kai said.

"Sure." I finished unloading the back of the wagon.

"She stored most of your grandfather's furniture with my dad." Mickey trapped me with her gray-green eyes. I'd always loved green eyes.

The wagon bumped into my ribs.

Kai said, "Beep, beep," and pushed me down the aisle and away from Mickey. "I'll pay, you bag."

Mickey's hand shot out to stop me. "Please don't. My manager would be furious if I let a customer bag stuff."

"We wouldn't want to get her in trouble. Would we, Oliver?" Kai asked.

She was giving me angry eyes. Damn. I loved blue eyes the best.

Too late, my wife muttered in my head.

As soon as Mickey finished ringing up our groceries, Kai swiped her credit card.

"Must be hard to furnish that old farmhouse with what you had in your tiny New York apartment," Mickey said. "If you want to look at your grandpa's furniture, I have the spare keys to my dad's place."

"I'd love to. Give me your number and I'll call you," Kai said.

"Oliver already has it." Mickey bagged our stuff.

The awkwardness thickened like cornbread. I was about to say something to slice through it when a little boy barreled into my leg. He bounced onto the floor butt first and sat there, looking stunned.

"Hey kiddo, you okay?" I reached out to help him up.

He peered up at me with Mickey's eyes.

She rushed out from behind the register. "Are you alright, Lukas?"

"I'm okay, Mommy."

Mickey scooped him up and ran her hands over him. "Any ouchies?"

He pointed to his butt.

Mickey's concern melted into annoyance as she scanned the store. "Where's your Gammie?"

Mickey's mom came bustling through the crowd of shoppers. "I'm sorry he got away from me again. He squirrels off when he sees Mommy." She mopped at her face with a handkerchief, sounding winded.

"Ma, you have to watch him more closely," Mickey said.

"I never lost sight of him." Mrs. Fuchs had that calm that comes from successfully rearing six kids. When she noticed me, her eyes brightened and her voice jellied. "Oliver Richter come over here and give me a hug."

"Mrs. Fuchs, great to see you again." She was a third mom to me after Aunt Ines. Her heart-nourishing hugs lasted minutes.

She let me go and asked, "What brought you back to town? Or should I say who?" She winked at Mickey. "You know Michaela and

I always figured you'd find your way back to us."

Kai stepped forward and slipped her arm through mine. "Honey, you haven't introduced us."

I looked from my third mom to my wife. "Mrs. Fuchs, this is my wife, Kai."

Mrs. Fuchs's forehead rippled and she blinked six times before she wrapped her hands around Kai's and pumped it. "So you're the girl who stole Oliver away from us."

"And you're the woman who helped raise him," Kai said.

"He was the sixth son I always wanted." Mrs. Fuchs patted at her neck with her handkerchief. "You were living in New York, last I heard."

"We needed a break." Sounded way better than I hijacked my wife and held her hostage the past week.

"The town hummed with rumors, but I figured Kohler was at it again," Mrs. Fuchs said.

I laughed. "Some things never change."

"The important things don't. Like Friday dinners at the Fuchses' house."

"You still make spätzle?" It was my favorite as a kid.

"This Friday's spätzle and jägerschnitzel. You have to come," Mrs. Fuchs said.

Images of egg noodles with veal in a mushroom cream sauce ran through my mind. My mouth salivated. For ten years, I'd longed for home-cooked Austrian food.

Kai tucked her hair behind her ear. "We couldn't impose."

"I'd take it as an insult if you didn't," Mrs. Fuchs said.

The Fuchses' family dinners accounted for 60% of my good Butternut memories. I'd loved all the noise when I was a kid. So different from the imposed silence of my father's house.

Kai squeezed my hand. "Can we bring anything?"

Mrs. Fuchs's gaze skimmed over Kai's petite figure. "You cook Austrian food?"

Kai blushed. "Not well."

"Come early, I'll teach you. Bring a big appetite and a nice Riesling and we'll get along great."

"Sure," Kai said.

"I'll make my kaiserschmarren for Oliver," Mickey said.

I'd loved her shredded pancakes longer than I loved her. "With homemade plum compote?"

"Is there any other way?" Mickey smiled like we shared the best secrets.

Kai tightened her hold on my hand.

CHAPTER 25

Kai

Of all the ways I'd imagined my husband opening up about his past, not once did I think I would confront it in the check-out line at the grocery store. I'd expected the revelation would come in pieces over the years. Possibly on the anniversary of a loss. I thought I'd have time to accustom myself to the idea of his life before me.

Instead, I came face-to-face with real people who now populated our present. People I never knew existed. People who still meant something to him.

Deep down, I always knew that the key to understanding him was buried here. It was why I wanted to visit Butternut. Because the part of Oliver I didn't know existed here. And I wanted to know all of Oliver.

I shoved the groceries in the trunk and got in the passenger seat. Oliver slid into the driver seat. I hated seeing the strand of emotion that linked Oliver and Mickey. It sparkled like tinsel across the checkout line, glints of friendship and affection. Mrs. Fuchs believed he'd come back for Mickey. As if they were the greatest love story yet to be told. Rendering me a marker on their road back to each other.

I didn't know what to do. Suddenly, there were books before the story of us. Not just a prologue, but an entire series of novels that didn't include me. Stories of how Oliver became who he was. Stories that included Mickey. Stories I'd never heard.

An earthquake had hit the epicenter of us, opening a chasm of uncertainty.

Oliver was about to pull out of Super One Food's parking lot when I blurted out, "You lost your virginity to her?"

He jerked his eyes off the road to look at me. I stared right back at him, daring him to deny it.

Lying is pointless with a telepath, he thought.

"Insulting, actually."

I hate when you do that.

"Then stop telegraphing your thoughts." I hugged my purse.

Granite bees swarmed around him, encapsulating his thoughts in their hive. "I was fifteen."

"Were you in love with her?"

His jaw tightened. "It's complicated."

"It's a yes or no question."

"We grew up together. She was my best friend."

I stamped my foot. "Answer the damn question."

"Yes."

One word became a serrated blade plunged into my stomach and yanked back out again. My breath hissed through my teeth.

"You had boyfriends before me. Everything with Mickey is in the past," he said. His thoughts remained encased in granite.

"Why didn't you tell me about her?"

"She wasn't in my life when we met."

"You want to have dinner with the guy who deflowered me?" I asked.

"I'll cancel."

"We're going."

He threw his hands up, but grabbed the wheel when we drifted too close to the center line. "What do you want me to do? Go back in time and save myself for you?"

"I can't believe you prefer those Listerine green eyes." My vision blurred. I blinked rapidly, shoving the stupid tears back behind my eyeballs.

"I didn't mean to hurt you."

"How did she know about the water and electricity?" I asked.

"What?"

"You think she's gorgeous." I hated the quiver in my voice.

"We've always greeted each other that way. It didn't mean anything." His thoughts wafted out a tiny window in his hive. *Oh God, is it that time of the month?*

"Did you see me buy tampons?" The tears escaped my eyes. I hiccuped and wiped the back of my hand across my face.

You're the only woman I know who looks pretty when she cries.

"Don't even..." I scavenged in my purse for a tissue. "How long has it been going on?" I struggled against another round of tears.

"Huh?"

"How long have you been calling her?"

He chuckled. "Since never."

"Don't bullshit me."

He tossed his phone into my lap. "Check the call log. She's not in there."

I skimmed through the numbers. He was right. But he'd added her to his contact list.

"How long have you had her number?" I asked.

"Well, Officer, it would be about three days ago. I was buying groceries and our paths crossed at the checkout counter. She slipped me her number in case I needed help settling in."

"While you left me locked in the bedroom?" I sniffed.

"Right after you broke the tree branch and threatened to impale me on it."

"Can't you take a joke?" I grumbled.

"You're the only woman I've broken multiple laws for."

"You should have heard her thoughts."

"Is that what's eating at you?"

I opened my mouth and Mickey's words flash-flooded the car. "She couldn't believe you were gay because you were such a horn dog with her. Even if it were true, she decided to bring you back."

"Luckily, I'm straight and married."

I imagined a window in my shield and opened it an inch so I could hear Oliver's thoughts. "She hoped she'd see you again after San Diego. What was that about?"

Oliver stared at the road. His granite hive stayed in place and his window disappeared. "She came to visit once, but nothing happened."

"When we were together?"

He shook his head.

"Why didn't you tell me about her?"

He shrugged. "Some things have to be left in the past. She was one of them."

"Until now." I'd told him about most of my previous boyfriends. The important ones, anyways. I played with the cup holders between our seats. "You know she wants you, right?"

"Doesn't matter. I want you."

"Even without green eyes?" I asked.

"Ocean blue are the kind I can swim in forever."

His words were absolutely, positively what he believed to be true. I couldn't fight him on it. But I would have to fight for him. Mickey's thoughts made that clear. I leaned across the armrest and gave him the kind of kiss he loved. Intense, deep, breath-stealing. He had to pull over to avoid running down a cow on the Wiesner farm.

"I love how you can go from sad to passionate in under 10 seconds flat." His palm cradled my face.

My hands wandered lower. It had been eight days since I'd touched Herr Peoples. Eight days of agony for him. And me.

"Let's go home," he said.

"I don't think you can make it."

"All I need to do is clear the property line."

"Deal." I stroked his thigh.

He pulled back onto the road and sped off as though his life depended on getting home in the next five minutes.

CHAPTER 26

Oliver

"LicD license and registration, son." Officer Lainer, who resembled a Shar-pei more than any person I'd ever met, stood on the other side of my car door.

I didn't know about the speed trap near Apple Street. Three blocks from Cherry Lane. Two minutes from Richter property. My wife rifled through the glove compartment for the registration, while I extracted my license from my wallet.

Officer Lainer examined my driver's license. "Richter. Oliver." He leaned in the window. "You Reinhard's boy?"

My first lesson in life? Always answer an officer's questions. "Yes."

"He was a great chief. Still had years left in him when that heart attack took him," Officer Lainer said.

That was my dad, a cop for most of his life. The chief of police just the last twelve years of it.

Lainer looked around. No witnesses, but for some cows and farm posts. "Son, I clocked you at 68 in a 55."

Give me the ticket so Herr Peoples can get down to business, I wanted to scream. Instead I said, "It didn't feel that fast. Sorry."

"They taught you to read at that fancy California university Reinhard sent you to?" He wasn't going to let me off the hook.

"I never got to meet my father-in-law." Kai's tone was lobster-bisque smooth. "His dad wanted the best for Oliver. I think I would have liked him."

"They didn't come more dedicated to their family than Reinhard," he said.

"We moved back here to fix up the family farmhouse." She leaned into me to look up at Officer Lainer. "This is such a nice town."

He stared down at her. She smiled back at him. I'd swear he was about to let me off with a warning until his radio squawked. He walked out of earshot, but came back with a resigned expression. "Son, I clocked you doing 13 above the speed limit. I have to write you a ticket."

"I understand. It won't happen again," I said.

He scratched away on his notepad and handed me the ticket. "Chief wants you to stop by the station Tuesday."

"Who's the chief?" Dread climbed my vertebrae.

"John Schneider," he said.

My father's best friend. My honorary uncle—not by blood or marriage, but because of the steel bond of their friendship. Dread tripped, tumbling down to my gut. "What time?"

"Ten in the morning. You remember how to get there?"

I nodded. Who could forget the place my father loved best?

My wife didn't say a word the rest of the drive. She got my need to be alone with my thoughts. Even went so far as to lock herself out of my mind so I could think. Sometimes, she knew me better than I knew myself.

I didn't want to think about my father. I'd buried him long before he died. Some deeds are unforgivable. Deeds there was no redemption for. My father did one of those deeds.

I didn't want to see Detective, shit, Chief of Police Schneider. I hated pretending my father was a great man. I never had to do it in New York. There, I could forget who the Richters were. What Reinhard had done.

I slammed my palm against the steering wheel. Tuesday morning, I'd go see Schneider. Then I'd come home. Kai and I would work on the house. I'd forget about everything else. I was damn good at forgetting.

The car rumbled to a stop in front of our farmhouse. Kai eyed me as I cut the engine. Without saying a word, we got out of the car and unloaded the groceries. I left her in the kitchen to unpack everything and headed straight to Grandpa's study for a shot of Jack. I threw back two and waited for them to take effect. Stared out the window at the remnants of Grandma's garden. Weeds had conquered the vegetable patch and gutted her flowerbeds.

I thought after all this time, I could come home. My father had been dead nearly nine years, but he remained alive in the minds of the people of Butternut. Their great chief of police. The upstanding man who fought for justice. What a crock. But something inside me refused to tell the truth. Even after his death, I couldn't go against the old man. I slammed my fist on the desk.

Shitfuckingdammit.

"Try not to break your hand, we don't have insurance anymore," Kai said from the doorway.

I rotated my chair around to face her. "Groceries done?"

She nodded. "Jack helping?"

"Not so much."

"I've got an idea." She moved toward me like a Bengal tiger stalking an axis deer.

"A distraction?"

"Better."

"What'd you have in mind?"

She straddled my legs and leaned in, giving me a great view of her tits. A full C-cup practically tumbled out of her tank top. Herr Peoples stirred again.

She came close enough to kiss me, but at the last minute skipped my lips and went for my ear. "Let me show you."

The things Kai's tongue could do. I didn't think any woman ever spent so much time on my ears. As she licked and sucked, her hand grazed my lap.

I groaned and dropped my shield.

She sent the images into my mind. Showing me what she wanted me to do to her. Handcuffs…whipped cream…the thing I'd dreamed about…

It was too much. Herr Peoples wasn't going back to sleep anytime soon.

Her lips moved onto my neck. She was definitely going to leave a mark, but all that mattered was that she kept going.

And then she was coaxing me out of my shirt. Unbuckling my belt and sliding my pants off. The woman had me down to my boxer briefs before I realized it. Mischief dimpled her smile. "I've been a bad wife lately, haven't I?"

I gulped. Game or trick question?

Game, she replied in my mind.

"Now, it's time to take your punishment." I tried to sound stern. She liked to pretend I was a cold German who barked orders at her. Whatever turned her on.

Her laugh stroked my skin. She spun around and raced out of the room. Herr Peoples impeded my pursuit. I almost caught up to her on the stairs, but decided to let her get all the way to the bedroom before I grabbed her.

She gasped as I tackled her to the bed. My fingers fumbled with the button on her pants. She whipped her tank top over her head in a deft movement, reached around and unhooked her bra one-handed. It whizzed past my shoulder.

Her voice filled my mind, *Let me undo my button.*

"THANK YOU."

She giggled as my mouth came down on hers. My hands went for all those forbidden parts I loved to touch.

She moaned and let me deeper into her mind. Sensations inundated my brain. Her pleasure, my desire, all rolled into one giant ball of ecstasy. The great little pill we used to take in our club-kid days. That's what sex with my wife felt like most of the time.

She made one of those cute noises that let me know I'd found the right spot. Not that I needed it. Her excitement electrified the hairs on my body. Oh, it was the spot all right.

I nearly lost control of Herr Peoples as she came. I loved how she could decimate my self-control. She was mind-shatteringly amazing.

I try.

You succeed.

Rubbing, teasing, licking, sucking, fingers, tongues. It all melded together. She took mutual pleasure to a whole new level. Changing the rules of the game so I shared in her multiple orgasms.

Herr Peoples couldn't take much more. But I held out, wanting to prolong each second of pleasure until it skipped along the border of pain. No one compared to Kai.

Not even Mickey?

Never.

Her mouth. Dear God. That tongue. What a way to die.

We collapsed onto the bed drenched in sweat and sex. Sex was always an adventure with Kai. How far she'd push it. How deeply our minds would intertwine until the pleasure became more than either of us could handle. The sum always being greater than each of our parts. I stretched against the ache in my legs and back. Every muscle had strained itself for maximum satisfaction.

Her hand inched toward mine. When her fingers laced through mine, I pulled her toward me. She lay there, tracing designs on my chest with her nails. "Happy?"

"Completely satiated." I yawned, stroking her back.

"It was really good."

"One of our top five."

"Top five of your life?" she asked.

"Do you want me to score you against Mickey?"

She plucked a hair out of my chest.

"Ow, what the hell?"

"Don't be crude."

"I'm not the one measuring performance. I distinctly remember you giving yourself an 8 and hoping I thought it was a 9."

She pulled away.

"Trust me, when I'm about to come, hearing you thinking about your performance kinda kills the mood," I said.

"As much as you chanting *don't blow my load* over and over does." She crossed her arms, forming a platter for her breasts to rest on.

"You wanted me to come quickly? I held out for you."

She slid off the bed and started looking for her clothes.

God, she had a great ass. "Honey, come back to bed."

She refused to look at me.

I got out of bed and walked toward her. She tried to duck me, but I wrapped my arms around her. "She was a vanilla 6. You're a 10 and like rocky road."

Her arms snaked around me. "Wait 'til you see what I have planned for your birthday."

Several fantasies two-stepped through my thoughts.

Kai murmured, "Not even close."

CHAPTER 27

Oliver

At 9:30 a.m. on Tuesday morning, I left Kai to sleep in. She earned it. God, did she earn it. By 9:50 a.m., I stood outside the two-story brick building that housed Butternut's police station, town hall, and fire department. The tiny town's police force existed by covering the neighboring towns of Glidden and Mellen.

I checked my watch. Three more minutes to question what Schneider wanted. Everything had been settled before I left for college. My silence was bartered. Maybe he wanted to remind me of what was at stake. His cushy position. Dad's reputation. The life I'd built.

I fiddled with my cell phone until 10:00 a.m. Then I took a deep breath and pulled open the glass doors. I made my way to the receptionist, Betsy Lainer. She'd been my dad's secretary and probably remained the spinster sister of Officer Lainer.

Without looking up from the message she was jotting down, she asked, "Hello. How can I help you?" mimicking the tone of a GPS navigator's voice.

"Here to see the chief."

She raised her precise gaze to meet mine. "I heard about your speeding ticket. Is that how you announce your homecoming?"

Betsy had scolded me every time I got a B in school.

I studied my shoes. "I was in a hurry."

She tutted. "This isn't New York. You could have killed a cow or one of the Wiesners' grandkids."

She still made me feel like that dahlia-murdering little boy. I hung my head. "I won't do it again."

"Your father would whoop you if he were here."

"My wife's none too thrilled."

She clasped her hands together. "Do you have a picture?"

"Sure." I fumbled through my wallet and handed Kai's picture to her.

"She's a pretty one." She ran her finger over the photo. "Your dad would be so proud."

"Thanks." I rocked on my heels. "I think the chief's waiting."

Betsy buzzed the chief's secretary and slid the picture back to me. A few minutes of small talk later, the door to the police department swung open.

The younger and prettier version that replaced Betsy said, "Come with me."

Betsy smirked, believing Schneider would administer the lecture I deserved. She was still under the misapprehension that he was one of the good guys. Once upon a time, he had been. Back when I still called him Uncle John.

I followed his secretary past a couple cubicles and back to the chief's office, my father's old office. My mouth felt like I'd eaten a dozen shortbread cookies. I swallowed and rubbed my tongue over the roof of my mouth. The parchedness lingered.

Dad had spent more time in the chair behind that desk than in our house. Now Schneider sat there. The promotion to chief had destroyed his waistline and his face sagged under the inertia of small-town politics. The moustache he'd grown didn't help matters. Neither did his thinning dirt-colored hair. The ghost of old Uncle John haunted his Cheshire-cat smile.

He gestured for me to take a seat. "Oliver, my boy, still up to no good? My officer clocked you breaking the sound barrier on Creamery."

"Nobody got hurt."

He sucked his front teeth and made that annoying thunk sound.

After his secretary shut the door, I leaned forward. "What am I really doing here?"

His sausage fingers played with a quarter, rolling it between them. He'd taught me that trick when I was 10 and desperate to be a part of my dad's poker nights. "Is that any way to greet your uncle?"

"You stopped being my uncle 10 years ago." When Dad and he sent me away to college and I promised to never speak of what they'd done.

His smile faded. "Oliver, we did what was best. I thought you understood."

"Tell that to the Hoffmanns."

"Leave the past where it is. They've made peace with it." He kept rolling that quarter along his bloated fingers. On his other hand, he wore the ring he'd been given for 25 years of service. My dad had the same one. I'd buried it in a cigar box at the bottom of my closet.

"I'm not here to cause trouble." A part of me wanted to tell the truth. But his word still outweighed mine and my father's reputation still eclipsed mine.

He leaned back in his chair. "I knew one day you'd come around. Told your daddy so."

"Leave him out of this."

"It wasn't right, you missing his funeral."

I gritted my teeth. "You know why I couldn't come back." Death rendered my father's fall from grace complete. He could never undo what he'd done. What he'd made me do.

He sucked his teeth again. "I'm willing to leave it alone, if you are."

"Done. Are we finished?"

Schneider laughed. "You're as stubborn as your daddy was. No forgiveness in you."

"You want forgiveness? Tell the Hoffmanns what really happened to their son."

"Christian is gone. Nothing can change that."

"We could clear his name." That meant something around here. Too much to the older generation.

Schneider kept playing with that damn quarter. "Boy, keep your nose clean, focus on your future with your pretty wife, and we'll get along just fine. Talk about what happened and we're going to have a problem."

"I got nothing to say." I headed for the door.

As I twisted the doorknob, he said, "Reinhard was a good man. He did the best he could for you after your mama died."

The muscles in my shoulders bunched up. His words shattered a wall of glass inside me, sending shards in every direction. I yanked the door open and slammed it behind me.

CHAPTER 28

Kai

I jitterbugged around the kitchen in Oliver's blue button-down shirt, making breakfast. It was the only meal that came naturally to me. The coffee machine slurped and the butter crackled.

I heard Oliver's thoughts before he arrived. They rolled ahead of him the last half-mile drive to the house. *I want to crawl back into bed and forget myself with Kai.*

I considered turning everything off and waiting in bed for him, but sex was a Band-Aid to an eight-inch knife wound. We needed to start facing his past together.

His key jangled in the lock and his footsteps hesitated near the kitchen. *I should have taken a longer ride. Yeah, to Alaska and back. Do I still have time to escape?*

Before he made up his mind, I turned and smiled at him. "What happened, Honey Bear?"

"Nothing much, Sugar Tongue." He headed to the living room.

I turned off the burner and trailed behind him. When I caught up to him, I walked my fingers up his arm and around his neck. "Why were you thinking of running out on breakfast?"

He pulled back. "I hate when you do that."

"Then shield your thoughts. The less people in the room, the easier I hear you. All the time alone here makes me more sensitive. I think I might have picked up a bear's thoughts yesterday—or at least images from its mind." They were primal. Raging. Violent. I shuddered. "Why does this Schneider guy get under your skin?"

"I don't want to talk about it."

"You never talk about it."

"I can't."

"There's a big difference between can't and won't." I bit my lip to stop the lecture from leaving my tongue. I wanted to be in his world like he was in mine.

He walked over to the fireplace and picked at the flaking paint on the mantle. *Why can't you stop pushing?*

"Because I want to help."

The peeling paint came loose and fluttered to the floor. Marble imprisoned his thoughts.

"Marble? That's impressive," I said.

"I've been experimenting with different rocks."

"So we only talk about my problems? That's not much of a partnership." I perched on the couch's armrest.

"I'll be fine."

I stared at his back, willing him to turn around. "You don't have to be."

"Christ, can't I have something that's mine?" He slammed his fist into the wall.

"You have your entire childhood, which you don't talk about. Then there's your father. Now Schneider. I'm starting to lose track of what I can ask about."

The marble thickened, entombing his thoughts. "I'm Austrian. We're quiet people." He prowled around the living room.

119

"Do you think it was easy to let you in?"

He stopped. "You made it look easy."

"It was the biggest gamble of my life. But I wanted you in my life, which meant sharing all the messy goo with you." I rubbed my palms over my thighs.

"Maybe I'm not ready."

"Maybe you'll never be ready. Maybe you like holding back. That way you never risk your entire self on me."

"Is that from your freshman year psych class?"

"Years of observing and listening."

His tone flat-lined. "There are things I can never talk about with anyone."

I didn't want to ask. Didn't want to hear the answer. But I had to know. "Does Mickey know?"

He raked his hand through his hair. "She grew up with me. She knows what she saw. That's it."

My chest seized up, like sucking air through Saran Wrap. I watched the seconds tick by on the clock on our mantle. Their passing didn't ease the tightness. "Maybe you should go have a heart-to-heart with her."

"I don't want to tell anyone."

I whispered, "Do you remember when my grandma died?"

He nodded.

I hardly spoke of it. The words reopened every wound and left me to bleed out. It took so much for me to mention her passing. To remember what happened afterwards.

He came and sat beside me. His marble prison melted away. His thoughts of that time flowed over me.

You were so close with your grandmother. You tried to bring her back to health and nearly followed her into death. I stopped you. When they revived you, you were catatonic for weeks. Then inconsolably depressed. Your mom wasn't equipped to deal with it. So she put you in that institution. I thought your sanity was gone. I thought you were gone. It took months to get you back and free you from that place. I married you to make sure it never happened again.

That I never lost you again.

I struggled to find my voice. "I remember you coming to see me and promising it would be alright."

"And it is. You're okay."

"But you aren't. You hide it way better than I did, but your past is gnawing away at you," I said.

"Kai, I can't."

Something inside me shriveled up. "Oliver Richter, why don't you trust me?"

He pulled me into his lap. His palms cupped my face. "Kai Dorian Guhn, I need you to trust me the way you did when you were in that institution. Believe in me like that. I can get through anything with you."

I wrapped my hands around his and squeezed. "I'm sure I can figure a way out of whatever is going on."

"You're beautiful when you're fighting for me." He kissed the top of my head. "I love you too much to let the past get in our way."

Frustration warred with faith. I wanted to believe him, but I couldn't ignore the voice inside me. The one that kept asking which of his secrets might destroy us.

"You'll be the first person I'll tell," he promised.

I wrapped my arms around his neck.

He licked his lips. "Something you wanted?"

"You. Always." I kissed him the way I did on our first date—zero hesitation, but with uncertainty over how long it would last.

CHAPTER 29

Oliver

T wo days later, I was patching up the living room wall and Kai was picking out drapes from the JCPenney's catalog when someone knocked on the door.

"Wonder who that is," Kai said.

"It's not Mickey." Please don't let it be Mickey.

I opened the door to see Aunt Ines standing there in all her floral grandeur. Her love of bright colors hadn't changed much in the past ten years. She wore a giant floppy hat with red and orange fake dahlias along the brim. The floral pattern on her long dress matched her hat. Her orange wool sweater coat balanced all the red. She finished the outfit with a peony print handbag and shiny red shoes.

Aunt Ines didn't smile. She didn't extend her arms for a hug. "Oliver, it's about time we talked face-to-face." She sailed into our living room.

Kai stood up and started toward her.

Aunt Ines stopped. "This must be your wife."

"I'm glad to finally meet you." Kai gave her a genuine smile. No teeth. Just lips offering a gentle welcome.

"Me too. Dear, I need a few moments with Oliver. Could you make us some tea?" Aunt Ines asked.

Are you okay with this? Kai's question echoed in my head.

Give us half an hour, I thought back at her.

Kai headed into the kitchen.

Aunt Ines put her purse on the couch and shrugged out of her sweater coat.

"When did you get back?" I asked.

"This morning." Her gaze flickered around the living room she'd grown up in. "The house looks nice."

"We're working on it."

"Grandpa was ill the last year. He couldn't keep it up. Wouldn't let me help."

"I know how he could be," I said.

"He missed you."

"I talked to him on the phone." After I left for college, I couldn't bring myself to return to Wisconsin. It was the only way to keep my father's secret. By never stepping foot in this town. Not to visit his house. Not to see Aunt Ines. Not even to help Grandpa.

"It wasn't the same. I never understood you cutting your daddy off, but that was between you two. After he passed on, why didn't you come to see Grandpa and me?"

"I couldn't." All those lies and secrets. I hated maintaining them. Especially since they weren't mine to keep. The only reason I'd come back here was to save Kai's life.

Wisps of gray wove through Aunt Ines's brown hair and tiny wrinkles spider-webbed around her eyes. The time I'd missed had marched across her face.

"It was the only way I could deal with what happened with Dad," I said.

"Grandpa kept the house because of you. He wanted you to have a place to come home to." Her hands knotted around each other.

I rested my hand on hers. "I'm sorry. I missed you both."

She inhaled the tears. "Oliver, I am glad to see you. But you left a pile of hurt behind."

"I know." I braced for her response. "But I'm here to make amends."

"Tomorrow morning, I'm going to the cemetery to visit Grandpa."

"I'd like to come," I said.

"He'd like that."

"Can I bring Kai?"

She nodded. "Your daddy is buried beside him."

"Right next to Mama." Something inside me went super nova. I slammed marble around it. "I can't, Aunt Ines."

"You don't have to. But someday you might wish you had."

She didn't know what he had done. The suffering he'd caused. I wouldn't ruin her memory of her brother, but I couldn't perpetuate it. "Baby steps."

"Baby steps." She patted my knee.

CHAPTER 30

Oliver

The last name carved into the gray granite headstone read *Richter*. Beneath it, in smaller script were written *Muriel Elisabeth* and *Heinrich Oliver*. The grandmother who tucked me in when my mother no longer could. The grandfather who looked after me when my father no longer would. They lay side by side under the fast departing leaves of a giant sugar maple.

The fall breeze ruffled Aunt Ines's hair. A smile tiptoed across her lips because she took it as a greeting. "Papa, I brought Oliver to see you."

I placed a bouquet of white lilies by the headstone and stepped back.

Kai laced her fingers through mine and squeezed.

For months, I'd stumbled over the fact of his death and then plunged into a memory of him. He remained alive in my mind. Somehow the gravestone made his death inescapable. He hadn't just left his house. He'd left the earth. He'd left me.

As a child, I came to this cemetery often. My mother lay one plot over, underneath the white headstone. Every time I visited her grave, I hoped to feel closer to her. To catch ahold of her lingering spirit or feel it brush past me. Anything to prove she wasn't gone.

I no longer believed the dead lingered with their bodies. It sounded too terrible. To be trapped in a decaying body stuck seven feet under the ground. Aunt Ines, however, took comfort in thinking something of Grandpa lingered here. Not in the casket, but around the grave. That he wasn't completely gone.

She needed me to believe it too. I cleared my throat. "Grandpa, I'm sorry I never came back to see you. You're the one who taught me what it was to be a man. To stand strong and love well. I can't thank you enough for that."

Grandma passed away during my sophomore year of high school. She wasn't alive to see the disappointment my father became to me. "Grandma, I'm sorry I haven't visited in years. You've never been far from my thoughts."

Kai squeezed my hand. *You're doing great.*

Thanks. "Grandpa, I'm going to restore the farmhouse to what it was." It was the only way I could make amends now. "Don't worry, I know I'm not the best at building, but I'll hire people to help me."

"I'm sorry we never met in this life," Kai said. "You raised a wonderful grandson. A man who has loved and taken care of me more than anyone ever could."

Aunt Ines's eyes misted over. "I miss you both every day. Mama, I still can't make marillenknödel as good as yours. Papa, you were right about the house. It was always Oliver's."

I slid my other hand into Aunt Ines's. "I'm sorry for staying away. For the time I missed with both of you."

"The calls were nice. The gifts were thoughtful. But all we wanted was you."

Dumplings of regret lodged in my throat, making it harder to get the words out. "Can you forgive me?"

Aunt Ines said, "You're the last of my kin."

"I'd like to be a family again." I tightened my grip on their hands.

The two of them were the only family I had left.

"It would be wonderful to have an aunt to show me around," Kai said.

Aunt Ines reached out and took Kai's other hand. "It's what Grandpa and I always wanted."

It was more than I ever dreamed possible. To be in Butternut. To see Kai healthy again. To have my aunt back in my life.

The white headstone six feet over would have to wait for the day I could face my parents' ghosts.

Dan Fuchs had always had a man crush on me. Mickey teased him about it mercilessly, but that didn't stop him from showing up on my doorstep the next day, twenty minutes after Aunt Ines whisked Kai away for lunch. Three years younger, Dan had tagged along with Mickey and me on our adventures. He was a good kid. And a little hero worship was nice every now and again.

Though he'd turned into a hulking man. I only recognized him because he had the same curly mud-pie colored hair and Golden Retriever brown eyes. He barely said a word to me as he surveyed the entire house from bottom to top.

After we descended the stairs back to the foyer, he headed to the kitchen. "We start work in the basement."

"I was working on the wall in the living room."

"Cosmetic stuff might make the wife happy, but we have to make sure the foundation is good first. Electrical wiring, pipes, heating. The basics."

I nodded, without knowing what we were looking for. I was an Excel guru, not a home improvement guy. I asked the first question that came to mind. "How much is this going to run me?"

"Mickey asked me to help you out. The consultation is free, the labor comes cheap, but you'll have to cover all parts."

Thank God for Mickey. "I owe you."

"Got any tips on the market?" Dan asked.

"Buy commodities." I had managed my little portfolio for a while. A nest egg for our kids. If Kai ever agreed to have kids. We fornicated like bunnies, so it was only a matter of time. Yeah, I was praying for that 1% chance of the pill failing. She kept claiming it wasn't the right time, but maybe it would be soon.

"Who got the water heater up and running?" Dan asked.

Shit. What was his name? "He's in the phone book."

"Ackerman and Sons?"

Sounded right so I nodded.

He tinkered around for a while checking different gauges. "They do good work."

I breathed a sigh of relief. One less drain on the bank account.

He strolled around the basement, examining the pipes that ran along the ceiling. "Problem."

I came over. "Serious?"

"Nah, but it will set you back several hundred." Dan ran his hand over the connector between two pipes. "A few of these need fixing and some sections of pipe need replacing."

By the time we made it outside, we had several thousand dollars' worth of work to do without even touching the landscaping. I'd taken a weed-whacker to everything growing too close to the house. The rest, I planned to deal with in the spring.

"The roof is good," Dan said. "Your grandfather replaced it a few years back. I worked on it."

"How's the job market?" I hoped things were better than I remembered.

"We don't have a stock market here. Mrs. Kohler wouldn't let you near her husband's bank."

"I'm branching out. I thought I'd try my hand at farming," I said.

Dan laughed. When he saw my expression wasn't changing, he stopped. "Oh wait, you're serious. Sorry, man. Just remembering the time you tried to milk the cow and it turned out to be a bull."

"Mickey set me up."

"What about the time the chickens refused to lay eggs until you left the farm?" he asked.

That was the worst summer job on the Wiesners' farm. "Temperamental beasts."

"How about the paper route? People still haven't found their papers."

"Okay, I get it." Maybe I wasn't cut out for country life back then, but I could learn.

"Dad might need some help at his place. People like to store stuff here. It's really cheap," he said.

Manual labor was not my specialty. "Does he need a bookkeeper?"

"Alex takes care of that." Dan slapped me on the back. "City living's made you soft. I'll talk to Dad and see what we can do. No promises."

"If you hear of anything around town…"

"You'll be the first to know."

And the last to be hired, given my track record.

CHAPTER 31

Kai

Certain occasions demanded makeup: work, anniversaries, family holidays, and dinner with my husband's first love. Oliver preferred me without it. Barefaced, he swore I could still pass for sixteen. He wasn't a pervert, well, not that much of one. He said he loved the way I looked first thing in the morning. I think he loved not getting powder or lip-gloss smeared on his face when I kissed him.

With makeup strewn across the bathroom counter, I sprawled across the sink. My face had to be inches from the mirror to make sure each stroke was applied properly. All to make it look like I was naturally gorgeous and hadn't spent an hour doing my makeup.

"You're taking this dinner more seriously than most generals do a battle," Oliver said from the bathroom doorway.

"Warpaint." I twisted the base of my lip glaze and waited for the pinky gloss to saturate the brush. My bee-stung lips were my best feature. Covered in gloss, they were more desirable than a glazed donut.

"Can I get in there for a 10-minute shave?" He hovered behind me, stroking his stubble.

I coated my lips in shininess and rubbed them together. "What's wrong with the dresser mirror?"

"I like the steam in the shower." *I'd like a few minutes with those lips too.*

The other bathrooms weren't operational yet. "Then you'll have to wait for the bathroom and my lips."

"I can be patient about the lips." He winked at me. "But at the rate you're going, we'll miss dinner."

"Would that be so bad?" I stopped dabbing at the gloss under my lip and stared at him.

"I don't want to hurt Mrs. Fuchs's feelings."

"Like that's who you're worried about." I closed my right eye and meticulously shaded the lid to give me Japanese-anime-wide eyes.

"A dry shave is better than no shave." He stood behind me, leaning right and left and trying to get a glimpse of himself in the mirror.

"Oliver Herwig Richter, we have two other bathrooms with mirrors. Use one of them."

His jaw dropped. *No one knows my middle name. Except…*

Aunt Ines. I smiled.

What else did you find out?

"Wouldn't you like to know," I said.

Not the bedwetting story.

Poor wittle Oliver. Such a teeny tiny bladder.

He turned his shaver off. "That stays between us."

"What about milking the bull?" I asked.

"A beginner's mistake."

"At twelve? You had to know what a dick looked like." I stared at him in the mirror. "I'm sure the Fuchses know all about it."

"The bull, yes. My middle name, sorta. But the bedwetting is top secret."

I gave him the thumbs up and waved him away with my hand.

He backed out of the bathroom, muttering, "Why did I let you go off with Aunt Ines?"

"Because you love us."

He snorted.

My hand slipped and I nearly tumbled into the sink. "This isn't exactly easy. Especially with an audience."

"You need my grandma's vanity."

"Nice idea, but not helpful right now." I stretched closer to the mirror.

"Your bathrobe is not really suited to that task." *It makes me want to wrap those gorgeous ankles around my waist after dinner.*

"Oliver," I squealed, kicking the bathroom door shut.

CHAPTER 32

Oliver

fter dinner at the Fuchses', my wife slammed the car door and stomped into our house. I sat in the car, debating my next move. I could take a ride around town to let her cool off, but this was Kai. Even if I went to Midlothian and back, she'd still be angry. I put the keys in my pocket and trudged into my house.

The clomping on the floorboards upstairs told me she'd made it up to our bedroom. Darth Vader's theme song played in my head as I mounted the stairs, knowing that somehow this would be all my fault. Again. Women were so hard to live with. No wonder gayness was on the rise worldwide. When I touched the knob, something smashed against the door.

I pushed the door open. A plastic figurine lay on the floor. Kai slammed the bathroom door. Her clothes were strewn all over the room. She knew I hated that.

A couple minutes later, the toilet flushed, and she stormed out of the bathroom to face me. "If you think about how irrational I am one more time, I swear to God I will never speak to you again."

Great opening line. But I had no idea where to go from there. "I think I missed something."

"No, I caught too much."

She pushed past me in only her bra and panties, stalking toward the dresser.

If I threw her on the bed, maybe I could distract her?

She slid her nightgown over her head, undid her bra and tossed it aside. "If you touch me right now, I will hurt you."

This would be the worst time for me to get angry. But that pissed me off. "I'd like to see you try."

She came at me. After she flipped me onto the bed and knocked the wind out of me, I remembered her green belt in karate. I lay there, realizing Dan was right. I was too soft.

She leapt away from me. Her voice shook as much as her hands. "Give me the keys. I have to get out of here."

"In your nightgown?"

She grabbed her jeans from the closet, shoved her feet into them, and hopped around to get them over her butt. She held out her hand. "Keys."

"Come and get them."

She edged toward the door. "Throw them to me."

"Tell me what happened."

"Did you think my telepathy wouldn't work in a crowded room?" she asked.

"Figured you'd shield."

"I could, but I wanted to test myself," she said. "The time alone out here sharpened my skills. I isolated each stream of consciousness at the table without straining my shield."

Mickey must have thought something bad.

"She did, but she always does." My wife's body trembled from the effort of holding in her emotions.

"Who offended you?" Maybe Dan or Alex?

Kai blew out her air in one angry stream. "It's you, asshole."

136

"What did I do?"

"Are you kidding me?" She stalked over to me.

I yanked her onto the bed. She squirmed and fought back. She was a tigress tonight. Too bad we wouldn't get to use that energy for something fun.

Tigress? She sank her teeth into my neck.

That hurt. I let her go and touched my neck. Felt the indentations her teeth left in my skin. "You bit me?!"

She rolled to the other end of the bed. "You shouldn't have grabbed me."

I pulled the keys from my pocket and tossed them at her. "You've seriously lost your shit tonight."

Something flashed in her eyes. It might have been panic, but she hid it so quickly I couldn't be sure.

"Don't do that," she said. "Don't act like this is all in my head. You thought it. I heard you."

"Before you sentence me to a hanging, can I get a trial?"

"Let's start with how many times you wished you had a normal life. With a normal wife like Mickey and a big normal family like the Fuchses." She knelt on the bed, staring at me.

"Maybe it ran through my head tonight. I'm not going to apologize for wanting a family."

Kai punched the mattress. "It's not that you want a family. It's that you want her family. You want her mom to be your mom." Her voice broke. "And her son as your son."

"I've always wanted a big family. I never hid that from you."

"You wanting a family is old news. YOU WANTING HER FAMILY IS WHAT HURTS ME."

"I never said that."

"You thought it. I felt how much you wished Lukas was yours."

"He's a great kid."

Her eyes glistened. "That's all you have to say?"

"I've always been up front about wanting kids WITH YOU."

"How many times have you thought of having a family with someone else?" The tears spilled over. She impatiently wiped the back of her hand across her cheeks.

I didn't know what to say. I mean, sure, sometimes when I passed a family with a stroller I wondered what it would be like to be that husband. Not because I wanted another woman, but because I wanted to have a family. A nice normal family.

Her shoulders started shaking and a sob escaped her lips. I hadn't seen her this upset since we left Manhattan.

"I'm too much?" She curled her knees into her chest and leaned against the footboard.

I hated when she was this hurt. Especially when I'd done it. Even if it was an accident.

"You don't want me anymore?" she asked between gulps of air.

"I love you."

Tears streamed down her face. "But you love her too." She got so riled up she couldn't speak. *You love the idea of a simple life with no telepathy. A husband and wife and a house full of kids. You see how much easier it would be with her and you can't help wondering what if.*

That's not true. Everyone wonders. It's what I do that matters. I edged closer to her.

She didn't move. The tears didn't stop.

I was supposed to rescue her from the pain. Not be a new source of it. "I'm a guy, we think things all the time but never act on them. Sometimes on the commute to work, I'd think about what it would be like to screw a hot blonde or get some sexy brunette to suck me off."

My wife choked on another sob. "Not helping."

"Be honest, don't you have thoughts about other men?"

She studied the duvet cover and sniffed several times. "Not about the exes who still want me."

"Wait, who?"

"I have a past. Guys I loved and slept with."

138

"Right." I guess I always thought of Kai as mine. "You in contact with any of them?"

She wiped her face on her nightgown. "Some facebooked me. One or two call on my birthday. But they aren't a part of my daily life."

"Neither is Mickey." After nine years, how could she doubt our relationship?

"Because it's been five years of hell for you. I'm not stupid. Mickey must be looking really attractive now."

I stood up. "Thoughts don't count. I can't believe you would use mine against me. That's not fair."

"Not fair? Not fair?" Her voice rose each time she said it. "Life is not fair, Oliver. Hearing everyone's thoughts even when you try your best to shield—that's not fair. I had to sit by and do nothing while that bastard raped his own daughter. I'm not going through that ever again."

Rage sliced through my words. "Are you equating me with a pedophile?"

She raised her chin. "I won't sit by and watch ever again."

"I won't talk to you when you're like this." I stormed out of the bedroom, galloped down the stairs, grabbed my jacket. I hit the night air and started running. Right now, I needed to be anywhere but here.

CHAPTER 33

Oliver

I
t might have been my choice to sleep on the couch the past three nights, but that didn't help the crick in my neck. It didn't help the silence that stretched between Kai and me either. She wandered ahead, perusing the aisles of Grandpa's stuff laid out at the Fuchs Storage Center, selecting what she wanted brought back to the house. An activity we should be doing together, we did separately and simultaneously.

Alex, my high-school buddy and the second oldest Fuchses' son, took notes on his inventory sheet while two high school kids carried the items out to the delivery truck. So far we had a leather sofa, queen-sized canopy bed, a dresser, several lamps, end chairs, end tables, a kitchen table and a dining room set.

My wife laughed with Alex. His blond hair and blue eyes made every woman glow in his presence. Even one that was still fuming at me. How had I become the outsider in my own marriage? We never stayed angry like this. She ignored me; I didn't talk to her. My expectation of an apology diminished with each passing day.

I caught up to Kai and Alex in time to hear him ask, "How'd Oliver land a woman like you?"

"Right time, right place." Her fingers swept over the carvings on an armoire. She opened the doors to look inside. "We'll take this too."

He jotted it down.

She wandered ahead of us. Her red turtleneck sweater and black pencil skirt embraced every inch of her.

Once she was out of earshot, I asked, "What happened to my grandma's vanity?"

He scanned the list of items. "It should be coming up."

"That's a definite take."

He whistled. "You're a lucky man, Mr. Richter."

I followed his gaze. Kai had bent over to examine the legs of a chair, giving us a great view of her ass. I cleared my throat. "She's taken too."

Alex laughed. "You make that clear to Mickey?"

"We're just friends."

His voice dropped several stories to a basement quiet. "Nathan did a number on her. She's still not over it."

Mickey dumped me for Nathan the beginning of our senior year. After I left, she married him and they had Lukas.

"What happened?"

"He ran out on her when Lukas was a few months old. Tread lightly," Alex said.

"Understood."

Alex hadn't just been Mickey's older brother; he'd been like mine too. I never competed with him for a girl. The minute any female met him, it had been an instant forfeit for me.

We turned the corner and caught Kai sashaying in front of an antique mirror.

I burst out laughing. Alex grinned. She flushed salmon pink.

Alex asked, "The mirror too?"

She studied its frame. "Nice craftsmanship. This will look great in the bedroom."

Alex tucked the clipboard under his arm and walked over to it. "My grandfather made it."

She glanced at him. "Is everyone in your family as gifted with their hands?"

"We have our talents," he said.

Was she flirting with him right in front of me? Either she'd taken crazy pills or the revenging had begun.

She caressed the wooden frame of the mirror. "You'll have to show me some time."

He leaned closer and slipped her his business card. "Happy to help fix up the old farmhouse."

STOP IT RIGHT NOW.

What? She asked in my mind.

Flirting with him.

I'm just making friends with the Fuchses. Same as you.

Unbelievable. The first time we'd spoken—well, shared thoughts, anyway—and this is what we talked about.

She put his business card in her wallet. "Is there anything we missed from the list?"

"Boxes of books, kid's toys, knick-knacks, linens, and of course the gun collection." He read off his inventory sheet.

"Gun collection?" She raised an eyebrow.

I stepped between them. "My grandfather loved old guns, especially the Wild West ones. He has one that belonged to Doc Holliday."

"Can we shoot it?" Her face shone with excitement.

"That's a take," I said to Alex.

She tried to shrug off my arm, but I steered her back to my Cherokee.

"And the books," she shouted over her shoulder.

"Should be there in a couple hours," Alex said.

CHAPTER 34

Kai

After he corralled me into the car, Oliver didn't say another word. The vein in his temple pulsated. I'd served him an adrenaline cocktail spiked with jealousy. It might have been wrong, but I needed him to feel what I felt. To understand what Mickey and he did to me.

A mile of dirt road from the farmhouse, he cut the engine and hit the locks. "What the hell was that all about?"

I pulled on the lever to open the door. It didn't. I tried again.

"Child-proof locks."

I folded my hands in my lap and stared straight ahead.

He slammed his hand against the steering wheel. "Shitfuckingdammit, Kai. Talk to me."

"The delivery guys will be here in a couple hours. We should get home and figure out where we want everything." I mimicked customer-service calm.

"Is that all you have to say to me? It's been three days."

"I hauled out my sex toys."

"I'm not talking about that. Wait, which ones?" He wiped his hand over his face. "Don't get me off track. We need to talk."

"About what?" I wanted him to say it. To acknowledge it.

"About Alex. What the hell were you doing back there?"

"Proving a point."

He scratched his forehead. "Which was?"

Venom sank into my words. "It sucks to watch the person you love flirt with someone else. Hurts to think of them wanting another, doesn't it? Welcome to my pain, Oliver."

"Are you going to suck one of those high school boys off next?" he asked.

"Depends. Did you go down on Mickey already?"

"I haven't laid a finger on her," he yelled.

"I had to endure you flirting with her. I listened to your thoughts about each other."

"What's it going to take to even things out? Do I have to watch Alex screw you?"

"Don't be ridiculous. But every time you flirt with her, I will return the favor." I clenched my hands in my lap.

"That's disgusting. He's like my brother."

"Which makes Mickey like a sister. Talk about disgusting."

I DON'T WANT MICKEY.

"You don't want me either," I said.

He unbuckled his seatbelt and climbed over the armrest. His knee slipped into the cup holder.

"What are you doing?"

"If you won't listen, I'm going to show you." He straddled me and pressed the button to make my seat recline.

"In the car? We haven't done that since college." Anticipation stole my breath.

He clicked the button to release my seat belt. "Your choice: front seat or back?"

"Seriously?"

He nuzzled my earlobe. "Front seat it is."

I didn't want him using sex to win the argument, but I didn't want to miss out on car sex.

"You need this as much as I do." His face hovered inches above mine, waiting for a response.

I wanted him. Always. "Kiss me."

Is this another game?

"Show me how much you want me." I rocked my pelvis against his. "I want you inside me." I started unbuttoning his shirt.

"Kai, I…"

I pressed my fingers to his lips. "No talking. Just fuck me."

He sucked on the middle of my upper lip. I moaned and melted into the seat. He nibbled on my lower lip. I wrestled with his belt. He slid his hand under my sweater, fumbling with my bra. Thank goodness, I wore a skirt today. He shoved it up to my waist and pushed my panties aside. He played with me, teasing me, taunting me. I undid his pants and strained to free Herr Peoples from his boxers.

"Get inside me now," I said.

"Demanding today, aren't we?"

He moved onto my neck and I whimpered. The wall between us gave way. His thoughts and mine melded. I crashed into his mind as he pushed into me. Deeper and deeper. The desire, the need, the want—it had never been so intense. Waves of pleasure rode us.

Oliver, Oliver, Oliver.

Kai, you're so beautiful.

Don't leave me.

I love you.

CHAPTER 35

Oliver

When the delivery truck rumbled up in front of the house, I stepped onto the porch to watch them unload.

Alex slid out of the driver's seat. "Dan mentioned you were looking for work."

"Yeah?" Didn't explain why Alex had left his office to oversee our delivery.

"You've got an audition. Show me what you can do."

I was still buzzed from showing Kai exactly what Herr Peoples could do. "I don't follow."

Only one high school kid got out of the truck.

"This is your trial run to prove that you can work for Fuchs Storage Center." Alex tapped his pen against the clipboard.

Kai joined us on the porch. "What's going on?"

Alex flashed his bookshelf-straight teeth at her. "We're going to oversee Oliver and Jimmy as they unload everything."

Kai rubbed her hands together. "Sweet. Can I tell him what to do?"

Don't be dirty.

You wish, she said inside my head.

"He has to do whatever you tell him," Alex said.

Her smile radiated out of her eyes. "This is awesome. I haven't the faintest idea where I want the dining room table."

My muscles ached from car sex. Especially since I'd done all the thrusting.

Alex looked at his clipboard. "Well, ma'am, they'll just have to keep moving it until you're satisfied."

I swore she was laughing at me when she asked, "So satisfaction is guaranteed by your company?"

"We aim to please," Alex said.

"Better get started." I followed Jimmy to the back of the truck and eyed all the items inside it. "What's first?"

He threw a pair of work gloves at me. "Just don't drop anything. Or you're paying for it."

Four hours later, the dining room table had moved from the kitchen to the dining room, where it changed positions eight times before Kai settled on the first one. Then we unloaded Grandma's kitchen table from the truck.

While we furnished the spare bedroom, I second-guessed our decision to have a queen-sized canopy bed for guests. Jimmy and I spent an hour getting all the pieces into the room. Luckily, he knew how to assemble them.

I was distracted by Alex and Kai talking in the hallway. They made a gorgeous picture. Their kids would be fair skinned and blue eyed. Maybe have strawberry blond hair. When Kai touched his arm, I lost my grip on the screwdriver and the screw rolled into oblivion.

"Alex can't help it, but he'd never cross a buddy like that," Jimmy said.

I eyed the burly 16-year-old boy. Either he was insightful or I was obvious. I took his place holding up the frame and waited for him to tighten the bolts. I couldn't see the hallway from this position. Didn't know what they were laughing about.

Alex stuck his head in. "We'll be right back. Kai wants me to help her with something."

It damn well better not be what I helped her with in the car.

Ten minutes later, they returned with a pitcher of iced tea, several egg salad sandwiches, and Oreos.

Jimmy and I emptied the pitcher of iced tea in three seconds.

"Everything's in and nothing got broken," Alex said.

"Good job!" She almost did her happy dance.

Jimmy shuffled his feet. "No big deal."

"Thanks for all your hard work. Everything looks great." She handed him fifty dollars.

I held my hand out. She slapped me five. "Good job, Honey Bear."

I winced at the nickname.

Alex coughed. "We'll be needing an extra guy on our next move. Any plans for Wednesday and Thursday, Honey Bear?"

I shook my head, knowing I'd never live that name down.

"It's an overnighter. We have to go into Minneapolis and pack up a couple houses. You up for it?"

I glanced at her. We'd never spent a night apart since we were married. Would she be okay in this house alone?

She smiled. *I bet your aunt Ines would love to have a sleepover. Just us girls.*

Don't pick her brain.

I can't make any promises.

"I'm in," I said.

"I'll check on Kai while I'm helping Dan with the repairs around here," Alex said.

"Aren't you coming to Minnesota?" I hated the idea of him having more time with Kai.

"Nah. Pete likes to oversee the big moves." Alex leaned in. "I think he's got a girl stashed away there."

"Pete's your older brother, right?" she asked.

He'd been out of town the night we had dinner with the Fuchses.

"Yeah. We both work for Dad. Though sometimes I help Dan out," Alex said.

Funny, Dan never mentioned that.

"See Oliver. I'll be fine. Big strong men protecting me during the day and Aunt Ines and Grandpa's gun collection here at night," Kai said.

"Great." Not sure what bothered me most—that my wife could substitute my good-looking friend, my just-reconciled-with aunt, or an old gun for me. Maybe it was how easily she could spend a night without me.

CHAPTER 36

Kai

I hadn't been a big cook before Butternut, but after meeting Mickey, cooking Austrian food took on a new importance in my life. Aprons securely in place, Aunt Ines and I started preparing wiener schnitzel at the kitchen counter.

"I used to make this for Oliver all the time." Aunt Ines pounded out the veal cutlet. "It's his favorite."

I measured out the seasonings and breadcrumbs and poured them into a Ziploc bag. "I've always wondered what Oliver was like as a child."

"Sweet. Quiet. Slightly diabolical." She chuckled.

"Do you know what happened between his dad and him?" I asked.

"I wish I did." She moved on to the next cutlet and flattened it out.

I waited. Hoping she'd tell me more.

"Don't think I didn't ask." She sighed. "Oliver and his daddy are the two stubbornest men I ever knew. Well, aside from my daddy."

She glanced at me. "Did he tell you anything?"

"His childhood is off limits." I poured flour into the bowl.

"And you don't mind?"

"Secrets have a way of creeping out at the worst times. Not talking about things always makes them seem worse."

"Every time I asked Reinhard, he'd say, 'Oliver's got to be Oliver.' Then he'd change the topic or leave the room."

"Did you ever ask Oliver?" I asked.

She hmmphed. "He was more tight-lipped than his daddy. When Oliver was still here, I'd ask and he'd leave the house. After he left town, anytime I hinted at it on the phone, he hung up."

"Stubbornest man in the world," I muttered.

"I wish they could have worked it out before Reinhard passed."

I rolled a cutlet in flour, making sure to coat both sides. "Do you have any idea what might have happened?"

She shrugged. "Nothing concrete, just an idle old mind leaping to possibilities."

She was one of those people who projected her thoughts. They slammed into the window in my shield, begging to be heard. When I opened the window, they leapt inside.

Reinhard closed himself off after his wife died. It was how he dealt with the loss. But when he pulled away from us, he pulled away from Oliver too.

We did our best to step in. Papa and Mama and me. I think it helped. Until his friend died. Oliver was only twelve. Too young. Reinhard didn't see how much it impacted Oliver. He didn't reach out to his son. Eventually, Oliver stopped trying with his daddy. He and Reinhard stopped speaking. Neither able to bridge the distance caused by unsaid words.

Out loud she said, "Teenagers and parents. They have falling-outs. Theirs was just made permanent by my brother's unexpected death."

"I guess that's why Oliver couldn't come back to Butternut."

"My daddy and I liked to think so. We hoped he didn't lump us all together and decide we weren't worth being around anymore."

"Whatever Oliver had to run from, it wasn't you or your dad," I said.

Her lips tipped up, but her eyes remained weighted with sadness.

"I hope someday you can get him to talk about it. He needs to tell someone."

"He's lucky he had you growing up."

"It wasn't easy letting that boy go. But we loved him so much, we wanted him to be happy even if it was without us," she said.

"I'm glad we came back here."

"Me too." She sniffed and wiped her eyes on a dishtowel. "Veal juice got in my eye."

"Let's blame the lemons."

She laughed. "We haven't started cutting them up yet."

CHAPTER 37

Oliver

Four days later, as I trudged up the front steps, certainty washed over me. I'd always be a failure in Butternut. Though I was still hazy on what happened with the chair. The piano I remembered in vivid Technicolor. Probably because I dropped it on my foot. This had to be a world record—fired four days after I was hired.

The front door swung open. Kai slipped out onto the front porch. "What happened? I could feel your depression rolling in like a thunderstorm."

"You wouldn't believe it," I muttered.

"Honey Bear, it's easy to drop a piano. That's heavy. But how did you manage to set a table and chair on fire?"

"You tell me, Ms. Knows-It-All."

Her forehead scrunched up. "You were pretty murky on the details."

I still didn't know how I did it. "The lady had one of those essential oil things you love on the end table beside her lamp. I went under the table to unplug the cord. Someone kicked my foot and I bumped my head on the table. The oil spilled everywhere. I guess it dripped too close to the socket."

Kai nodded.

"I yanked the plug out of the wall. Bam. It sparks and burns along the oil trail to the table—wait for it—igniting the chair."

She bit her lip to stop from laughing. "How much did it cost?"

"The Fuchses ate the loss, but had to let me go on the spot to make the client happy." I hung my head. "I had to wait for a ride back here."

She hugged me. "My poor baby. Come inside, Mama will make it all better."

It was one thing to mess up, another thing to cost the Fuchses money. I felt like I'd pick-pocketed my family.

I stepped into our house. Saw the candle-lit living room. I was getting laid tonight.

She slipped her hand through mine. "Count on it." Then she pulled me into the kitchen.

I smelled—no, it couldn't be—wiener schnitzel?

"Aunt Ines spent all night teaching me how to make it. I hope you like it." She smoothed her hair back from her face.

"It smells delicious."

She pushed me toward my grandma's rectangular kitchen table. It sat six, but was set for two. "Sit. I'll bring everything to you."

When she scooped the side of potato salad next to the breaded veal cutlet, I almost wept. She even knew to place a slice of lemon on top of the wiener schnitzel. And the bottle of ketchup sat on the table. It was essential with this dish. At least, the way we Richters ate it.

The first bite—a slight crunch then succulent.

She opened a bottle of Riesling and filled my glass. "We'll dip into our savings to pay back the Fuchses."

"What about fixing up the house?" Her parents were visiting in a couple months.

"We'll use the savings to tide us over until you get a new job."

"Why don't I solve the Middle East Peace Crisis while I'm at it?"

"Then you can get going on reuniting North and South Korea." A smile grazed her lips. "Don't worry." I started to relax until she slipped in, "Aunt Ines is helping me find work."

I clenched my knife and fork. "You are supposed to de-stress. Do some writing." She never finished her novel. The one she started in college. The one she stopped writing when her grandmother died.

"I'm going to help out at a daycare center a couple days a week," she said.

The food in my mouth tasted like Styrofoam. My stomach recoiled. "No, you aren't. That will push you right back toward the edge."

"I'm doing okay. My shield is repaired." She leaned forward.

Her breasts practically tumbled out of that low cut purple top. She'd worn it on purpose to distract me. It was working. Damn it. "And too much stress, A.K.A. PEOPLE, will tear it apart again."

"I can't be stuck in this house anymore."

"Someone has to oversee the contractors." I took a gulp of wine.

"You mean Dan? He could be running a poker game out of our basement and I'd never know it." She forked her potato salad.

"Whose idea was it?"

"Aunt Ines gets how much I miss my job. Helping out at the daycare made her transition from teaching to retirement easier. She said they are looking for more help."

"How many kids are there?" I asked.

"They range from babies to toddlers."

"How many?"

"About 40." She rearranged the potato salad on her plate.

"That's 10% of the town's population." Seemed like a huge number for our miniscule town.

"Some of the kids are from Park Falls and Glidden."

I whistled. "That could be 125 people when you factor in the parents plus the other teachers." Way more minds than she dealt with on a daily basis. Way less than she dealt with in New York. Still the strain on her shield might start her back on that path to self-destruction.

She studied her plate. "It would only be three days a week."

"No way."

"They pay $10 an hour and need me 15-20 hours a week."

$600 to $800 a month. Almost tempting.

Her lips curved into serenity. "I knew you would understand."

I dunked a piece of wiener schnitzel in my ketchup pool. "The answer is still no."

"You drag me out here, lock me up in the house, and won't let me get a job. When did we travel back to the 1800s?"

"Remember how you got started at Children's Services?"

Her lips thinned, swallowed by annoyance. "This is different."

"You wanted to save kids, the way your grandmother saved you and Caleb. But it didn't work out that way. Every time you lost one, I nearly lost you."

She stamped her foot. "DAYCARE center. These kids are not in jeopardy."

"That's how it will start out. But you'll sniff out the kid in trouble and then you'll try to fix everything."

"Is that so awful?" She spoke so softly her words barely reached me.

"No." I reached for her hand, but she shoved both of them under the table. "It's what happens when you can't make a difference. I can't watch that happen again."

"I can't hole up here and write. I haven't written anything except case reports for years."

"Don't you miss it?" I asked.

I fell in love with her writing before her. Back in college, we'd hole up in her dorm room, where she'd light a circle of candles around us. I'd twist open Boone's Farm Strawberry Hill wine—her choice, not mine. She'd read aloud her poetry and short stories, encouraging me to share my favorite poems by Frost and Cummings.

"Remember junior year when you started your novel? You'd text me in the middle of class just to tell me you'd finished a scene." I rushed back to the dorm and made her read it to me. I missed the way her entire face lit up when she added a new twist to the plot.

She pushed her wiener schnitzel around on her plate. "I'm not the same girl. I can't be her again."

"Start small. Poetry. Short stories." Her writing had been so important to her. To us.

She rested her fork on her plate. "You understand why I have to help them."

"Because of your grandmother. She taught you and Caleb how to control your abilities."

"We thought we were freaks. Ostracized at school. Outsiders in our own family. She gave us what every child needs. Love and acceptance."

"And you loved her back. You nearly died with her. Isn't that enough?"

"Caleb donates half his bonus to children's charities in the UK. This is what I do." She stalked over to the sink and stared out at our backyard.

"Things are broken in you. You have to stop and repair them."

"I'm fine," she said.

"You're always fine. Until you aren't."

She slapped the counter. "What do you want me to do?"

"I want you to love and nurture Kai. I want you to be selfish and take time for yourself."

She turned around to face me. Her fingers clutched at the lip of the countertop. She pleaded like a child. "If I stop helping them, I don't feel her anymore. Please, don't ask me to give her up."

Tears trembled on her lower lids and slipped over. They ran down her cheeks. She used her knuckles to brush them aside.

Shitfuckingdammit. "Two days a week and you only work with the infants." Their thoughts were so rudimentary, she'd be okay.

"Okay," she said.

"You promise to keep your shield up around the adults. No eavesdropping. Ever."

"I promise." She wiped her face on her arms and started toward her chair.

"And the minute you start getting depressed, you quit. No arguments."

Her smile faltered. "Fine."

She sat back down and devoured her wiener schnitzel. I tried to enjoy the rest of the meal, but I couldn't. It was like a psychic had predicted a bomb would obliterate my life. I could hear the ticking, but I had no idea when it would explode. Just that it would.

The next day, Dan and his toolbox camped out in my downstairs' bathroom. Alex was nowhere in sight. I lingered in the doorway, trying to assess the damage I'd done to my friendship with the Fuchses.

Most of Dan's torso lay inside the cabinet beneath the sink, where he tinkered with the pipes. "Something you wanted, Oliver?"

"You still talking to me after I messed up the move?"

"Pete took a chance bringing you in on such big moves. Should have started you off with a simple one. His mistake."

"I cost your family three grand." He couldn't be okay with that.

"She was a rich lady. We padded the estimate a thousand and still were the lowest bidder."

I let my breath out. "So we're cool."

"You and Me? Yeah." Dan put his wrench down and reached for another tool. "But Pete caught hell from Dad. Took it out on Alex. Give them a few days."

"Will do." I tried to sound casual. "You know of anyone in town willing to take a chance on me now?"

Dan's chuckle reverberated inside the cabinet. "The Wiesners need a hand around the farm. It's grunt work. No skills required. Stop by and talk to Mr. Wiesner."

Dan didn't clarify what grunt work entailed. It didn't matter. I needed cash to pay for all the repairs he made to my house.

He slid out of the cabinet and sat up. Searched through his toolbox until he found something and tossed it at me.

I fumbled but caught the tiny jar in the crook of my elbow. "Tiger Balm?"

"Bring it to Wiesners'. Smear it under your nose."

"Why?"

"Trust me. You'll need it." Then he grabbed a flashlight, rolled onto his stomach and went back to work under the sink.

I swallowed my breakfast and my pride before I showed up at the Wiesners' farm on Monday.

Though balding, Mr. Wiesner had the build of Genghis Khan's father. He looked me up and down. "$6.50 an hour, 35 hours a week."

"That's $227.50 before taxes." Which was $910 a month. If I lasted a month.

"You deal with the government." He handed me a shovel. "Payday is Friday."

The fluttering curtains in the front window of his house distracted me. Mrs. Wiesner peered out. Probably had the phone pressed to her ear so she could fill Mrs. Kohler in on my activities. Both delighting in my fall to manual labor.

"Great." I tried to sound optimistic. "What do you need me to do?" Please no milking cows.

He pointed to the barn. "It needs mucking."

"Is there anything I can do outdoors?"

He shook his head. The sun had carved lines so deep around his eyes, I couldn't make out what color they were. "You work seven hours a day. Half hour for lunch. Bring your own."

I headed toward the barn. With each step, the stench of manure grew stronger. By the time I opened the door, the putrid scent of cow dung conquered my nose and invaded my mouth.

There were mounds of it. Everywhere.

I got out the Tiger Balm and smeared it under my nose. Maybe the Fuchses held a grudge. Or maybe this was the safest thing for me to do. No chance of destroying anyone's property. An hour into it, I reapplied the Tiger Balm and hoped for the destruction of my sense of smell.

Eight days later, I quit. Not because I couldn't handle the work. No, I turned out to be pretty good at mucking out the barn. Seemed I had a knack for shoveling shit—whether it was in barns or at banks.

It was Kai. She refused to let me near her. Even after three showers, she couldn't stand it. She caught a whiff of me and doubled over the toilet the first night I came home. We thought it was the manure. I stripped off all my clothes in the car. She still hugged the bowl whenever I came near her.

Evidently, cows were an emotional bunch and I somehow carried their fears and anxiety home. The psychic stench was unbearable for her. Neither one of us understood how. There was no one to ask whether her abilities were evolving or if cows were just huge telegraphers.

After the seventh night of sleeping in the spare room without sex, I made up my mind. The job wasn't worth it.

Next morning, I stood in front of Mr. Wiesner and said, "I quit."

He didn't look the least bit surprised. "You lasted longer than anyone expected."

"It's my wife. She can't stand the smell." Or the psychic stink for that matter.

"Takes a special woman to love a mucker," he said.

"Is there anything else I can do?" I asked.

"I still remember that summer you worked on my farm."

His chickens hadn't laid an egg until I left their coops for good.

"I can't afford to have my chickens upset," he said.

I hung my head. Unemployed. Again. Twice in two weeks.

Mr. Wiesner rubbed his callused hand over his face. "I told your daddy you weren't meant for this life. He knew you were more like your mama's folks. You should be behind a desk somewhere. There's no shame in that. We all have to do what we're good at."

It was the most he'd ever said to me. "You knew my mom's parents?"

He almost smiled. "Your grandpa Eder was a darn good lawyer. Helped me out of a bind or two."

They died in a car crash before I was born. "Why'd they move back here?"

"Your grandpa loved this town. Thought it could be more than it was." He looked off in the distance as if replaying that time in his head.

I wanted to ask him more about them, but one of the other hands yelled, "Calf's coming!" and Mr. Wiesner took off for the barn.

Word of my unemployment circulated faster than Kohler's rumors of my gaydom. Mickey called, trying to soften the blow. "You were never cut out to be a farmer."

"A job's a job." I tried not to sound relieved. I'd gotten used to Mrs. Wiesner spying on me and reporting everything back to Mrs. Kohler. Truth was I hated the smell of mucking, but Mr. Wiesner had been a decent boss. Though I enjoyed catching up on all the sex I missed that week.

"With your brains, you need something more challenging," Mickey said.

"Got any ideas?" I leaned back on the couch, cradling the portable phone against my shoulder.

Kai rearranged the living room knick-knacks for the umpteenth time.

"We have an opening for a stock boy at Super One Foods. Let me know and I'll put in a good word for you."

"I'm letting you know."

Mickey giggled. "You're such a dork. Come in tomorrow to meet the manager and fill out the application."

Kai would kill me.

Mickey took my silence as needing further incentive. "They have insurance after you work 1000 hours and you can move up to a cashier eventually."

"You think I'll last that long?" I didn't. I seemed destined for desk jobs. According to Mr. Wiesner, it was in my blood.

"With me there to help you? You might make assistant manager." Mickey made it sound so tempting.

"What's the pay?"

"Eight dollars an hour plus time-and-a-half for holidays and overtime. And fifty bucks worth of groceries a month."

"I'll give it a try."

Kai slammed the bull and bear brass figurines down on the mantle.

CHAPTER 38

Oliver

Two weeks passed without any problems, or maybe Kai just hid them better than she used to. I know I sounded paranoid, but when you've watched a loved one come undone, you're always looking for the early warning signs.

She worked Tuesdays and Thursdays at the daycare center. I worked six days a week, with Thursdays being my only day off. Yep. New guy got the second shift all weekend at the grocery store. Third shift three nights a week. Even though Super One Foods closed at 8 p.m., I cleaned the store and restocked the shelves into the darkest hours of the morning.

On Tuesdays, Kai finished her breakfast as I dropped the keys on the counter and headed to bed. On Wednesdays, I had the evening shift, which should have meant afternoon sex for us. Except Dan had a habit of showing up Wednesday mornings to work on the house all day. And Kai refused to have sex with him around. Thursdays, I slept in, while she went to work. I made dinner at night and she showed her appreciation in the bedroom.

The entire time, I worried. Mostly about her sanity.

I still remembered the woman I fell in love with. The woman she'd been before her grandmother died.

The summer after sophomore year, I studied abroad in Austria. Kai came with me by convincing her parents it was educational. The girl hadn't studied a word of German in college. One afternoon in Vienna, it took us two hours to find Peterskirche.

"I'm so glad we found Peters Kirsch," she said in her Gerglish, a mix of bad German and English.

Peters Kirsch translated into "Peter's Cherry" in English. I burst out laughing. "We didn't find Peter's virginity, we found his church: kirche."

She responded by kissing me speechless.

I realized I wanted to marry her. To spend my entire life with a woman who made German adorable.

Her smile filled her eyes. "I'll never find anyone else who loves my poetry."

We didn't set a date or anything. We were twenty and the future remained a hazy dream. After we graduated, we moved to the Big Apple. Marriage was a distant eventuality. I climbed the corporate ladder at Sterns Brothers, a multi-billion-dollar investment bank. She started at the New York Times as a fact checker, using her daily commute to draft new scenes and edit old ones in her novel.

Her grandmother's death changed everything. That's probably what morphed her telepathy. Sent her into the mental institution for months. We should have moved to the desert or a ranch in Montana when she was released. But she had one condition before she'd marry me: We had to return to New York. Otherwise, it was no.

We returned to New York a married couple, but she stopped writing her novel and left the New York Times. Said she was done working for "The Man" and enrolled in a graduate program to become a social worker.

I figured she was rebelling. Her parents thought she was ridiculous. Caleb encouraged her. Like he knew her better than me. Maybe he did.

That ate away at me. The severe migraines she suffered during grad school should have been a red flag for all of us.

She finished her master's, and started working at Children's Services. Gradually, she lost her ability to shut out people's thoughts and feelings. The downward spiral continued with episodes of depression that grew so frequent, happiness became the aberration. Her emotions intensified. They didn't just affect loved ones. They spread to those around her, especially during the bouts of depression. I tried talking to her about it. Flushed the anti-depressants when she tried to overdose. Neither of us could take much more.

When I inherited the old farmhouse, I saw it as my chance to save Kai. Part of me hesitated to strip away my wife's free will. But eventually, it had come down to her choosing to kill herself and me deciding that wasn't going to happen.

So I brought her to Butternut.

Stocking cans on aisle seven was a huge demotion from managing my own audits at Sterns Brothers, but the life we were building out here was worth the pay cut and having to report to someone who couldn't spell Manhattan.

"You're mixing green beans and diced tomatoes again." Mickey came up behind me, reaching around to move the cans to their proper places.

I flinched, knocking the cans out of her hands.

She knelt down to pick them up. "Dented cans are deducted from your $50 grocery allowance. Robert said you're at $20 already this week."

Robert Lainer, Betsy's nephew, had been an annoying pissant in high school and now managed the grocery store. "Kai likes dented cans."

"Not if they start coming out of your paycheck," Mickey said.

"If somebody didn't sneak up on me..."

"You'd have to restock this entire section."

"True." She made sure my mistakes were never caught by the annoying pissant.

Mickey's cell rang, playing "She's a Brick House." She said, "It's my mom. I need to take it," and made her way to the employees only area in the back of the store.

By the time she got back, I'd sorted out the cans. Her face scrunched up in concentration and she sighed.

So un-Mickey. "What's wrong?"

"Nothing." She chewed on the inside of her right cheek.

"Then why do you look worried?"

"Mom got a part-time job. Tuesday and Thursday. The two days I have to work. I don't have anyone to look after Lukas."

"What about daycare?"

She looked at me like I told her to leave him in the woods alone.

"Kai works at The Children's Corner twice a week. She said it's super clean and the kids have a ball."

"What days does she work?" Mickey tapped her finger against her lips.

"Tuesdays and Thursdays."

"He's only four. I'd feel better if someone he knew kept an eye on him."

"Kai works with the babies, but I'm sure she'd check in on him too."

"Thanks. I may give it a trial run." Mickey squeezed my arm. "I'm glad you're here. I missed you."

Kai would kill me for saying it, but… "I missed you too. It's almost okay to be home."

CHAPTER 39

Kai

The silence when everything is roaring inside my head—that's the hardest part of the argument. Knowing that it's coming. It's inevitable. And trying to maintain some self-control while I secretly want to stab my husband's hand with my fork.

"How was work today?" Oliver asked.

"Fine." I speared my chicken breast.

"How were the babies?"

"Fine." I wrestled with my anger and pinned it beneath me. Momentarily, anyways.

"Did robots take over your body?"

I dropped my fork. "What?"

He waved his hand in front of my face. "Earth to Kai? What's going on?"

"Did you tell Mickey that I would watch over Lukas?"

He sipped his wine. "I told her you worked at the daycare and could check in on him."

The chair screeched across the floor as I leapt up. "Do you remember

167

the terms of me taking this job?"

"Of course."

I splayed my fingers on the table and leaned toward him. "Didn't you demand that I only work with infants?"

"So?"

"SO?" I ticked off the reasons on my fingers. "So you made me promise to only work with babies for my own good. So I told my boss I was bad with toddlers, but great with infants. So then you changed your mind the second Mickey needed something."

"I was trying to help."

"By throwing me under the bus?" I stormed to the garbage, scraped the food off my plate, and tossed the dish and fork into the sink.

"Did you get in trouble at work?" he asked.

"I looked pretty bad when Lukas became my shadow."

"What do you mean?"

I leaned against the counter and blew my hair out of my eyes. "The other kids wouldn't play with him, so he begged to spend the day with me in the nursery."

"Why wouldn't they play with him?"

"How should I know? Kids are cruel."

"Speaking from experience?"

"He's a good boy. But he should be with the other children," I said.

"Maybe he felt safe with you? This was his first time away from his family."

"Why do you think I let him hang out with me?"

He brought his plate to the sink, sliding his arms around my waist. "Ya big softy." He nuzzled my ear.

I couldn't help giggling. "Stop it. I'm not done being mad at you."

He gave me his serious face. "Do you want to spank me?"

My pulse triple-dog dared me. "You deserve it."

"I'm willing to take my punishment."

I pushed against his chest. "No sexy time. I'm annoyed at you."

"You'd feel better if you spanked me while lecturing me."

I paused to consider it. "Possibly maybe."

"I'm sorry I offered your help without checking with you. I didn't realize it would make things difficult for you at work. If you want, I'll have Mickey talk to Lukas about leaving you alone."

I shook my head. I'd already figured out how to fix this. "I'll keep helping out in the nursery and I'll watch over Lukas and I'll even forgive you for being a thoughtless ass..."

"If?"

"I can work an additional half day with the toddlers."

"I hate your fine print," he said.

I tapped his forehead. "If you weren't so thoughtless, you wouldn't have to make deals with me."

"Tonight, I'm paddling you."

I slipped out of the circle of his arms and ran to the kitchen doorway, pausing just long enough to say, "Only if you can catch me, old man." Then I sprinted toward the bedroom.

CHAPTER 40

Oliver

Kai wanted a quiet Thanksgiving in our new home with Aunt Ines. Mrs. Fuchs insisted that we stop over, but Kai held firm that we have a family dinner. She gave in on dessert with the Fuchses. She scoured websites for the perfect Thanksgiving feast, finally settling on a Martha Stewart Thanksgiving. No pressure or anything. The grocery list she gave me rivaled a six-year-old's Christmas wish list.

She insisted on a twenty-pound turkey. She was flexible on the organic thing. I refused to eat 20 pounds of hormones. The organic bird was $4.00 a pound. And I still had to get everything else on Kai's list. Phil the deli guy offered a solution. For cash upfront, he could get me an organic bird for $2.25 a pound and his buddy would deliver it to my farmhouse free of charge. I jumped on that deal.

Three days later, the delivery truck rumbled up to the house. I was in the shower, so Kai went outside to deal with him. Half an hour later, I came downstairs to find Kai in the living room with a turkey. A live turkey.

She petted his feathers and crooned away to him. "Who's a pretty bird? Herbie is. Yes, he is."

The weird part? The turkey liked it. He ducked his head so she could rub it.

"What's going on?" I asked from the base of the stairs.

The turkey shuddered and flew at me, making this scary putt-putt noise. He chased me into the dining room.

Kai giggled. "Herbie, shhh. It's okay. That's just Daddy."

I'd swear he cackled. I tiptoed into the hallway and stuck my head around the living room doorway. Kai coaxed him onto the couch beside her. The bird made his version of a purring noise.

"Is it safe to come out?" I asked.

She ignored me. "Who's my good boy? Sitting with Mama on the couch."

I took a step into the living room.

The turkey growled.

She petted his back. "It's okay."

"There must be a mistake. I didn't order a live bird."

She continued crooning to the turkey. "Daddy didn't realize what he was doing, being cheapy cheap. Nobody's gonna touch you."

My stomach rumbled. "What about dinner?"

"Go buy a ham."

"Grocery store's closed for the holiday."

"Then we make do."

"He looks like a perfectly good bird..." I refrained from saying *to eat.*

"Don't even think it. That'd be like having Alex or Mickey as our main course."

"This is our first Thanksgiving." Thanksgiving without turkey was like Halloween without candy.

My wife stroked the feathers on his back. "He's going to need a pen and a house of some sort. What do turkeys live in?"

"Barns."

She looked at the turkey. "Isn't that sweet? Daddy wants to build you a barn."

Herbie cluck-purred at her.

"Wait a second. We need to get him back to his owner." I moved toward the couch.

The turkey puffed up his feathers and made that putt-putt noise again.

"Herbie's protecting Mommy. Good boy!"

I rolled my eyes. "Did you get the guy's contact info?"

"He said he was delivering what you ordered. I signed for it, and Herbie popped off the truck."

"He can't live in the house."

"Don't be silly." She jumped off the couch and disappeared into the study.

Herbie stared at me, daring me to make a move. I didn't. Three words: claws and beak. Kai came back with her laptop. He fanned out his tail for her.

She tucked the laptop under her arm and clapped. "Who's my pretty bird?"

He purred at her. Freaking purred at her.

I rubbed my forehead. My wife had adopted our dinner.

She flipped open the laptop. After a quick Internet search, I was dispatched to set up a tarp outside for him, while she went to gather our fresh fruit and veggies for his lunch.

I was still trying to secure the tarp to the side of the house, when Aunt Ines pulled up in her tomato red Dodge Durango. I rushed over to open her door. She spilled out of the car in a purple wool coat and lemon yellow scarf. She topped it off with a yellow hat decorated with peacock feathers.

"I brought some sweet potatoes and a green bean casserole," Aunt Ines said. "I hope Kai doesn't mind."

"It may be all we get to eat." I picked up both Tupperware containers.

"Oh no! Did she have a problem with the turkey?" Aunt Ines looked worried. "They can be troublesome."

"She befriended him," I muttered as we made our way to the front door.

"What?" Aunt Ines followed me inside.

You could hear Kai singing the "Itsy Bitsy Spider" song in the kitchen. We got to the doorway and the turkey was sitting in her lap, cuddling with her. Aunt Ines burst out laughing.

Kai looked up, enveloping me in her smile. The one that reached all the way to her eyes. The turkey clucked a few times.

"Did you get the tarp up for Herbie?" Kai stroked his feathers.

"It's a work in progress." I put Aunt Ines's dishes on the counter.

"What have we here?" Aunt Ines asked as she walked over to the turkey.

"Aunt Ines, this is Herbie. Herbie, be nice to Aunt Ines." Kai acted like the proud mama.

It was pretty cute. Except she had Rosemary's baby.

Aunt Ines put out her hand and he licked it. She was a convert in 30 seconds.

My stomach whined. "What about dinner?"

Kai wrapped her arms around Herbie and shot me a not-my-baby look. Like I planned on serving him up now.

Aunt Ines pulled a chair out and sat down. "I suppose we could bring a couple bottles of wine and crash the Fuchses' dinner."

CHAPTER 41

Oliver

As good as she was at making Austrian food, Mrs. Fuchs's true talents shone through in her holiday fare. Her turkey was moist and tender with crispy golden skin. Her homemade gravy had the perfect thickness, promising deliciousness to everything it touched. The mashed potatoes had the right ratio of creamy to chunky. The candied sweet potatoes were carnival sweetness. And the stuffing. A man wouldn't care if he died and went to hell after a meal like that.

Sounded impossible, but dessert almost topped dinner. Cherry squares with crumbly topping, pumpkin pie where allspice blended with evaporated cream to charm the taste buds, tartly-sweet apple pie, and linzer torte cookies dusted with powdered sugar.

The meal came to an end when Mr. Fuchs set down his coffee. "An excellent job, my dear." His gaze drifted to the door leading to the garage.

Mrs. Fuchs tapped her teacup. "Time for you and Dan to go work on the car."

"What do you say, Dan?" Mr. Fuchs asked.

Dan looked to his girlfriend.

She stared back at him. "I guess I should get over to my parents."

Dan patted her shoulder as he got up from the table. "Tell them I said hello."

The girlfriend's expression warned that she might never come back, but Dan didn't notice.

We dispersed from the table, and I ended up in the living room. It hadn't changed much in the ten years I'd been gone. Some things had been worn and torn and replaced. The same brick fireplace held up the wall at the end of the room, its mantle crowded with decades of family photos. A shot of Mickey and me at junior prom still sat up there.

Kai was off in the corner with Lukas building a Lincoln Log farm. They had finished constructing the cabin and were working toward a barn. I hoped he got her biological clock ticking.

Alex sat on the sofa, watching football with Pete. What game? I couldn't say. Thomas, the bookishly serious Fuchs, had taken his six-month pregnant wife, Irena, on a short stroll. Kevin, being the youngest, disappeared into his room right after dessert.

Which left one Fuchs, Mickey, to lounge on the armrest of my La-Z-Boy. "I can't believe how much Lukas has taken to your wife."

"She has the Snow White effect." Great with kids and animals.

"How could Phil not mention you were buying a wild turkey that had to be killed and prepped?" Mickey touched my arm.

The years hadn't dimmed the warmth in her eyes. "He rattled on about the quality of the meat for a while. Maybe I zoned out."

Mickey laughed. "How can you miss the words *live bird*?"

I shrugged.

"Poor Oliver. What are you going to do now?"

"Get used to having a pet." Once Kai got it into her mind to do something, there was no way around it. You either got on the Kai train or you found yourself run down by her.

"That's a change of pace for you." Mickey pushed my hair off my forehead.

It felt nice. "What?"

"I remember when I told you to do something, you did the opposite. Always."

Back when Reinhard ruled my life with an iron fist. "Guess I grew up."

"That you did." She trailed her eyes over me.

It made me almost uncomfortable. I glanced at Kai. Her head was bent so close to Lukas, you'd swear they were conspiring to take over the town or sneak a few cherry squares. Wonder if she noticed Mickey.

I noticed. And if you don't do something soon, Empress Qi Qi won't be talking to Herr Peoples for a long time, Kai said in my head.

I leapt up. "Gonna hit the bathroom."

I stayed in there a good ten minutes. If Mickey were still near my chair when I came out, I'd go watch Dan tinker with the old car or play Lincoln Logs with Kai.

Smart move, Kai's voice echoed in my mind.

CHAPTER 42

Kai

No matter how old we got, the girls and boys separated at every get-together. That was how I found myself sitting around the kitchen table with the Fuchs women, Aunt Ines, and Lukas. The kitchen was done in shades of peach and beige and light pine. It should have felt welcoming. But Mickey's frustration boa-constricted around my shield and her jealousy bit into it.

I opened the window in my shield and let her thoughts dart in. *How does she do it? Oliver and Lukas wrapped around her finger. My brothers liking her. My own mother making her feel at home. In my home. It's not supposed to be this way. Oliver was supposed to come back to be with me.*

I was about to shut my window and tune her out when I felt something. A hurt that bit into the marrow of my bones. Anger that simmered in my heart. Someone I'd never felt before. I pushed my window open, trying to catch the breeze of hatred. It blew through my hair, tangling the ends.

He has to pay. The thought skittered through my head.

The more I tried to focus on it, the faster it disappeared. That scared me. Almost as much as the emotion behind the thought.

Lukas slapped his hand on the table and startled me out of my head. He sat on Mickey's lap across from me. "Do the hand thing, Kai," he said like we rehearsed.

"Maybe later." I hunched my shoulders forward and played at embarrassed.

"What hand thing?" Mrs. Fuchs asked.

I smiled, inviting her in on the silliness of it. "My grandma taught me some palm reading when I was little."

"Pleeeeaaase, Kai," Lukas asked.

The emotions circulating at the table vacillated from yellow to green, slightly interested to terribly fascinated. One by one everyone asked me to do it. You know, for fun. Everyone except Mrs. Fuchs, the one person who needed her palm read.

"Mrs. Fuchs, can I start with you?" I asked.

She was too good a hostess to say no. Hesitantly, she placed her hand on the table.

I studied the lines on her palm. "I see a life full of family and friends. You are very lucky."

The corners of Mrs. Fuchs's lips curled in relief.

I stretched out her palm. "But you are prone to breathing problems."

"A little shortness of breath and dizzy spells," she said. "Just part of getting older."

Lukas squirmed in his mom's arms. I winked at him, and he relaxed.

"You should go for a checkup. These are warning signs." I paused. "Things will become more serious. Make sure the doctor tests your thyroid and pays special attention to your throat."

Mrs. Fuchs tried to withdraw her palm, but I held on to it. "Do it for your family. You are their heart and soul. Irena is going to need a lot of help with your first granddaughter."

Mrs. Fuchs gasped, "Granddaughter?"

Irena's eyes went egg-round. "How did you know? We just found out a few days ago."

I rubbed my lips together. She'd been broadcasting it in her thoughts all day. "I peeked at your palm during dinner. I'm sorry. Were you waiting until the baby was born?"

"Thomas wanted to, but I was dying to tell everyone," Irena said.

"Blame me," I said.

Irena laughed. "Mrs. Fuchs, you're my witness."

"I'll tell Thomas the fortune teller revealed it," Mrs. Fuchs said.

Oliver's thoughts tapped on the window in my shield. Without looking, I knew he'd entered the room. I opened the window.

His voice whispered in my head, *What are you up to?*

I'll explain later.

Kai...

Shhhh, I need to concentrate.

I stared into Mrs. Fuchs's palm. "You've been thinking about starting a new business. Hold off on that for six months. You're going to need some time to take care of your health problems. Plus, by then the money will be available."

"My mother had thyroid problems," Mrs. Fuchs confessed.

"All the more reason to be proactive, Anna," Aunt Ines said. "I have to schedule my annual soon. Let's go in together."

"I'm sure it's nothing." Mrs. Fuchs tried to deny any hint of wrongness inside her.

Lukas sat up very straight. "Gammie's sick. I don't want her to die."

"Don't worry, I'll make the appointment." Mrs. Fuchs shot me a withering look.

Lukas grinned at me.

Mrs. Fuchs got up and gasped. "Oliver, what are you doing in here?"

Oliver rolled up his shirtsleeves. "I was raised by two amazing women, who taught me to always do the dishes after dinner." He walked over to the food-encrusted dishes, gunked-up pots, and grease-coated pans surrounding the sink.

I came up behind him and rested my chin on his shoulder. "Everything has to be prewashed. You need some help?"

"You offering?" He leaned his head against mine.

"Of course." I opened the dishwasher. "You rinse, I'll load."

Mrs. Fuchs tried to shoo us away, but I wouldn't budge. "It's the least we can do since we crashed your family holiday."

Mrs. Fuchs rubbed my arm. "You're the newest addition to our family."

Lukas asked, "Can Kai be my aunt?"

Mickey bounced him in her lap. "Would you like that?"

"Yes," Lukas said.

For his sake, Mickey pronounced me "Aunt Kai" and my husband "Uncle Oliver."

Which left me with one question: How would I explain all of this to Uncle Oliver?

CHAPTER 43

Oliver

My wife sat at her vanity, dawdling over her dangly earrings and lapis pendant. Something was on her mind. She was determining whether she'd keep it to herself or share it.

I lounged on the bed in my boxers. "Gonna tell me what you were up to at the Fuchses?"

"They are quite a family." She made eye contact with me in her mirror.

Where was she going with this? "Lukas and Alex are certainly taken with you. Should I be worried?"

She winked at me. "About Alex? Nah."

"What about Lukas?"

She studied the bottles on her vanity. "Have you seen my makeup remover?"

"Yeah, I borrowed it after a night out on the town."

She turned in her chair and stuck her tongue out at me.

"Kai…"

She went back to searching the top of her vanity.

Something was definitely up with Lukas. I stared into her vanity mirror, but she refused to meet my gaze.

"Anything you want to tell me?" I prayed it wouldn't take too long. We were ten minutes away from fornicating.

"About?" She opened her jewelry box and started arranging her rings.

"Lukas." Yep, we were having this conversation. Pause on the sexy time.

She pursed her lips, oblivious to how her robe slipped open.

I couldn't stop staring, anticipating a glimpse of her tits. "Does this have to do with you reading Mrs. Fuchs's palm?"

She did that when people had crazy ideas in their heads and she wanted to sway them away from it. It was a good cover. She could give advice without ever outing herself as a telepath.

"Sort of." She bit her lower lip and rolled it between her teeth.

I walked over to where she sat and rested my hands on her shoulders. "Tell me."

"Lukas is a special kid."

"I've said that since day one." No big deal. Sexy time back on.

Kai squirmed beneath my hands. Keeping a grip on that black satin robe proved challenging.

"No, I mean special-special." She half-whispered, "Like me."

"Are you saying he can read minds?" I laughed. I'd never met anyone outside her family that was like her.

"Not everyone has the same skills. Look at me and Caleb."

I was still pissed about her brother invading my dreams. "I'd rather not."

"We're different in what we can do, but we can do something no one else can do. I think Lukas is the same way."

"Why?" I'd never noticed anything weird about him.

"His thoughts are different. Harder to read. Almost like he broadcasts on another frequency."

"I thought we agreed no listening to anyone's thoughts at the daycare?"

She studied her nails. "I don't. For the most part. Only with him. And I have to work to tune him in."

"That's pretty rare for you."

"Try *he's the only one.*"

My fingers tightened around her shoulders. She winced.

I let go and walked around the room. "This is not good."

Kai swiveled in her chair to watch me. "That I have trouble reading his thoughts or that he is special?"

"Both."

She went quiet-before-the-hailstorm silent. "Don't you want to know what he can do?"

"Huh?" I was too worried about what would happen if Mickey and her family found out.

"Aren't you curious about what his gift is?" she asked.

"Yeah, but even more curious about how you discovered it."

"He can see people's illnesses—as colors over the affected body part. It's like reading an aura, except he only sees illness. But he's really young so it may develop into more."

"How did you find out?" Schist walls slid into place in my mind. I knew this job would be too much for her. Shitfuckingdammit. It was going to happen all over again.

"He sought me out. I think he felt a pull to me." She paused. "One of the babies was crying and Lukas told me her ears hurt."

"Don't most babies have ear problems?" Schist walls morphed into a cave. This was the beginning of her getting too involved, which would lead to another depression. I had to stop her.

"Except this baby's ears were pink as pink can be. When I showed Lukas, he told me her ears were bright red and pointed to the right as being much worse than the left. He said she needed a doctor."

"He's got an overactive imagination. I used to think I was invisible when I was five." No way I'd let all the progress she'd made here in Butternut evaporate.

She chewed on her nails. "Two days later, the baby was out sick with a horrible ear infection."

"That it?" I folded my arms.

"A few days later, one of the teachers complained about a stomach ache. Lukas told me it wasn't her stomach but the tubes below needed to be checked out fast. He said they were purple."

"Let me guess, she ended up having something wrong with her intestines?"

"She had to have part of her intestines removed—diverticulitis," she said.

"Sounds like a coincidence."

"Then I'll just shut the hell up, I guess."

First smart thing she said all night. "Why leap to the conclusion that he's like you?"

Kai whirled around in her chair, giving me her back. She jerked open the vanity drawer and grabbed her hairbrush. The brush whipped through her hair while she stared at the wall. "He knows about my problem. He said my head was light pink and I needed to rest more."

I forced a laughed. "You really are taking this way too seriously."

"He told me his grandmother's throat was purple. It really scared him because purple is bad, worse than pink or red. No one listened to him, so I promised I'd talk to her."

"I knew you were up to something with the palm reading," I said.

"I was helping Lukas and your beloved Fuchses." She slammed her brush on the vanity.

"Why are you so worked up over this?"

"Because you won't believe me." She gave me her fuming face.

"It's more like I can't."

"I am so sick of you hiding behind that word." She stalked over to the dresser.

"What's that supposed to mean?" I knew we were crossing the overpass into fight territory, but I couldn't apply the brakes.

184

"Would it be that awful if Lukas were different? Would you love him less?" Her hands froze in the dresser drawer.

"I'd still care about him. It's not like he's my kid."

"And if he were?" she asked softly.

"Don't go off on a tangent." I raked my hand through my hair. A schist avalanche encased me. Mickey and I ended years ago. I hadn't seen or heard from her since we said goodbye in San Diego.

"God forbid people find out I'm a telepath. Are you that ashamed of me?" Kai's eyes filled with tears.

How the hell did she come to that conclusion? I held my head with both hands. God, the woman gave me headaches.

She stormed into the bathroom and shut the door with such vehemence that it vibrated in its frame.

I waited a few minutes. Nothing. No water running. Ten minutes later, I knocked on the door. "We aren't done talking." I tried the handle, but she'd locked herself in.

Five more minutes passed before she emerged from the bathroom, grabbed her book from the nightstand, and marched toward the door.

"Where the hell are you going?" I asked.

She didn't bother turning around. "I can't talk to you when you're like this. Forget I said anything."

"I can't do that. Come on. Let's talk this through."

She spun around. "You're an asshole, who doesn't believe what his crazy telepath of a wife says."

I gritted my teeth. "I never said that."

Her broken laugh bounced off the walls. "Not in those words, but the sentiments are there."

"I'm looking out for you...for us."

"If saying that makes you sleep better, go ahead. It doesn't make it true." Then she walked out of the room and down the hall. Nineteen seconds later, the door to the guest room slammed shut and the lock clicked into place.

CHAPTER 44

Oliver

Black Friday was known for ridiculous lines forming at ungodly hours in front of most stores. Most stores not including grocery stores. With a fridge packed full of Thanksgiving leftovers, people hunted for electronics and clothes. The trickle of customers into Super One Foods stopped at 11 a.m. By 1 p.m., the pissant let me and the other stock boy go home, but docked us two hours' pay. Happy Freaking Holiday.

Key in the ignition, I sat in the Super One Foods's parking lot, dreading the discussion Kai and I had to have. Seemed marriage was a series of discussions punctuated with sex, food, sleep and work. At least, ours was lately. The only way I might win this battle of silence was with a surprise attack.

I visualized myself encased in a marble cave-in the entire ride home. Tons of rubble compressed to seal me away forever. I parked the car a quarter mile from the house and made my black-ops approach. No turkey in sight. Probably because he was inside, making goo-goo eyes at my wife.

I slipped through the front door. No sign of my wife. She had to be on the phone somewhere. She loved to vent after we fought. Maybe she'd called her mom or dad. I tiptoed down the hall. Her voice wafted toward me through the half-open study door.

"Sometimes, I hate being right," she said.

Caleb responded, "I told you he wasn't good enough for you."

She was skyping with Caleb. Rat bastard Caleb.

The turkey purred at him in agreement.

I stopped a little ways down the hall. Close enough to hear, far enough to remain unseen.

"What am I going to do?" Kai asked.

Herbie clucked at her.

She murmured, "You're such a pretty bird." To Caleb, she said, "If he can't, no one can."

"Isn't it better to know than to have a child and see him react like Mom and Dad did to us?"

"I'd been thinking it could be different here. And now I know we can never have one." She couldn't talk and cry simultaneously. The effort made her gasp and hiccup.

"He's an idiot," Caleb said.

The hiccup-gasps continued.

He tried again. "An asshole. A tool. A booger brain."

"A booger brain?" She sniffed. "You haven't called anyone that since I was ten."

"Booger brain squared."

"Caleb." Her giggle shifted into a sob. "It hurts so much."

"You want a baby? We'll get you a sperm donor or adopt one. I'll buy you a private castle somewhere in the hinterland of Scotland."

Closer to his London residence and further from my Wisconsin home.

"Can Mom and Dad visit?" She blew her nose.

"Mom can."

"Can't you forgive Dad?"

"Never."

His dad had called him a sell out when he became an investment banker, but that wasn't the cause of their rift. Caleb hadn't spoken a word to him since his father let his mother institutionalize Kai.

His mom's fears about Kai's abilities were understandable. She was ungifted. But his dad, he should have understood. Granted his dad's telekinetic abilities were easier to repress, but he still had them. That alone should have made him the perfect person to handle things. But his dad didn't know what to do to save her.

"I forgave him," Kai said.

"You've always been way better than me."

"I couldn't do any of it without you."

"Just reciprocating." I heard the grin in his tone. "Have you told Oliver you're thinking about having kids?"

"I never got that far."

"Are you going to?" Caleb asked.

"I know what he thinks about special kids like Lukas and us. He'd say he wanted the child, but I'd know he didn't." She sniffled. "It would be pretty heartless to bring one into this world knowing what he would face. It was a selfish idea."

"Could be like Naomi," Caleb said.

The normal kid in the Guhn family.

"You want me to roll the dice with my baby's life?" she asked.

"I'm guessing no."

Her voice fractured, not a clean break but a messy splintering. "Why can't he be okay with Lukas?"

"You know what I think," Caleb said.

"Not when you're an ocean away."

Caleb chuckled. "Come visit me. I'll send a private plane."

"I can't leave Lukas."

"He's got a mom."

"How'd that work out for us?" Bitterness salted her words.

"Point taken."

"Besides, all I have to do is loan her Oliver and she gives me an all-access pass to Lukas."

"Aren't you worried?"

She chewed on her nails. "Most of the time."

"Grandma wouldn't want you risking your happiness and your sanity. She wanted you safe and happy."

First smart thing Caleb said today.

"She wanted us to be a family too," she reminded him. "Why are you waving a white handkerchief at me?"

"Truce. I'll stop talking about kids and you stop talking about Dad."

"Only if you pinky swear to visit me by New Year's."

"Done. I've got a meeting. Hugs and kisses," Caleb said.

"Love and misses."

That was their signature goodbye.

Kai typed away for a while.

I hoped she was working on her writing, but worried she might be drafting a *Dear John* letter to me. Christ, I was clueless. We were never fighting about Lukas, but about our future children. Needed a decoder ring for our discussions lately.

I had no idea how I was going to fix this mess. But if she found me here, I'd have a better chance finding a pig who spoke Chinese while making tamales. Slipping out of the house, I snuck back to my car. I started the engine and drove to the one person who might be able to help.

CHAPTER 45

Kai

I was an aquifer mined dry. I had no words. No adjectives. No verbs. No way to put fingers to keyboard. I was empty. Devoid of that spark. That magic that once made me write.

I stared at the blank computer screen. Stupid empty page of a stupid empty unnamed document. No point in saving something that had nothing in it.

I wanted to write a short story or a poem. Something to prove that I could. That my writing hadn't died with my grandmother. But the words refused to come. My imagination had nothing to spin into story string.

I'd always known all of me didn't come back. That what happened was not something every part of me could survive. And the gentlest part. She'd been butchered.

If only I could resuscitate her. But she was a Frankenstein monster and no matter how many times I tried to sew her back together again, the pieces never fit. She never came back to life.

I hated losing that part of myself. The part Oliver first fell in love with. But I couldn't bring her back. Sometimes life strips away pieces of you. And you can't save them.

That's not quite true. I stood by and watched as she was brutally sacrificed. Never knowing how to deal with her blood on my hands. I pretended she was asleep. But I knew the truth. I pushed that part of myself out into the executioner's hands. I traded her for me. And the me that made it through, she's not who I'd like to be. She's who I had to be.

My fingers tapped away on the keys, trying to find words. But they couldn't. Even after all these years. I couldn't talk about what happened to me. And I drowned a little each day in my silence.

CHAPTER 46

Oliver

I nibbled on my third chocolate chip cookie from the plate that Aunt Ines had laid out in front of me. She refilled my glass of milk and poured herself another cup of tea while we sat at her kitchen table. The metal chairs had iridescent-yellow-sparkly cushions. Not sure where she got them, but they suited her. The whole kitchen was pure Aunt Ines—shades of sunny yellow and crisp white with accents of turquoise.

"Oliver dear, if you don't tell me what happened, I can't possibly help." She spooned two sugar cubes into her tea and stirred them.

I needed her help, but didn't want to out Kai. I took a gulp of milk. My eyes drifted to her daffodil print curtains.

"Did you have an argument?" Aunt Ines asked.

"Sorta."

"What happened?"

"Kai thinks I don't want to have kids." That was the truth…at least part of it.

"Why would she think that?" She put down her spoon.

"We were talking about kids with special needs and she thought I wouldn't want one." I shoved half a cookie in my mouth.

Confusion swirled across her face. "Why would she think your child would have special needs? Is there some sort of genetic disorder on her side?"

"Yeah." Okay, so I had put telepathy and dreamwalking under the header of genetic disorder.

"Would it bother you?" Aunt Ines peered at me over the rim of her rose-patterned porcelain teacup.

"I don't think so." I paused. "Depends on how bad it was. I mean I'd love the kid because it was ours."

"I see why Kai might have concerns."

I grabbed another cookie, broke it in half, and dunked it into my milk. We used to do this after school. Aunt Ines always made sure to have a snack ready for me. Maybe she thought it would hide the fact that my mom wasn't there. "How do I convince her I'd love our kid, no matter what?"

"Give her time." She patted my hand. "You planted a doubt in her mind and it has taken root. You can't just yank it out."

"Shouldn't we talk about it?" I asked.

"Go in there like a bull in a china closet, and you know what will happen."

"Things will get broken."

She pointed at me. "Bingo."

I leaned back in my chair and looked up at the ceiling. "Is that yellow and turquoise glitter imbedded in the white paint?"

"Do you like it?" she asked.

"Definitely dresses up the ceiling."

"That's what I told the painter."

"So what do I do?" I sounded like a 10-year-old whining about some problem at school.

"What sort of birth defect are we talking about?" She was a stickler for details when dispensing advice.

I couldn't keep dodging the question. "Kai's not like other people."

"She's a remarkable woman."

"She's extraordinary," I said.

"My apologies, she's amazing."

"No." I leaned in. "She can do things other people can't."

My aunt flushed. "Oliver, I don't want to know anything about what goes on when you're alone."

I was screwing this up. I blurted out, "She's a telepath."

She blinked. "That's not a genetic disorder."

"She inherited it from her dad's side of the family."

She stared into her teacup as if answers lurked just beneath the surface. "Do you remember my good friend, Sabine?"

"Not really." Though I was confused by the sudden topic change.

"She used to see the future."

"Seriously?"

"Her mother sensed when earthquakes and floods were going to happen." She stirred her tea.

"How long did you know?"

"Sabine told me when she was twelve." She smiled at the memory.

"Did Dad…" I couldn't imagine Reinhard being okay with it.

She waved her hand in the air. "Of course not. God rest his soul, but your father was never an open-minded person. Too much of my daddy in him for that."

"Could we call her?"

Her eyes looked softer than caramel and stickier than molasses. "She passed on five years ago."

"Did she have any children?" I'd never met anyone outside Kai's family with abilities like that.

She shook her head. "Sabine saw her gift as a curse."

"Kai never wanted kids until she met…"

"Lukas?"

"How'd you know?"

She stared into her tea again. "He's like her, isn't he?"

The cookie slipped through my fingers and sank to the bottom of my glass of milk.

"His grandmother mentioned how he finds sickness before others do. She thinks he'd make a great doctor one day."

I borrowed her spoon to scoop the cookie out from my glass.

"Sabine's last name was Hoffmann. Her nephew was Nathan. It runs in their blood."

The same Nathan who stole Mickey from me and fathered Lukas.

She must have taken my silence as forgetfulness. "He bullied you in high school, dear."

"That was before my growth spurt." Nathan might have been a year younger, but he was a decade tougher. "Did Nathan have special abilities?"

She shrugged. "I'd known Sabine since the third grade, but she rarely talked about her own, let alone anyone else's."

"You see what a mess I'm in." I got up to grab the chocolate syrup from the fridge. This was serious. Chocolate time.

"Didn't I teach you every mess can be tidied up with enough effort?"

CHAPTER 47

Kai

Rearranging the living room didn't clear the clutter out of my head. Though angling the couch 30 degrees away from the wall created a cozy atmosphere. A couple chairs and an end table around it, and we had a u-shaped sitting area atop the toffee-colored rug Aunt Ines gave us. The rest of Grandmother Richter's furniture went into a reading space and a workspace. I kitty-cornered her secretary desk to the right of the picture window to take advantage of the natural light.

The living room had come a long way from my first night here: barely inhabitable to shabby chic. The hardwood floor shone, the crown molding gleamed, the walls glowed a warm eggshell, and the fire crackled in the fireplace. All the cleaning and decorating didn't fix things between Oliver and me.

I plopped down on the couch and immersed myself in *The Picture of Dorian Gray*. Anything to escape the thoughts in my head for a few hours. At first, I thought the darkness I felt was Dorian Gray's. Then mine. But it wasn't. Something was on the farm. Shrouded in a haze of frustration and rage. A need for revenge. A desire for retribution. It didn't feel quite human. A rush of fear jolted through me.

It reminded me of that bear. But it wasn't pure visceral reaction. More like what I'd encountered on Thanksgiving. I didn't know this person. This mind. It was different. I couldn't get a lock on it. I dropped my shield completely.

He must suffer. Pain for pain. Blood for blood. Truth for truth.

A ferocious pounding at the base of my skull. A pressure inside my temple. Like my own mind couldn't contain these thoughts. Shadows tunneled my vision. I squeezed my eyes shut and prayed it would pass.

It didn't. Not until I raised my shield and shut the mind out of mine.

Slowly, I opened my eyes. My vision was normal. The thoughts were gone.

I ran upstairs and peered through every window, trying to catch a glimpse of who might be on our property. I didn't see a single person. Maybe my telepathy was evolving. Maybe I was losing my mind. Neither thought brought me any comfort.

Oliver's car rumbled up the driveway an hour later. I didn't hear his thoughts with my shield up. We'd kept our minds locked up tight since the last fight. Neither ceding an inch to the other.

He came in. "The room looks great."

I didn't look up from my book.

"Let's go get a Christmas tree," he said.

I flipped the page. "Maybe tomorrow."

"Be ready in five minutes."

I didn't move.

"Or I'll toss you in the Cherokee. Your choice."

I stomped to the hallway closet to get my winter gear. It was just like him to not talk about our issues. To pretend them away.

When we met by the front door, he shoved his knit cap on his head. "Ready?"

I followed him outside.

"Herbie's all set?" he asked as he locked the front door.

"Fed and watered and out in his house." Dan had built Herbie his own shelter. Took Dan an entire morning, but Herbie loved his new place.

"This will be our first real tree," he said.

Usually, I was big into firsts. I remembered the street we first kissed on, the beach where I first went down on him, even the name of the dorm where we first had sex.

"I liked our fake tree in New York," I said.

It was a Duane Reade special—three feet tall with colored lights already strung on it. Pull it out of the box, plug it in and hang a few ornaments. Instant Christmas.

"It served its purpose," he said.

I slammed my door and secured my seatbelt without looking at him. I pitied the tree that ended up with us for the holidays.

CHAPTER 48

Oliver

We started out with fading daylight and followed boot prints already carved into the eight inches of snow. In search of the perfect Christmas tree, we wandered out amongst the trees to untouched whiteness.

An hour later, we still hadn't found our tree. We'd come across several that were too small, a dozen that fit the too-blue category, and one that wasn't green enough. None to my wife's liking. The snow crunched and iced together beneath our boots.

"I thought you'd been here before," Kai said as we trampled through the darkened woods.

"My dad used to take me here to pick out our tree." Aunt Ines always packed a thermos of hot apple cider and sugared donuts before shooing us out into the night. She said it was the last thing he promised my mom. To let me pick out a live tree every Christmas.

I shook off the memory. We weren't just temporarily misplaced. We were lost. Totally lost in the woods after dark. Everything looked familiar except the route back. Temperature was supposed to go down into the teens tonight too. At least, I'd brought the cider and donuts in my backpack. We wouldn't starve. Though, we might freeze to death.

"Oliver, just admit it. We're lost." Kai's foot slid and she grabbed my arm. The second she regained her footing, she let go.

Maybe it was a guy thing; maybe it was a pride thing. Schist all around me. I lied, "It's starting to look familiar."

She swung around to block my path. "You said that half an hour ago."

"Think of it as a story to tell the grandkids."

She flinched. "Yours and Mickey's?"

"Mine and yours, dumbass."

"I'm the dumbass? Who dragged us out here to freeze to death?"

"That was my idea. So is having kids with you."

She stamped her foot in the snow. "Not if they aren't normal."

"Stop putting words in my mouth."

She stalked off. I let her calm down, which meant she was pretty far ahead of me when she stopped. I caught up to her in front of a morbidly obese tree. Had to have a radius of six feet.

"You like it?" I asked to be sure.

"It'll do."

"I don't want to cut it down unless you love it."

"I like it."

"Maybe we should keep looking?"

"Give me the saw." She thrust her mittened hand at me.

This ought to be good. I passed her the saw. "Ever cut down a tree before?"

"There's a first time for everything." She crouched beside the tree to examine the trunk. "Have you?"

"A few." I stood there, waiting for her to make the next move.

She gave a soul-expelling sigh. "I don't want to hurt the tree. How do you do it?"

I squatted beside her. "Give me the saw." I had no idea how to get us, let alone the tree back to the Cherokee. Or where the Cherokee might be. But that was a worry for later.

I pressed the saw's teeth to the trunk and made the first cut. After twenty-seven minutes sawing through the thickest Christmas tree trunk in the world, I housed a sweat lodge beneath my clothes. I lowered the tree onto the tarp. "Get the netting and rope out of my backpack."

Her teeth chattered. "Here you go."

"Get the thermos out and eat a donut."

"I'm watching my weight."

"Eat the damn donut. You'll burn it off walking back to the car." I struggled to slide the netting over the tree's branches. It was Spanx for the tree, making it easier to wrap in the tarp.

With each bite, Kai made the little noises she makes when she's happy—a meowlike-humming.

Once I had the tree all bundled up, she handed me the hot apple cider and a donut. We sat on a rock and finished our snacks.

"Should be fun to decorate," she said.

The tree was easily eight feet tall. "I don't think our ornaments will cover it."

"I bet Aunt Ines knows where to get ornaments."

"I'd like to invite her to the tree trimming." I'd missed a decade of holidays with her.

"I planned to," she said.

"You don't mind it being the three of us?"

"It's her first year without her dad. She should be with us."

I sidled closer to her. "You know I love you more than anything else in this world."

She studied the patterns her boots had made in the snow.

"If our baby had five arms and three eyes, I would love it. Because it's ours."

She refused to meet my gaze. "You say that now..."

"And I'll say it again and again until you believe me."

"I can't let my child go through what I did," she said.

201

"Would you rather have never been born?"

She didn't say a word.

I let the silence linger. She needed to find the answer.

She whispered, "It would have been better for everyone."

"Not for me or Caleb. Definitely not for your grandmother. She loved you more than anyone."

Tears flooded her eyes. "I was too much. She gave so much of herself to me, there was none left."

I looped my arm around her. "Sweetheart, loving you gave her life meaning. She fought the cancer as long as she did for you."

Tears raced down her cheeks, trembled on the cliff of her jaw, and disappeared into the crevasses of her scarf.

"What about Lukas and Mrs. Fuchs? Where would they be without you?"

She tried to pull away.

I crushed her against me. "You gave me a place where I belonged."

She wrapped her arms around my waist. "I love you, you know. It makes me so afraid of losing you."

"Don't you think I worry about that too?"

She nuzzled my neck and pushed my hat aside to suck on my earlobe.

"Honey, it's freezing out here," I said.

"So?" She pulled my scarf down.

The air chilled my skin. Her lips warmed it back up.

"I don't want you getting colder," I said.

Her teeth grazed my neck. The nip of encouragement sent blood rushing to my extremities.

"Heat me up," she said.

Such the pragmatist. "Kai…"

Her warm breath filled my ear. "We'll be really quick."

"But on a rock?"

She straddled me. "Don't worry. I'll do all the work."

She stuffed her mittens into her pockets. Her fingers scrambled under my coat, immediately at work on my pants. I heard the zipper and felt her hands reach inside. God, her hands. She kissed me fiercely, plunging her tongue into my mouth. It didn't take long for Herr Peoples to wake up. She struggled to get her pants out of the way so she could get closer to me.

I pulled my glove off and slid a finger inside her. Then a second. And a third. She bucked against my hand. Everything went active-Mount-Vesuvius inside her. I slid my fingers out and Herr Peoples in. She clutched at my shoulders, sucking on my neck. I lost control and surged into her. She pushed against me, rocking back and forth. Trying to reach that place. Where everything stopped and nothing mattered but us.

My fingers hunted for the spot that would get her there. She whimpered. Her shield crashed down. Her thoughts swarmed in my head. Suddenly, I was being penetrated. Being stretched, yet aching to be full. Needing to erase that emptiness inside me. More than anything, needing this.

Minutes after she collapsed against me, she scampered off and shimmied her pants back up to her waist. I tucked everything back into mine.

"Sorry about your neck." Her smile was repentant, her eyes defiant.

The spot she'd nipped was barely tender. "Sorry we didn't have more time."

"Sometimes I like it a little rough."

"Duly noted."

"Don't you?" she asked.

"I didn't want to hurt you."

"I'm not that breakable." She walked over to the tarp and grabbed the side of it. "Ready?"

I grabbed the other side. Together, we dragged that tree.

A half-hour later, she stopped and checked her cell phone. "You're kidding me."

"Still no reception?" I already knew the answer.

"I'm getting tired," she said.

Through the break in the trees, I'd swear I saw a hill. "I think I know where we are."

"If I had a dollar for every time you said that..."

"This time I mean it," I said.

We dragged the tree toward the hill. As we closed in, I saw lights and figures moving way up at the top.

Kai said, "Oliver..."

I dropped the tree and yelled, "Hello! Can you help us?"

I ran up the hill. Had to be a quarter mile to the top. Hampered by the snow, I was sucking wind by the time I got there.

The Fuchs clan, Kai said in my head.

Why didn't you say something?

I tried. Someone wouldn't listen.

Alex was the first to greet me. "Oliver? What are you doing out here alone?"

Looking over my shoulder, I realized Kai had stayed with her fat Christmas tree. "Kai's..."

"You left her behind?" Alex acted like she might become a coyote's dinner and took off toward her.

"Catch your breath." Mickey pressed a Styrofoam cup into my hand. "Alex will take care of her."

Just one sip couldn't hurt. Mickey still made the best hot chocolate I'd ever tasted. "What are you doing up here?"

"Pete takes the family sledding after every good snowfall." Mickey's breath frosted in the air.

When I was a kid, I'd been invited along for Fuchs family sledding. Back when her parents bundled us into their trucks. "Haven't had a winter like this in a long time."

She offered me her mom's homemade linzer torte cookies.

"No thanks." After a few more swallows of hot chocolate, I handed the empty cup back to Mickey. "Got to go help the wife."

Downhill momentum slid me through the snow toward Alex and Kai as they made their way upward. Of course, Alex pulled the tarp by himself.

As I got closer, I heard Kai say, "You have no idea how long we've been lost."

I missed Alex's reply.

Kai doubled over with laughter. "So true!"

By the time she righted herself, I was in front of them.

I reached for the side of the tarp. "I'll take the tree."

"I got it." Alex continued his ascent.

"Nice of you to remember me." Her cheeks might have reddened from the cold, but her face tightened from annoyance.

I gestured at Alex. "I got help."

"Alex, thank you so much for coming to my rescue. I couldn't pull this tree all by myself." She gave him her best smile. The one she usually reserved for me.

"Can't imagine why anyone would leave you stranded in the snow," he said.

I exploded. "I didn't leave her. I ran up a hill and had to catch my breath."

"With Mickey?" he asked.

Kai gave me her people-are-noticing look.

"What are the chances of catching a ride back to our car?" I asked.

He adjusted his grip on the tarp. "Kai already secured a ride for her and the tree."

"What about me?" I asked.

"I'm sure Mickey would be glad to help you," she said.

It took ten minutes to reach the top. Ten minutes of Kai and Alex making small talk and me trying to get a foothold in the conversation.

When we rejoined the Fuchses, Lukas ran up to us. He wrapped his arms around Kai's leg, dragging her toward the sleds. "Aunt Kai, ride with me."

Kai smiled at him. "I'd love to sweetie, but I don't know how to sled."

"Everyone knows how to sled when they get big," Lukas said.

Kai knelt down in front of him. "I grew up surfing."

"You've never sledded?" Lukas asked.

"I've been snowboarding on vacation," she said. "We didn't get much snow where I'm from."

Lukas frowned. "No snow?"

"She's from Southern California," Mickey said, "which is a lot like Florida..."

"Where it never snows," Lukas finished. "Aunt Kai has to sled with me."

"I'll take you two on the next run," Alex said.

Mickey patted Alex's back. "He taught me everything I know about sledding."

Kai snorted. "I guess that makes you an expert?"

"I've taught Oliver a thing or two," Mickey said.

I blurted out, "But I still can't steer the thing."

Mickey laughed, tucking her hand in the crook of my arm. "I'll help. Let's race them to the bottom."

Lukas jumped up and down. "I wanna race. I wanna race."

I ended up on a sled, sitting in front with Mickey's arms and legs wrapped around me. She whispered in my ear, "Remind you of anything else we used to do?"

I gulped. "Not really."

She laughed. "We're going to let them win."

"Sounds good." My eyes darted over to Kai.

Alex had his legs and arms encircling her. She held Lukas in her lap. I was still watching them as someone gave us a push and we took off down the hill.

Right until Mickey said, "Eyes forward, mister," and kissed me on the back of my neck. "For luck."

CHAPTER 49

Oliver

Pete's brake lights flared a few times before his GMC pickup disappeared into the darkness.

Alex tugged at the ropes securing my Christmas tree to his Land Rover's roof. "I'll bring you back to your car. Kai and I will meet you at your house with the tree."

I didn't like that plan. "We'll take it from our car."

"Can we swing by the McDonald's in Park Falls on the way? I'm starving," Kai asked Alex.

Alex opened the front passenger door. "As the lady wishes." His grin widened as I yanked at the rear passenger door.

We'd been driving long enough to take the chill out of the car before Alex asked, "You enjoy the sledding?"

"Best part of the night," Kai said.

"What do you think of Wisconsin's winter?" he asked.

"I started to hate snow after someone got me lost in the woods." She jerked her thumb in my direction. "But Lukas and you reminded me how fun it can be."

I envisioned granite all around me. When Kai was hurt, she lashed out verbally. Rarely needed to throw something. Not when she fired buckshot words.

"Oliver?" Alex asked.

"Yeah?"

"Do you or don't you?" He sounded annoyed, like he'd already asked the question.

"What?" Maintaining the granite shield while angry and thinking about Kai required most of my attention.

She fiddled with the radio, hunting for a station she liked. "Pretty sure he doesn't have a tree stand."

He made eye contact in the rearview mirror. "Guess we're boring you."

"I'm a little worn out. Worked all day, hiked most of the night." With some quick outdoor sex in subfreezing temperatures. Then sledding. "Cut me some slack."

"I'll pick a stand up at my parents'." He drove down the path that chains and tire treads had pressed into the snowed-over, dirt road. He came to a stop beside our lone car.

"Thanks." I let my walls of granite melt away. Who cuts down a tree without a stand to put it in? If I were a cartoon character, I would slam my head against a desk.

Silence. No reply in my head. I shifted forward to kiss Kai. She leaned in to change the radio station.

"See you soon." I patted her shoulder.

"It might take us a while to eat and find a tree stand," she said.

"We should be there in an hour or so," he said.

I got out of the car and slammed the door hard enough to rock the vehicle.

CHAPTER 50

Kai

I found an ally in the most unexpected place—sitting by the window, eating fries at McDonald's.

Alex wiped his mouth with the napkin and muttered, "It's always been this way."

"What has?" I asked.

His voice dipped low, tugging me toward him. "Mickey and Oliver."

"They've been close for a long time?" I asked.

"Since we were kids. It fell apart senior year."

"They seem to be putting it back together," I said.

"Mickey likes to push the limit."

I coughed. "That's a nice way to describe it."

"She's my sister. I love her. I'll have her back," he said. "But I'm aware of her faults."

"Why can't she get over Oliver?" I asked.

"He was always her Plan B."

"But it's been a decade since they saw each other." That was a long time to expect Plan B to wait.

"After her husband left her, she needed something to believe in. Something that was solid."

"Oliver and her?" I asked.

"I saw the kiss she snuck. It wasn't Oliver's fault...this time."

"It's not just a one-time thing though, is it?" The heaviness of my realization flattened my voice.

"Things never got settled between them."

"Should I be worried?"

"I don't know." He grabbed some of my fries and dunked them in ketchup. "Oliver wasn't a cheater. But we haven't been close in 10 years."

"He's been a good husband." Up until now. "But your sister keeps pushing."

"She sees them as star-crossed lovers. It's irresistible."

"And I'm the wicked woman trying to steal her man?" I asked.

"You're the obstacle to her happiness with Oliver."

"What do you think of me?" I imagined a peephole in my shield to hear his thoughts.

"I've never met anyone like you before." *It's got to be hard to be the outsider in your husband's past. That's why I don't mind you using me to make Oliver jealous. Especially if it keeps him away from my sister.*

"Is that why you flirt with me?" I asked.

"Oliver needs a reminder that he doesn't have a lock on both of you."

I never thought I'd lose Oliver to another woman. I always pictured him leaving because of my telepathy.

Tears stung my eyes. "You think jealousy is the best way to keep him?"

"What's your other option?"

I looked up at the fluorescent lights, begging the tears to evaporate. "And you don't mind helping me?"

"Oliver's like my little brother. I'm always up for teaching him a lesson...or playing a prank."

I laughed. "Thank you."

"Just out of curiosity, if you weren't married, would I have a snowball's chance in hell?"

"Oh, you'd have a snowball's chance in the middle of a Wisconsin winter."

CHAPTER 51

Oliver

A ccording to the clock, one hour, twenty-seven minutes and thirty seconds had passed since I last saw Kai. What the hell was she doing with Alex? My imagination slapped me in the face with an image. Her straddling him in the front seat.

No. She wouldn't do that. It would mean the end of us.

Alex's SUV rumbled up the driveway. No doors slamming. Nothing. Channeling Mrs. Wiesner, I stalked to the picture window to peer around the curtains.

The interior light illuminated the front seat where they sat facing each other, talking like old friends.

Or soon to be lovers, my insecurities whispered.

Kai leaned over and kissed Alex on the cheek. He hugged her.

Bastard.

They got out. Alex worked on freeing the Christmas tree from his roof. Kai held a flashlight. Not once did she glance at the house.

Herbie came out of his turkey hut to check on the commotion. He flew right over to Kai, ducking his head so she would pat it. Alex

212

stopped untying the knots to greet our turkey. The Judas bird waited with Kai while Alex extricated the tree from his SUV. Trotted beside them as they headed toward the house.

I let the curtains fall back into place before they saw me, grabbed the nearest book, and threw myself on the couch. I looked up from my book when they came in. Kai held the door open for Alex. He carried the tree into the living room. Herbie pranced behind him.

Her lips bunched when she saw me on the couch. "Nice of you to help us with the tree."

"You should've beeped. I didn't know you were out there."

"Enjoying the book?" Alex asked.

"It's a thought-provoking read."

She giggled. He smirked at me.

"Something funny?" I asked.

"Did you get to the part where Lord Hampton ravishes the innocent Penelope? Where he thrusts his thick sword into her tiny, wet sheath?" she asked.

I slammed the book shut and checked out the cover. A blonde with breasts about to tumble out of her dress was in the arms of a shirtless hunk tugging at her bodice. "I like to see what Kai's reading."

"Never knew you went for romance novels. Wait until I tell Dan," Alex said.

She touched his arm. "He loves the regency period best. All those dashing noblemen ravishing the innocent ladies of society."

I dropped the book on the coffee table and stood up. "You got the tree stand?"

She held it up.

"Great. I'll take it from here." I headed toward the tree.

"Alex lugged it in. He remembered the tree stand. I'm trusting him to set it up while I make the hot chocolate." She left the tree stand on the floor and headed back to the kitchen.

Herbie followed her.

Alex gave the tree a little shake. "So where do you want it?"

"Didn't you and Kai already decide?"

He kicked the tree stand into the room and picked up the tree. "You've got a wife most men would kill for and you're messing it up."

"What do you know?" I scooped up the tree stand and positioned it in front of the picture window. Same place Grandpa always put his. Hoped she agreed to this location.

The diameter of the tree required pushing the couch back against the wall. That meant the rug, the end tables, the chairs, and the coffee table all had to be adjusted to re-balance the room.

"I feel like I'm stuck in one of those home design shows," he said.

"She'll be pissed if the tree throws everything off kilter." I finished re-arranging the furniture and stood in front of him.

"As pissed as when she saw Mickey kiss you? I'm starting to wonder if New York rubbed off on you a little too much." He frowned at the tree stand. "You going to unscrew it, so I can slide the tree in?"

I wanted to throw him and that damned tree out of my house. Instead, I found myself on my hands and knees turning the eyebolts so the trunk could fit into the stand.

Alex picked up the tree and slid it through. "Now screw them into the tree's trunk to keep it in place."

"I've had a tree before." I twisted the last eyebolt tighter. "So you like my wife?"

"There's a line of guys in town who like your wife," he said.

I stood up, brushing my hands clean on my thighs.

"She's completely in love with you. But keep pushing, she might fall into someone else's arms."

"Mickey's a flirt," I said.

"When she's encouraged."

Kai came into the room with a serving tray and placed it on the coffee table. "Marshmallows, Alex?"

"Sounds great." He crouched down, checking the eyebolts.

She tossed a marshmallow at Herbie and he caught it in his beak. Then she put a handful of mini-marshmallows in Alex's hot chocolate and swirled the whipped cream a good four inches high.

As soon as Alex got up, she handed him the mug. "Thanks for everything. You're a lifesaver."

He sipped his hot chocolate. "Glad to help."

She poured her mug of hot chocolate, tossed a couple marshmallows in, and topped it off with Redi-Whip. She made an *mmmhm* noise when she took a sip.

The third mug sat empty on the tray. She'd forgotten to make mine. I cleared my throat.

"You never like the way I make it," she said.

Alex licked his lips. "It's got a nice kick. What's your secret?"

"A dash of cayenne pepper and shot of tequila." She blushed. "It's my grandmother's recipe."

I made my own, giving myself a good handful of mini-marshmallows before I reached for the Redi-Whip. I turned it over and pushed the nozzle. Air gushed out with wisps of cream.

"Oopsy. Guess I used the last of it." She blinked at me with practiced innocence.

"I'll pick some up tomorrow after my shift."

"Are you coming by tomorrow to finish up in the bedroom?" she asked Alex.

I spit my hot chocolate back into the mug. "What?"

"I'm doing some work for Kai," Alex said.

"By yourself?" Tomorrow was Sunday. Dan only came on Wednesdays and Saturdays.

"It's a little side project." He popped a marshmallow in his mouth.

"I thought the upstairs was done." That was what Dan had said, anyway.

"This requires Alex's special touch." Her eyes laughed behind her mug.

215

"What sort of work?"

"Shelving for my closet," she said. "Alex is better at accommodating my needs."

I gritted my teeth. He'd be in our bedroom. With Kai. When I wasn't home. It wasn't that I didn't trust them. It was more about how far she might push things, trying to get back to even.

By the time Alex left, Kai had taken her pint of blood from me and sauntered off to bed. I escaped for a couple hours of House of the Dead on my Wii.

I crashed on the old leather couch in my study. Hell, at the rate we were going, we should just call it Oliver's bedroom and move all my clothes in there. The downside of all this space? We had room to run away from each other.

The next day, I came home from work to ornaments galore and holiday tunes. Aunt Ines had brought four boxes of decorations for our tree trimming. Kai had found some of my grandma's ornaments in the boxes we hauled out of storage. Plus she had our Duane Reade and Lot Less balls, bells, and snowflakes from New York. My wife whipped up her slice-and-bake version of sugar cookies. Aunt Ines made the eggnog and dusted it with nutmeg.

Kai and I completely forgot the lights since our Duane Reade tree came pre-lit. But Aunt Ines had been doing Christmas for decades longer than us. She had an arsenal of lights: white, multicolored, blinking, twinkling, large, tiny. We opted for multicolored, tiny, and twinkling. Aunt Ines and I strung the lights while Kai walked around the room giving us her input on spacing considerations. Afterward, each of us took a box of ornaments and shifted around the tree, making sure all sections got a mix of the old, the new, and the cheap.

When it came time for the star, Aunt Ines insisted Kai put it there.

My wife needed the ladder to reach the top of the tree. I steadied her as she climbed up and down. She smiled at me when the star blazed atop our tree. I wanted to take it as a sign of things to come, but I knew it was just a moment. Sometimes, those are all you get.

So I grabbed her hand and squeezed.

She glanced over at me.

Aunt Ines pronounced it, "Absolutely gorgeous."

If you ignored the tension between Kai and me, it was a pleasant afternoon. But I knew it wasn't over. Just a temporary ceasefire in our ongoing skirmish. Still I enjoyed the day. You have to take advantage of the family moments, even the ones that are forced or faked.

CHAPTER 52

Oliver

Mondays, Mickey and I worked the same shift, reminding me of back when we'd sold friendship bracelets. She excelled at division of labor. Knew my weaknesses, compensated for them, and accentuated my strengths. We had been an unstoppable team. Still were.

She explained where everything went in the stock room before I started on my section. Somehow, she always finished her area and found time to adjust everything in mine. So far, the pissant seemed pleased with our work.

She stepped back to run her eyes over the rows. A smile flitted across her face.

This section was done.

Her cell phone rang, playing "She's a Brick House."

I couldn't make out what her mom said. I didn't need to.

Mickey's eyes bulged. A wave of worry splashed across her forehead. Something was wrong. Really wrong. I put my hand on her shoulder.

"Ma, slow down. What happened?" The blood fled from her face.

"What do you mean Lukas is gone?"

This had to be a mistake.

"Where are you?" She paused. "I'm on my way."

Her shoulder turned to shale beneath my hand. Hard and shatterable. "What happened?" I asked.

She whispered, "Lukas is missing."

This couldn't be happening. Not in Butternut. Not to Mickey. "What?"

"My son is gone." She pulled away from me. "I have to go."

"Where?"

"My mom's," she said.

"I'll drive." I put my arm around her and guided her through the shoppers toward the store's exit.

The pissant's stance told me he was preparing to stop us.

"My son's missing," Mickey said.

No one could mistake the aura of petrified anxiety around her. Even the pissant's tiny heart had to go out to her.

He stepped aside.

"My son's missing." I wasn't sure if she was telling me or trying to convince herself. She kept mumbling it between bouts of silence on the car ride.

The car hadn't come to a complete stop at her parent's house, but she leapt out and raced toward the front door. I parked and ran up the walkway, hoping this was all a big misunderstanding. Kids loved to play hide and seek. Or maybe he ran away to get attention. I'd done that a few times. Except I was nine and twelve, not four.

Officer Lainer sat in the living room, jotting down notes on his pad.

Mrs. Fuchs's bloodshot eyes and rubbed-raw nose signaled that Lukas was gone.

The minute she saw Mickey, she shrank into the couch. "I'm so sorry. I don't know how this could have happened."

Mickey snapped. "Why weren't you watching him?"

Mr. Fuchs stood between them, towering over his seated wife and his seething daughter. One hand remained on Mrs. Fuchs's shoulder, the other he extended to Mickey, offering whatever comfort he could. "This isn't your mother's fault. Lukas was in his room playing. It couldn't have been more than half an hour."

Mrs. Fuchs hid her nose in a tissue.

"When she went to check on him, he was gone. The doors were locked. We don't know how he got out of the house," Mr. Fuchs said.

Mickey turned her fury on Officer Lainer. "You have to find my son."

"We searched the entire house. We're organizing volunteer search parties to comb the area," Officer Lainer said.

"He's four years old." Mickey's voice crumbled.

It was already dark outside with the temperature dropping by the hour. If Lukas had wandered outside alone, this was life threatening. God help us, we were hoping for a kidnapping.

"How long has he been gone?" I asked.

"Near as we can tell? Two hours," Officer Lainer said.

"Do you think someone…took him?" Bile sloshed against my back teeth.

"His bedroom windows were locked from the inside. The bathroom window was unlocked, but too high for a four-year-old to open and climb out on his own," Officer Lainer said.

"Could someone have taken him out through the bathroom window?" I asked.

"Maybe." Officer Lainer rubbed his forehead. "The area around the house is all tracked up. No clear foot trails."

"We looked everywhere when we couldn't find him," Mr. Fuchs said.

"He might have wandered out on his own. The back door was ajar when I arrived." Officer Lainer refuted Mrs. Fuchs's story.

Mrs. Fuchs clenched her tissue. "Because we opened it to go look for him. I always keep the doors locked when he's here. The house is too close to the road."

"Front and back?" Mickey asked.

Mrs. Fuchs looked shell-shocked. "Yes."

"Basement?" Mickey asked.

"We already looked down there," Officer Lainer said.

"What about the tunnel in the crawl space? It leads out of the house." Mickey marched toward the basement door.

"I sealed that off years ago," Mr. Fuchs said.

She stopped. "Then where is my son?" Her eyes were wet, but she didn't let herself cry.

She'd told me when I was eight and she found me crying at my mother's grave that it's always okay to cry for dead people. But Lukas wasn't dead. And if she cried, it would be like letting the possibility become more real.

She stared at her parents. "How could you lose him?"

"Honey, we don't know what happened," Mr. Fuchs said.

"What do we do?" Mickey asked.

"The boys are already out searching," Mr. Fuchs said.

Officer Lainer got up. "Stay here and mind the phones." He zipped his jacket. "I've got to get back to the station."

Mickey was already zipping up her coat. "I'm going to find my son."

I wasn't about to let her go traipsing off alone. "We'll need two flashlights."

As soon as the front door shut behind Officer Lainer, Mr. Fuchs pulled me aside and handed me a gun. "You know how to handle one of these, right?"

I nodded.

"Don't care what Lainer says. I know my wife and I know Lukas. He didn't wander off. Someone took him."

I swallowed. I had no problem putting a bullet in Lukas's kidnapper. I was more afraid of finding that little boy under an ice-covered pond.

221

CHAPTER 53

Kai

When I freeze my husband out, I can't sleep without a little help. A few glasses of wine delivered me into dreamland. The phone rang at 7 a.m., and I wasn't surprised to find myself alone in bed. He'd taken to his study when we fought. The space helped us to stay angry.

He didn't pick up the phone. By the fourth ring, I grabbed it.

"Kai, I'm sorry to wake you, dear," Aunt Ines said.

"Do you need Oliver?" I asked.

"He's not there," she said.

My insides froze in a moment of perpetual fear. "Is Oliver okay?" I whispered.

"He's fine. It's Lukas, dear. He went missing last night," she said.

I clutched the phone. Why didn't Oliver call me? He knew I was the one person who might be able to find Lukas. Or at least catch his thoughts or the kidnapper's. How could he forget about the Miller case where I was out all night searching for that little girl? I'd felt such relief bringing her home to her mom. It was the best thing that came out of my telepathy.

"Kai, are you still there?" Aunt Ines asked.

"I'm here." I took a breath. "Did they find him?"

"Not yet. They have search parties combing the town. I thought you might like to help."

"Definitely. Can you pick me up?" I asked. "Oliver has the car."

"He left it at Super One Foods," Aunt Ines said. "He was searching for Lukas all night with the Fuchses."

And Mickey. Regret crushed my toes. "Can you give me a ride to the grocery store to pick it up?"

"I'll be over in twenty minutes."

I hung up the phone and got dressed. My thoughts jumped from Oliver to Lukas. We'd lost a night already. A night Oliver and Mickey shared in fear. A night Lukas spent terrified. A night I could have been searching.

CHAPTER 54

Oliver

Every two hours or so, Mickey and I managed to get cell reception and called back to the house for news. There wasn't much, so we went back to searching for Lukas.

On our third call, Mr. Fuchs reported that the cops had interviewed all the neighbors, but no one had seen Lukas leave the house. No one saw him being taken. We had no leads. No clues. Just a missing boy and a devastated family.

I don't know how Mickey kept it together. If my little boy disappeared on a winter night, I don't think I could.

At the park, she clutched a KitKat wrapper she found near the slide. "His favorite. He got a bunch for Halloween. He was a doctor this year."

We walked the perimeter, calling his name for an hour. Nothing. We headed into the nearby woods, where she found a red mitten.

"Is it his?" I asked.

"Could be."

"Does he have red mittens?"

Her eyes begged me to believe her. "Maybe someone gave them

to him. And he dropped it so we could find him?"

I couldn't give her false hope. "But there aren't any small footprints in the snow."

"They must be carrying him."

"There aren't any big footprints either. Just ours."

"It's a sign."

I nodded. I couldn't take away that shred of hope she clung to as tightly as the mitten in her hand.

We put in nine hours searching before we circled back to her parents' house. Her father insisted she get some rest. She compromised, making me pancakes and coffee. As close to rest as she could get.

I sat at the counter. "We'll find him."

She concentrated on the frying pan. Sliding the flipper around the edge of the pancake, testing if it was ready to be turned over.

I racked my brain for something to do. "Want me to call into work for you today?"

"Yeah." She didn't take her eyes off the pancakes like she was atoning for the one second she hadn't been completely focused on Lukas.

I picked up the receiver from its cradle on the wall.

"No," she yelled.

I dropped it back into place..

"Keep that line free."

"Sorry. I'll use my cell." I pulled it out of my pocket, but the battery was dead. "Can I borrow yours?"

She slid it across the counter to me. "Just click over if anyone else calls."

I dialed the main number at Super One Foods and left a voicemail that we wouldn't be in work today.

"He's coming home." She flipped the pancake over with a shaky hand.

I knew that fear. The feeling that the most important person in your life wasn't coming back. When I lost my mother, Mickey was there. When Kai was locked up and I lost all hope, Mickey was there. Each time, she said the words I needed to hear: You aren't alone in this.

225

She sniffled. "He's okay." She put the flipper on the counter.

"He's a Fuchs. He's going to be fine." I came over to the stove, wanting to help her, but having no idea how.

Tears slipped down her cheeks.

I wrapped my arms around her, pulling her back against me.

"Why?" She clutched my arms. A sob escaped her lips. "Who would take my little boy?"

"I don't know. It's not fair."

She hiccupped. "What if he's..."

She doubled over. I held her and we slid to the floor. She fell to pieces in my arms, sobbing like a lost little girl. I rested my chin on the top of her head and rocked her until the sobs turned into gasps.

"It's going to be okay. I promise." God, I hoped I wasn't lying.

"If anything happens to him. I can't. I won't..." Her voice trailed off.

"Nothing is going to happen to him." Please, don't let anything happen to Lukas.

She turned in my arms, looking up at me with haunted eyes. Needing me to fix this. To take away the fear.

"You aren't alone in this," I said.

In that moment, I'd have done anything to erase her fear.

God help me, I kissed her.

CHAPTER 55

Kai

T he boxes of Dunkin Donuts coffee and munchkins slipped from my grasp and thudded against the floor. "Tough night?" Oliver tore his lips from Mickey's. Their limbs disentangled, but wisps of pink cotton candy swirled around them. Love linked his heart to hers.

My husband.

Kissing her. It was too much, even for me. Especially for me. Because I knew their bond was stronger than he admitted. Not that it mattered. Each day, I felt their emotional tie re-knotting like a cheese grater to my heart. Now, he julienned my heart with a chef's knife.

Oliver made it to his feet first and helped her up. Something in me snapped as he jumped away from her.

Maybe it was the way he said, "Kai, don't. We were out all night searching," while his mind scrambled to find an excuse for their kiss. *The moment. Exhaustion. I was trying to comfort her. It didn't mean anything. Don't know how it happened.*

"And you thought a little make out session would rejuvenate you?"

Rage bled over my words. I blinked away tears. I'd die before I let her see how much this got to me.

"Let's talk about this at home." His eyes flickered to her.

His concern for her shattered the last of my self-control. "My mistake. Is the Fuchses' kitchen just for cheating?"

She put her hand on his arm. "It's my fault. It was a momentary lapse in judgment."

"Funny, what can happen in a careless moment." My voice went cast iron-cold. "Maybe your son would be here, if you weren't so caught up in my husband?"

She started crying. I wanted to chalk it up to an act, but I got swept up in her undulations of absolute guilt.

I already swam in the love she felt for my husband. Her need for him. I had to block her out. I imagined millions of crystals swirling around myself. Coalescing into a solid eggshell. Impenetrable. I focused on my own feelings. Humiliation and betrayal strangled logic and reason.

"Her son is missing. How can you be so cruel?" he asked.

Cruel? You want to see cruel? I sharpened the image of Alex and me ripping each other's clothes off on the bedroom floor and torpedoed him with it. It hadn't happened...yet. But I wasn't done. I'd heard Mickey's worst fear.

"Are you sure he didn't run away from you?" I asked.

She choked on a sob and scampered out of the kitchen.

Evidently losing her son and kissing my husband were the limit for her. For me too.

Oliver hissed, "Stop it. What's wrong with you?"

"My husband just cheated on me."

"It was a kiss."

He kept throwing that bullshit excuse at me. Like his refusal to admit it was more could stop it from being more.

I needed to hear his thoughts. To know where his head was. But when I visualized a window in my crystal shield and opened it, his

228

thoughts didn't come streaming through. Outside my window loomed a granite tower, a barricade he'd erected against me.

The Fuchses' thoughts whistled through the opening. Mickey's fear that I was right about her being a bad mother. Poor Mrs. Fuchs tortured herself with the "If Only" game.

I couldn't help them now. I slammed the window shut and layered crystal bricks over it, blocking out everyone in the house. "If you can't see what that was, there isn't any hope for us."

The months I pretended my jealousy was in my head. Pointless. I was done ignoring the inevitable. I stormed out of the kitchen and stalked out the front door. I had to get out of there. Away from her. Far from him.

His feet pounded behind me on the road. He grabbed my arm and spun me around. "What do you mean?"

"I felt what was going on in that kitchen. It wasn't desperation. You broke your promise to me." The words clawed their way out of my throat and went for his eyes.

"I get that you're hurt. But don't overreact." His breath came in clouds of frustration.

My laugh ping-ponged from frustration to hysteria. "I've been under-reacting for months. I'm through giving you time to sort things out. You want her? You got her." I wrenched my arm free from his grasp.

He grabbed both my arms. Bad idea. I chopped my hands into his elbow joints and shoved him with all the hurt I'd held inside. He flew back and landed on his butt.

"Don't ever touch me like that again," I said.

"You want out? You got it."

"I'm gone."

Shock froze his face.

"Guess we're both breaking promises." I sagged in exhausted relief. Like I'd lanced an infection and the pus could finally drain. Sure the pain short-circuited my brain, left me lightheaded and dazed, but afterward...

I hightailed it to the car.

His chaotic thoughts swarmed me as I neared the driver-side door. None of them penetrated my shield. My hand shook as I tried to get the key in the ignition. They say after a shock, auto-pilot can kick in. It did for me.

I concentrated on getting through the next five minutes. Remembered what Grandma always told me about silver linings not being visible for at least three days. I slammed my foot on the gas and forced myself to drive. Three miles later, I gave into the tears as the realization pummeled me, shattering a few ribs: This time I might lose him.

Caleb's words ran through my head: Get out and get your head on straight before you consider talking to Oliver again. I stormed around the bedroom, throwing clothes and toiletries into my two suitcases. Caleb had secured me a room at the local B&B, Deer Haven Lodge. It was on Highway 13, the main route in and out of Butternut. I'd be several miles away from Oliver and have time to figure out what came next.

Thank God for Caleb.

I contemplated staying with Aunt Ines for all of seven seconds. That would be too weird. No matter how much she liked me, she'd have to be on Oliver's side. And despite my burning-oil-field of rage, my resolve was too fragile to stand up to her interrogation. When it came down to it, I was weak. Miserably, wretchedly weak. I'd come to depend on Oliver too much, becoming what I feared most. A burden he could no longer handle.

I tried not to think about Mickey on the drive to the B&B. I focused on picking up people's thoughts, straining to hear Lukas's or the kidnapper's. My telepathic radius of half a mile meant diddly-squat here. I could drive all over town and open up my mind, but that didn't guarantee I'd find him because most of the farms were double digits of acres. He could be smack dab in the middle of one and I'd never hear his thoughts from the road.

Still, I had to do something, so I opened the window in my shield several inches and listened. Drove around for hours, picking up stray thoughts like *If I make steak tonight will my husband kiss me?* or *That poor child still hasn't been found, soon they'll search for a body.*

Staying busy kept me emotionally removed from my reality, like a photographer hiding behind his lens during September 11th. It allowed me the luxury of pretending not to feel. It wasn't until I'd checked into the B&B, unloaded my suitcase, and sat down on my bed that it hit me.

The physical pain came first. As though an invisible hand slipped under my skin and through my ribs to squeeze my heart. Then the burning ache inside my chest, like I was drowning on all the unshed tears. Despair dragged me down. Nothing would ever be right again. I curled up on the bed and sobbed into the pillow for everything I'd lost that day.

"Interesting form," Caleb said.

I looked down and found I had my nine-year-old body in this dream. "I liked being nine." The last year of ordinary in my life.

"I wasn't that fond of ten and three-quarters."

I twirled my long hair around my finger. "My dream, I get to pick what we look like."

"Fair enough." A honey-colored ringlet slipped in front of his eyes and he blew at it. "I hated the ringlets back then."

"I loved them. Why do you put all that gunk in your hair now?" I climbed up on the flat rock by the pond in Grandma's yard. I loved how my legs dangled over the edge without touching the water. Thrilled at the changing patterns of shade the ancient oak beside us cast on the surface. It was our favorite spot. The one place we could be ourselves.

"You look pretty wiped out." Caleb scrambled up the rock to sit beside me.

"I haven't slept alone in years." I stared out at the water's surface, willing it to be still.

"What about when he worked for the moving company?"

"That was one night." Not the rest of my nights.

His arm came around my shoulder. "You'll get through this."

"I left my husband. Probably lost him for good." My lungs expelled hopelessness.

He squeezed my shoulder. "And the little boy?"

"Oh God, I'm so selfish." Poor Lukas was lost or kidnapped, and I was worried about my marriage.

"You've got a lot going on." My brother's hand stroked my back as if he were petting the feathers of a wounded bird. Gentle, tender, hesitant to harm.

"Everything's a mess." I crumbled into his arms. Faucets of sorrow ran from my eyes.

Caleb rested his head against mine, rocking me as he hummed "The Itsy Bitsy Spider."

Gradually, my sobs gave way to hiccups. "I lost him."

"You gave him time to think."

"I served him up on a platter to her."

"Clinging to him wasn't working. If he comes back, then he's yours." He rubbed my arm.

I choked back a fresh sob. The loneliness loomed. The knowledge that Oliver wasn't beside me ripped into me. His absence felt incomprehensible.

I started babbling. "I'll miss the way he snipes at me when he first wakes up. The way he talks in his sleep in German. How he sleeps in the middle of the bed. How he brushes his teeth for ten minutes. I'LL MISS HIM." How could I face a lifetime without him?

Caleb was quiet for a moment.

I thought he would share some brilliant insight when he finally spoke.

"Ten minutes? Doesn't his hand get tired?"

I laughed. "You'd think, but no."

"You want to go play?" Caleb laced his fingers through mine. "It's your dream. We can do anything you want."

"Anything?" I asked.

He groaned. "I'm not wearing a dress to your tea party."

"But the blue one brings out your eyes and the crown looks so good on your ringlets." I squeezed his hand, hoping he'd give in.

"You can't tell anyone."

"It'll be our secret." I tried to smile as if my heart weren't being dismembered.

CHAPTER 56

Oliver

Time stopped in front of the Fuchses' house. I didn't know what to do about Kai and me. I was too angry, she was too hurt. If I followed her, the next fight might be our last. I wouldn't lose the most important person in my life.

Not like Mickey had lost Lukas. She didn't deserve that kind of pain. No one did. I had to help her right now. I owed her that. My feet took me back into the Fuchses' house. I found Mickey in Lukas's room, curled around his stuffed rabbit.

"Mickey, it's not your fault," I said.

Fresh tears streamed down her cheeks.

"You're a terrific mom. We'll find him."

"I've been thinking about you too much," she said.

I laughed. "You always put Lukas first."

"I've been a bad mom."

I knelt down beside her. "Kai lashes out when she's hurt. She didn't mean it."

"I saw her eyes. She meant it." She hiccupped.

"I don't think it's your fault." I sidled closer and put my arm around her. Now wasn't about the mistake we'd made in the kitchen. It was about helping her through the worst moment of her life. "What happened in the kitchen was my fault. 100% me."

"I didn't stop you." She sniffled.

"Fair enough. 14% you." I stroked her back.

She gasp-giggled. "14%?"

"Yup."

We stayed there until her breathing calmed. She wiped her face on her sleeve.

After she'd pulled herself together, I said, "You need to shower, change clothes, and eat. Then we'll get back out there, okay?"

Her smile wavered. "What about Kai?"

"She and I can work it out after Lukas is home safe and sound," I lied. I was worried about my marriage. But right now, Lukas's life was at risk.

"Are you sure?"

Mickey had been there most of my life. All the days my mother wasn't. After Reinhard splattered my world like a bug on his windshield. Mickey came through for me when I needed her. I had to see her through this.

"Remember when you came to San Diego?" I had no way to stop Kai's parents from institutionalizing her five years ago. She was only my girlfriend. I spent weeks trying to reach her in that institution. The doctor gave up hope. The weekend I thought I'd lost everything, Mickey was there for me.

"You helped me through the darkest hours. You gave me the strength to keep fighting. I told you I'd never forget that," I said.

"I owed you after how I ended things."

"We were kids." Seniors in high school when she told me she didn't want me anymore. That we didn't work. Then she took up with Nathan. That's why Alex dragged me to Chicago to meet girls. To get my mind away from Mickey. "You've been there for me every time it really counted."

"Thanks." She tried to smile, but her lips couldn't hold that pose.

"Let me be here for you now." I stood up and tugged her to her feet. Focusing on the wildfire of Lukas's disappearance, I tried to ignore the hurricane tearing along the coast of my future with Kai.

CHAPTER 57

Kai

Half asleep, I groped for my husband on his side of the bed. I had a moment of euphoric ignorance before I rolled into his vacant spot. The quiet pressed in on me. Gray hopelessness enveloped me. Tendrils of depression reached for me.

It would be so easy to surrender to it. But I wasn't the coming-undone woman I'd been in New York. Because of Oliver. His ability to stand up for me when I couldn't. To do what needed to be done.

But he was gone. Four little letters paralyzed me. Made it impossible to get out of bed. My head settled deeper into the tear-crusted pillowcase while the B&B owners' thoughts trickled into my head.

Must get the coffee started for our guest, Mr. Hoffmann thought.

Where is my grandson? Is he alright? Why is this happening? Mrs. Hoffmann asked herself. She was Lukas's other grandmother.

That poor little boy was out there somewhere.

I groaned and threw the pillow over my head. I'd indulged in my self-pity party all night. My depression must have leaked out and made sleep more impossible for them. Yet they'd dragged themselves out of bed to make breakfast for me. I was beyond self-absorbed.

Guilt was the only thing that could prod me out of that bed.

A shower and change of clothes later, I sat upstairs at the dining room table. The open floor plan allowed me to sit at the head of the table and see straight into the kitchen. A quick turn to the right and the entire living room was on display. If I twisted in my chair, I could see out the wall of glass to the back deck.

Mrs. Hoffmann forced a smile, but her eyes were reflecting pools of misery. "Cream in your coffee, dear?"

"Please."

She bustled over to pour some for me.

"I love your place." The log cabin walls, vaulted ceiling, and antler chandelier all contributed to the perfect rustic getaway. "Especially the deer-themed items. Charming." I wished I could enjoy it.

"Did you get a chance to try out the swim spa or the hot tub?" Mrs. Hoffmann tucked her brown bob behind her ears.

Oliver would love them. I tried to infuse my voice with cheerfulness. "Not yet, but I will tonight."

She went back to the kitchen. Her thoughts were like a hummingbird's wings lashing the air. *Should I ask about Oliver? I don't want to upset her. She looks like she was up all night crying.*

I should have put on makeup. I didn't have anyone to impress, but it would have hid the evidence of my brokenness.

Not that I could hide what happened in a small town. Everyone knew everyone's business. Made me long for the anonymity of New York.

Mr. Hoffmann flipped a pancake on his turn-of-the-century-style stove. He eyed the skillet crackling with bacon. Images of two dark-haired boys beside the stove flittered through his mind. A memory of years past. *Nathan loved almost burnt bacon. Used to raise a fuss when I made it any other way. Damn him for walking out on his family to see the world. This right here was the only world that should have mattered to him. His dreams may have cost us our only grandson.*

"Do you like preserves?" Mrs. Hoffmann buttered my toast. *She looks like she doesn't eat enough. I hope Lukas has something to eat.* She closed her eyes against a rush of despair.

It wasn't just her pain. Mine was trickling out again, permeating their home. "What kind?" I conjured up my crystal Fabergé egg, sealing my emotions inside. Protecting the Hoffmanns from my despair. I could keep it airtight for weeks with only a few people around.

"I make my own. Strawberry and blackberry." She pulled out her canning jars.

"Both."

I grabbed today's *Park Falls Herald*, needing a safe conversation starter. Splashed across the front page was the headline, "Toddler Gone Missing." Inside me, something screamed, This can't happen. Not here. Not to Lukas.

Before Mrs. Hoffmann saw the front page, I flipped the paper open and folded it over. Pretended to peruse the second page. How did I not see this coming? Lukas never thought about running away. At least when I was around. He loved Gammie and Mommy too much. Which meant someone took him. But who?

Mrs. Hoffmann slid a plate of scrambled eggs, fluffy pancakes, crispy bacon and golden toast in front of me. An emotional eater, I devoured everything on my plate while she went to work on the dishes.

In the kitchen, her husband prepared a dozen baby bottles.

"You have a lot of babies to feed." Weird. I hadn't seen or heard any here.

"We consider them our babies," Mr. Hoffmann said.

"Didn't you read about the fawns? Feeding them is a part of the B&B experience," Mrs. Hoffmann said.

"Cool." I'd never had a close encounter with a deer. Caleb must have planned the distraction for me.

After I finished breakfast and bundled up, we went outside to bottle-feed the fawns. I tried to stay in the moment, focusing on getting the fawns as much milk as I could. They were skittish at first, so I stayed in place. I opened the window in my shield and sent out calmness to them. Once they caught that and the scent of the formula, they made their way toward me. I tilted the bottle at a sharp angle and they sucked it down.

For twenty minutes, I lost myself in their joy. Animals are wonderful like that. Willing to share their happiness with others. Most humans are calmed by their presence. Me, I was buoyed up by their kindness.

When we came back inside, Mrs. Hoffmann surprised me by printing out pictures she'd snapped while I was feeding the fawns. My eyes lingered on the photo of me laughing while the fawn pawed at my leg, demanding more milk from his bottle. I never thought I would smile on the morning after my world collapsed.

"How did you get into raising deer?" I asked her.

"We wanted more children, but they never came."

"Oh."

Her eyes misted over. "I had two sons. Good boys. Christian was my eldest. Brought home our first fawn and nursed him back to health. Nathan was the athlete. Loved to compete."

"Do they live around here?"

"Nathan's work took him to South America a few years back." She sipped her cocoa. "Christian died in middle school."

"I'm sorry."

"You never expect to bury your children." Her voice sank under the burden of that reality.

I wondered what happened, but a death that young always remained a pocket of pain. I didn't want her to have to re-open it. "No one should have to."

Her face trembled. "Now Lukas..."

I reached over and squeezed her hand. "There will be time."

"I wished we'd seen more of him. It was so awkward," she paused. "We thought in time Michaela would come around."

I leaned forward. "You know, my best memories are of my grandmother, and we didn't get close until I was ten."

Television didn't provide the distraction I needed. My thumb ached from pressing the channel up button. I was about to take the car out for another round of telepathic eavesdropping, when someone knocked on the door. Mr. Hoffmann greeted him.

Alex's voice echoed in the B&B's entryway. "We've been at it all day and night. My group just finished canvassing the woods across the street."

I unlocked the window in my shield and eavesdropped on their thoughts.

This is a nightmare. Lukas gone. Seeing the Hoffmanns. But Kai's here somewhere, Alex thought.

I switched off the flat screen TV and sat up in the leather recliner.

"Any news?" Mr. Hoffmann asked. *They have to find him. My wife can't take much more.*

"We're hoping it's a kidnapping. At least then Lukas would be safe indoors." *I'll kill anyone that hurts Lukas.*

Mr. Hoffmann said, "If there's anything we can do…" *Not that you'd ever ask. Fuchses are so damn proud.*

"We've got it under control." *We don't need you anywhere near Mickey right now.*

Alex came into the living room. His navy blue wool coat and rosy cheeks accentuated his gorgeous Larry Hagman blues. I had on my oversized UCSD sweatshirt and baggy jeans. Not a stitch of makeup and my hair in a finger-combed ponytail. Thor meets troll girl.

He smiled at me and a swoon-inducing dimple popped out. *Even on her worst day, she's a hottie.*

"What are you doing here?" I stood up, smoothing down the bumps in my hair.

Had to get away from everything. "I needed a break from searching."
He pulled his gloves off and unbuttoned his jacket. "Unless you'd
rather be alone."

"I could use a distraction."

"Coffee?" *And time to tell me why you're staying here.*

"Give me ten minutes."

He slid his gloves back on. "Meet me in the SUV."

I ran down the spiral staircase to my room, brushed my hair,
switched to a white cable knit sweater and skinny jeans, and smeared
some lipgloss on. Then I joined Alex inside his car.

I buckled my seatbelt. "Was that awkward?"

"Always is." He shifted into gear. *Hoffmanns never accepted that their
son was the bad guy with Mickey.*

"Does Lukas's dad know what happened?"

"The real question is would he care?" *The only good things he gave
her were full custody of Lukas and the divorce papers.*

"I think the Hoffmanns contacted him."

"Hmm." Alex stared at the road ahead. *I hope that douche bag never
comes back.*

"What happened?"

Alex frowned. "Mickey said things weren't working out between
them." *Bad judgment. He was a jerk. She wasn't over Oliver.*

"You didn't push?"

"Do I seem like the type?" he asked.

I laughed. "You haven't asked about Oliver and me."

"How are you?" *You look good.*

I studied my chewed-raw fingernails. "I've been better."

You don't deserve this. "I'm sorry."

"Not your fault."

"I wished I'd been wrong."

"Me too." My voice dropped an octave.

"Oliver's a fool." *Why do women fall for him?*

"Things haven't been easy with us for a long time."

"That's no excuse to kiss another woman." He slammed his palm against the steering wheel. "Like Mickey's head isn't confused enough."

My darkest memories suckerpunched me. Oliver's face haunted me. The stark horror when he had pried the razor blade from my fingers. The agonizing stoicism when he forced me to vomit up the sleeping pills. His voice breaking when he pleaded with me to move away.

"I can see why he might give in to the impulse." Admitting it cut me deeper than a 24-inch blade.

"Really? Cause from where I'm sitting he's an idiot." *Risking his marriage for a woman who left him in high school.*

"There's a lot you don't know." So much I should have done differently.

"Enlighten me." He pulled into a mom-and-pop shop in Glidden, the town north of Butternut. "Let's get the coffee to go." *Can't sit still today.*

"And take a walk?"

"It's like you can read my mind." *Copper Falls Park is 20 minutes away.*

If only he knew. When I tried to tell my boyfriend in high school about the telepathy, he branded me a witch and things went from hearts-to-hatred in fifteen seconds. Safer to keep it to myself. So I did most of the time.

I hadn't felt the urge to confide for a long time after that. Until that night on the rooftop when I met Oliver. And now Alex. Something about him made me want to spill.

Look how things turned out with Oliver, my insecurities reminded me.

I kept the conversation light until we arrived at our destination.

He turned the ignition off. "Copper Falls Park."

"Oliver promised to take me here."

"It's one of the highlights of the Northwoods."

Oliver-emptiness enveloped me. I struggled to regain a foothold in my world without him. Cold radiated from my marrow.

I blurted out, "I'm a telepath." My body lurched back to the moment. The warmth of confession.

No way.

"Way."

He stared at me. *Coincidence. She can't be.*

"I can and I am."

"Prove it," he said.

My fingers twisted together in my lap. Disappointment rolled over me.

"Remember when you were picking out furniture at the storage center?" he asked.

"Yes."

What was I thinking when you examined the mirror?" he asked.

I rubbed my lips together. No polite way to say it. "You thought Oliver had struck gold and that you'd tap my tight little ass if I wasn't his wife."

Alex had the grace to blush. "Sorry."

"I've heard people's thoughts most of my life. It's worse than eavesdropping." I shrugged. "You can't get mad for what people keep inside where they think no one can hear them. They're thoughts, not actions or spoken words."

"That's mighty big of you."

"What's the alternative? To live my life in constant shock and anger? No thank you."

His eyes brightened. "Have you heard Lukas?"

"I've tried. But I can only hear people within a half-mile radius."

"Does Ines know?"

"Just my family and Oliver," I said.

"And me."

I toyed with my scarf.

244

"What am I thinking right now?"

"You're praying Lukas is alright and scared to death you might have to tell Mickey it's changed from a search and rescue to a recovery. And you think this sweater doesn't do justice to my rack."

He let out a breath. "That's amazing."

No trace of fear in his thoughts. I listened in to be sure. Nope, not an ounce of afraid there.

"Is that how you knew my mom was sick?" he asked.

I studied my mittens. "Not exactly."

"Lukas?" he asked.

I jerked my head up. "You know?"

His palms smoothed over the steering wheel. "Before my neck started acting up, he warned me that the stack of books holding it up was about to fall over."

"And?"

"Turned out I'd had a herniated disk for years. A compressed nerve finally caused enough pain to get me to a doctor. MRI confirmed what Lukas said. I stopped lifting and started managing the storage business with Pete a couple months ago."

"Did you tell anyone about Lukas?"

"The family chalked it up to coincidence. Said he must have seen me massaging my neck or something."

"Did you agree with them?" I asked.

"Seemed the easiest thing to do for everyone."

"But you knew…"

"They weren't ready to face that possibility," he said.

"Were you?"

"I'd do anything for Lukas."

"So would I."

We got out of the car and walked along the snow-covered trail, following the Diet-Coke-colored water of a copper-infused river. I slipped, but Alex caught me, steadied me, secured my mittened hand into the crook of his arm.

He never asked me how to shield his thoughts.

We came around a bend in the path and stopped at the viewpoint. Copper Falls was magnificent in winter. Partly frozen, it reminded me of a ginormous root beer float.

His thoughts were so clear. *If she wasn't Oliver's, I'd kiss her.*

I turned to face him. Stood on my tippy toes and pulled his face toward mine.

"What are you doing?" His lips were two inches from mine. "Kai?" His warm breath defrosted my nose.

I filled his mind. My face. My eyes. My smile.

Closing the distance between us, I pressed my lips to his. My tongue traced over his upper lip. His lips parted.

He wanted me. Just me. No one else. I deepened the kiss, clutching at his coat. Desperate to stay in that moment. Blocking out everything that was wrong. Burying it in my cemetery of bad memories.

Oliver, Alex thought. A picture of Mickey, Oliver, and him filled his mind. Tall and lanky, I recognized the teen version of Oliver. Alex stroked the beginnings of a goatee. Mickey sported bangs.

Desire warred with integrity. Guilt wrapped around him. Choked him.

He tore his mouth away. "We shouldn't."

I stepped back, whispering, "I'm sorry."

"Me too."

"I shouldn't have dragged you into this." I clutched at the wooden railing. I'd made a bigger mess of the pigsty my life was becoming.

"I knew you were vulnerable."

"Your nephew is missing." I said.

Alex's eyes seared mine. "We used each other."

"I guess so." If I hadn't been so caught up in believing the lie, I might have noticed the puff of silver evaporating above us.

CHAPTER 58

Oliver

I ran out of excuses to not go home. When I pulled up to the house in Aunt Ines's car, all the windows were dark. No matter how many times I called his name, Herbie didn't come out of his hut. Aunt Ines had kept him fed and watered while I searched for Lukas. Herbie probably blamed me for Kai's absence.

I trudged up the stairs and into my house. It didn't quite feel like a home anymore. A part of me hoped Kai would leave for a day and come back. Be waiting to talk to me tonight.

Foolish optimism, I suppose. I went into the kitchen to scrounge up a meal and found an envelope on the kitchen table. *Oliver* was scratched across it in Kai's handwriting. I dropped into a chair and unsealed it.

Dear Oliver,

I don't know how to do this anymore. I tried pretending Mickey didn't matter. I tried everything I could to get you to understand. It was never in my head. It was always in yours. Your feelings for her. They were never settled.

And I can't settle them for you.

You need to figure out who you want. Staying here and watching is too painful. I'll be at the Deer Haven Lodge.

I'm not giving up on us. But I'm giving into the reality of what is going on. I can't make you stay with me. I want it to be your choice to be with me each and every day. Just as it has been my choice to be with you each and every day.

Yours,

Kai

I crumpled the letter in my hand. She'd left me. Not to get back to New York. Not because she'd lost her sanity. Not because she didn't love me. She'd left because of me.

CHAPTER 59

Kai

While Alex's Land Rover traversed the back roads between Copper Falls and Deer Haven Lodge, I scanned every mind I could reach for thoughts from Lukas or his kidnapper. Straining to find them. Five hours of searching yielded nothing. My brain pulsated against my skull. Beating out a steady rhythm of "CAN'T FIND HIM." A side effect of telepathic fatigue.

By the time Alex dropped me back at the B&B, I cradled the side of my head. I trudged down the shoveled and sanded walkway to the back entrance, skirting the hot tub on my way to the sliding glass doors. I should have gone to bed, but I couldn't. Not to that empty bed. I searched my suitcase for Aleve and found the items Caleb insisted I pack: my bikini and my flask.

I changed and went out to the hot tub. I slid into the simmering heat, sinking down until the hot water lapped at my collarbone. The bubbles tickled the back of my neck. The steam warmed my cheeks.

I had kissed another man. Oliver had kissed another woman. Two wrongs made things five times as bad. I tried to consider Alex a lapse of judgment. Mickey wasn't. I'd seen the love swirling between them. Even if they never admitted to it.

I massaged my temple with my thumb. The vein tapped against my fingertip. I welcomed a full day of work tomorrow. Just had to get through tonight. I eyed the drink tray. Glided over and splashed some rum into half a cup of Diet Coke. The first sip tickled my throat. My gaze drifted above the snow-covered yard and frozen pond to the silver-speckled indigo sky. This could have been bliss.

A car door slammed in the driveway. Boots scraped along the back sidewalk. I couldn't hear any thoughts, but I saw the schist tower. Oliver coming toward my almost oasis.

Crystals writhed around me, thickening into an egg-shaped barrier. It wasn't just his kissing Mickey. Or my kissing Alex. Symptoms of our deeper issues. His shrouded-in-secrecy past overtaking our present. My powers making normal impossible for us. We faced 15,000-foot-tall obstacles.

Oliver trudged toward the hot tub. I took another swig of rum and Diet Coke. Stared at him over the rim of my cup. He didn't strip down to his boxers and plunge into the hot tub. He didn't even pull up a chair and sit near me. He stopped a foot away from me.

"Having fun?" he asked.

"Relaxing after an afternoon of searching."

"I didn't see you at the checkpoint."

"I wasn't going near Mickey after yesterday." My voice turned six-pack-a-day-smoker harsh.

"You wouldn't let me explain."

"If you found me making out with my high school sweetheart, what would you do?" I put my cup on the drink tray.

He blew out a cloud of white. "Smash his face in."

"And then?"

"Sleep on the couch."

I raised an eyebrow.

"Go stay at a hotel for a while."

Which is exactly what I did.

He stared at me. "You've made your point."

"You get why I can't come home?"

"Ever?"

"For now." I sat on my hands to resist reaching out to him.

He looked at his watch.

"Somewhere you need to be?" He wasn't due at work for hours.

"I promised Mickey I'd help with the search."

"Lukas is the most important thing now." But spending more time with Mickey? Double slap in the face. I blurted out, "Alex stopped by to see me."

"When?"

"This afternoon. He took me to Copper Falls." I let my fingers glide along the water's surface.

"Guess the search isn't a priority for him."

"He needed to talk."

"I'm sure he did." His expression rendered an indictment. "What did you do with him?"

"You broke my heart. You destroyed the trust between us."

"With one kiss?"

"Does a kiss really matter that little to you?" I cocked my head to the side, dangerously close to testing that theory.

"Yes."

I visualized a cannon built in my crystal wall, pushed the image of Alex kissing me into a ball, and fired the memory at him. It burrowed through his schist tower.

Oliver's jaw dropped. "You kissed him?"

"But it doesn't matter, right? Just one kiss."

"You did it to get even."

With Oliver, you couldn't just explain. Sometimes, you had to teach him a lesson.

253

"You've been fawning over Mickey since we arrived. Wishing my telepathy would go away. Wanting me to be a different person."

He rubbed his forehead. Dark circles ringed his eyes.

I rested my chin on the warm water. Closed my eyes so I could get the words out. "We're broken. And I don't know how to fix us anymore."

"Neither do I." His voice crashed down on my head like a four-foot icicle.

"Maybe I should go to London for a while."

"With Alex?"

"Would it matter?" Tears stung my eyes.

"How can you ask that?"

I looked down at my wedding ring. "I can't make you stay with me."

Oliver grabbed my towel and held it out. "Come home to me."

"We've been through so much. Maybe too much. You have to be sure I'm the one you want."

He stripped off his left glove and wiggled his ring finger. "Already decided."

"You kissed another woman. And don't tell me it was a heat-of-the-moment thing. I heard your thoughts."

"It was for me."

"Then you're lying to yourself." And me. "Your emotions were all laid out in Technicolor."

"What about Alex and you?"

I still hadn't wrapped my mind around that impulse. "I shouldn't have done that. And I wouldn't have, if you didn't first."

With each word, he shoved the towel toward me. "Come. Home. Now."

I shook my head, unable to say those words. To tell him I wouldn't be with him, when I wanted to be with him more than I wanted to be right.

He draped the towel across the chair, giving me his cold German face. The one that always made me worry about what I'd done wrong.

"I love you," I whispered.

"Not enough." He marched back to the driveway.

The beaches of Southern California always smelled of home to me. No surprise that the dream me stood on Torrey Pines Beach, watching the tide creep out to sea.

My brother snuck up next to me. "Nice to see you, again." The corners of his eyes crinkled up, laughing at me.

"I know. Two nights in a row. Kind of intense." But I needed him.

"I'm not complaining." He looped his arm around my shoulder as we started walking south along the beach. "Just think how great it would be if you lived near me."

I shook my head, unwilling to have that argument tonight.

"So what's up with Alex?"

I turned to face him. "How'd you know?"

"You were thinking about him when I walked into your dream."

The sand beneath our feet sparkled and shimmered with flecks of gold and silver against tan and black. "This has to be the most gorgeous shoreline in San Diego county." My toes burrowed into it.

Caleb waited.

I bit my lip. "I kissed him."

"Wow. Never saw this coming."

"Like I did?"

"You're a telepath." He grinned. "You had to have an inkling of his feelings for you."

I stared at the waves pulling away from the shore. "I never would have done anything if Oliver hadn't kissed Mickey."

"Two wrongs…"

I squinted at the biggest playboy in the western hemisphere. "Since when did you become the moral police?"

"No judgment here." He started walking and I fell in step beside him. "Did you like it?"

"It was nice."

He rolled his eyes. "Such a girl."

"What do you want me to say? I loved how he plunged his tongue into my mouth?"

"TMI," Caleb chuckled. "But I prefer the honesty. You've been hiding from your feelings about him for a while."

I exploded. "What feelings? He's gorgeous and flirts with me to make Oliver jealous."

"But you get all flustered when you think about the kiss."

I whirled around to face him, shoving my pointer finger into his chest. "Don't you go sneaking into my dreams and rifling through my head." His eyes were the most amazing shade of turquoise. Reminded me of Kata Noi beach in Thailand.

"Thanks. That was a great family trip. Best surfing ever. And it's not my fault you dreamt about him."

I threw my hands up in disgust. "If only Oliver hadn't kissed Mickey."

"That's your story?" He strolled ahead, whistling to himself.

In-fur-iating. He meandered along the shore. The water lapped up to his ankles before racing back out to sea. How did he see right through me when I didn't even know I was putting up a façade?

With a growl of annoyance, I ran to catch up with him. "What did you mean?"

He glanced at me. "You're attracted to Alex."

"No, that's…no."

"You and Oliver have been through so much together." Caleb's voice was stiller than a tidal pool.

"He's my heart and soul. Nothing can change that."

"One kiss seemed to unravel everything."

"I don't love Alex."

"Not yet. The real question is: Do you love Oliver enough to fight for him?" He pointed toward the cliffs. Mother nature crafted a hundred-layer Thanksgiving cake made of dirt the color of turkey, corn, sweet potato, and gravy all precariously stacked a thousand feet above us. "That cliff is ready to return to the ocean on a whim. Or remain in place another twenty years."

"Meaning?" I hated when he got all philosophical on me.

"Everything has a tipping point."

"Don't Yoda me."

He picked up a rock and skipped it across the shallow water.

Around the bend, another beach loomed. Black's Beach, the nude beach we'd snuck onto as kids.

"Remember the saggy-assed guy that asked you what time it was?" he asked.

I giggled. "And I said, 'Time for me to get home.'"

"You ran back to Torrey Pines faster than a cheetah on the hunt."

"I didn't see you lingering behind."

"You were always scared of going too far," he said.

"And you always had to exceed the limits."

He touched my arm. "Remember what Grandma used to say?"

I whispered, "All the important answers are inside you."

He pulled me into one of his hugs. The kind that withheld nothing. "Take your time. But listen to what's in there." He rested his head on top of mine. "I'm worried about you."

"I'm tougher than I look."

"Do you still hear those thoughts?"

I slipped out of his hug and walked into the water. My toes sunk into the buttery sand. I crouched down to pick up a coral-colored rock. I struggled over the words to describe what it was like.

"It's not a constant thing. More like I pick up a frequency that I'm not supposed to. Or one that eludes my senses." Blood-spattering emotions that burst the capillaries in my brain.

"Can you figure out what it is?"

"I can't pinpoint the source." Every time I tried to hone in on them, I lost the signal.

My brother's jaw pulsated. Worry singed his lips.

I tried to make it sound less bad. "It never lasts more than a few minutes. There are days of nothing. Then bam it comes again." The cloudless blue sky couldn't banish the sick feeling inside me. "I get swept up in hatred. Like I'm on the verge of rage, but those are someone else's feelings, not mine." I stepped further into the water, letting it wash over my feet.

"Do you think it's connected to Lukas's disappearance?"

"I hope not."

"Does it feel like a person's mind?" he asked.

"Sort of. Everyone's mind feels different. Like seashells." No two were completely alike.

"Anything like mine and Grandma's?" He handed me a white clamshell and a black mussel shell.

I cupped the shells in my hand. With Grandma and Caleb, I was a magnet for their thoughts. "It's nothing like you and Grandma."

"Maybe this guy's got some gift of his own." His expression slid toward thoughtful.

"People like us are pretty rare." Besides my family, there was only Lukas.

"You were a bit preoccupied in New York. Would you have noticed a mind you couldn't tune in when you were struggling to tune out tens of thousands of Manhattanites?"

"You think this person is like us?"

"Purely conjecture." He picked up a flat black stone and skipped it out to sea.

"Should I be worried?"

He wrapped his arm around my shoulder again. "Maybe."

We strolled onward to Black's Beach.

CHAPTER 60

Oliver

Today, we found more places Lukas wasn't. I came home to Aunt Ines holding court over my kitchen table.

"Oliver, we need to talk." She ladled wiener kartoffelsuppe into a bowl for me.

Viennese potato soup was hearty winter food. Exactly what I needed after an exhaustive day of searching.

I grabbed some apple juice and joined her at the table. "It's nice to have dinner with someone."

"It must be lonely here without Kai. Herbie really misses her," Aunt Ines said.

The turkey never let me near him. I'd hoped in time he'd come around. The likelihood of that diminished daily.

"It's not the same without her." Every time I walked into our house and she wasn't there, imaginary torturers jabbed bamboo sticks under my fingernails.

Aunt Ines sat down next to me. "You miss her?"

"She's my wife." I slept diagonally in our bed to fill the space. It took everything I had to not sniff her pillow when I climbed into bed. This morning, I woke with my head buried in it.

"Why did you kiss Mickey?" she asked.

"I don't know."

"You'll never get Kai to come home with that answer."

"It was the heat of the moment. I was trying to ease Mickey's pain. Distract her from the fear. Let her know she wasn't alone. It was a stupid mistake."

"Sounds pretty thought out, actually," Aunt Ines said.

"You don't understand." I raked my hand through my hair. "Mickey's always been there for me. I was just trying to repay the favor."

"Hmmph." Her lips stretched downward like a grumpy turtle.

"What does that mean?"

"You broke trust. You crossed a line. You made a mistake."

"Right."

"And you need forgiveness." She stirred her soup.

"Exactly."

"Which isn't something you give easily," she said.

"No one should grant it too easily."

"Did you apologize?" she asked.

"Of course." I dipped a bread dumpling in my soup.

"You said the words: I am sorry?"

"I think so." I replayed the moment in my head. Kai had to know I was sorry.

"Thinking you said them and saying them are the difference between a lake and an ocean." She added softly, "The difference between your daddy and you."

"It's not the same," I said.

"If he'd apologized, could you have forgiven him?"

She didn't know what he'd done. How unforgivable it was. "I don't live in hypotheticals."

"You betrayed Kai and lost her trust," she said.

"I didn't sleep with Mickey," I grumbled.

She chuckled. "I really hope that is not what you lead with next time you talk to Kai."

CHAPTER 61

Kai

Microscopic trolls chiseled their way out of my skull. End-of-the-work-day migraine. Not from all the kids yelling and crying at daycare. That I could handle. No, I had the brilliant idea to drop my shield and listen to everyone's thoughts. Which meant I got to experience the tides of their strongest emotions. For the entire workday.

I'd forgotten how much it drained me to hear and feel everyone around me. Sorting out each strain of consciousness made me feel like the hallway monitor at a Brooklyn public school. Yet another thing Oliver was right about. I hated when he was right.

After the last child had been picked up, I tidied the room for tomorrow morning. Anything to avoid returning to my empty room at the B&B. Tripping on a foam block, I scooped it up. When my arms reached overladen, I headed to the containers where the toys should be stored.

How can this be happening? They were so happy together. It has to be Michaela. That little troublemaker. Aunt Ines's thoughts announced her arrival.

I plastered a smile across my face as she bustled into the room.

She threw her arms around me, smothering my face in her ample chest. "You poor thing, what was Oliver thinking?"

A doll's plastic toes jabbed into my ribs.

She held me at arm's length and looked me over. "Why did you move out?"

He's still in love with the she-demon. "I think he has feelings for Mickey."

"He loves you." *She was never good for him.*

I walked over to the bins in the corner and deposited the toys in their proper place. "How's Herbie?"

"Missing his mommy."

"I miss him too."

She pulled off her fuchsia gloves, shrugged out of her purple coat, and unwrapped her lime green scarf. She laid everything over a kiddy chair. "You should be staying with me."

I prayed for some of Caleb's strength. "My brother booked me into the Deer Haven Lodge for the week."

Her eyes sugared with worry. "You should be with family now."

But not Oliver's family. "The Hoffmanns need me."

Her face fudge-rippled with confusion. Then it smoothed out. "They must be worried sick about Lukas."

I laced my fingers together. "Having a guest gives them something to focus on."

"You're such a good girl."

Guilt nipped at me. Using the Hoffmanns to duck staying with her. Awful, but effective. "Just trying to make the best of a bad situation."

"Are you sure you want to leave Oliver all alone?" She plopped down into the teacher's chair.

Being together hadn't stopped him from kissing Mickey. "It's for the best. We both need time to figure things out."

"How can you work things out when you aren't seeing each other?"

I squirmed under her gaze. "I can't make his feelings for Mickey go away. He can't make me trust him again. Those are things we have to work on alone."

"In my day, you stayed together and fought your way back to each other."

Things would be different if we had kids...

Pain seared the center of my scalp, bringing me to the brink of tears. I blinked them back.

She rubbed my arm. "What are you going to do?"

My forehead throbbed. "I don't know." I sat in one of the kid's chairs.

"You shouldn't have to go through this." Her lips sank toward her chin. "What is this world coming to? And poor Lukas is missing."

"It's terrible." I felt useless. Despair welled up inside of me.

I thought it was mine. Until Aunt Ines faded away. The room disappeared. And the familiar blackness closed in. I'd lost everything that mattered. Everything had been eclipsed by an insatiable blood lust. *Oliver will pay. He will suffer as I have. Lose what he loves.* If I'd had a gun, I'd have unloaded a round of bullets into his body.

Soul-melting emotions consumed me. I'd swear they were my own. But they weren't. They were someone else's. Woodsy smells assaulted me—dank earth and kindling fire. These were a man's thoughts.

If I conjured up my shield, I could get away from his mind. Save myself. But if he wanted to hurt Oliver, I had to stop him. Reaching out with my mind, I tried to pinpoint his thoughts and get a picture of who he was.

This time he didn't disappear.

My world drowned in purple-blackness. Anger split my spine. Fury engulfed my heart.

A hand snaked around my throat. Fingers bit into my skin. Cutting off my air supply. Weightlessness stole over my body. My mind blanked. One word flashed like a neon sign: Dying.

My shield flared around me. Everything became speckled colors.

In the distance, I heard Aunt Ines's voice. "Are you all right?"

I blinked, trying to bring the room into focus. The children's playroom. I wheezed and coughed my way back to life. The rawness in my throat robbed me of words.

She thrust a glass of water into my hand and pressed her palm to my forehead. "What was that?"

"Dizzy spell," I croaked.

She scrutinized my face. "Bull."

I took a few sips of water and rested my head against my palm. "Low blood sugar?"

"Don't fib to me, missy."

Not like she believed anything I said. "I'm telepathic."

"My best friend saw the future."

I nearly sprayed water across the room. "She what?"

"Every time she saw a horrific event, she'd go white as a sheet and fall into a trance. Just like you did." She frowned. "Though she never acted like she was choking. Is that normal?"

"I can't see the future."

She rubbed my back. "I know, dear. Whose thoughts did you pick up?"

I'd never connected with anyone like that. Even in my dreams with Caleb, nothing stuck. I'd cut my foot on a shell and wake up with no sign of injury. No one had ever been able to physically harm me through my telepathy. "I'm not sure."

She snorted. "I taught elementary school for 20 years. Try again."

"Lately, I've been feeling someone's emotions, but I can't figure out whose." That was the simplest explanation.

"What's this person feeling?"

He made my worst depression seem like a walking tour of Central Park. I put the water on the table and whispered, "Despair. Complete loss of hope."

"That can't be good." Her lips compressed in concern. "Any idea why this person affects you so much?"

265

"No." I wasn't sure if he hated Oliver, or if his hatred ignited mine and it was really me who hated Oliver. Neither answer would make me feel better.

I sat on my favorite rock in Grandma's backyard, gazing out at the sparkle-kissed pond. A warm breeze brushed my hair from my face and ruffled the leaves above me. My adult legs dangled over the rock and my toes swirled in the water. My throat still burned from the attack. Purply bruises had manifested in a blurred handprint around my neck.

Caleb and I swam here every summer. To the other side and back three times proved who was the best swimmer. I slid off the rock and into the water. Crisply cool if I stayed in place; barely comfortable if I crawled frog-like across the pond. Not the fastest or the prettiest stroke, but the most maintainable. I looked down through the water as I swam, trying to make out the sandy bottom and the rock clusters. Something glinted up at me. I dove under the water to recover it.

As I got closer, brightness blinded me. I squeezed my eyes shut and swam toward the light. The water warmed with each kick. Weird thing? I didn't need to breathe. Usually, the dream me followed the basic laws of nature.

Orange light filtered through my eyelids. It penetrated every cell in my body, warming muscles, tendons, and vertebrae. Eradicating fear. I never wanted to leave this place, but my lungs began to burn, screeching for air.

My eyes flew open. Venetian blue water swirled around me. Bubbles passed through my skin. I clawed at the water. Desperate to find the surface. Panic powered my movements. I kicked and thrashed. My head burst above the water and I gasped for air. Minutes passed before my lungs were consoled.

The shore stretched miles away from me. Unreachable. I squinted against the sun, making out a rowboat in the distance. I waved my hands to get the rower's attention, treading water until his arrival. Once the boat pulled up beside me, relief washed over me.

The rower asked, "Kai, how did you get here?"

"Grandma?" I hadn't heard her voice in five years.

When her hand reached out for me, I recognized her labradorite ring. My fingers laced through hers and she pulled me into the boat as easily as a bass she'd hooked.

The minute I emerged from the water, my clothes went instantly dry. "Where are we?"

"In-Between," she said.

Not heaven, not earth. Neither the land of the living nor the dead. I'd been here before. The day she died.

I threw my arms around her. The scent of rose water still clung to her. "I miss you so much."

She rubbed my back. "I've been watching over you."

"Am I doing okay?"

She squeezed my hand. "Oliver's right. You've been going about things the wrong way."

I stared at the bottom of the boat. I thought she'd be proud of me.

"I am very proud of you and your brother. But he understood that saving someone else at the expense of his sanity was never acceptable." She tipped my chin up so I'd look into her eyes.

The same dark blue as mine.

"You're much too much like me. Trying to fix everyone," she said.

"I had to continue your work."

"Do not follow in the footsteps of the wise, seek what they sought." Grandma loved her ancient proverbs.

"Zen koan?"

She patted my knee. "You have no idea how many times I repeated it when I was frustrated about where my life was going. Until I met your grandpa."

Grandpa Guhn was my step-grandpa, a Korean immigrant who raised my dad and loved us grandkids more than our bio-grandfather ever did. "Is he with you?"

Her lips crescented. "I can't tell you how things work on the other side. But he never left any of us. Ever."

"I wish you hadn't died." I needed her so badly in my world.

"I fought the cancer for years. You and Caleb kept me going long after I would have quit." She took my hand in hers. "You both needed a safe place. That's why I left my house to Caleb. You will always have a piece of me there."

It wasn't enough. I needed her with me. Teaching me. Loving me. "I don't know what to do anymore."

She traced her fingers along the bruises on my throat. "You must be more careful."

My throat stopped throbbing. "What did you do?"

"My healing abilities are still strong. Especially effective against a psychological attack."

"How did he hurt me physically? That's never happened before." I shivered despite the warmth of the day.

She caressed my cheek. "There are people out there with different abilities. Some interact with ours, yielding unexpected results."

"How do I stop it from happening again?" I didn't want him killing me from a distance.

"Don't ever reach out to him. You created a link and he used it." Her fingertips swept over my forehead. "Keep your shield up. No windows. Peepholes only when absolutely necessary."

"But I think he wants to hurt Oliver." I twisted my hands in my lap.

She cradled my face in her palms. "You cannot control everything in this world."

I pressed her hands to my face. Burning the feel of them into my memory. "I have to help the people I love."

"You're as stubborn as Grandpa. And as foolish as I was."

"You were the smartest person I ever knew."

She laughed. "Always my Sweet Pea."

My eyes swam in tears. "I'm so sorry I couldn't save you."

"You saw me into death, handing me off to the next world."

My shoulders shook and five years of guilt escaped in a sob. "I let you die."

She gathered me into her arms. "You did no such thing." She ran her hand over my hair. "Kai Dorian Guhn, don't you blame yourself. You gave me a reason to fight. You and Caleb were the best things that ever happened to me."

I sniffled. "I don't want you to be dead."

"It's not so bad on the other side."

Her face was free of the pain that had stolen over it those last weeks of her life. Her smile brimmed with affection. Faint white hairs streaked through her thick auburn locks. Her skin glowed with an inner light, like it had before the illness. I memorized every laugh line radiating from her eyes. Every freckle on her nose.

"Sweet Pea, you have to go now," she said.

"Why?"

"Time passes differently for the dead and the living in the In-Between."

"I don't want to leave you." I snuggled closer to her.

Her warm lips pressed against my forehead. "I'm always with you. If you found your way here, you'll do it again."

"Wait. What about Lukas? Is he…on your side now?"

Fierce concentration sharpened her features. "I don't think so." She looked away, like she was hearing a distant voice. "No. He's still in the realm of the living."

"Where?"

"He's trying to reach you."

With those words, the sun became so brilliant I couldn't see anything. Grandma disappeared. The boat overturned, tossing me into the lake.

I tried to swim back to the surface, but lost my way.

The water swirled around me like giant waves breaking on Martha's Vineyard, pulling me under and obscuring the sky.

Everything went midnight blue.

CHAPTER 62

Kai

I took my first breath in absolute darkness. Was I in San Diego? No. East Village? Later than that. Butternut farmhouse? Closer, but not quite. I fumbled for the nightstand lamp. Flicked it on. A moose silhouette appeared on the cream-colored shade. The chest of drawers beside the bed was sea green with a moose stenciled on it. Moose Room. Deer Haven Lodge. Butternut, Wisconsin.

I didn't think it was possible for a dream to transport me to the In-Between. Then again, it's not like my abilities came with an owner's manual. I was still learning my limits. The worst part? They continually evolved. What was impossible at age 12 became doable at 15.

My abilities had developed slowly. I was a normal dorkasaurus before the car accident. Sure everyone said I was a sweet kid. But a few months after the accident, my teachers began to praise me for being insightful. My mom thought I had a knack for reading emotions on people's faces. No one realized emotions manifested as colors that only I could see. They evolved to affect my own feelings. A few months later, snippets of people's thoughts filtered into my mind. Grandma said it was always a matter of when and never if.

I pushed the covers off and hopped out of bed. My leg and shoulder muscles ached. My throat, however, felt fine. I staggered to the dresser and looked in the mirror. All the bruises around my neck had disappeared.

I should have been happy. But the near-strangulation gnawed at me. He'd done something I didn't think anyone could, which begged the question how he might evolve by our next encounter.

It had been four days since Lukas went missing. Still no sign of him. No word from a kidnapper. The Hoffmanns knew how critical the first 24 hours were. What it meant when the child wasn't found.

I lingered over my morning coffee, picking at my fruit cup. Helplessness over Lukas battled worry over Oliver. Looming decisions filled me with indecision.

My gaze wandered to the wall of windows, past the porch swing beyond the pond to the treetops. The winter blue sky promised clarity.

I stood up. "Think I'll go for a walk in your orchard."

Mr. Hoffmann looked up from his paper. "Best be back before dark."

It was only 10:30 a.m. "I'll be back before three."

Mrs. Hoffmann continued crocheting. "We own hundreds of acres. They stretch beyond what you can see."

"I'll stick to the trail you showed me," I said.

"Bundle up, dear," she said. "Don't forget your snow boots."

"I won't."

She stared at the clock on the wall. Time ticked by. Time she would not spend with her grandson. Time that made his return less and less likely.

I was wrong about the winter sunshine. It didn't penetrate or warm. My boots squished the snow into footbeds of ice, and my breath came out in wisps of white. My tingling cheeks and nose spurred me on. Recognizing my shortcomings as a granola goddess, I aimed to walk two hours straight ahead on the trail and then double back. No way I could get lost.

With my route determined, my mind was free to try to straighten out my life. The wind whistled through the ice-glazed branches. Reminded me of my Christmas tree hunt with Oliver. If I stood still, I could feel the warmth of his lips on mine. The strength of his body beneath mine.

I missed him.

Up until Mickey came into our lives, he'd been the best husband I could ask for. Probably should have told him that more often. All those years he stood by me, putting me back together when I came undone. How did I not see what I was doing to him? Stupid, stupid girl. I let work get between us. I let my fear of him leaving drive him away.

Granted, he kissed Mickey. There was no excuse for that. But Lukas's kidnapping presented extenuating circumstances, pushing it into the realm of gray. Why couldn't it be black and white? Because I couldn't imagine my life without him. I had to find a way to make this okay and forgive him. Or else I had to let him go. And that wasn't something I was willing to do.

It was just, well, my pride. My need for justice required he hurt as much as I did. But that left room for Mickey to move in on him. And Oliver had a tendency to fix broken people. He'd done it with me.

Even if we could get beyond the kiss, we still had the issue of starting a family. He wanted one so badly and I was the only thing keeping him from it. Everyone needed roots. How could I deny him his?

The answer lay in my memories of middle school. Kids had taunted me all the time. Months of Caleb fighting them for me, coming home with split lips, swollen jaws, and raw knuckles. Their words still rang in my head. *Freak girl. Crazy. Lunatic.* Most lunches, I sat alone in the cafeteria, hearing what they thought. It was way worse than what they said. At night, I cried myself to sleep, praying I'd wake up and the telepathy would be gone.

Things never got easier. I just got more used to it. Caleb became popular and I became something they whispered about. I dressed goth in high school, embracing my role of an outsider and creeping them out even more.

I had a way cooler secret than them. I was a telepath. My brother a dreamwalker. My grandmother a healer. Dad had telekinesis. We were freaking superheroes come to life.

I learned to recognize the darkness in people. Instead of cowering at rude, cruel or dirty thoughts, I accepted them. The way they never accepted me.

Because of Grandma.

It had been nearly five years since she died. I'd wanted to see her for so long. Every day I was locked away in that institution, I wished for her to visit me. One would think with my mind in tatters, I could've had one comforting hallucination. But all I saw were others' fears. My daily visitors were their demons. I didn't have it in me to keep fighting, but Oliver refused to let me go. He bound me to his reality.

When I was released, he married me and brought me back to New York despite his misgivings. Several months later, the migraines started, and I begged for Grandma's strength. Every time I failed a child, I asked for her forgiveness. I wanted to continue her work, proving that all the time and energy she invested in me was worth it.

Oliver voiced concerns, but he didn't get in the way of my work. Not until I began unraveling. We fought a lot the past year. Me refusing to see what I was doing to us. Him trying so hard to find a work around. God that man had the patience of Buddha. And the mouth of Kanye West.

I turned back to check my progress and realized I couldn't see the lodge anymore. Just a single set of snowy footprints along a path rimmed with trees. A person could get lost so far out. That thought beat like a Kodo drummer against my skull. Refusing to quiet down.

I hugged the memory of last night's visit with Grandma. Her warning about the stranger echoed in my head. I visualized a one-inch glass peephole with a cover in the middle of my shield. I lifted the cover. Images of snowy trees flittered through my mind. Probably some animal's thoughts again. Had to be a side effect of the lack of people. I looked around for a deer, but the woods dulled everything to gray.

I ducked to avoid a branch and kept walking.

Fear trickled through the peephole. Faint enough that I considered going back because I mistook it for my own worry. I stopped and checked my watch. It was barely noon. Timewise, there was no need to turn back yet. I pulled my cell out to call Oliver—total reflex reaction. That would have been awkward. Luckily, I had no bars.

The fear cha-cha'ed over my skin. I didn't want to be there anymore. I turned to retrace my steps. Tripped over a tree root hidden by the snow and fell on my palms and shins. Dazed, I knelt in the snow. Coldness seeped through my jeans and mittens.

My pulse hopped up my wrist and danger permeated my pores. Nothing had changed in the woods around me. Everything had changed inside me. I dropped the cover over my peephole. The fear dissipated, which meant someone else was scared out there. Shit shit shit.

I cupped my hands around my mouth and shouted, "Hello? Is anyone there?"

Silence came back through the trees.

I shouldn't drop my shield, but I couldn't leave someone out here alone in the Wisconsin cold. I stood up, dusted the snow from my jeans, and opened the peephole again. Fear came whistling through. Couldn't tell if it was a boy or a girl. The person had to be at the limits of my range. I took a few steps forward. Sweat beaded over my upper lip.

Who was it?

I widened the hole, focusing on locating the person. Another hundred feet and the thoughts tugged me off the path and into the woods. I stopped. It was a double bad idea to leave the path and traipse through the snowy woods alone.

I was in mid-swivel when I heard one word.

Mommy.

I'd recognize Lukas's thoughts anywhere. I stretched the peephole to its limit.

I want Mommy.

I walked faster, trying to find him. Trees barricaded me in. No path. Just obstacles of branches. Think, Kai, think. Tracking people by their thoughts required maximum coordination.

I visualized my shield. A clear crystal egg, cocooning around me. Carefully, I stretched it like a bubble. Except instead of wrapping around me, I forced it to bend outward to block out the rest of the world and create a clear path between me and Lukas.

I imagined my shield as a tunnel, spanning through the trees with Lukas at the end of it. I still had no idea where he was, but I went bloodhound, following the scent of his thoughts.

Why doesn't Mommy come get me?

My heart cracked. He didn't understand what was happening.

I trampled through the snowy underbrush, tethered to his thoughts.

I tried something I'd only succeeded at with loved ones. I sent my thoughts to him. *Lukas, it's Kai. Can you hear me?*

Nothing. A branch scraped at my face. I shoved it aside.

I want to go home, Lukas thought.

You will.

Silence.

Lukas's thoughts popped into my head every few minutes. Like a radio station I couldn't quite tune in.

I needed to get closer so he could hear me. I stumbled over uneven ground. Had to slow down or neither of us would make it out of these woods okay. I looked at my watch: 1 p.m. I checked my cell. No bars.

The base of my cerebellum imploded. I fell against a tree as a blast of emotion tore through me. Children panic in a way we can't understand. Their thoughts literally collapse onto each other. My world became a frenzy of fear.

Lukas, Hold on!

Aunt Kai?

Yes, it's me. I'm on my way.

I'm scared.

I pressed my hand to my head and started moving toward his thoughts. *It'll be okay.*

I was close enough to hear the commotion in his head. It sounded like Midtown at rush hour.

I want Mommy.

She misses you too. You'll see her soon.

Promise?

I promise.

The dense walls of woods gave way to a clearing. A one-room shack sat in the middle of nowhere. With no road in or out. No way Lukas had gotten here on his own.

I stopped and crouched down, surveying the area. The woods were silver-lavender bark against white starkness. Footprints circled around the shack, leading off in another direction. The sky burned azure blue.

No sounds. No birds. No squirrels. No one.

The hairs on my neck stood up, preparing to march off my body in search of safer ground.

Aunt Kai?

I'm here, Lukas.

Hurry up.

Are you alone?

I think so.

On my way.

I crept up to the shack to peer through the window, but it was covered over. I sensed Lukas's mind inside. I widened the link between Lukas and me to encompass the entire building, trying to figure out if he was alone. All I picked up were Lukas's thoughts.

Honey, can you come outside?

No.

Why?

He didn't have the words to describe what had happened. Images of duct tape appeared in my mind. What kind of monster duct-taped a toddler to a chair? I shivered. One last look at my cell phone. Zero reception. Shit shit shit. I slid it back in my pocket and made my way to the door.

I reached for the door handle. A pain grenade burst in the back of my head.

Lukas screamed.

I plunged into darkness.

CHAPTER 63

Oliver

Four days ago, Kai walked out on me. She swore it was for my own good. I might have believed her if she hadn't kissed my best friend the next day. After nine years together, she decided we needed time and space. Death blow to most relationships. Ours settled into a tug-of-war silence.

Most of my time went to helping Mickey search for Lukas. We both called out of work. The job didn't matter. Lukas did. I'd seen more of Butternut in the past four days than I did during the 18 years growing up here. The search and rescue dogs only found traces of him around the house. Then the trail disappeared. No one understood how. It shouldn't have been possible.

That afternoon, after we finished searching our section of woods, Mickey said, "Take me to the police station."

"Why don't you go with Alex?"

"Can't you take me?" Her voice hitched on *take* like the word stole her son all over again.

I swallowed the golf-ball-sized *No* in my throat. "Sure." We'd get in there, corner Officer Lainer and leave without Schneider seeing me. That was my plan.

She, however, veered around Officer Lainer's cubicle and headed for the back wall to invade Chief of Police Schneider's office. I trailed behind her, knowing what awaited us.

His secretary raced after Mickey. "You can't just barge in here without an appointment." She tried to corral us back out the door.

Mickey held up a picture of Lukas. "This is my appointment."

The secretary took two steps back. "I didn't realize it was you, Mrs. Hoffmann."

Mickey eye's lasered her.

"I'm sorry, I mean Ms. Fuchs." The secretary inserted herself between Mickey and the chief. "But you can't storm into the chief's office."

Mickey advanced on the secretary. "Get. Out. Of. Here."

The secretary glanced at Schneider. He sat behind his desk. He flicked his fingers in a silent dismissal. She scurried out the door.

Schneider smiled his official smile. "Mama bears always protect their cubs."

Mickey's voice shot up three octaves. "What are you doing to find my son? It's been four days."

Schneider waved us toward the seats on the other side of his desk. "As much as we can."

Mickey sat on the edge of the chair. "Not enough."

"We've got our officers combing the area. We called in a search and rescue unit. State police scoured the area with their heat-seeking devices. Flyers are up all over town." Schneider leaned back in his chair, daring her to ask for more.

"Why isn't there any contact from the kidnappers?" She gripped her armrests.

"Either they're trying to get you good and riled up, or there isn't going to be a ransom demand," Schneider said.

"Which means?" A tremor scissored through her.

He looked at me.

I squeezed her hand. "Why don't you go ask Officer Lainer if he's got any leads?" I could take Schneider's brand of truth. Mickey couldn't.

"I need to know," she said.

Schneider raised his eyebrows.

I nodded.

His eyebrows collapsed around his nose. "Best case scenario? They keep the boy or put him up for an illegal adoption."

Tears filled her eyes. "Worst case?"

Schneider took a sip of his coffee. He stared at his paperweight. *25 Years on the Force* blazed across it in Garamond Bold script. "The boy is dead."

Mickey shot up out of her chair. "No!"

I tugged her back down. "He's out there."

Schneider rested his hands on his desk. "Everyone wants that to be the case."

"He's not dead," she said.

"Why haven't they found anything?" I asked.

Schneider sipped his coffee. "Best guess?"

I nodded.

"Whoever did this planned it out. Took his time, making sure to cover his tracks." Schneider looked every one of his 55 years today.

Her hands balled into fists. "How do we get him back?"

"We're working on it," Schneider said.

This had to be how the Hoffmanns felt when Christian went missing. It took two weeks to find his body.

CHAPTER 64

Kai

Tridents of pain speared through my brain stem. Colors club-kidded through my mind. This kind of pain demanded a world coated in tar. No sounds. No dreams. No images.

"Ms. Guuuuuhhhnnnn." Her voice echoed in the emptiness. "Ms. Guuuuuhhhnnnn."

"Jenny?" I whispered. She'd been dead a few months. Because I failed her.

"You have to get up."

I struggled to move, but my body wouldn't listen. I floated out of it and looked down at myself lying below. Freaky. This didn't feel like a dream. If it was somewhere Jenny could meet me, I had to be in one of the places in between.

"I'm so sorry I couldn't stop your father."

Her voice wrapped around me. "It wasn't your fault."

"I should have done more," I said.

"You did more than anyone else."

The darkness rippled and Jenny emerged, transparent, like a picture imposed on top of another one. Not quite here. Not really there. Her long black hair was split into two French braids tied with pink ribbons. She wore a pink dress with white patent leather shoes. Everything about her exuded contentment.

"You look beautiful."

She played with her braids. "Mama does my hair."

"Is she with you?"

Jenny hunched her shoulders. "I'm not supposed to talk about it."

Right. Rules of the afterlife. "Are we in the In-Between?"

"Sort of."

"Why's it so dark?" Grandma and I had met out in the sun.

"You were too hurt to come all the way through. I had to come to you."

"What happened?" I asked.

"You're in trouble."

My body lay doll-like below me. "Am I dying?"

Jenny looked down at the tips of her shoes.

"How much time do I have?" I asked.

"It depends on you."

"What do I have to do?"

"Fight and stay awake from now on."

"No dreaming?"

"You might not ever wake up," she said.

"I hit my head?"

"You've been out too long. It feels like a few minutes here, but it's been a lot longer in your world."

A sharp pain shot around the right side of my head to my temple. I pressed against the back of my head and yelped. I sank to the ground beside my body. "I have to climb back inside?"

She nodded.

"Thank you for helping me." I held out my translucent hand.

She squeezed it. "I wanted to see you again. I've tried a few times. But it's hard to get through to your world."

"I'm so sorry you died."

"It's not so bad." Jenny gave me a brave smile. "You need to help Lukas now."

"Is he okay?"

"Go back and you'll find out." Jenny started to fade into the void. She sounded so far away. "Don't give up."

My head throbbed. I tried to open my eyes, but they wouldn't budge. Fog swirled around my brain, creating a layer between reality and me. I couldn't find my way through it. Fear trickled down my back. Someone else's emotions tugged me toward reality. I tried to open the peephole to hear them. But it wouldn't budge. Damn. Damn. Triple Damn.

Memories resurfaced. Snow. Woods. Shack. I was rescuing Lukas when everything went blank. Now things were gray. Heading toward white. Okay, Kai push your way through.

I groaned and rolled to my side. It took a minute for things to come into focus. In the darkness, shadows ringed me. The faintest scent of copper reminded me of my fingers after I'd finished counting what was in my piggybank.

Aunt Kai.

Lukas. I tried to figure out where he was, but I couldn't see through the darkness.

"Aunt Kai?" he whispered.

"I'm here," I whispered back. *Are we alone?*

No.

The head injury couldn't be too bad. My telepathy still worked. *Try not to speak. Just think at me.*

Okay.

Where are you?

In the corner. I thought he killed you.

I'm still here. My fingertips grazed the back of my head as I struggled to sit up. Matted hair and a tender bump. Definite blow to the back of my head.

I'm scared. Lukas's thoughts grounded me.

Me too. But we're here together. I crawled toward him. *Can you follow my thoughts and come closer?*

Something scurried out of the corner and flew at me. Lukas.

It's going to be okay. I promise. I gathered him in my lap. Tucked his head under my chin like a kitten. And rocked him in my arms.

I thought you were gone. His tears wet my neck.

No way I'd leave you here, I thought.

Why'd he hurt you?

I wasn't paying attention.

Because of me.

I was stupid. I'm going to talk out loud so he doesn't wonder what we're doing. "Where are we?" I asked.

I don't know.

"Is there a candle or a flashlight?"

Lukas pressed a small tube into my hand.

I clicked the button and light flared from a mini-flashlight. The beam swept the room. Or rather the cave. It was the size of an eight-by-eight-foot room. The rock ceiling drooped a mere seven feet above us.

I trailed the light up and down the walls as I looked for some clue about where we were. Pieces of rock glittered amongst the earth. Reminded me of the fool's gold Caleb and I found at a California gold-mining camp when we were kids. The floor was dirt and rock. Two sleeping bags and a small portable toilet lay in separate corners. This was a carefully planned kidnapping.

The beam illuminated the opening. Grimy metal bars held us inside. Chains snaked around the bars with a solid padlock at the head. I shivered. No way out. No breeze, no outside light. We were prisoners.

I tried to sound calm. "Are you thirsty?"

Lukas nodded.

"Can we please have a bottle of water for the boy?" I asked.

No reply. A few minutes later, a bottle of water rolled through the bars. I snatched it up and checked the seal. Unbroken. Lukas settled into my lap. I undid the cap and gave him a few sips.

"Have you eaten?"

Lukas nodded again.

It's okay to speak. Just use your thoughts for secret stuff.

Lukas nodded.

I smiled. *Out loud, sweetie.*

"Yes," Lukas said.

Nausea obliterated my appetite, but my last meal had to be hours ago. I tried to check my watch, but it was gone. I slid my hand in my coat pocket. My cell wasn't there anymore.

"Can I please have a snack?" I asked.

Something landed next to me. I shined the flashlight on a Twix bar and checked the wrapper for puncture marks. When I didn't find any, I tore the wrapper open. I forced myself to eat one bar, saving the other for later. Hoping there was a later.

"How long has it been?" Lukas asked.

I hugged him to me. "A couple hours."

His voice quivered. "No, since I left Gammie's."

"Four days."

"I want Mommy."

"Honey, she's been turning this town upside down searching for you," I said.

"I want to go home."

"Me too."

Why'd he take us? Lukas's question echoed in my head.

Are you sure it's a he?

He's got a dark beard.

How did he get you? I asked.

I don't remember.

Were you at Gammie's house?

I don't remember. Lukas started shaking.

It's okay. He got me too. I rubbed his back.

He's mean.

Did he hurt you?

He scares me.

I rocked Lukas in my arms. Kept my shield up so he wouldn't catch a stray thought. He didn't need to know his would-be rescuer and only protector was freaking out. I tried humming to him. It always soothed me as a kid. Poor little guy nodded off quickly.

My head settled down to a dull pounding with the occasional ear ringing. Definitely not a mild concussion. I didn't have time to dwell on it. I had a child to save. I had an unknown kidnapper to overcome. I had no idea where we were.

Being locked in this cave left me one option. But I was petrified of what I'd encounter if I reached out with my mind. This guy had duct-taped a toddler to a chair and bashed an unarmed woman on the head. We had no choice. By the time Lukas woke up, I needed to have a plan.

I opened up the peephole in my shield. Nothing. Maybe the kidnapper had left us behind. A few deep breaths later, I widened the peephole in my shield. Didn't pick up any thoughts. Time stretched like a triathlon before me. I remember reading about how people lose their minds while being held hostage. Me, I'd never felt more sane.

My entire world shrunk down to three minds—the kidnapper's, Lukas's and mine. When Lukas dreamed, his thoughts were lost to me.

I closed my eyes. Split my shield down the middle and searched for another mind. I made myself as receptive as I could. He'd come to me. All I had to do was wait.

Death. Drowning in anger. Rage erupted from the depths of my soul. Found him. Sweat broke out in the small of my back. His thoughts weren't really developed, but closer to pure emotion. Not normal. Eavesdropping wouldn't be enough. I'd have to reach into him. Touch his mind. Let him touch mine.

I dropped my shield completely. My mind trickled into his. Sunlight warmed my skin. I stood in a field of wildflowers. The sky blazed blue. He remained on the periphery, a shadow under a towering oak tree. No form. No function. No reality. I tiptoed toward him. The shadow coalesced into the shape of a man. The shadowman leaned a shoulder against the tree, playing his flute.

I shouldn't have been there, but his song compelled me forward. Too late I realized my self-control had gravitated to him.

The shadowman smiled.

Faceless terror gripped me. I tried to pull back but I fell further into his mind. Tumbling through purple emptiness. My arms stretched; my hands reached out. But there was nothing to grab on to. No way to stop my descent into his madness.

Pain must be returned in kind. Oliver must pay. Aren't you tired of suffering?

I was sick of being in pain. I never wanted any of this. Damn Oliver for dragging me out to this hicksville and kissing Mickey. He obliterated my trust. He deserved to die.

These weren't my thoughts. But I couldn't disentangle my mind from his.

Grandma's warning rang in my head, *Don't drop your shield around him. His powers interact with yours.*

He wasn't just the man who kidnapped Lukas. This was the man whose hatred had reached for me. His thoughts had nearly strangled me. And now he had me—and Lukas.

What did he want with us?

Bargaining chips in a hand of poker.

His excitement became mine. His desire for revenge tasted of summer strawberries on my tongue. I savored it, wanting more.

Lukas's hand touched my face. With my shield down, physical contact served as an anchor. He pulled me back to myself, back from a mind more insane than the worst insanity of the institution. A mind eaten up with revenge. Worse than where my own mind had gone five years ago. There was no road back from his break with reality.

My teeth chattered.

Lukas's small hands held my cheeks. He whispered, "It's okay, Aunt Kai."

Tears weighed on my lashes. "No, it isn't."

He's sick, Lukas thought.

How do you know?

His head is dark purple. His brain is broken.

How did he handle all this?

Mommy and Uncle Oliver will find us.

They will move heaven and earth for you.

And you.

Lukas sat up and asked, "Water?"

I handed him the bottle, but he said, "Drink."

"What?"

Your head's dark pink. Drink.

I'm okay. Dizzy, but okay. The back of my head felt mushier than cereal left soaking in milk all day. I took a sip of water. I had to find a way to protect Lukas. To warn Oliver. To save myself.

One phrase kept rolling around in my mind: *bargaining chips.* Did you kill them after you played them? Did you torture them as part of the game? If only I could walk around and process my thoughts. The space was too small for serious pacing, and my legs were too shaky to support me. Besides, Lukas remained curled up in my lap, needing human contact.

Another trip into that man's mind would mean the end of me.

His insanity awoke that part of me I'd tried to destroy, the part that reveled in my self-destruction. When Grandma died, I had shattered. My world stopped making sense. I stopped making sense.

But his insanity felt like the sum total of his being. Like that was who he was. Dread crept up my spine and wrapped its bony fingers around my neck. We were in the hands of a person capable of anything and culpable for nothing.

And yet…he gave us water and food. Somewhere underneath there had to be a shred of humanity.

I cleared my throat. "Hello?"

Nothing.

"My name is Kai and this is Lukas."

Boots shuffled over dirt, but I couldn't see him. Made me think we were sequestered in some offshoot of the main tunnel.

"Why are we here?"

A shadow hovered outside the bars.

"Please, let the boy go. You only need one captive, right?"

"I have everything I need." His calmness wafted through the bars.

"Where are we?"

"Safely tucked away." His deep voice tunneled through me.

Goose bumps cascaded across my skin. Lukas huddled closer to me.

I tightened my arms around him. *It's okay. I'm just trying to figure out what he's up to.*

His voice scares me.

I dropped a kiss on the top of his head. *Me too.*

"How long are we going to stay here?" I asked.

"Until this is over," he said.

Great. We'd been kidnapped by the Riddler. "Can I go to the bathroom?"

"Use the portable toilet in the corner."

I grimaced. "Will you please let the boy go? He's scared and he doesn't understand."

"He'll learn." His footsteps faded away.

CHAPTER 65

Oliver

Eating at the kitchen table without Kai was like a voiceover on repeat, announcing, "You're Alone Now." I'd taken to my study with microwaved leftovers, thumbing through the channels until I settled on a documentary about funnel-web spiders on The Discovery Channel. During the commercial break, I dropped my dishes in the sink, poured a glass of milk, grabbed the tin of Aunt Ines's chocolate chip cookies, and slunk down on the leather sofa.

I kept thinking Kai would call. I even checked my cell. One missed call. I didn't recognize the number. The voicemail was from Mr. Hoffmann, the owner of Deer Haven Lodge. He said Kai hadn't come back tonight. The timestamp was 9:17 p.m.

It was after 11 p.m. now. She had to be back. I hung up and dialed her cell. It went to voicemail. Nothing to worry over, she usually ducked my calls when we fought. I texted, asking if she was okay. Waited ten minutes. No reply. The heaviness in my gut had nothing to do with my dinner.

My phone rang.

"Oliver?" a man asked.

"Yes."

"This is Keith Hoffmann from Deer Haven Lodge."

My mouth went Anza-Borrego-Desert dry. "I just got your voicemail. Is everything okay?"

"Kai never returned from her walk this afternoon," he said.

"What?"

"She said she'd be back around three. But we haven't seen her. Her car's still in the driveway, so we thought she went out with a friend."

"Did anyone stop by to see her?" Please let her be with Aunt Ines and not Alex.

"I don't know. Mrs. Hoffmann and I were helping with the search all afternoon."

"When's the last time you saw her?" Panic bubbled up my esophagus.

"A little before eleven this morning," he paused. "Your wife makes hot chocolate before bed. When she didn't, we went to her room. Doesn't look like she came back from her walk."

"Did you call the police?"

"They said to check with her friends and family. Then someone would have to go to the station to file a missing person's report."

Shitfuckingdammit. "Did you talk to anyone else?" Alex and Aunt Ines were her only friends in town.

"We thought she might be with you."

"I haven't seen her. I'll call around and call you back." I hung up. It was 11:15 p.m. I tried Aunt Ines first.

She answered on the third ring. "What's wrong?"

"Is Kai with you?"

"No. What happened?" The concern in her tone rekindled my anxiety.

"The Hoffmanns haven't seen her since this morning. She's probably with Alex." First time I wanted her to be with him.

"Maybe she took a drive to clear her head?"

292

"Her car's still at the B&B." I paced the room.

"I'm getting dressed."

"Don't panic," I said.

"I'll be ready in 10 minutes." She hung up.

I'd hoped she'd volunteer to call Alex. The next call would either destroy my marriage or mean Kai was in serious trouble. Which one I hoped for, I couldn't admit. Not even to myself.

Alex answered on the second ring.

"Have you seen Kai?" I asked.

"No," he said. "Something wrong?"

"When's the last time you saw her?"

"Yesterday."

"When you kissed her?" My anger splattered on him.

"No, when I dropped her back at the B&B."

Neither Aunt Ines nor Alex had seen her. Skeletal fingers crawled up my spine. "I gotta go."

"Wait, what happened to Kai?"

I hung up without answering.

Half an hour later, I left Aunt Ines sitting beside the fire at Deer Haven Lodge with Mrs. Hoffmann, while Mr. Hoffmann and I trudged down the path he'd seen Kai take this morning. The snow had started falling around 2 p.m. and the wind picked up after dark. By now, Kai's footprints were covered over. We walked and called her name for an hour.

No sign of her.

Mr. Hoffmann stopped. "We should head back and get help."

Wandering through the woods at night was a bad idea. But if Kai got lost out there, we needed to find her. "I've got to find my wife."

"There are no tracks to follow," he said.

"If it were your wife, what would you do?"

He handed me his pack. "I've got a compass, some coffee, a chocolate bar, and a flare gun in here. Stay on the trail. Otherwise, we'll be searching for another person come morning."

"Thanks."

He disappeared into the yawning darkness, tracing his footsteps back to his wife. My flashlight barely illuminated a way forward to mine. I scanned the trail and the blackened woods.

I yelled, "Kai!" until my voice rasped her name.

Where could she be? I didn't see anyone out there. Just stark trees and a down comforter of snow. Kai wasn't an outdoorsy girl. Manhattan had been a poor training ground for a Wisconsin winter. She'd know to seek shelter, but Mr. Hoffmann didn't know of any buildings near the trail. Images of her lying in the snow—unconscious and alone—ripped through my mind.

I hadn't saved her from New York to lose her to Wisconsin. If only we hadn't fought. None of this would have happened if I'd kept my lips away from Mickey. I didn't know how much was at stake. What I was risking. That one moment might cost me everything. Whatever happened to Kai tonight fell on me.

I'd have kept going all night. But I had no way of telling if she'd stayed on the path or gone off into the woods. Leaving the trail sounded like a dangerous choice. But this was Kai. Safety usually came last.

At 2:30 a.m., another beam of light crept up behind me. I swung around, hoping for Kai. I found Alex. "What the hell are you doing here?"

"Hoffmann said you needed help looking for Kai."

"Not from you." Anyone but you.

"Have you found anything?" he asked.

I kicked at the snow. "No."

"Has she contacted you?" Alex shoved his hands in his pockets.

"There's no cell reception out here." Dumbass.

"I mean, you know," he looked away and dropped his voice, "mentally."

"What?"

"Using her telepathy," he said.

No one here knew about that. Except me and Aunt Ines. The fact that Kai had shared her lips with him infuriated me. But her telepathy too. It shoved me over the rim of anger and into the abyss of fury.

My fist leapt at his jaw. The blow vibrated through my knuckles. Alex stumbled back. I took another swing. He blocked it, kicking my legs out from under me and shoving me back into the snow. I collapsed inward like a box dropped ten stories. The air whooshed out of my chest. It was a couple minutes before I attempted to get up.

"Stay down. You only get one pass today." He rubbed his jaw.

I slipped on ice and flopped onto my back.

"Is this helping Kai?" he asked.

No. But it felt damn good. Minus the falling on my ass part.

"I deserved that for kissing Kai. But fighting me won't find her." He extended his hand to help me up.

I slapped it away and struggled to my feet. "We're not done."

"I know."

"I'll find her."

"Right now, we need to get back to the Hoffmanns' and come up with a plan," he said.

I wasn't leaving my wife in this frigid cold. "Kai's out here."

"You know where?"

"No."

I stared at the dark trees silhouetted against the darker night sky. His words penetrated my hat and sunk through my skin and wormed into my brain.

There wasn't much sense in walking and screaming her name. Sixty percent of me knew I needed to file a missing person's report, but forty percent demanded I find my wife.

"Let's get the cops involved. They can send a search and rescue dog over," he said.

"Aren't they all looking for Lukas?"

"We've got six dogs. We can spare one for Kai."

I knew how to spark a blaze under Schneider. That was the only reason I went back to the Hoffmanns'.

CHAPTER 66

Kai

I craved sleep more than freedom. Fuzz-filled head and dizzified eyes. Tides of nausea completed the trifecta of a concussion. No sleeping for at least 24 hours.

Sensing the passing of time without a watch was difficult. Unless you had practice. Four months, two weeks, three days, eleven hours, and sixteen minutes in the mental institution. I'd been tied to the bed for sixteen days. Locked inside that room for thirteen weeks. Complete loss of control over my own body.

Now, it was happening again. The darkness pressed in on me as if hundreds of shadow people crowded me into the corner of the cave, swallowing all the air until my breath came in shallow gasps. I tried not to look at the bars. It didn't help. Panic isn't something you can run from. It's internal. My mind screamed for the only comfort I had—dissolving into a memory of when I'd lost everything. Dislocating from the current pain and returning to the worst carnage of my life.

My descent into madness started the day I said goodbye to Grandma in her hospital room. My powers flared and I leapt into her mind. I couldn't let her go. Not to death. We took every journey together. Part of me thought I could pull her back from death's clutches. No idea of how insignificant I was. Does anyone at 23?

I trailed her toward the light. "We need more time."

Each step eased the pain in her expression. "You have to go back."

"Not without you."

She grabbed my arms. "It isn't your time. Let me go."

Tears blurred my vision. "I can't."

"Sweet Pea, you have everything you need inside you." Her palm cooled my cheek. "Go and live your life. There's so much before you."

"Stay with me," I begged.

"I've fought as long as I could. Now it's your turn."

The light grew brighter. I blinked and lost my grip on her. She headed toward it. I ran after her. The distance between us grew exponentially. The faster I ran, the farther she got from me. The light flared around her and dissipated, drowning me in inky darkness.

I screamed, "Grandma," until my voice splintered.

She never answered me.

I was In-Between. Limbo. No way to reach her. She'd gone beyond. To death. Summerland. Heaven. The Afterlife. Didn't matter the name. They all meant the same thing. Unreachable.

I collapsed. Time slipped away from me.

I cocooned in emptiness.

From miles away, I heard Oliver's voice. "Kai, don't you leave me." Where was he? Not here. No. I was completely alone here.

I had no idea how long it was before I got up and took that first step toward his voice.

For Oliver, two weeks had passed at my bedside while I remained catatonic. For me, a mere day had passed since Grandma died. When I woke up in the hospital bed, I wished I'd stayed in the In-Between.

Things got worse after I was released. I couldn't get out of bed, didn't dress myself, wouldn't shower. Dad was lost in his own grief.

Mom reached the end of her understanding. They never told Caleb how bad I was. I lied to him in my dreams. He might have been able to stop me if he knew.

The day I stole my mother's Vicodin and my father's rum, I blended up my own special cocktail. Then I got in bed and waited for everything to stop. I wasn't prepared for the pain. Everyone thinks you just fall asleep. You don't.

My diaphragm relaxed to the point where I started to suffocate myself. A five-thousand-foot mountain collapsed on my chest. I wheezed through bronchial tubes the size of coffee stirrers. Cold fear sprung up, condensing against my skin. I tried to relax and let go.

But panic forced me toward movement. Made me sit up and wrestle for each breath. It was only a matter of time. Eventually, I'd stop breathing. Until then, every second reminded me that I was miserably alive.

That was when Oliver found me.

No one cared about what I wanted after my failed suicide. My mother gave up and committed me. My father didn't stop her. He didn't understand what it meant for a telepath. Caleb never forgave him. Sometimes I wonder if I really did.

They locked me away because I scared them. My telepathy always made them uneasy, forcing them to constantly guard their inner thoughts. But now, I became the monster in their closet.

Tied down to a bed. A necessary precaution, the nurse said. Needles. Needles. Needles. They shot me up with so many drugs to keep me docile. I couldn't form a shield with that in my system. I struggled to keep my sanity. After the third day of counting ceiling tiles, I gave up. Let the insanity come for me. Show me its darkness. No desire to continue, I plunged into the madness. Death my sole desire.

But the institution forces you to endure your misery. They never gave me enough pills to finish me off. Everything about that place centered on control. Losing myself in the other patients' illnesses was my escape.

I stopped speaking. Therapy sessions were an absolute joke. The doctor kept thinking about what he wanted to do to me if I weren't so crazy. I fantasized about jabbing his pen through his hand.

I kept count of the days as they lingered. Gauged time by the nurses' thoughts. Oliver's visits. He couldn't see. He didn't know. I'd lost all hope when I came back from the In-Between. My life had entwined so deeply with Grandma's. I couldn't just be resuscitated and return to normal. Something of me stayed behind. Not the kind of sickness doctors could heal.

Caleb understood. Slipping into my dreams whenever he could, reminding me I wasn't alone. That his pain ran as deep. He came home to see me, bringing me rose water and brushing my hair. He didn't ask anything. Just gave me everything I needed.

Oliver pushed me. He'd come in and throw his thoughts at me. Engulf me in his guilt. His fear. Make me feel things I didn't want to feel. I preferred madness and numbness. But he wouldn't allow that. He sat there without saying a word and thought about every happy moment we shared.

Fifty-nine days of silence before I asked, "Do you have any cherry candy?"

Oliver stared at me. "Cherry?"

"I miss the cherry cobbler we ate in Vienna."

He smiled. "You remember how many times we went back to the Leopold Museum?"

"Because it was the only place you could find."

He reached over and took my hand. "I'll bring some tomorrow."

I studied his face. "You're pretty tan."

"Summer job walking dogs."

Summer. "I missed the River-to-River festival?"

"Let's go next year." Oliver entwined his fingers with mine. "Promise me, we'll go next year."

Convincing the doctor to release me required considerable effort. Caleb, Oliver and I formed a reluctant triumvirate. Caleb worked on the doctor in his dreams. I played along in the sessions. Oliver became my loudest advocate.

I remember the day Oliver dragged my parents to see me. To prove I was sane again.

My father said, "I didn't know what else to do."

My mother hugged me and whispered, "I knew this was the best place for you."

I bit my tongue and tasted the iron in my own blood. "I don't want to be here anymore. I know what I need to do with my life."

My parents exchanged worried glances.

Dad was the one who asked, "What?"

"Help kids. I'm going to be a social worker."

"What about becoming a reporter?" Mom asked.

It was what I'd been working toward in New York. Mom loved the idea of my name in the *New York Times* byline.

"I need to do something important. I think Grandma would approve," I said.

Dad blew out his breath. "She's gone, Kai."

"I was there when she crossed over." I stared at him until he looked away.

Mom gripped the table's edge. "I don't think we should talk about this."

Oliver squeezed my hand.

I forced a smile. "You're right. She's gone. We need to move forward."

"What does your doctor say?" Dad asked.

"I'm making progress. If it continues, I can be released in a few weeks and do outpatient treatment."

"And you'll do that?" Mom asked.

Oliver squeezed my hand again.

"I need it. I want to get better." Because now I had a reason to keep going. In memory of Grandma.

Footsteps outside the bars yanked me out of my head and thrust me back into my cave prison. Earthy dampness clung to my skin. The kidnapper kept checking on us, as if escape weren't impossible. I didn't have Oliver and I couldn't contact Caleb. Just a toddler and me. And I was hurt.

Lukas remained bundled in his sleeping bag. I moved him off my lap and onto the floor. He stirred but stayed safe in his dream world. I slid on my butt across the floor toward the wall. Bracing my back against it, I pushed myself to my feet.

The room topsy-turvied. I melded against the cave wall, waiting for the world to right itself. Even breaths were essential. Too deep and the dizziness thickened. Too shallow and the darkness smothered. I tucked my hair behind my ears.

Once the cave stopped rotating and the ground no longer undulated, I flicked on the flashlight and sized up the floor. Uneven and rocky. Focus, Kai. I took a step. Then another. My legs shook, but I forced each foot off the ground and back down again. I walked to the other side of the cave and slid down the opposite wall and switched off the flashlight.

Progress. I reached into my coat pocket and ate the other Twix. While Lukas slept, I made myself walk the entire length of the cave. Over and over again. Until my balance returned. I had to learn how to see in the dark and navigate without light. I had to be ready when the time came.

Jenny's warning echoed in my head. I couldn't risk falling asleep. Unable to contact Caleb, I plotted ways to get out of that prison. Evaluated how to disable our kidnapper. To get Lukas home safe. I didn't think about me. Everything I loved in my life. I couldn't. If it came down to it, I'd sacrifice myself so that Lukas could get away.

There were so many things I meant to say to Oliver and my family. Things they needed to know. I made my way to the bars, determined to do something right. "Can I get a pen and paper, please?"

It took a couple minutes for his footsteps to reach me.

"Why?" His voice ground over my skin like gravel after a spill from my bike.

"In case something happens. I need to tell my family goodbye."

A few minutes later, a bright light shined into my eyes. "Back away from the bars."

I took three steps back.

Something slid through the bars. The light disappeared. Air balloons of color superimposed over everything. When they cleared, I clicked on my flashlight, went to the bars and picked up a small notepad and pen.

Lukas rolled over. Half asleep he asked, "What's happening?"

"I'm having trouble sleeping," I lied.

He struggled to unwrap himself from the sleeping bag.

"It's okay." *Better for me not to sleep with my head problem.*

"Come here."

I walked over and dropped down next to him.

I love you.

I rubbed his head. *I love you too.*

A few minutes later, he drifted back to the security of his dreams. Alone, I crafted my first good-bye letter.

Dear Oliver,

I am so sorry for how we left things. I made a mess of it. You hurt me and I lashed out. Like I've been known to do.

My heart has always been yours. If there was one reason to continue in this life, it was you. You are the best thing that ever happened to me.

If you're reading this, I'm probably dead. Understand it was my choice. I saw no other way out. I had to protect Lukas and give him a chance at escaping. I couldn't let the kidnapper hurt him. I knew what I was doing.

I accepted the risk.

You have to live for both of us. I want you to find happiness. I want you to have those five children you always dreamed of. I think Mickey might be the one to give them to you. Lukas already adores you.

I need you to have a place to call home. Because the past nine years, you have been mine.

All My Love,

Kai

I tucked the note inside my jacket pocket and began writing the next one.

CHAPTER 67

Oliver

I monitored the bars on my cell phone as Alex and I trudged back to Deer Haven Lodge.

Three bars finally appeared when we reached the front porch. "I need to call Kai's brother."

"Then we go to the police station," Alex said.

The muscles in my neck bunched up. "I go to the police station."

"You aren't in this alone."

"I have Aunt Ines."

He stayed on the porch.

"I need to call Caleb." I scrolled through my contact list. "Without an audience."

"Is this best for Kai?"

"Don't lecture me about my wife." Fury liquefied my veins.

He must have heard it in my voice because he went inside. I paced the porch, trying to find the words to tell Caleb I'd lost his sister. I bit the inside of my mouth. My last hope hinged on Kai contacting him by phone or dreamwalking. The 6 a.m. on my watch translated to 12 p.m.

in London. About time for Caleb to rise and trade the U.S. markets.

He answered on the third ring. "This better be important, Oliver."

Forget about breaking the news nicely. "When's the last time you heard from Kai?"

He paused. "Why?"

"Just answer me."

"What the hell is going on over there?" he asked.

"She's missing." Two words obliterated both our worlds.

"We talked on the phone two days ago. Dreamwalked that night."

She always made time for Caleb. "What about last night?"

Caleb hesitated.

"What?"

"I couldn't find her."

"What does that mean?" I asked.

"She didn't dream."

"All night?"

"Yeah," he said.

"Why didn't you call me?"

"She gets insomnia under stress. You dropped a hundred kilos' worth on her." Before I could respond, he added, "I left her a voicemail this morning."

"Can you contact her when she's awake?"

"Dreamwalking requires that she be dreaming," he said.

"I'm going to the cops."

"When was the last time anyone saw her?" he asked.

"Yesterday morning."

"Call me the minute you hear anything."

"You'll do the same?" I asked.

"I'd do anything to help Kai." He hung up on me.

I snuck into Schneider's office at 6:30 a.m. with the cleaning crew. No one stopped me. Not that they could have. I didn't care what happened to me. All that mattered was finding Kai.

Schneider showed up as I finished my third cup of coffee.

"Oliver, what an expected surprise." He unbuttoned his coat and hung it in his closet. He made his way to the coffee I'd brewed and poured a cup.

I threw myself into a chair. "You heard about Kai?"

He added sugar, shook some non-dairy creamer, and stirred. "Heard she left you."

I slammed my hand on the armrest. "She's lost out in the woods."

He leaned against the filing cabinet. His girth rolled over his gun belt. "How can you be certain?"

"That's the last place Mr. Hoffmann saw her."

He walked over to his desk. "The entire town is out looking for Lukas." He sighed and sank into his chair. "He's been gone five days. The chance of him being alive decreases by the hour. I've got a crazed mom breathing down my neck. What do you want from me?"

Lukas was important. But Kai mattered too. Too much for me to wait. "Can't you look for her?"

"Don't have the evidence or the manpower to support doing that right now." His gaze locked on mine. "You want me to bend the rules for you?"

I knew I shouldn't ask, but for Kai I'd ask anything. "Yes."

"You nearly castrated your father for doing the same."

"This is different." I was trying to save someone. Dad had covered for a friend.

"Feels that way to you, eh?" he asked.

"This isn't like my wife."

He rubbed his chin. "Woman probably needed to clear her head."

"She didn't take her car."

"Your car," he reminded me.

"It's not like that. No one's heard from her." Frustration bled into my words.

"Son, I know you're worried, but wives have a way of turning up. Four-year-olds don't."

"She hasn't contacted anyone."

"You can file a missing person's report now and I'll send an officer out to the Hoffmanns' later."

"What about a search and rescue dog?" He'd be able to find her in the woods.

"We have them focused on Lukas."

"Can't you pull one for Kai?"

He sucked on his teeth. "Could." Silence filled in the rest of his sentence.

"What do you want?"

"A little respect for starters," he said.

I gritted my teeth. "Done."

"A written statement that your father killed Christian."

"Why?"

"Insurance," he said.

"I promised I'd keep my mouth shut."

"Just in case your conscience acts up."

I'd spent the past 12 years not destroying my father's reputation. That statement would forever blacken it. Signing that document would make it impossible to ever do the right thing. Refuting a statement rendered me an unreliable witness. Schneider knew that. "If I don't?"

"We'll fill out the missing person's report. And get to work on it as soon as the manpower is available."

He'd let Kai die.

Bile burned the back of my throat. Singeing every word I wanted to say.

I'd always held on to the possibility of salvation. That one day I would speak out against my father and set his wrong right. The *might* that lived in tomorrow. Schneider would take that from me.

"You'd really let your dead best friend stand trial for your deeds?" I asked.

"He may not have been guilty of the fact, but he was guilty after the fact."

"He did it to protect you."

Schneider sucked on his teeth. "He'd understand I'm protecting all of us."

I never realized what a monster my "uncle" was. The tides in my stomach shifted, slamming against the walls of my gut. I tried to think up options, to weigh scenarios, to evaluate the choices. But everything led to the same conclusion: Finding Kai outweighed everything else. "Deal."

Schneider smiled his Cheshire cat smile. "You can start by calling me Uncle John again."

"Uncle John, the clock is ticking."

He handed me a pen and paper. "Then you'd better write quickly."

By 2 p.m., all the paperwork had been filed, the search and rescue dog had arrived with his handler, and we'd been in the woods an hour. But we found zero proof that Kai ever walked along the Hoffmanns' trail. The snow had buried my tracks from last night before it tapered off this morning.

The dog should have scented Kai. I gave his handler Kai's pillowcase. The bloodhound left the trail, but then doubled back and crossed to the other side. I watched everything. Waiting. We'd find her. We had to.

Two and a half hours later, dusk threatened and hope flittered away.

Mickey's primal scream of "Oliver, you are dead!" reached me from twenty paces away.

I left the dog and the handler to avoid distracting them and met Mickey on her way to me. She didn't bother speaking before she hauled off and punched me. She still had a killer right hook. Twenty inches of snow cushioned my fall backwards.

"Feel better?" I asked from my mattress of snow.

She planted her hands on her hips. "Someone had to knock some sense into you. Give me Lukas's search dog back."

I rubbed my jaw. "You have five dogs looking for Lukas and an army of people."

She shook the hand she'd punched me with and flexed her fingers. "Don't give me another reason to hit you."

"We've got to find both of them." I started to get up.

She shoved me back down. "Your wife's been gone a day, not days." She hardened the "s" in days so it buzzed and stung my ear.

"If I thought that one dog would help find Lukas, I'd never have borrowed him," I said.

"Everything matters. It all counts." Her body trembled. "He's my baby."

"She's my wife. I have to look for her."

Mickey leapt on top of me. "She's an adult." She slapped my head. "She can survive a few days on her own." Hit my shoulder. "He's four, Oliver. FOUR!" Pounded a rib.

I used my arms to deflect the rest of her blows until someone hauled her off me.

"Michaela Fuchs, you should be ashamed of yourself." Alex restrained her.

She squirmed, trying to break his hold on her. "Don't you dare side with him over me."

"This isn't helping anyone. Pull yourself together," he said.

"He stole a search dog from Lukas." She kicked snow into my face.

I wiped it away and got up. "That's not true."

He pulled her further back. "I okayed one dog to Oliver."

"YOU WHAT?!" she asked.

"We have plenty of people searching for Lukas. We've got five dogs full time."

Alex's logic couldn't penetrate Mickey's bank vault of rage.

"You bastard." She threw herself to the left to escape his hold. Then she knocked his feet out from under him.

Wished I'd been the one to do that.

When she lunged at him, he rolled to the side. Then he rolled back and pinned her down. "Get a hold of yourself."

Her limbs twitched beneath him.

He sat on her stomach. "I miss him too. I want him home. Oliver has done everything he can to help. Now it's our turn to help him."

"I just needed the dog to do one trip," I said. "He's coming back in two hours. Then he's all yours."

"He'll need to rest," she yelled. "Hours lost, Oliver. Precious hours."

Taking the dog from Lukas's search made so much sense at the police station. But now. Shit. Lately, all I'd done was make the wrong call.

"His wife is missing," Alex said.

"Probably ran away from him," she spat out.

I deserved that. But Kai didn't. "Something's wrong. Really wrong." My voice faded in and out like an old radio signal.

Mickey stopped trying to get away from Alex. "I need the dog back."

The desperation in her voice mirrored mine. She would do anything to save her son; I would do anything to save Kai. I couldn't give Mickey the dog, but I could show her some compassion. "Let her up."

He raised both eyebrows. "You sure?"

I nodded.

He slid off Mickey.

She scrambled to her feet. "You better pray my son is alright or I will never forgive either of you for putting your dicks before a child's life."

CHAPTER 68

Kai

There was something unnatural about living humans under
the earth. Like a fish stuck up in a tree or a mole in the ocean.
Wrongness I had to fix.

I smoothed Lukas's hair back from his forehead. We'd spent the
last four hours building to this moment, creating a natural progression
toward illness. *Sweetie, you've got to sound really sick.*

I don't want him touching me. He burrowed into my arms.

Me neither. That's why I need you to run when I attack him.

Where?

Out of here.

He'll get mad, he thought.

He'll be too busy fighting with me to come after you. I paused. *It's the
only way to get you home.*

What about you?

I've got to stay here. I'd follow if I could.

Aunt Kai, I'm scared.

I pulled him closer. *Me too. But we can't just wait for him to hurt us.*

Don't you want to be like your Uncle Alex? He wouldn't wait. He'd take action.

What if I can't find a way out?

Hide. Don't let him find you.

His arms snuck around my neck. His warm lips found my cheek. *Be careful.*

You too. I kissed the top of his head. *Ready?*

He started moaning.

"Lukas, what's wrong?" I made sure my voice hitched with fear.

He whisper-groaned. "It huuurts."

"Where, sweetie?"

"My tummy."

I pressed my hand to his forehead. "You're warm."

He whimpered, "It hurts bad. Make it stop."

Good job. I raised my voice to the kidnapper. "The boy's sick. We need help."

Silence.

Lukas called out, "Mommy."

It twisted at my heart and I knew he was faking. The kidnapper had to have a twinge of conscience. He had to.

Boots scuffled over the ground outside the bars. "What's going on?"

"He hasn't been right today." My voice wobbled. "He's running a fever. His stomach. Something is wrong."

"He's homesick." The deep voice rippled into the cave.

"No, he's ill."

The kidnapper shined his flashlight into our cell. "Bring him to me."

I hadn't thought of that. *Pretend to puke.*

"I'm gonna be sick." Lukas twisted out of my arms and made retching noises.

The words rushed out of my mouth. "He's getting worse. I don't want to move him."

The kidnapper's voice never wavered. "If you're faking, there will be serious consequences."

I shivered, tightened my shield around me, and lied, "He's sick. Hospital sick."

"Get against the wall."

I scuttled back until rock bit into my spine, leaving Lukas on the other side of the cave.

Kai, I'm scared.

You are so brave, just a little longer.

The kidnapper shined a flashlight into my eyes as he opened the padlock and came into our cell. Lukas huddled closer to the wall, shaking.

The kidnapper mistook it for illness. His tone softened a fraction. "Turn over."

Lukas moaned and made more vomity noises. My fingers curled around the jagged chunk of rock behind me. The kidnapper crouched down to roll Lukas onto his back.

In that moment of distraction, I launched myself at him, using both hands to aim the rock at his head. Except he moved a split second faster than me. The rock slammed into his shoulder.

Run, Lukas. RUN.

Lukas scurried out of there.

I leapt onto the kidnapper's back. He moved from side to side, trying to shake me off. I locked my feet around his waist and dug my fingernails into his neck. I thought I had a chance of taking him down until he slammed me into the wall.

Galaxies exploded in front of my eyes.

My hands wouldn't clench up. My feet refused to kick. My body didn't know how to fight anymore. He reached around, pulled me off his back like an ant, and threw me to the ground.

He grabbed my left wrist. "Get back here, boy." He twisted it until I screamed.

Run, Lukas.

But he's hurting you.

I'll be okay. Just get away.

The kidnapper promised, "I'll break her wrist and snap every bone in her hand if you don't come back." He gave each word equal weight. "Don't make me hurt her."

Run, Lukas. Don't come back here.

He exerted pressure until my wrist couldn't turn anymore.

Pain lanced up my arm to my shoulder. I howled. Bit my lip and tasted blood. Heard a delicate snap. A sobbing that must be me. The pain cut through the universe I was seeing. Long enough for me to elbow him in the thigh.

He grunted and snapped my pinkie finger.

Pain jolted though me.

"Stop it!" Lukas yelled.

The universe exploded in purple.

At Grandma's house, I sat by the pond, wanting a swim despite the ache in my wrist. And my pinkie. I didn't remember hurting them. I looked down at my left hand and saw my wedding ring. Seemed a lot of things were breaking lately.

My mouth tasted of caramel apple and my mind felt like spun sugar. But nothing stuck there. I giggled. Something was wrong with me. Seriously wrong. And I didn't seem to care.

"Kai, where are you?" Caleb sounded like the disembodied voice of a nearly-extinct god.

"Where are you?" I giggled again.

"What's wrong with you?"

Tears trickled down my cheeks and laughter stole my breath away. "What's wrong with you?"

"You'renotmakingsense." His words ran together.

I couldn't seem to muster up any concern over what was happening to me. Had happened to me. Besides, it was such a nice day to sit by the water. Wonder if Grandma would bake her mascarpone cheesecake cookies. I loved weekends at Grandma's.

Caleb's voice broke through again. "Are you hurt? What about Lukas? Aren't you going to help him?"

That name. Lukas. It triggered something in me. The giddiness drained away, allowing the pain to rush in. "He was with me when…" I howled. Pulled my injured hand into my lap. "You have to help him."

Caleb's image came through. Like a cable channel you didn't pay for. Garbled and not quite there. "I'm trying to. Where are you?"

I looked around. "Grandma's backyard."

Caleb sighed. "Not right now. *You and Lukas.*"

Invisible needles plunged into my brain. Blood stained my shirt. "I'm hurt."

"I figured. You're pretty incoherent. And hard to reach."

So hard to remember. "I got hit on the head. Twice."

"I don't know how long we have. Troublereachingyou. Where are you?"

So hard to respond. Answers slipped away. "Underground."

"Where?"

I shook my head. Felt my brain rattling around up there. Saw the trees waltzing and the ground skipping along.

"The hater, he kidnapped Lukas and me. We're his poker ships." My words slurred. Not ships. Chips. But my mouth wouldn't form the word.

Caleb's voice distorted into white noise.

"What?" I blinked, trying to bring my mind into focus. The water was sparkling and clear. So inviting. I bet it was warm. A swim would be so nice.

Caleb's voice crackled. "Kai. Focus. Show me where you are. Conjure up the image and throw it at me."

My eyelids drooped. I strained to keep them open. Tried to send him the images of the cabin and the cave. The bars. The walls. "Caleb?"

No answer.

The water turned murky. Clouds streamed across the sky, blocking out the daylight. Wind lashed at the trees, whipping my hair against my face.

I should go. Now.

Something snaked around my ankle and pulled me into the pond.

Underwater, a scream is barely a gurgle.

CHAPTER 69

Oliver

I sat at my kitchen table with a bag of frozen peas embracing my jaw. "Mickey still has her death-strike fist."

"I never liked her. More boy than girl if you ask me," Aunt Ines said.

Thirty-two hours without a sign of Kai. The search dog found nothing. "How is that possible?!"

"What, dear?" Worry lines cracked across her forehead.

I'd started the conversation in my head. Kai usually heard it. Aunt Ines couldn't. "The search dogs, how can they come up with nothing?"

"The snow covered everything up." She toyed with her bracelet.

"They should be able to scent her."

She bit her lip. "Maybe it's because she's not completely human."

"She's a telepath, not an alien."

She stared down at her fuchsia fingernails. "I remember one time my…Sabine got lost. No one could find her. Even her own dog couldn't scent her. Two days later, she found her way out of the woods."

If only I'd had that information eight hours ago. The whole incident with Mickey could have been avoided. My jaw wouldn't be throbbing. "You think Kai's untrackable?"

"I'm not certain, dear. No one understands how these things work. But it may be why they can't find Lukas either."

It made a bad sort of sense. The kind you don't want to accept because of the implications. "How do we find them?"

"Did you talk to her parents? They must know more about it than you or me."

The last time they got involved, she got committed. "Caleb prefers to leave them out of it."

Her shoulders straightened.

To avert the oncoming lecture, I said, "Her mom freaks out about her abilities and her dad generally pretends he doesn't have his."

"Sounds like Kai had a wonderful support system growing up."

"Everything was great until her abilities surfaced. The first 10 years of her life sounded idyllic."

She hrumphed. "Most families can survive the good times."

"Did ours?"

"Your mom doted on you so much." She patted my knee. "I think it was because Reinhard was so closed off. But with her, he was different. If she had lived, he'd have been a different man."

"I doubt that."

"Lord knows my brother had his faults, but he loved your mother. He never recovered from her death."

I wish I'd met the man she remembered. Maybe her memories were of who he would have been. The mind has a kindness in restoring the past, sanding down the splinters and rounding the sharp corners.

I needed to focus on the present. I might lose my wife forever. Fear tumbled around in my gut. I wondered if this was what my father felt when he found out Mama's cancer was incurable.

After Aunt Ines left, I showered and changed and prepared to head out again to the Hoffmanns' woods. It was the only lead I had. I pulled out the maps Schneider got from the town clerk this morning. Surveyed the possibilities. Their land stretched for acres and acres.

The clock in the living room counted away the time I had left to find her. No one could survive more than a few days out there. Lukas was already heading into day five.

Two missing persons in the same town. Reinhard would say it couldn't be a coincidence. He saw the connections others couldn't. That's why he was so good at hiding what Schneider did. Reinhard knew what evidence needed to be there and what couldn't be there. I didn't want to think about what they did to make it seem like Christian had an accident.

When my mind got stuck on something that horrible, it took everything I had to turn away from it. I couldn't help Christian, but I could try to find Kai. I stared at the maps, waiting for enlightenment to brain me.

Nothing happened so I headed to the Hoffmanns', thinking I'd find something. By 1:36 a.m., I still had no idea where my wife was. The snow fell in cotton balls. My cell battery died. Not wanting to become missing person number three, I trudged back toward the Hoffmanns'.

Their lights were out. No one cared that Kai had gone missing. No one but me, Aunt Ines, and Alex. I turned on my Cherokee, plugged the charger into my phone, blared some drum and bass, and tried to figure out my next move.

The roads were empty. A Stephen King time of night.

I was almost warm when I pulled up in front of my farmhouse. There was nothing to do but go inside. I didn't flick on the light in the living room. I couldn't look at our Christmas tree, so I followed the hallway to my study. The TV filled the house with false company.

Something to distract me from the lack of Kai. I must have nodded off during the Pompeii documentary because I woke to lions mating and the phone ringing.

I fumbled for my cell and knocked it onto the floor. I grabbed it and said, "Hello?"

"She's in an underground cave," Caleb said.

"What?" I rubbed the crusty stuff from my eyes. I had to be alert. Caleb only said things once.

"She dreamed. Sort of. She's hurt Oliver. And she's with Lukas."

"Kai found him?"

"The kidnapper has them both."

He explained how she'd been in the woods, heard Lukas's thoughts, been knocked out, woke up in a cave.

"Do you know how many caves and underground tunnels there are in the area?" I asked.

"Not my problem. Find her."

"It could take weeks."

Caleb snarled. "She doesn't have that kind of time."

"What?"

"Two blows to the head and her telepathy is all screwy. Think about it."

"Did she give you anything else to go on?" Something to help narrow down the search.

"It's weird. I smelled pennies and saw gold bars."

"What the hell does that mean?"

"Her mind was projecting everything it had. Might be a clue," he said.

"Or a misfiring."

"I don't know, Oliver. Explore every possibility until you find her. Because when I get to Butternut, she better be safe or you're dead."

I might have spent the rest of my predawn hours dreading Caleb's arrival, if I hadn't been trying to figure out what the smell of pennies and gold bars had to do with Butternut. If it meant anything. On a whim, I scooped some pennies out of the change jar and sniffed them. Coppery. Maybe it was copper?

This was beyond the scope of my abilities. Someone in town had to know something about the local topography. A well-connected retired schoolteacher would know who to call. Aunt Ines needed her rest, but I needed to find Kai. I thumbed through some of Grandpa's files, looking for old land maps. Each minute waiting felt like it took three laps of the second hand around the clock. The town clerk's office might have what I needed, but it wouldn't open until 9 a.m.

At 4:59 a.m., I broke down and dialed Aunt Ines's number.

She answered on the second ring. "Oliver, what's wrong?"

"Who's a local geology expert?" I asked.

"What?" Her voice bubbled up three octaves.

"I need to find a cave with copper and gold in it."

She spoke each word with caution. "Did you sleep last night?"

"A few hours."

She hesitated. "Maybe you should get some more rest and call me back."

"Caleb called."

"Did he hear from Kai?"

"Sort of." I explained about the almost dream with the horrible reception where he couldn't really connect with Kai.

"You know, Michaela's dad dabbled in rock collecting. Mostly on public lands."

Didn't sound promising. Who would hold people captive in a public area?

"Wait. Thomas was the assistant to the soil scientist and county surveyor."

"Thomas Fuchs? The accountant?"

"He put himself through night school. That was a few years back. But he might be able to help." The sounds of papers shuffling and pages flipping filled the phone. "I've got his number here somewhere."

"It's okay, I'll call Alex." I'd have to go through him. I couldn't tell Mickey, I know where your missing kid is. Yeah, he's been kidnapped along with my wife and hidden in a cave with gold and copper. Fruitcake with a scoop of delirium, anyone?

I had no evidence to secure their assistance. Alex would need to explain things and make them believe me. If what Caleb said was true, we didn't have time to debate things. Kai was in serious trouble and Lukas was only a whisper away from danger.

At 6:31 a.m., Alex's SUV rumbled into my driveway. He cut the engine and stomped up the front stairs. I had the door open before he knocked. He handed me a cup of hot coffee and came into my house.

I started to shut the door behind him, but Herbie shot out of his house. Damn turkey had ignored me since Kai left. Didn't matter that I offered food and water or tried to coax him inside with treats. He refused to acknowledge my existence without Kai. Only took sustenance from Aunt Ines. For Alex, he came right up the front steps.

"Hey, Herbie." I pitched my voice toward welcoming.

The turkey growled at me and ducked his head under Alex's arm. Alex rubbed his head and stroked his neck. Herbie purred.

Alex looked into my darkened living room. "Can we sit?'

"Yeah." I headed back to my study.

When we got there, Alex sat on the leather couch. Herbie climbed up beside him. I headed for my chair.

"I don't know how we'll get Thomas to believe us," Alex said.

"Lukas's and Kai's lives are at stake. Lie if you have to." I was starting to sound like Reinhard. I didn't care if it saved two lives.

"I don't lie to my family."

"Tell the truth then. Do whatever it takes to get his help," I said.

"I called Dad. We're having a family meeting in an hour. Everyone will be there."

"Good." I sipped the coffee.

"That includes you."

They'd think I was insane, but there was no other choice.

"I'll take the lead," he said.

"I never expected otherwise."

"You know you're asking a lot of my family."

"I know." I was asking them to believe in the unbelievables, to accept that a dreamwalker communicated with a telepath, to stop thinking Lukas was normal. They would have to put aside the world they knew and follow me into a world of unknowns, taking time away from their search and diverting it to mine.

But I didn't have a choice. I needed their help.

He pointed to the framed picture on my desk. "Vacation picture?"

"Wedding photo." I picked up the picture of Kai and me.

We wore jeans and sneaks. Badwater Basin stretched out behind us. Kai had a secret smile for photos. Her lips curved up slightly, but never revealed her teeth. Like she didn't rely on them for her beauty. My arm wrapped around her, anchoring her to me. Her palm rested on my heart.

"Really?" he asked.

"Kai's choice."

He finished his coffee. "Ready?"

I took another swig of mine. "Come on Herbie, outside time."

The turkey fluffed up his feathers and growled.

"Herbie, time to go back to your home," Alex said.

Herbie hopped up and trailed him outside.

On the ride to the Fuchses', I made every turn and stop on auto-pilot while my radio blared. My thoughts revolved around one fear:

The Fuchses would never believe me.

Everything hung on them. If they believed in me, I'd make things right with Kai. I had to. Second chances don't come often. Sometimes, you get one opportunity. One moment to make it right. And then the window gets bricked over.

I wouldn't lose Kai. I'd bartered my integrity for Schneider's help. I'd give my life for hers. I'd get my wife back. And I would never let her go again. I pressed my foot down on the gas pedal. Alex be damned. I passed him going 70. I was taking the lead on this one.

Mr. Fuchs assembled the family around the dining room table, where they'd enjoyed hundreds of rowdy dinners with lightning rounds of banter. Today, they had to hear about my telepathic wife and their youngest being a seer-of-sorts. Both were in serious trouble and the only clues I had to find them sounded straight out of *Harry Potter*.

Alex finished explaining everything and sat down.

I waited.

Silence ticked by.

Mr. Fuchs covered his mouth, refusing to speak. Mrs. Fuchs blinked rapidly as if the information had short-circuited her brain. Mickey shook her head, a clear dismissal of everything Alex had said. Dan gave me the indulgent, you've-lost-it smile. Pete snorted and bit into a danish. There was no eye contact from Kevin. Thomas gripped his wife's hand.

Thomas's wife, Irena, was the first to speak. "So that's how she knew about my baby being a girl?"

I nodded.

Mrs. Fuchs tentatively asked, "And my illness?"

"Lukas was so worried about you, he confided in Kai," I said. "She pretended to read your palm to tell you what he saw."

Mrs. Fuchs rolled her lips outward, but no words came.

Mickey slammed her hand on the table. "Bullshit. I'd know if my son had special powers."

"Didn't you?"I raised an eyebrow.

"No." Mickey's voice defied anyone to question her. "Because it's all a lie. What game are you playing, Richter?"

I winced at the use of my last name. She only reminded me I was Reinhard's boy when she was furious with me.

"Why were you so hesitant to let others watch him?" Alex asked. "Come on Mickey, you sensed something."

Mickey crossed her arms. "He's perfectly normal."

"We can all agree he's an exceptional little boy," Alex said.

Mhmms, yeahs, and grunts ranging from whole-hearted to hallelujah came from everyone at the table.

A glassy layer hardened over Mickey's eyes. Her body vibrated with anger.

Kevin fiddled with his butter knife. "Silver lining—Kai's with him. This is good, right?"

"We just need to find them," Alex said.

Mr. Fuchs cleared his throat. "If we believe Oliver."

Everyone had an opinion. Fuchs family discussions always descended into debate matches without a moderator. Mr. Fuchs questioned my sanity and Pete discounted what I said. Thomas raised concerns about this being the best allocation of our time. Alex stood strong about how we had to pursue every lead, even those that might be fruitless.

None of it helped Lukas or Kai. These filibusters could drag on for hours.

I stood up. "Help me or tell me to leave."

Mr. Fuchs stared me dead in the eyes. "You've blitzed our family. We can't pretend away the fallout from what you've told us."

I hated telling him these things. But I had to. To save Lukas and Kai. "You've known me since I was a kid. You had Thanksgiving dinner with my wife." Was that enough to make them believe me? "I want

Kai and Lukas home safe as much as you do."

"Oliver's our best lead, " Mrs. Fuchs said.

When the muttering began, she silenced them by saying, "Everyone at this table has kept a secret. Myself included. Lukas was right about my thyroid. I didn't want to worry any of you," she paused, "but if I hadn't gotten medication, I'd be dead now. Lukas and Kai saved my life."

Irena patted her baby bump. "She's 100% girl. I was thinking about it on Thanksgiving, wanting to share the good news. Kai must have heard my thoughts."

Mrs. Fuchs smiled at her. "Let's take a vote."

Mr. Fuchs's hands curled into fists on the table. "We aren't ready for that."

"A preliminary vote," Mrs. Fuchs said. "Show of hands. Who wants to find Lukas?"

"Ma, that's not fair. We all want to find Lukas," Mickey said.

Mrs. Fuchs ignored her. "Show of hands, Fuchs family."

Everyone raised their hand.

"Excellent. Who wants to help Oliver find Lukas?" Mrs. Fuchs asked.

Mickey rolled her eyes.

Alex's and Irena's hands shot up. Kevin's came next. Mrs. Fuchs raised hers. I lifted mine. That left Dan, Mr. Fuchs, Mickey, Pete and Thomas. A tie.

"And by helping Oliver, you're guaranteeing a place in your mother's heart," Mrs. Fuchs said.

Dan's hand crept up into the air.

"By family vote, it is decided. We help Oliver." Mrs. Fuchs came over and rubbed my shoulder. "We'll get them back."

"Thanks."

"Family helps family," Mrs. Fuchs said.

Mickey stomped out of the room. Mr. Fuchs followed his daughter.

Irena latched on to Thomas's arm. "You'll help Oliver, won't you, honey?" Her tone implied dire consequences if he didn't.

Thomas's Adam's apple bobbed up and down. "Of course, sweetie." He knew better than to argue with a severely pregnant woman.

I looked at my watch. Even with their cooperation, I wasn't sure we'd be able to conquer our biggest threat: time.

CHAPTER 70

Kai

I spun like a drill bit, tunneling through water. The screams torn from my mouth were shrill sounds encapsulated in bubbles. Like a wounded dolphin being yanked further into the depths of the Venetian blue.

Light, radiant white light, burst around me. Scooped me up and deposited me in the desert. Scorpions and lizards click-slithered across the barren land. Unplowed snow-white sand dunes. Unrelenting sun sizzled my skin.

Grandma's dark blue eyes peered into mine. "What did you do to yourself?" She crouched beside me and pressed her palm to my forehead.

I opened my mouth, but the words wouldn't form.

She chewed on her lip. "Sweet Pea, this is serious." She took my pulse and stared into my eyes. "Your pupils. That's not normal."

I blinked, trying to fix them.

She chuckled. "If only it were that easy." She rifled through her burgundy carpetbag of herbs. The same one she'd consulted to cure every illness I had when she was alive.

"Sorry," I wheeze-whispered.

"If I weren't dead, you would be the death of me." Her lips twitched, the barest hint of a smile.

I wanted to laugh, but my brain felt like chicken that had been microwaved until it exploded.

She tsked at me. "I hoped to see you again, but not because you were so injured you ended up back here."

I tried to smile, but my facial muscles ignored my command. Nothing seemed to work right. Grandma puckered her lips, shook her bag, and reached for something at the bottom. Her auburn braid fell across my shoulder as she worked. The smell of roses engulfed me.

I want to let go, to stop fighting, to stay here.

"What about Lukas?" She shifted to examine the back of my head.

Hers were the gentlest of touches, but the throbbing returned. Worse than before. I swore my head split open, and with each beat a piece of my brain leapt outside my skull.

My mouth flooded with saliva. The nausea came so violently, I barely had time to roll to the side before my spine arched and green vomit spewed from my mouth, my nose, my eyes.

Purple and yellow irises bloomed in front of me. They shifted into a starry night sky. Van-Goghed into swirls above sweeping trees. I couldn't feel my palms clutching the hot sand beneath me anymore.

I floated out of my body.

"Kai, don't you dare give up." Grandma's words looped around my ankle, trying to ground me.

I kicked them away. I wouldn't return to lie in a pool of green vomit and shake uncontrollably. All spasms and shudders. I was tired of fighting and losing. It was all I ever did. *I could stay here a while. A long while.*

"Kai Dorian Guhn, you get your butt back here. I can't clean up this mess by myself," Grandma said.

I didn't want to be sick. I didn't want to go back. This was...well, extraordinary. Better than life. So much easier that I ever thought it would be. The letting go. The ending. Dying.

I sensed my grandfather. Not the bio-grandpa that abandoned Dad. No, my one true grandpa, Grandma's second husband. He wanted to parent my father even if he wasn't his kid by DNA. He had died in the car accident when I was ten.

His honey-spun voice immersed me in calm. A hint of his Korean accent lingered in his words. "Sown-yah, what are you doing?"

My whole life, he called me "Granddaughter" in Korean. "I think I'm dying, Grandpa."

"Have you lived enough already?" His tone was neutral, wanting me to reach a conclusion on my own.

"It's been so hard since Caleb and I developed these powers. At first, all I wanted was for them go away."

"What about Caleb? Can you leave him all alone?"

Images of my brother—memories of us—raced across the screen of my mind. Summers building sand fortresses at Torrey Pines Beach. Winters snowboarding in Mammoth Lakes. Photographing spring wildflowers in Death Valley. Gorging on Ghiradelli sundaes during San Fran's fall.

He'd left me for London six years ago. We fractured to live our lives.

"He's always been more self-sufficient than me. Not so much his own island, but his own solar system," I said.

"He doesn't need you enough?" Grandpa asked. "I used to think that about your father."

"All Dad's lectures end in *like Grandpa said*." My entire life was guided by those principles.

"It wasn't always that way. Caleb and he are a lot alike. Both afraid to show weakness. Both desperately needing to belong."

Hard to picture my dad caring what anyone thought. "He's never needed any approval from Caleb or me."

"He can't. He's the parent. But he did from your Grandmother and eventually me."

Dad didn't cry about Grandma. Didn't even speak at Grandpa's funeral.

"Ever wonder why Caleb could be so strong?" Grandpa asked.

"Cause he's more like Grandma."

"Sown-yah, such a quick tongue." He laughed. "Everyone needs someone to believe in them. To love them. He had you."

Sadness cluttered my throat like forgotten boxes piled in the basement. "Why can't I see you?"

"You're In-Between, on the cusp of my world."

"I'm dying." Dying. Dying. Dying.

"You seem to be headed that way. Unless you change course."

"Is that possible?"

"Can you hear people's thoughts? Can Caleb dreamwalk? Can your father move objects with his mind?" Grandpa asked. "What, my dear girl, isn't possible?"

"Seeing you."

The sky rippled a few yards to my right. And for the briefest of seconds, a doorway opened. Or rather a sliding glass door. And he was right there. With his gray hair combed over, gentle smile, and black mustache. Perfectly pressed white dress shirt and gray slacks.

"Grandpa!"

He waved at me and winked. "Anything is possible, Sown-yah."

The glass fogged over and faded back into the tumultuous sky. Midnight blue swirled with black. Yellow stars shone back at me. He was gone.

And I knew what I had to do. Where I had to go. What came next.

CHAPTER 71

Oliver

Thomas unrolled the geographical maps across the Fuchses' dining room table. Thousands of wavy lines with subtle shading. I had no clue what any of it meant. He'd spent hours digging them out of the basement. Mementos of a career that wasn't.

"There are five possible locations where you'd find chalcopyrite in this area." Thomas's fingers grazed over each one.

"What's chalcopyrite?" I asked. "Aren't we looking for copper and gold?"

Thomas sighed. "It's a copper ore with a strong copper scent. It's called yellow copper because of its gold-like color."

He'd taken Kai's clues further than I ever could.

"Here in Ashland county, there's a site up in the woods behind Butternut Community Park and one near Mineral Lake in Mellen," Thomas said.

I nudged Dan. "He said five, right?"

"What gives, Thomas?" Dan asked.

"Three sites are unofficial. They didn't get entered into the geological reports."

"Why?" Alex asked.

Thomas shrugged. "Landowners are perversely private. They let us take soil samples and survey their land as long as the information never made it to the county level."

"So Kai and Lukas might be kidnapped by people we know?" I couldn't believe anyone in Butternut could hold a boy and a woman captive.

"They might be on someone's land. We're talking about hundreds of acres around here." Thomas eyed the maps. "No one knows everything that happens on their property."

"So who are we looking at?" I asked.

"The vein up in the woods by the park is deep underground. No caves or tunnels nearby. Mellen's is similar. Nothing like what Caleb described." Thomas rolled up those maps and put them aside.

"The other three?" I asked.

"Kohlers', Wiesners', and Hoffmanns' properties."

The biggest landowners in Butternut. "Can we narrow down the locations?"

Thomas's lips thinned, preparing me for less than stellar news. "On the Kohlers', we only found one specific deposit. It's a hike, but we can rule it out in a day. The Wiesners' have a few locations. That may take a couple days." He pulled off his glasses and rubbed his eyes. "The Hoffmanns' property is riddled with deposits."

I raked a hand through my hair. "How long?"

"With help from the police?" Thomas asked.

"They'd never believe us," I said.

Mr. Fuchs muttered, "Better to go it alone." Lukas's absence had only enforced his dislike of the local law.

Thomas tapped his pen against his lips. "The Hoffmanns' could take us several days to a week."

"We'll do it in pairs." Alex said, "Dan and I will check the Wiesners'."

"Kevin and I can start at the Kohlers' and then work on the Wiesners' too," Thomas said.

"I'll do the Hoffmanns'." It made the most sense for me to be there.

"I'm taking the Hoffmanns'. I've spent the most time there." Mickey had joined us a few minutes ago, after spending two hours holed up in her room. Alex, Mrs. Fuchs, and Aunt Ines all took turns talking to her. Not sure if any one of them made a dent or if it took all three to break through.

Mr. Fuchs cleared his throat. "We can do two teams at the Hoffmanns'. Mickey with me. Who'll partner up with Oliver?"

"You sure you want to go to the Hoffmanns'?" Alex asked.

Their son had abandoned Mickey and Lukas. Bad blood splashed between the families after each sided with their own child.

I thought about Kai and Lukas. What was in their best interest. "Alex, maybe you should team up with Mickey. And Dan can work with me."

"I'm not staying home," Mr. Fuchs said.

Mrs. Fuchs patted his hand. "You and Pete can go to the Weisners'."

Aunt Ines already offered to sit with Mrs. Hoffmann to calm her nerves and smooth the situation over. This was going to be awkward enough, asking people to search their land for my missing wife.

"How are we going to get the landowners' permission?" I asked.

"The Weisners won't be a problem. They let me go rock sampling on their land," Thomas said.

"Thomas will tell the Kohlers there's a discrepancy in the maps and he's clarifying it as a favor to his former boss," Mr. Fuchs said.

Thomas stared at me. "Tell the Hoffmanns you're still searching for Kai. They won't question that."

"How do I explain Mickey being there?" When she should be off looking for Lukas.

Thomas chewed the inside of his mouth. "She'll go to the Weisners' instead."

"The hell I will." Mickey jerked and coffee sloshed over the sides of her mug.

Thomas passed her a napkin. "Michaela, it's for the best."

"We need more searchers covering the Hoffmanns' land. I'll wear a hat and sneak on with Alex." Mickey's eyes simmered in mutiny.

"She'll do it anyways. Better I'm with her," Alex said.

Mickey smiled. "I knew you'd see it my way."

I looked around the table. Determination filled everyone's eyes. We were ready to start our search based off Caleb's clues. I couldn't believe how easily the Fuchses believed me. How much they trusted me. I didn't deserve it. Not after I perpetuated Reinhard's lies. Let Schneider get away with murder. Maybe I deserved to lose Kai, but not like this. She didn't deserve to die for my mistakes.

Twenty-five known deposits spread out across the Hoffmanns' property. Few of them near each other. We hiked through the snow-camouflaged woods for hours. Dan and I had ruled out one location so far. No clue how Mickey and Alex were doing. The lack of civilization made our cells useless. Had this happened to Kai?

If only she'd been able to send me images. Caleb's words couldn't capture everything she'd seen. She might have included a miniscule clue that would only make sense to someone who knew the area. Something tugged at the back of my mind. The minute I tried to zero in on it, it fled.

Dan and I took a break. Gulped coffee from our thermos. Gobbled down cookies. Dan wasn't about to give up. Neither was I. We both had someone we loved at stake. By the time the sun dipped on the horizon, we'd still only ruled out one mineral deposit.

Fear shadowed our footsteps. The temperature dipped. Eventually, we had to rest. And Kai would have to survive another night with the kidnapper. We found the second site after dark. Flashlights shone into every crevasse. Nothing big enough for a child let alone a woman to crawl through.

"Where's the nearest site?" I asked.

"I'd estimate it's a two-hour hike from here. In daylight." Dan checked his watch. "We should head back. Get some rest and start at daybreak."

"You think they have the luxury of us sleeping?"

"We have to rest. Even if we keep at it all night, we'll be useless when we find them."

I heard the sense in his words. Felt the logic permeating my panicked haze. Finding Kai and Lukas was the first half of our task. We also had to rescue them from the kidnapper. Dan carried a rifle. Reinhard's loaded pistol remained holstered against my chest. Beside my heart.

The kidnapper wouldn't survive this. I prayed Kai and Lukas did.

CHAPTER 72

Kai

Turned out it wasn't green vomit. I mean it looked like it. To me. Because my mind couldn't process what it was. Refused to watch myself dying. Dark red blood had spewed from my mouth, poured from my nose, spilled from my eyes. I caught a glimpse of my body in a puddle of burgundy before I slipped back inside and everything went dark.

I woke up to Grandma singing "Twinkle Twinkle Little Star." My head rested in her lap. All the blood had disappeared. A pearly moon replaced the blistering sun. Diamonds twinkled down at me, reminding me of the promises I had to keep.

Grandma brushed the hair back from my forehead. "Look who's finally awake." Love stretched my heart to capacity. A Thanksgiving feast for my soul. "Am I still alive?"

"You came back, didn't you?" Her eyes were darker than the night sky.

"I saw Grandpa."

"He misses you so much." Her voice was like jam on toast, filling in all the cracks and crevasses. Smoothing everything over.

"I wish you were both still alive," I whispered.

"Can you sit up, Sweet Pea?" She handled me more delicately than her ivory chopsticks.

"I think so." I wanted to stay in that moment of us. But I decided to go back. It was something I had to do for Lukas and Oliver and Caleb.

She helped me stand.

"How long have I been here?" I touched the back of my head. Tender, but more like three-days-later sore.

"Half a day in your world. Hours in mine." She tilted my chin, forcing me to look into her eyes and see the darkest truth there. "No more hits to the head. I've patched you up, but you need a doctor."

"Am I going to die?"

Her fingers waffled through mine. "We all will. But let's make it a long time from now."

"I'll do my best." Being with her made what I had to face more bearable. I squeezed her hand. "I'll see you again."

"Bring Caleb next time you sneak through," she said.

Heat radiated from her hand into mine. Sprinted up my arm to my head, dove down into my chest, burrowed all the way into my baby toes. Bright light blossomed between us. Her fingers started to slip away.

I tried to hold on, but my muscles were too relaxed to cooperate. "Wait, Grandma, how do I get Caleb here?"

The light wrapped around me, cutting off all contact between us. I tried to fight it, but my body had committed to the warmth. The trip back wasn't peaceful. The desert's heat couldn't sustain me. I plunged back into cold water and my body tensed. I sank deeper and deeper... back to the pain I'd run from.

Waking up wasn't an instantaneous thing. Not when your body was as banged up as mine. More like a gradual returning to the pain.

Reconnecting with the world around me in accretions of agony.

Voices registered like sounds underwater. No meaning, just vibrations that barely reached my ears. I waited. The voices grew clearer. I found meaning in the syllables, but I still couldn't speak or move.

They say when one sense is weak, the others compensate. Mine became hypersensitive. Lukas whimpered from three feet away. It minced my heart. I wanted to wrap my arms around him and promise everything would be okay.

A deep baritone eight inches from my head said, "She'll be fine. She just hit her head."

"You…hit…her head…again," Lukas whispered.

"Because she attacked me." The kidnapper smelled of Frankincense, but not in a revolting potpourri way. More like an incense-inducing meditation.

"She tried to help me." Lukas sniffled.

"She'd be better off if you'd both behaved. I didn't want to hurt her."

"Her wrist…" Lukas's question lingered in the air.

"Broken." He stumbled over broken, catching himself like he didn't mean to do it. "She won't try to escape again." His voice came from beside me now. "I'll set it."

Oh God, I didn't want to feel this. Pain jolted my shoulder and webbed out to my fingertips. I shrieked and my eyes flew open.

The cave blazed with soft lantern light. Siberian-Husky-blue eyes peered at me. "About time you woke up."

Lukas scurried over. Grabbed my good arm. "Aunt Kai, are you okay?"

I gasped and wheezed my way through the pain. The electric shock in my fingers eased, but the horrible ache wouldn't recede.

"I'll survive," I rasped with a throat drier than the dunes I'd returned from.

"Give her a sip of water, boy," Husky Eyes said.

I tried to raise my head, but it felt heavier than one of the unmovable boulders in Arches National Park. Husky Eyes slid a hand between my sleeping bag and my shoulder and lifted me upright.

"Thanks." I studied his face. A black beard engulfed his jaw, encroaching on his lips. Deep squint lines radiated around his eyes, testifying to years spent in the sun.

Lukas brought the water. It tasted of epiphanies. My eyes slipped closed, and I contemplated chugging the entire bottle.

"That's enough for now." The kidnapper took my water away. "Get her a Pop-Tart."

"What happened?" I whispered.

"You hit your head on the wall," he said.

A whiff of blue escaped from the corners of his eyes—sadness, potent and enduring. So much suffering lurked there. In the depths, I recognized the spark of it. I'd seen it before. In my own eyes, five years ago. Insanity.

"Who hurt you?" My voice threaded through the words, dropping stitches.

"Let's get this wrist fixed up."

"Who are you?"

"It doesn't matter anymore." He tucked his hair behind his ears.

"Please. I need to know." He'd nearly killed me. I deserved a name.

"You can call me Chris."

"Chris," I said. "Why are you helping me?"

He wrapped my wrist in a makeshift splint. "People need to be held accountable for their actions."

"But I tried to escape."

"I stopped you. More aggressively than I should have." He concentrated on securing the wrapping around my wrist. As if he were doing penance for a mortal sin he'd enjoyed too little.

I hesitated. "You didn't hurt Lukas, did you?"

"No." He sounded disgusted by the thought. "The boy followed your bad example." His fingers tangoed with mine, testing the joint in my pinkie.

341

My finger throbbed. "It was all me. He just wanted to go home."

"I have to rebreak your pinkie now."

"I know."

I heard the kkkrik. Pain lanced through my hand. Bone-deep agony. My shriek echoed in the cave. Sparklers brighter than the Fourth of July filled my vision before I passed out.

I didn't dream; I sunk into oblivion. The sleep of the dead, Caleb called it. Because you were unreachable. Untouchable. Like being buried alive in a cave.

Except I went willingly. No recollection of anything. Until I rolled onto my broken wrist and screamed. Jarring myself back to consciousness.

Lukas leapt up. Flicked on the flashlight. "Aunt Kai, it's only a dream."

I panted through the pain, like a dog trying to shed heat. "My wrist."

He bit his lower lip. "He broke it because of me."

"Not. Your. Fault." I forced the words out.

"I shouldn't have run."

I groped for his hand. "Lukas Fuchs, you are the best little boy in the world. I'm the adult and everything, *everything*, that happened here is my fault. I tried to escape. I attacked him. It was all me."

"I thought you were dead." Lukas wiped his nose on his sleeve.

I pulled him close. "I'm okay."

He curled up in the crook of my good arm and laid his head on my chest. "He got worried. He thought he killed you."

And that upset him?

Lukas didn't think anything back at me.

I whispered, "Did you hear my thought?"

"Yup." He sat up. "Didn't you hear mine?"

"No, my head's a little broken lately."

Lukas cupped his hands around my ear and whispered, "He said it wasn't part of the plan."

Did he say what the plan was?

"No one had to die yet." Lukas shivered.

I curled the edge of my sleeping bag around him and stroked his hair until his breathing slowed to sleep. We stayed that way for hours. I dozed into darkness. No dreams. No Caleb. No Grandma. Whenever I slid back to consciousness, I thought about Oliver. Wondered if we'd ever get to say everything we needed to say. Doubted whether any of it was worth it.

I walked out on my husband over a kiss. He'd stuck by me through suicide and insanity.

If I could talk to him right now, I'd forgive him for kissing Mickey. Go back home, rent a horror movie, bring Herbie inside, eat a ginormous bowl of my olive-oil popcorn together.

The holidays would be here soon. My parents were supposed to bring Naomi to visit. And Caleb said he'd try to stop by. Aunt Ines would be with us. Herbie. We were supposed to have a family Christmas. Dad and Caleb's feud and Naomi wishing we were a normal family—it all sounded so wonderfully trivial.

CHAPTER 73

Oliver

I slammed on my brakes, coming to a body-jerking halt 25 feet from my house. The headlights illuminated a parked black Mercedes SUV. At midnight, every bulb in the farmhouse blazed.

I groaned.

Caleb had arrived. He hadn't opted to stay at Deer Haven Lodge or a nearby motel. He could afford a rental cabin or ski lodge. But then I wouldn't have been forced to trudge up the steps and through the front door to face my wife's brother.

He lounged on my living room couch with the tree lit. Aunt Ines's cookie tin sat on the coffee table in front of him. Herbie rested his head in his lap.

"Did you find my sister?" Caleb asked.

"Don't you think she'd be with me if I had?"

Caleb shrugged. "Not even a blow to the head could make her forgive a cheater."

My fist clenched around my keys. The grooves bit into my palm. I didn't relax my grip. "How did you get here?"

"I flew into Minneapolis and chartered a helicopter to Butternut." Caleb's voice sported the brand of condescension only affordable to multi-millionaires.

"So you could sit on my couch, eating my cookies?"

"I've hired a search team to start in the morning. They'll be here at 5 a.m." He flipped the lid off and grabbed a chocolate chip cookie from the tin.

"How'd you get in HERE?" Locking the door was a New York habit.

Caleb's turquoise eyes were six, maybe seven shades lighter than Kai's. But they contained none of her love. "My sister and I have no secrets. She hid the key under a rock beside Herbie's house. Rather brilliant of her."

"Part of why I married her."

"And why you betrayed her?" he asked.

"It's not that simple."

"Tongue enters mouth of another woman. Pretty cut and dry if you ask me." He tossed a piece of cookie into Herbie's mouth.

"Nice that you decided to help her through this crisis. Slow time at the office?" He'd been in London through most of Kai's mental breakdown in San Diego. Rode in on his white horse for the final stages of her recovery.

The corners of his mouth levitated into a magician's smile. "You lied back in San Diego too. Told me Kai was all right while she unraveled. You let her rot in there for months. I'd have gotten her out in weeks."

The blood rushed to my head along with the certainty that I could take him. I leaned back against the wall. *Don't kill him. Don't kill him.* "Maybe if you and your Dad could play nice, your parents would have told you your sister lost her mind."

He laughed. "I've been inside your mind. I didn't abandon everyone I loved because of my daddy issues. Keeping your wife at arm's length like your father did with you."

Dread balled against my lower back. "You abandoned your entire family for London."

"I'm in touch with Mom and Naomi and Kai. They all have a standing invitation to visit me."

I rested my head against the wall. He made me feel a ten-year-old's need to prove myself.

"This isn't helping Kai." He frowned down at his phone. "What time are you gathering to search tomorrow?"

"Six. We already sectioned out tomorrow's search sites."

"We?" he asked.

"The Fuchses are helping me."

Caleb's perfectly groomed eyebrow arched upward. "Mickey too?"

"It's her son."

"Kai's gonna love that." He snickered. "You sure know how to nail yourself into a coffin."

"She'll understand." I prayed she'd understand.

"How many searchers do you have?" He typed away on his phone.

"Eight."

"And the cops?" he asked.

"Would never believe a dreamwalker figured out where a missing woman and boy are."

He didn't bother looking up. "I've got a dozen men coming in tomorrow."

"We might be able to check every location."

"That was my plan." His tone added *dumbass* to the end of his sentence.

I headed toward the stairs. "See you in the morning."

"Pleasant dreams." The rocking tone of his voice haunted me all the way into my bed. No way I could fall asleep with a dreamwalker in my house.

Thomas poured over the maps with Caleb's crew of geologists and former CIA guys. When they finished, Caleb mandated that every group carry a walkie-talkie so we could keep in contact. One of his lackeys circulated the equipment to each team. In six hours, Caleb had taken charge of the entire search and rescue operation.

Mickey was the only one to openly question Caleb's authority. He stared at her until she looked away. I'd never seen her back down before. Then again, she'd kissed his sister's husband. Caleb was intimidating under the best of circumstances.

He would die for Kai. So would I. But it might not be enough to bring her back to me. With Caleb here, she'd have another place to run to. A place to feel safe. He had a lifetime of being her hero. Me, I'd waffled from hero to villain the past few months.

Alex clapped Caleb on the back. "Where'd you find all these guys?"

His crew remained silent.

"Called in a few favors," Caleb said.

"We appreciate it," Alex said.

"I'd do anything for my sister."

"Me too."

Side by side, they mirrored Viking warriors preparing to wage battle. All golden hair and blue eyes committed to rescuing the fair maiden and missing child. My intestines double-knotted at the thought of them partnered up in the search. The protective brother and soon to-be-lover.

It felt like our entire marriage hinged on me finding Kai. I hated myself for making my wife's rescue into a competition. All that mattered was that Kai and Lukas were safe. And that I be nearby when she was found. And that Alex not find her. But if it came down to saving her life, I'd rather have her alive with Alex than dead. Even if it killed me to imagine it.

The Viking team never came to be. Caleb preferred to work with his own guy. Imagine Caleb having no faith in anyone but himself and his lackeys. It was one of the reasons the guy pissed me off. Then again, on no hours of sleep, everything grated against my skin.

At the first site, could-we-find-them-this-soon warred with what-will-we-find. Dan and I eyed the narrow crevasse. Large enough for a person to slip inside the hill. Small enough to remain undetected to anyone but the avid searcher.

I projected my thoughts as loud as I could. *Kai are you here?*

The wind whistled through the trees. Dan's boots trampled the snow. And not a thought from Kai. Caleb said she'd been injured. That her powers were all haywire. Maybe she couldn't hear me. Maybe she couldn't project her thoughts back. Maybe she was…I wouldn't go there.

I squeezed through the space in the rocks, proving a child and woman could be here too. Dan followed me. It didn't matter if her telepathy was off-line. I'd search until I knew she wasn't here. I stumbled over the uneven ground and scraped my cheek on a rock outcropping. Resisted the urge to yell.

The passage tightened around us. We had to double over to fit through. We kept going until we dead-ended in solid rock. No way forward. Two hours wasted going backward.

Halfway to the next site, Dan's foot caught on a snow-insulated tree root. He went down hard, twisting his knee with a slurping-pop noise. He tried to stand, but collapsed back on the ground, blowing out long breaths of steam. His kneecap wasn't in the right place.

I swallowed against my gag reflex.

"I'll just lean on you." Dan braced his hand against the ground, determined to get up and continue the search.

"You can't put any weight on that. We gotta get you to a hospital." Shit. Shit. Shit. I couldn't waste time getting him back to the Hoffmanns'.

But I had Caleb's walkie-talkie. Thank God, he thought of everything.

I pressed the button and said, "Oliver here. We've got an injured searcher. Anyone near search site 16 or 17?"

Over the crackling on the walkie-talkie, Caleb asked, "Oliver, did you hurt yourself?"

"Dan's kneecap is in the wrong place. He can't walk on it."

"Mickey and I are nearby," Alex said.

"We're about a mile from site 16 along the path Caleb's guy drew," I said.

"We're on our way," Alex said.

Forty-seven minutes later, I heard them coming. Mickey's tone bordered on irate. "I am not giving up the search."

"He's our brother," Alex said.

"You don't need me to help carry him." Her cheeks reached boiled-lobster red.

"You want to stay and search with Oliver? That'll be great. Just what Kai needs."

"I don't give a damn about Kai. I have to find my son. Your nephew."

"Over here, Alex," I yelled and waved.

Dan tried to get up. The snow he'd piled over his knee in a makeshift ice pack fell away. The second he tried to shift weight onto it, his leg buckled and he fell back onto the log. His face paled in pain.

Alex stormed toward us. "Dan, stop it."

Dan gritted his teeth. "It's not so bad. I can continue."

Mickey pressed her lips together.

Alex examined the area around the kneecap. "It's swollen and out of place. You can't walk on this."

"Danny, that has to hurt," Mickey said.

350

"It's nothing like the game where I was tackled by three guys," Dan said.

She blinked back tears.

"I need to keep searching. Can you take him back to the Hoffmanns'?" I asked.

"I'm not giving up the search," she said.

"Neither am I," I said.

Alex dragged us aside. "I have to get him to a doctor. I can't babysit you two. Can you work together?"

"Why don't we search separately?" I asked.

Alex blew out a long breath. "Because whoever has Kai and Lukas, probably has a weapon and can easily take out one person."

She crossed her arms. "I can take care of myself."

"Don't make this about you. Lukas needs his mom and Kai needs her husband," Alex said.

He'd always been the bigger, better person. I really hated that about Alex. "Fine, we continue on to site 17."

Mickey blanched. "I have two more sites to hit. We should go to site 13."

"You're closest to 17. Finish that and double back to the others," Alex said. "Mickey, you work with Oliver."

She hmphed at him.

He dropped his voice, confiding, "I have to get Dan help. I'll radio when I can re-join the search." He raised his voice to ask Dan, "Ready, buddy?"

"As I'll ever be." Dan's face was saturated with pain.

Alex pulled Dan to his feet, taking most of his weight onto his shoulder. "Let's go."

Mickey's boots chomped on the snow. She didn't say a word to me. Pissed off to the 90th percentile. It didn't matter what she wanted. We had a job to do. A search to complete. A missing woman and kid to find.

This rescue mission was so screwed up. I half-wished Caleb would radio that he found Kai and rid me of the acid inferno burning through my stomach lining.

I lengthened my strides. Sped up my pace. Anything to bring the distant hills closer.

"Are you running from me or to Kai?" Mickey asked.

"Both."

"I won't forgive you for taking the dog from Lukas's search party."

I scanned the ground as I walked. "I'm not asking you to. In your shoes, that would be unforgivable."

"It is."

"So it's settled?" I asked.

"Seriously?"

"I mean, we'll just move on."

She hesitated. "Are you trying to ask about the kiss?"

"The dog thing negates everything else."

"Always taking the easy route," she muttered.

I stared at the hill that loomed in front of us and checked the map. It would be another hour until we reached the next site.

She grabbed my arm. "Did you hear what I just said?"

"I don't have time to talk about it right now."

"Really?! Can't talk and walk at the same time?"

"I'm trying to move forward," I said. "Focusing on what really matters."

"By burying the past? Pretending the kiss didn't happen? Putting everything on me?"

"It happened. It's over." She was the one making a huge deal about it.

"Don't pretend it's an isolated incident," she hissed. "It's not the first time we kissed in a crisis. Probably won't be the last."

"You kissed me last time." For five years, I'd done everything I could to make amends for that one moment of weakness. The night I lost all hope in San Diego. The night I gave up on Kai and me.

"And you kissed me back," she said.

Kai had been locked away for two months, spiraling further into her insanity. She gave up on everything. The doctor gave up on her. I couldn't reach her. The woman I loved was gone. Without her, I spun out. Relapsed into my old world. Just for a moment. I needed someone to connect with. Someone to not be alone with. "We didn't get beyond first base."

"I wouldn't have stopped, you know." She sounded almost regretful. "I mean something to you. It doesn't negate what Kai means to you."

"We've always been each other's emergency exit." I never told Kai about kissing Mickey. Kai needed me to be strong and certain. I didn't want her to know that I had a moment where I let go of us. "We made a mistake."

"We were never a mistake." She stamped her foot. "Does Kai let you get away with this crap? Because I won't."

"Good thing we aren't together."

Pain bonfired in her eyes. "You are as cold as Reinhard."

A stone fist rammed into my gut. Crushing ribs and bruising organs. I pretended it wasn't a serious blow. "Cold enough to drive a husband away?"

"Whose wife moved out after you kissed me? Oh, that would be you." She slapped me with her words.

Everything stopped. I was rooted to the ground like one of the ancient sequoias in Yosemite, while Mickey threw every derivative of the f-word at me. Shook my arm a few times. I didn't say anything. Her tornado of anger ripped through me. Tore at my foundation, collapsing everything I believed to be true.

I lied. I kept people at arm's length for their own good. I abandoned all my friends and family in Butternut. Walked away from everyone that mattered to me. Built a new life with Kai and betrayed that too.

Reinhard never cheated on my mother. Reinhard had been destroyed by her death. But he'd never destroyed her.

Not like me. What I'd done to Kai.

I was worse than Reinhard. Bile burned the back of my throat. I swallowed, trying to push back the guilt. It clung to my tonsils.

I was what I hated most. I'd become my father. No. A man even my father would despise. "You're right."

She fumbled over the words. "I'm right?"

"I screwed up everything." I rubbed my hand across my eyes. I didn't want to see the way she looked at me.

She rested her hand on my arm.

I pulled away. "I deserve this."

"No one deserves to lose the person they love most. To fear they are dead." Her lower lip trembled. "Whether it be four days or eight days."

Eight days, she'd been without her son. And I was the one she comforted. What was wrong with me?

"I was wrong to kiss you. Wrong to take the dog from your search party. I was wrong to come back here," I said.

"Why did you?"

"I wanted to start over. I wanted…" To come home. "I thought…" I could fix things. Fix Kai.

"I'm sorry for what happened in high school. But not for San Diego. Never San Diego."

"We steered each other back to the paths we needed to be on," I said.

"What if we steered each other wrong?" she whispered.

"We didn't." The silence lingered between us until I said, "We've got to find Lukas and Kai. That's all that matters."

Mickey and I hiked upward through the woods for an hour. Neither of us spoke. The saids had exhausted us. When we reached the crest of the hill, I saw something familiar coated in snow. Our old oak tree with the giant symbol slashed across its bark. Fifty paces from the cave's entrance.

"Remember the day Christian did this?" She rubbed the snow off the tree, revealing the rune for protection.

"Yeah." Christian, Mickey and I were the treacherous trio back in elementary school. Complete with our secret cave. I hadn't thought about it in decades. Didn't realize this was the next site on my map.

"Caleb said something about gold bars?" Her fingers gripped my coat. "What if it wasn't gold bars, but metal bars on a door?"

"You mean…"

"What if it was bars holding her prisoner?"

"The little cave where we hid our loot?" I'd buried that memory with Christian.

"Who would keep Kai and Lukas there?" Confusion skipped over her features.

"I don't know." I surveyed the cave's yawning mouth. "But we need to find out."

CHAPTER 74

Kai

I must have dozed off, not into a dream, but that black pit of rest where your body heals. Or tries to at least. All I remembered was purple darkness before I woke up. Fingers prodded my head.

"You'll be fine," Chris half-muttered to himself.

I blinked. "Will I?"

He shined a flashlight into my eyes. I clamped my eyelids shut, shielding my corneas from the bright burn.

"Sorry." He pried one eye open and shined the light into it. He did the same to the other. "Keep them both open. I need to compare your pupils."

"Does it matter?" I asked. "I mean, I'm supposed to die. Isn't that what you planned?" I'd seen his face. There was no way he'd let me walk out of here alive.

Chris moved the flashlight's beam out of my eyes. "Your pupils are slow to react to light." He started to get up.

I reached out with my left hand. Forgetting. Until the current of pain sparked into my fingers and reminded me. Broken wrist. I sucked the air through my teeth, trying to contain the agony. To keep it from encroaching on what remained of me.

Chris rubbed my forehead. "Rest."

"Why?"

"We're almost done here."

"Dead done? Or go-home done?" I asked.

He headed toward the bars.

"Wait." I pushed myself up on my elbows. The cave tipped and rocked like the cabin of a Venetian water taxi on rough seas. "Please. What's going to happen to us?"

"That depends."

His steady pronouncement unnerved me more than a violent outburst. The seas refused to calm down. I swayed. "On what?"

The bars groaned in protest as they closed. "On what he does next." He snapped the padlock into place.

"He? Who? Wait."

Chris disappeared.

Leaving me locked in the cave again. Damn it. I had to save Lukas. Didn't matter if my brain was on the fritz, I had to use it. Reach out and send an SOS to Oliver. The only problem was finding a way to light the flare inside me. I'd never done anything like this on purpose. Probably wouldn't live to do something like it again. But today was going to be the day I tried.

Grandma told me the day of the car crash, she heard me screaming in her mind. Knew exactly where I was and how to get to me. I was fifty miles away. That was the power of a psychic scream.

Oliver would hear me if I could replicate that level of danger.

You couldn't fake it, though. For my soul to scream, death had to be imminent or I had to believe it was. I'd have to make Chris lose control and verge on killing me.

While Lukas ate his Pop-Tart and drank his water, I stroked his hair. Such a simple movement kept him relaxed and helped me to

357

figure things out.

I had to reopen the hole in my heart, the one that made death seem so much better than life. I had to meet Chris's pending insanity with my own.

Lukas, I gotta do something really scary.

"What?" he whispered.

I have to go into his head.

"How?"

It's hard to explain. But I need you to take your sleeping bag and flashlight and hide in that corner over there for a while. Don't come out. No matter what happens, okay?

"No."

Lukas, I'm serious.

"You're hurt. You should rest."

I wish I could. But the only way we can get out of here is if I scream really loud with my mind, and to do that I have to go after Chris.

I didn't mention what my grandmother called it. A death scream.

My abilities were all jumbled up. Nothing worked like it used to. It was like being 11 years old again, learning what I could and couldn't do. The limits of my powers. The weakness of a novice.

Except my frustration knew what I should be able to do. I concentrated on taking even breaths. In for a count of four, and out for a count of eight. When I visualized my shield, it wasn't normal. Not crystal but solid Manhattan bedrock schist. I poked at it. No give.

I had to split my shield. This time, I knew where my mind had to go. Who it had to go to. The shield fought me, refusing to let me wield it. It took more concentration and force than ever before.

A tiny fissure appeared. I pounded at it until that one crack birthed a web of baby fractures. Shoved against it until the shield finally gave way. When I pushed it apart, the shield exploded, leaving me without any protection.

That never happened before. Okay, new territory. Deep breath. I sent my thoughts in search of Chris. Dove inside his head.

Killing that woman wasn't something he relished. He'd tried to rationalize it away. They had to suffer. But she wasn't what he expected. She fought for a child that wasn't hers. Jeopardized her life for a kid that could tear her marriage apart. Stupid woman.

I plunged deeper into his insanity. It's easy to find the worst in people. Always has been for me. I spotted the festering puss, the illness that ravaged the mind.

No qualms. No second thoughts.

I flung myself into his swamp of sickness. Slime coated my skin. His murkiness oozed through me. Murder became justified. My death was simple justice for him. For me.

I wanted to help him. To die so that he could get better. It was so simple. My death avenged him. Made his entire world make sense again. And Lukas. Lukas might be allowed to live.

I plummeted.

Under his influence, I hated Oliver for taking everything that mattered. I hated myself for giving Oliver happiness achieved at other's misery.

Oliver had to lose what mattered most. It was the only way to right his world again.

Give me a knife, I begged Chris. *I can do this for you. I can make this right.*

He refused to get up from his chair.

We can make Oliver pay. I'll do it. I promise.

"Not time." His garbled words couldn't sway me.

It's time for me to die. Bring me the knife.

Chris shifted. Not a physical movement in his chair, but his mind turned away and sucked me into another place.

A place bathed in sunlight. The grassy meadow tickled my bare feet and swished against my skirt. I knelt down to pick a buttercup and twirled it between my fingertips.

A few gauzy clouds stretched across the cerulean sky. The perfect day for a picnic. Out across the field, a blanket and basket waited for me.

When I skipped up to them, Chris materialized on the blanket and held a hand out to me. "Join me."

"Of course." I slid my hand in his and lowered myself onto the blanket.

He wore a pale blue-and-white-striped seersucker suit. He checked his pocket watch before pouring our apple cider. "Why are you in such a hurry to die?"

I shrugged. "I thought it was what had to happen."

He gave me a tight smile. "And you want to do it on your terms. Now rather than later?"

I chewed my lower lip, trying to remember my reasoning.

"I thought you loved Oliver," he said.

"I do."

"But you're giving up. And he's looking for you."

"I have to." I couldn't remember why, but the need burned inside me.

"And the boy? Would you die for him?"

"Yes."

He frowned. The longest eyelashes, too pretty for a man, swept over his eyes. Then he leaned closer and scrutinized my face. "He's not even your child."

I shared a breath with him. "I know." The blue was so pristine it hurt to look into his eyes, but I couldn't stop.

"Why?" he murmured.

My eyelids felt so heavy. I fought the urge to close them and sink into his velvety voice. "I have to." I willed him to understand. "It's the only way I can stand living."

He leaned back. "No one has to die. It's Oliver's choice."

"You aren't planning to kill Lukas...or me?" I asked.

"All I ever wanted was the truth." Strings of unhappiness unfurled across his forehead. "I'm so tired of all the lies."

It was then that I felt Oliver. Not in Chris's head. No, nearby. I couldn't hear his thoughts, but something in me screamed he was coming. The part of me that always ached for him. I clamped down on that thought. I couldn't risk telegraphing to him. Not from Chris's head.

"You should go," Chris said.

Dark, menacing clouds streamed over us, obliterating the blue sky. "Why?"

He tucked a stray hair back behind my ear. "They're coming."

"Who?" Please don't let him sense Oliver.

"Get out of my head." The ground quaked at his vehemence.

"But..." I wasn't finished. I had to die.

"Go."

Golf balls of rain pelted me. Stung my skin with their coldness. Lightning shot from cloud to cloud. Sections of the sky blackened. I ran. But it was too late. A tornado touched down, swooping me up.

CHAPTER 75

Oliver

The gaping hole in the hillside had once housed pirate booty, miners' rewards, and ancient treasure protected by a torturous curse. In a child's imagination, anyway. Now, I hiked toward the kidnapper's subterranean crypt—the place I planned to kill him. I prayed I'd find Kai and Lukas first. I peered into the darkness, but it only shrouded rocks. Dampness clung to my face and seeped through my jacket, more chilling than the snow outside.

Mickey whispered, "It's a ways to where the kidnapper's holding Kai and Lukas."

If he hadn't moved them and if we'd guessed right. "I'll radio Caleb."

I pulled out the walkie-talkie to zero reception and had to retrace my steps into daylight. Mickey shadowed me.

"Oliver here. We're entering site 17. Mickey and I played here years ago. There's a tunnel that leads to a huge cavern with three outlets. The outlet furthest back contains a small-cave with bars and a padlock. Over."

"I'll send backup." Caleb asked, "How do we get to the cavern?"

"I only know the way by sight," Mickey said.

Caleb swore. Sounded like log duck. Probably pig fuck. Kai's favorite words.

"We're headed in. Oliver out." I turned the walkie-talkie off before he could respond. We didn't need any radio feedback warning the kidnapper of our approach.

Fifty or so paces inside the cave, the tunnel narrowed. We bumped hands and jostled elbows until we single-filed to a curve in the tunnel. Mickey halted, shined her flashlight on the wall, and traced her fingers over the symbols. Symbols Christian carved to help us find our hideout.

"It's been 16 years since he died." Mickey's voice trembled on the "16."

"Remember how he laughed?"

"It always started with a snort."

I wished I could hear it one more time. "Why would someone hold Kai and Lukas here?"

Her pupils had devoured her irises. "I never told anyone about it."

"Me neither." We blood-oathed it to secrecy. At nine, the three of us pricked our fingers and swore to never divulge our secret hideout. "So who would know about it?"

"Mr. Hoffmann? Someone in town?"

"I guess." But something didn't sit right. Kai would say it was my intuition. Except I was the least intuitive person. The dud and the telepath.

Oliver? Kai's voice was a hoarse whisper in my head.

Kai? Honey, I'm coming, I thought back at her.

He wants to hurt you.

Are you okay? I asked.

He doesn't want to hurt Lukas.

Kai? Can you hear me? Are you okay?

You've got to help Lukas.

Her telepathy was broadcasting, but not receiving. No matter how hard I thought something back at her, she didn't respond to it. She had to be hurt bad.

Who is holding you?

He knows you're coming. Her voice sputtered out.

Damn.

I told Mickey what I'd heard. She didn't say a word, just studied the ground and trekked toward the colossal unknowns.

When the path widened and forked, I stopped, forgetting which way to go. We'd ventured here just once after Christian died. Mickey sang "Imagine" by John Lennon while I dug a hole and buried a box of our treasures where no one could disturb it. We promised never to return. It wouldn't be the same without Christian.

She scrutinized the wall, searching for the symbols he'd carved there. She'd admired his ingenuity in the design, treating him like a kid brother despite his being five months older than her. She murmured, "Sun sets and rises, east meets west, and then we take the path into darkness."

"What does that mean?" The rhyme sounded familiar, but the memory couldn't be conjured up anymore. Too many years spent actively forgetting.

"Shine your flashlight beam over mine on the wall between the tunnels."

I did and the faintest of arrows pointed left. "How'd he do that?"

She shrugged and veered left, tugging me along. Closing in on Kai and Lukas and the kidnapper.

I tasted tin in the back of my throat and pulled Mickey back toward me. Whispered, "Weapon?"

She reached for the gun lodged between her jeans and spine.

I pulled Reinhard's gun from its holster. Held it muzzle down beside me. The way he'd taught me.

We crept around the corner. Our narrow tunnel emptied into a monolithic cavern with three other offshoots. The one furthest away, the most isolated, was the one where our hideout lay, complete with bars. We'd never known who installed them or why, but we claimed them as ours. Or at least Christian did, and we followed his lead.

The cavern swallowed the tips of our flashlight beams. Mickey and I pressed back to back, circling toward our hideout. Our feeble light tunneled through the dark, but couldn't eradicate it. The beams illuminated a tent, a chair, scattered camping supplies. Never piercing the entire expanse of the cavern.

Fear pricked at the base of my spine and munched up my spinal cord. *Kai?*

No reply. Shit. Shit. Shit. She had to be nearby. I'd heard her thoughts.

Our down coats swished against each other as we spun toward the blackened tunnel opening. Back to back, we edged into the tunnel, turned right, and rounded another curve.

Mickey hurried forward, whispering, "Lukas? Lukas? It's Mommy. Can you hear me?"

I kept my gun and flashlight raised, aiming at the route back. "What do you see?"

"Sleeping bags, candy wrappers, water bottles. No Lukas. No Kai." Mickey's voice hovered on hysterical. "Where are they?"

"Watch the tunnel." I switched places with her. Yanked at the padlock, but it held tight. Rattled the bars. "Kai? Lukas? Are you here?"

Nothing. Except the faintest whiff of copper like a thousand pennies in a room. Something in the wall glinted in my flashlight's beam, glittered like gold. "They're here. Somewhere."

We crept back to the main cavern. The remaining two tunnels slithered deep underground with paths that branched off like tree roots. More turns than a Slinky. Christian had to rescue us from them once.

I started toward the tunnels. Bright lights burst to life throughout the cavern. Blinding me. Driving me back against the wall. Mickey stumbled, clutching at the back of my coat.

"Thank you for joining us," an unfamiliar male voice boomed across the chamber.

CHAPTER 76

Oliver

My left arm shielded my eyes from the glare. I pointed my gun into the light. "Where are Kai and Lukas?"

My pupils hadn't adjusted to the brightness when the lights went out, plummeting us back into the incoherence of darkness. A spotlight jarred the blackness, carving a circle of visibility. Illuminated Kai, my Kai, duct-taped and propped against the wall on a dirt platform. Twenty feet away from me.

"Kai," I yelled across the room.

She didn't move. I couldn't hear her thoughts. She had to be unconscious. The alternative was unthinkable.

Another light flared over Lukas. Ropes bound his wrists and ankles. Duct tape sealed his mouth shut. He blinked. Glossy streaks of tears crisscrossed his cheeks.

Mickey's voice cracked. "Baby, we're going to get you out of here."

Lukas trembled.

In the shadow between Kai and Lukas, the man said, "We have so much to catch up on."

Mickey gasped. "Nathan?"

A third spotlight came on over the still-water-trickling-insane voice. "Hello, my sweet. Did you miss me?" He trained his gun on Kai and fixed his gaze on us.

Jackal eyes sized me up. Same pale blue color from childhood. Now a dark beard wrapped around most of his face. But the eyes, the hatred there, I recognized it.

Mickey's grip on my arm slackened.

"Don't faint on me," I said.

She breathed, "Nathan."

Christian's brother. Lukas's father. "Let the boy go, then we'll talk about anything you want."

Nathan stroked Lukas's head. "We'll talk and then they'll be released."

The inside of my gloves went Florida-Everglades swampy. He'd hated me all through high school, picking fights with me wherever he could. Now he wanted to talk while holding my wife and his son at gunpoint. "Why isn't Kai awake?"

"She kept trying to get into my head," he said.

A splint supported her left arm. Her pinkie and ring finger were taped together. Dried blood matted her hair. She looked like a survivor in a zombie flick. "What did you do to her?"

"Chloroform. She'll wake up soon."

He was over six feet of malevolence and muscle. Mickey and I were too far away to charge him. We'd have to take him by surprise or he'd take us all out. "What do you want to talk about?"

"Drop your weapons."

I hesitated.

He pointed the gun at Kai's leg. "I can maim her." When we didn't react, he swiveled his gun toward Lukas. "Or him."

Out of the corner of my eye, I saw Mickey jerk her head in agreement and place her gun on the ground. I put mine beside it.

"Kick them over here," he said.

We did it. Now our weapons lay five feet beyond our grasp.

His voice remained diamond-stable. "We're going to discuss Christian's murder."

He'd never accepted the story about Christian being drunk and riding his bike off the cliff. He knew, God help me, he knew.

Mickey whispered, "What happened to you?"

His laugh ricocheted off the walls. Rebounding.

Mickey recoiled. "He's lost his mind."

"My beautiful loving wife." Each word sounded more lethal.

"Please, Nathan. If this is about Christian, don't bring Lukas into it."

"I have two things. One dear to Oliver and one to you. Leverage to compel you to give me the truth," he said.

"About what?" Mickey asked. "Christian's death was an accident."

His voice sheared the air. "Oliver. Truth or death?" He aimed his gun at Kai's head.

"Truth," I shouted.

"What happened to Christian?"

It was the truth I'd always wanted to tell. But not like this. Never like this. It came back to me in shards. Super Mario Brothers on my PlayStation. A bowl of Pop Secret half-eaten. "It was Saturday night. Christian was supposed to sleep over."

Nathan nodded.

"I didn't know he had a crush on Mickey. I mean we both liked her. But I didn't realize how much he did."

Mickey's fingers bit into my jacket. The gun remained inches from Kai's head.

"I told him Mickey and I were going out." I'd never forget the look on Christian's face, like I'd kicked his puppy in front of him. "He told me I screwed everything up. Then he grabbed his backpack and stormed out."

The scene unfurled in my head. "I tried to stop him. Told him it was too dark to ride his bike home. Said my dad would drive him later. But he wouldn't listen." He'd punched me when I tried to grab his bike from him.

"Then what happened?" Nathan asked.

Guilt crept up my throat. Swallowing didn't wash it away. "He went missing. Reinhard and Uncle John looked everywhere for him. It took two weeks before they found his bike by Witches' Rock."

"Tell me how he died." He cocked his pistol. "And don't leave a single detail out."

"It was a pitch dark night. Christian shouldn't have been out riding. That was my fault," I said.

His eyes glittered and hardened to double-paned glass. "Did you kill him?"

My tongue scratched against the roof of my mouth. "He was my best friend. I never meant to hurt him." But because of me, he'd been out on that road. "I don't know everything that happened. I thought it was an accident."

Until Uncle John and Reinhard's blowout four years after Christian died. A week after my 16th birthday, their argument smeared the truth across our walls and made it impossible to ever get over his death.

"Wrong answer," he said.

I blurted out. "John Schneider had been out drinking. He didn't see Christian." It all sounded so lame to my ears. "Never had time to brake. But he stopped."

"Christian was bleeding from his mouth and nose. He had no pulse. He wasn't breathing. John tried CPR. But there was nothing he could do." When said aloud, my words sounded inexcusable.

"He let my brother die." Nathan caressed the side of Kai's head with the butt of his gun.

"He was dead. Nothing could be done." That's what Uncle John screamed at Reinhard.

"What did your father do?" he asked.

369

"Reinhard found John with Christian's body. Reinhard didn't want John to lose his career. He'd just lost his wife and daughter in a fire. He was my father's best friend." I used the same justification that Reinhard gave me.

"What about my brother?" Nathan's words snaked around my conscience and squeezed.

"Christian deserved better. Reinhard made the wrong choice when he covered for John. He helped him move the body and set up an accident scene by Witches' Rock so your family would think Christian was out riding and missed a turn." The guilt inside me flatlined.

"And the alcohol?"

Nathan's words resuscitated my guilt.

"John had to make it look like an accident. Christian had to be drunk and ride off the road." And over the cliff.

"The blood on the tree trunk?"

"Your brother's. I don't know what they did to cover things up." I forced myself to look at him. "It was wrong."

"Why didn't you tell someone?" He poked at my complicity.

"I had no evidence. They'd staged it perfectly. Reinhard wouldn't betray John."

"My mother blamed herself. Did you know that?" His gaze fixed between Mickey and me. Watching both of us, connecting to neither.

I shook my head. "I'm sorry."

Oliver, how could you? Kai's voice threaded through my mind before her eyelids fluttered open.

"Do you see what kind of man you married?" he asked Kai.

Kai's bleary eyes focused on me.

"This is all his fault. Everything you've been through is because of him and his family." He pulled the tape from Kai's lips. "Let's hear what your wife thinks."

Kai's voice wavered. "Is this it? The secret you've been keeping from me."

"One of them." He bent to kiss the top of her head.

Her eyes rolled up to look at him. "What else?"

"Your turn, Mickey." He swung the gun toward Lukas.

Mickey gasped. "Don't. He's your son."

Nathan snorted. "Who's lying now?"

Mickey released my arm, distancing herself from the taint of me. "Please, Nathan. Whatever went wrong between us, don't hurt your son."

A fine tremor started at the crown of Nathan's head and rippled down to his boots. "Don't call him that."

Mickey took a step forward. "But he is. Lukas Christian Hoffmann."

"What about your weekend in San Diego?" Nathan asked. "Nine months before Lukas was born." He patted Kai's head. "When you were locked up in the institution, Mickey slept with your beloved Oliver."

Kai's breath hissed through her teeth. Like she felt every second of a kidney being ripped from her belly.

It's not true. I sent my thought to her, praying she would hear me. But no response came in my head. I shook my head, but she didn't seem to notice.

"I saw Oliver in San Diego. We kissed." Mickey amended, "Made out. But nothing else happened."

Kai's eyes became fathomless pools.

"Try again, Mickey," Nathan said.

"She's telling the truth. We didn't sleep together," I said. "There's zero chance Lukas is mine."

I was a mess back then. Kai had been so far gone, I never thought she'd come back. Forty-nine days of unresponsiveness obliterated my hope. Mickey showed up at my hotel, reminding me of the days she'd helped me survive without my mother.

Nathan's eyebrows arched to meet his hairline. "And I'm supposed to take your word for it?"

I was a liar. Twice proven. "No."

"I'm going to take away everything that matters to you. Your son.

Your wife. Maybe even your whore." He tossed his head at Mickey.

Lukas cringed into the wall.

"Wait. Please, wait." Mickey's hand darted out, fingers outstretched, trying to forestall him. "I can prove it."

Nathan lowered the gun. "How?"

"Lukas is special." Mickey's tongue twisted over the words. She didn't want to believe it. But she'd say it to save Lukas's life.

"He's like Kai," I said the words for her.

Nathan's face spasmed.

"Mickey and I aren't special," I said.

I stared at Kai. *Please help Lukas.*

No reply. Just a vacant expression.

Dread thunked down in my gut like a cold, hard block of cement. That face. I remembered it. She'd worn it at the mental institution.

Kai blinked and looked up at Nathan. The words scratched against her throat. "Lukas can see people's illnesses. I can hear people's thoughts."

"Your point?" Nathan asked.

"Mickey and Oliver can't do anything special. They're not like us," Kai said.

"I don't believe it," Nathan said.

"You don't want to." Kai struggled to sit up. "Because that makes you the monster terrorizing your own son."

"Don't play with me." Nathan leveled his gun at Kai.

She didn't flinch. "You're the one playing games. I've felt your mind. You have power. Abilities. Like me and Lukas."

I edged toward Nathan.

Two steps taken before he said, "One more and Kai gets a bullet in her special brain. Let's see how it works after that."

I froze.

"Back up." He didn't bother looking at me.

I took two steps back.

"Don't you think I know what happened? I'm an empath." Nathan swiveled the gun toward Mickey. "Do you know what that means?"

"No," Mickey said.

He shouted at her, "I felt how much you loved him. It lingered after we got married. He abandoned you, and you fell deeper in love with him." His nostrils flared and a vein in his forehead leapt out. "After you returned from San Diego, I felt everything you felt. The shame when you found out you were pregnant. You didn't tell me about the baby for weeks."

Tears soaked Mickey's cheeks. "Is that why you left?"

"Only a masochist would stay," Nathan said.

"I felt guilty that I'd betrayed your trust. Like a failure because I couldn't make our marriage work." Mickey gulped down a breath. "I didn't tell you about the baby because I had to settle things in my head. I had to let go of Oliver, so I could raise my son with his father. I was committed to us."

"Liar," Nathan said.

"Am I?" Mickey asked. "Can you sense lies?"

Nathan frowned and asked Kai, "What is she thinking?"

Kai shrugged. "I can't read her thoughts."

"But you've been projecting yours," he said.

"It's hit or miss." Kai's tone choked on indifference. As if a lunatic weren't holding a gun on her. As if her life weren't in danger. As if her injuries didn't matter.

"You came into my head," Nathan said.

"You're different. My abilities get skewed by yours," Kai said.

"What do you think of your precious Oliver now?" Nathan asked.

"I hate him," Kai said.

CHAPTER 77

Kai

"**I** hate him." My words echoed in the cavern, reverberating in the chasms of my soul. Oliver had made a mockery of us. Kissing. Touching. Her.

Images of them stampeded through my mind. I couldn't hear their thoughts. Couldn't see their memories. But my imagination filled the void. I heard him saying, "We shouldn't," but not stopping. Not yet. I felt his need to forget me. To ease the loss of me.

Except I hadn't died. I had been stumbling through my own version of Dante's *Inferno* inside the mental institution.

Longing. Desperation. Despair. Wisps of Oliver's old feelings inflamed my cartilage.

Emotions swelled up inside me. A tsunami in response to the earthquake of his unfaithfulness.

Rage. Blind rage. One desire—to hurt Oliver—obliterated every other impulse I had.

"How about I kill him?" Nathan's words fell like feathers on my head.

"Not in front of Lukas," I said.

"He's really mine?"

"I think so."

Something in me knew he wasn't Oliver's child. But Oliver wanted him to be. And he might have been. If Oliver's self-control hadn't returned in time. He'd lied to me about it for years. Betrayal shish-kabobed my heart. My fingers pressed against the invisible wound, trying to staunch the pain. When I was locked up, Oliver cheated on me. When we were married, Oliver cheated on me. Oliver's double treason ripped through everything we were.

"He is," Mickey said. "Nathan, he's your son."

She was worse than Oliver. They deserved each other. Lukas deserved a better mother. Someone like me.

Nathan stroked my hair. "We could raise the boy together."

"We could raise him right," I said.

"Kai, please, listen to me," Oliver said.

"Shut up," I yelled.

Nathan sliced through the duct tape on my hands and feet. "Take the boy out of here."

Lukas, it's going to be okay. But I need you to close your eyes.

Lukas clenched his eyelids shut.

I couldn't lift him with my injuries. "I need to untie him."

"Be quick about it." Nathan aimed the gun at Mickey. "Would you die for your son?"

I rolled Lukas into the tunnel behind us. *Stay down.*

And then I slammed into Nathan.

The gun roared.

I didn't know who was hit. Couldn't think about that now.

I sent one thought to Oliver. *Get Lukas out of here.*

Then I shoved myself inside Nathan's mind. Waded into the stench of his mental illness. Sank under the sludge to the event that started it all.

I stood in front of the closed silver casket that contained my brother's remains. He was such a mess we couldn't see him again. No amount of makeup and chemicals could fix his mangled body.

In a sea of mourners, vanilla-flavored guilt emanated from Officer Schneider. Lilac-scented remorse sputtered from Chief of Police Richter. Lavender regret leaked from Oliver. Blue Spruce sorrow wafted from Mickey.

Everyone's emotions swarmed me. Scents and tastes that produced electrical twinges along my skin. It worsened during the receiving line. Shaking hands. Pecks on the cheek. Touch intensified every emotion. I staggered through a minefield of feelings when all I wanted was to be numb.

The memories blurred as the years barreled by. Junior year, Oliver's vanilla-frosted guilt choked me. He knew something about Christian. It wasn't an accident. My brother wasn't responsible. The police said he'd been found with alcohol. That he must have been riding his bike drunk. But Christian wouldn't do that.

Oliver never came forward. Never spoke up for Christian.

I planned to take away what Oliver loved most. It was easy to manipulate Mickey's insecurities. To play on her fear that he'd leave her and this backward town behind when he went to college. Once he got accepted into the university in California, she was mine. Senior year, I gorged myself on Oliver's cinnamon pain and sipped on Mickey's blueberry depression.

After high school, Mickey said she loved me. I thought it might be enough. That I could build a life with her and let my brother go. So I married her. But it was never enough. She wasn't enough. I still needed answers. My brother demanded his name be cleared. He started appearing to me. The brain-grilling headaches came with him.

I couldn't trust anyone. Mickey betrayed me. A son that wasn't mine. The lies. Lies. Lies.

Oliver took everything from me. My brother. My wife. My son. My family. Gone.

He had to pay.

I raised the gun again. This time I wouldn't miss.

I leveled the gun at Kai's head. She knelt there with eyes unfocused. She didn't fight back. She didn't cower.

Will it end your pain? she asked.

Nothing will end my pain.

Your son needs you.

He hates me.

So fix it.

I can't.

I didn't shake or twitch. I couldn't because I was inside Nathan's head. I'd only done this once before. Projected myself into another body and tried to take control. To save Grandma. But I couldn't be in two places at once. I couldn't move my body out of the way. If he shot me at this range, I was dead.

I heard Lukas's thoughts. *Mommy, Kai saved me.*

I didn't know what happened to Oliver, but Lukas would be safe. That was worth my life.

I watched the tears pool in my eyes. Saw the fearless way I met my death.

And then a shot rang out. Hit me. No, Nathan. He twisted to see who'd shot him.

Oliver stood behind him with Reinhard's gun.

Nathan slumped to the ground. Oliver had shot him. Us. It was Baccarat-crystal clear to Nathan and me: He had a few breaths. I tried to get back to my body, but panic tripped me.

Nathan and I stood in a field of poppies with sunlight streaming down upon us. He picked a blood-red blossom and handed it to me. "Take care of my son."

And then he disappeared.

We died.

EPILOGUE

Kai

Bright white light. I blinked my eyes, expecting to see Grandma. She'd help me adjust to the afterlife. Except it wasn't.

Sterile. Pristine. Clinical. Hospital room. The faintest scent of sandalwood.

Sunlight streamed through the window.

Caleb grasped my hand. "Finally waking up, Sleeping Beauty?"

He hadn't called me that since I was ten. "Didn't I die?" I whispered.

"In a little coma for a week." The curve of his lips minimized everything. "A lot of people have been waiting to see you."

I rasped, "Not yet." My throat felt like I'd drank from the salt waters swirling beneath Badwater Basin.

He poured a cup of water and pressed it into my good hand. Not the one in the splint, but the one eviscerated with tubes.

Over the rim of the cup, I gazed at a face I feared I'd never see again. *This what I have to do to get you to visit?* I drank until relief trickled into my throat.

His fingertips swept the hair away from my face. "Do you remember what happened?"

Images piled up in my mind, fighting for dominance. *The kidnapping. The cave. Saving Lukas. Oliver's confessions. Nathan's death.*

"He's still in ICU. They say the bastard has a chance of making it," Caleb said.

"Oliver?"

"Stunk. I sent him home to shower." Caleb tapped me on the nose.

I cleared my throat. "Lukas?"

"He's telling everyone what a superhero you are. Kid's seriously in awe of you."

"Everyone's okay?"

"You had a little pressure on your brain but they alleviated it." Dark circles ringed my brother's eyes.

I held my good arm out and waved him in for a hug. "I'm okay."

"I know." He held on for longer than usual. *Don't do that to me again.*

I won't. I touched his hair. "I love the curls."

"I forgot my gel."

Oliver came in and shut the door. He leaned against it, gripping the door handle behind his back. "I'm so sorry."

"For?"

He rubbed his hand across his eyes. "Where do I start? For kissing Mickey. For letting you leave. For everything Nathan did to you. For all the lies."

I patted the bed. "Come here."

He shuffled toward the bed, sitting as gently as he could. "You're going to be okay?"

"Doctors say everything's on the mend." I drank in the sight of him. The man who'd been my safe house for nine years. I reached out and touched his face, proving he was here. The face I loved. The face that lied to me all these years. I dropped my hand back on the bed.

"I got your note," he said.

"There's more that needs to be written."

"Can you forgive me?" His hand inched toward mine on the bed.

"I don't know if it's possible." Or if I wanted it to be.

He touched my arm. "You did a dozen impossible things to save Lukas." Hope trailed behind each word.

"Maybe, I exhausted myself." I didn't pull away from his touch. Today, I'd just be grateful that we were both alive.

He hesitated before asking, "Tomorrow?"

I shook my head. I couldn't have that conversation right away.

"Can I do anything?" He lifted his eyes to meet mine. *I'll do anything.*

"Lay with me?"

He crawled under the covers. Laying on his side, he formed a careful *C* around me.

"When I thought you might die…" His voice cracked like a thirteen-year-old boy on the brink of manhood.

I did. Twice. Almost.

He buried his face in my hair. "I love you."

I sank into him, needing him more than I should. Less than I used to.

AUTHOR'S NOTE

After publication, I received several comments about the setting of the story. As this is fiction, I've taken some artistic license with the town. Some places are represented as they are, and others are completely fictionalized to suit the story's needs. I thought I should add an author's note in the second edition to help clarify things.

The town of Butternut, Wisconsin, is a real town with an amazing citizenry. I've been there a couple times to visit and am lucky enough to call many of its residents my friends. When I originally researched the town back in 2010, the population was at 407. In 2014, when I last visited it was at 375. However, the events of this book are taking place in 2012, so I kept the older population number.

The *Park Falls Herald* was the name of the local newspaper up until 2013. Since this story takes place in 2012, I continue to use that paper as it is historically accurate to do so.

There is no Butternut Police Station nor a Butternut police force. In reality, Ashland County provides police coverage for Butternut. The town hall is actually its own separate building, but that didn't work for my story, so I changed it. The fire station is beside Brennan's Green Brier, but it doesn't house the town hall and police station too.

There are sites with chalcopyrite in Ashland county. I embellished on their abundance.

Copper Falls is a beautiful state park and the water is indeed the color of root beer.

The Deer Haven Lodge was where I stayed in 2010 when I was doing research for the book. It is not owned by the fictional Hoffmanns. The B&B actually closed down in 2013. I have stayed faithful to my memories and photos of this amazing B&B.

Cherry Lane is a real street in Butternut, but you will not find the Richter house off of it.

There is a McDonald's in Park Falls. Super One Foods is the main grocery store in Park Falls and most people in Butternut drive down Highway 13 to get their food from this grocery store. The shift hours that Oliver and Mickey work there don't represent the actual store working hours. This was just for story purposes.

ACKNOWLEDGMENTS

There are so many people who helped me get this book out of my head and into your hands. First and foremost, I'd like to thank my mom, Sandra Tansley, for reading several drafts of this book, providing feedback even when I didn't take it especially well, holding my hand through the many rounds of rejections, cheering me on toward publication, and being a promotional magician. You gave me a place to call home. I couldn't have made it this far without you. To my dad, Michael Tansley, thanks for all your feedback on the original short story. You were the first person to say I had something worth pursuing there. Bet you never thought it would lead to endless hours spent toiling over the query letter and the synopsis together. Remember how you red-penned all my high school essays and papers? If I don't say it enough, I am a better writer because of it. Thank you for being my parents and my patrons.

To Katrina Bender—for wearing every hat I ever needed you to and doing it with style and grace—you are my critique partner, my writing buddy, my conference pal, my editor, and my dear friend. Thank you for tirelessly interpreting agent feedback and reading my revisions. Most of all for being my sanity. To my warrior lapdog, Emerson, who napped in my lap while I typed, snuggled my leg while I edited, and cuddled me through rejections. To Anthony Dvarskas, for putting me up in the city so I could attend writing conferences, supporting me in pursuit of my dream, believing in me when I didn't, and lending me his shoes when mine didn't fit. To Jian Chan, for designing my amazing website, original book cover, and bookmarks. Somehow you understood exactly what I wanted and matched it to what I needed. To Jennifer Fusco, for being my marketing Yoda. To Cindi and Amanda Garland, for helping promote the heck out of this book. To Pat Malloy, for patiently fielding all my police-related questions. To Paige Shelton and Jenna Bennett, for being the best mentors I have ever had. I was so blessed to meet you. I don't know how you found the time to give me advice on publishing, read my writing and provide feedback. Paige, your ABNA review is one I'll cherish forever. You believed in me when I doubted myself. That made all the difference in the world. I am so so thankful to have you both in my life.

To my awesome blog buddies, Cat, August, JM, Carrie, Kathryn, Phil, Jenny, Pete, Audrey, Berry, Kelly, Naomi, Laura, EllaDee, Victoria, Emmie, Anne, Winsomebella, and all the wonderful people who comment and read my posts—your words of encouragement gave me the confidence to publish this book. You kept me committed when giving up would have been the easiest thing to do. To everyone who read my ABNA excerpt and commented—THANK YOU! To OL, thanks for reading the original draft and believing in my writing. To BH, for being a great beta reader. To Zacharias, for all the dinners and amazing advice. To the Deer Haven Lodge for making me love Butternut. To Gene and Erik, for believing in me. To Amazon—being a 2012 Amazon Breakthrough Novel Award Semifinalist spurred me on to indie publishing. To all the agents who read the manuscript and gave me feedback—thank you for helping me grow as a writer. And most of all to you, my dearest readers. Thank you for taking a chance on a debut indie author. You have no idea how much it means to me. After years of laboring in solitude with a few beta readers and the occasional conference critique, it is absolutely wonderful to have you reading my words. Thank you!

READER DISCUSSION QUESTIONS

1. Look at the front cover. Compare and contrast the background with the foreground. Explore the symbolism of the colors and shapes of the clouds, the positioning of the couple, and the central image of the farmhouse and trees. How does the cover speak to the concept and themes of the book?

2. What does the author's use of flashbacks say about how we live? Does the past always impact the present? Is the past inescapable? Are all the moments of the future grounded in the past?

3. Given that the "Six Train" is a local subway line in Manhattan and does not run to Wisconsin — what conflicts does the title hint at?

4. The author does not use the characters' first names in the text until Chapter 20. What is her purpose in doing this? How does it contribute to the reading experience? Does it create more intimacy between the characters?

5. What does the enduring relationship between Kai and Oliver reveal about their individual character traits?

6. Why does the idea of having children bring about such different responses from Kai and Oliver?

7. Compare and contrast Oliver and Kai's family situations growing up. How did those experiences impact their interactions with each other?

8. Discuss why Oliver and Kai hold such different beliefs about suicide. Reconcile Kai's view with her inability to let her

grandmother go and Oliver's with the loss of his mother and best friend at a young age.

9. In what ways are Oliver and Kai well-suited for each other? How are they not?

10. What is the worst lie told by a character in the book? Who tells the lie? What makes it worse than any of the other lies told?

11. The book is filled with misunderstandings between the characters. Find three instances where loss seems to lurk in the characters honorable intentions and discuss the importance of this to the cohesiveness of the novel.

Want to have author Kourtney Heintz join your book club
discussion for THE SIX TRAIN TO WISCONSIN?
To learn more, visit
www.kourtneyheintz.com/contact

The Original Short Story Version of THE SIX TRAIN TO WISCONSIN

By

Kourtney Heintz

PART I

She didn't mean to do it, but she was at it again. Like any man, I love my wife; but these 3 AM suicidal thoughts were killing me. Her feelings seeped into my dreams and yanked me awake. Without looking at her side of the bed, I knew she was in the kitchen stirring her tea because the image passed through my head. Christ, she was out of control tonight. Another wave of misery hit me, and I kissed my last chance at sleep goodbye. Tomorrow's presentation was going to be shit. Why? Because my wife was a suicidal telepath.

Lately, it had become my job, nah, my sworn duty, to keep her from going over the edge. I saw our dead dog lying limp in the road. Oh fuck. She was projecting the worst shit. Wonder if old Mrs. Thompson next door felt it. Last time it got this bad, the entire building was depressed for a week. No one realized it was her feelings broadcast over a special bandwidth that fucked with their heads.

She couldn't help it. Hell, I didn't know how she did it. Everyone's thoughts and feelings beating around in her head all day while she kept her own under wraps. She probably didn't even realize she was doing it. I couldn't be mad at her. Annoyed, yes, but not mad.

By the time I padded down the hall to the kitchen, she'd already pulled out another mug and started making my hot chocolate—the one perk of a telepath. Maybe tonight wouldn't be so bad. She still heard my thoughts. Shit, not all of them. Please not all of them.

She looked up, plastering a smile on her tired face. Amusement lurked in her dark blue eyes. "Most of them. And I'm not gonna do that, so stop dreaming about it."

I laughed. She was good at distracting me when I should be worrying about her. I pulled out the stool and sat down. She pushed the warm mug of hot chocolate into my hand and perched on the stool beside me. Her fiery red hair fell over her face as she blew into her teacup.

"Rough night?"

"The usual." Her voice lost its warmth.

"Bad day?"

"Bad life."

Sadness punched through my defenses. The psychic shields she'd taught me to build were useless on nights like this.

"Sorry," she mumbled.

I reached out and she flinched.

"It's easier if you don't touch me," she reminded me.

"I'm already depressed," I said and pulled her into my arms.

She tensed, but I didn't release her. We'd been through this before. Minutes ticked by before she relaxed.

It wasn't easy being in love with a suicidal telepath.

PART II

I bet Jameson over there in his roomy corner cube never worries about his wife killing herself because of a four alarm fire on the news. Shaneeka in front of me is good for a crazy story about her boyfriend, but I bet she never has to hold him while he shakes for hours after a dead body is found in a 10-block radius. Murray's apologizing for another late night out with the guys—poker night my ass. We all know where he goes with that wad of dollar bills. But he'll sends roses, and she'll forgive him again. Then I get to hear about the makeup sex.

Let's not forget my boss, Mr. Gong, the littlest Napoleon on Wall Street. He doesn't chew his nails raw when there's a sick kid in his building. No, he comes out and hands me my ass on a platter, telling me I have to focus and be more ambitious. If only he had my ambition.

It's simple. I want to make it better for my wife. To take away the telepathy. But I can't. Next best thing? I've got a plan. So that new admin needs to stop flirting with me and put her boobs back in her shirt. Hell, buy a goddamned shirt. I don't have time for distractions. This is my wife's life we're talking about here. So the report due tomorrow, I'm not going to write it. I work best under pressure—they'll never know how much.

PART III

It wasn't always like this. In the beginning, she saved me. Eight Novembers ago. Christ, time moved too fast; but that night, it stopped. My life was in the shitter: screwed up a midterm, caught my best friend in bed with my whore of a girlfriend, and my dad died—all in a 24-hour period. It's what pushed me out on the ledge, ready to jump. (Okay, it was a dorm rooftop, but a ledge sounds better.) I looked down at the ground below, figuring the 10-story drop would do me in.

"Not always," said the red haired imp that popped up out of nowhere. I don't scare easily. I wouldn't be here if I did. "What the hell?"

"Who actually." Then she smiled at me with the most perfect...

"Dick sucking lips?" she supplied helpfully.

Shit. How'd she do that?

She rolled her eyes. "What brought you up here?"

"The lip thing, how'd you know?"

"I get it a lot," she tossed back at me.

She was creepy. Hot but creepy.

"Ditto," she replied.

"What?" I asked the total stranger who had trespassed on my private suicide time.

"When they find you on the pavement below, it'll be pretty public."

"Huh?" Somehow the crazy bitch was reading my thoughts. I was so out of here.

Then she smiled—the kind of smile that reached all the way to her eyes—and offered, "Millie and Al's?"

"What?"

She sighed. "I'll tell you how I do it, if you tell me why you're up here. Deal?" She wasn't taking no for an answer.

Might as well go and see what happened. "Coffee?"

"Dinner. And dessert. You're treat. Make that two desserts for saving your ass."

I looked back at the edge of the roof. Maybe she wasn't the lesser of two evils.

"The roof's gonna be here a while. You can always off yourself tomorrow," she threw over her shoulder as she headed toward the stairs.

She had a valid point, so I followed her. Best decision of my life.

PART IV

When the newsfeed hit CNN, I was trapped in a meeting with some prick relationship manager who'd gone all cowboy on us. Maybe the multi-million dollar bonus went to his head, but more likely he'd always had a god complex. He was going to fuck everything up for me, so I let my boss catch him. There was just so much necessary evil you could have in one bank and he put us over the limit.

Three more hours of my life wasted, I sat down in my cube for some email and web surfing—my version of a smoke break. I never made it to Youtube. When Explorer opened up, my eyes automatically scanned the local news for car crashes and suicides—the kind of things that set my wife off. That's when I read about six year old Jenny Montez being choked to death by her father. The article mentioned sexual abuse. Didn't say what. No one says what when a kid's involved. It's too horrific to contemplate.

Where they found the body set off alarm bells in my head. Third Street between Avenue B and C. Six blocks from my apartment. Fuck no. I didn't log out or grab my coat in my rush to get to my wife. One block from the office, the sky opened up, compounding the chaos of rush hour. You'd have thought it was acid rain the way everyone panicked about getting wet. Me, I plunged into the heart of it, jostling pedestrians, dodging cyclists, and darting between cars toward my destination: the 51st Street station and the downtown 6.

The rain had just started, but the subways already had delays. It took seven minutes for the train to show up. I couldn't afford to wait for the next one, so I shoved my way through the throngs of people and into the car. No need to hold on. There was nowhere to fall in the crush of bodies. At Grand Central, I held my own against the mass exodus that threatened to sweep me out onto the platform. By 14th, I was fairly certain I'd impregnated someone's purse. Two more stops to Bleeker.

PART V

I opened the apartment door and was greeted by grief slamming into my gut. I stumbled toward the light switch.

"Don't," she croaked from the corner.

I froze and waited for my eyes to adjust before edging toward the figure huddled in the corner.

"Stop," she pleaded.

I kept inching toward her like I would any wounded animal—without fear or aggression.

She buried her face in her hands, sobbing incoherently.

Why didn't I bring my Blackberry to the meeting? "Sweetie, what happened?"

She shook her head. Tears spilled down her cheeks. She'd smeared her makeup all over her face. She wore slacks and a blouse, which meant she'd gone to work today. Maybe it wasn't the kid I read about.

"Work?"

Another sob tore through her. Christ, she hadn't been this bad in months.

Okay, this was going to hurt. "Can you show me?"

I fell forward onto the carpet as images ripped through my mind. Jenny in my wife's office at Child Protective Services. Jenny's thin file lay on her desk. The interviews where Jenny never spoke a word. But my wife saw it all. Jenny's father liked to hurt her. He made her do things. Things that made her feel bad. He liked to make her scream. He always did it until she screamed.

My wife spent months trying to build a case against him. But there wasn't enough evidence. The original accusation was recanted. Without a witness, there was no crime. But my wife knew. Every time she did a home visit, he played the doting father. But he always thought about what he was going to do to Jenny later. My wife saw it all. And she was absolutely powerless to stop him.

"My fault," she whispered.

"You did everything you could."

"Not enough." Bitterness twisted her beautiful face.

I reached for her and she shrieked.

Right. Touching hurt when she was this far gone. Stupid of me to forget.

"My fault. All my fault." She rocked in place. Shock had set in.

I had to break through her misery, even if it was only for a second. Then she'd know things would get better. There was only one thing left to do. I gathered her into my arms and remembered our wedding day, replaying every detail for her. From Dante's Peak, Badwater Basin stretched out below for miles—straight out of some crazy sci-fi landscape. Except it was sunset in Death Valley, California. We'd tricked her younger sister into coming along, and she stood up for us. She loved being the only member of the wedding party. We had no guests. Well, besides the retired judge I'd corralled into officiating.

My bride wore white. Sort of. If you count my white wife beater. She paired it with jeans. She wrapped the blue-green silk scarf I gave her for her birthday around her neck and threw on her bright blue Nike sneaks. The wind whipped her hair around her face like wildfire. She kept tucking it behind her ears, but it refused to stay there. She'd never looked more beautiful to me.

She sighed in my arms. It was such a tiny sound that I thought I'd imagined it.

I concentrated, mentally reciting every vow she made to me. Her eyes looked right into mine. No trace of fear. No doubt. I had to keep wiping my sweaty palms on my jeans. When it came time to say my vows, the damned wind yanked my paper out of my hands and threw it off the summit. I didn't know how to continue. But she did. She took my hands in hers and smiled like we shared the best secret in the world. I winged it.

She sighed and burrowed deeper into my arms.

I promised to always wash my feet after a long summer day. I promised to not mention any weight gain. Then I got to the serious shit. I would be there every night when she fell asleep and every morning when she awoke. Most importantly, I would be there to catch her every time she fell.

I was going to keep that promise until my dying day.

PART VI

"I know what you're doing," my wife said while clearing the plates.

I got up to wash them, itching to avoid her gaze. "What?" Shit. I already sounded defensive.

"You can't fix me."

"Who's trying?" Think puppy dogs and balloons, not work, not the accounts. No. Focus on clowns and circuses.

She laughed. "Seriously? You're going soft."

Machine guns and *Platoon. Rocky.* Men being men. Blowing shit up.

"Not gonna work," she practically sang the words to me.

If she knew what I did, she'd....

"Think you were a wonderful husband." She left the glasses on the table to wiggle in between the counter and me. I dropped the plate back into the sink. Her lips tasted like cherries.

She looked up at me with her serious face. "Give it back."

"No." I skimmed a little money out of some high net worth accounts. "Trust me, they'll never miss it." I needed it to get her as far away from everyone as I could.

"A farm in Wisconsin? We'll go crazy there," she sputtered.

"We're going crazy here. New York is the worst place for a telepath,"

I shot back. She didn't see what it was doing to her. To us.

"Okay. We move to Wisconsin and what do we do? Shoot anyone that tries to get within two miles of me?"

"Better than losing you." Didn't she get it? I needed her. Fuck fiduciary duty. Fuck everyone.

She smiled. "I need you to be happy and Wisconsin ain't gonna cut it."

"But you can write." And we can live a quiet life together.

"We always promised our life would be remarkable and worth living," she countered, swaying slightly. Good sign.

"Key word: Living. You're barely surviving here."

"I don't want to go," she crossed her arms. Stubborn mode. Uh-oh. Had to keep her talking.

I smiled at her. "You don't have a choice. I always repay my debts."

She lost her balance and clutched at my arm. "What did you do to me?" Her pupils were dilated.

"Tranquilizers. You'll be out for a while." Long enough to get to Wisconsin.

"You're so dead," she promised as she collapsed into my arms.

"But you won't be," I whispered into her hair.

Turn the page for an exciting sneak preview
of the sequel to *The Six Train to Wisconsin*

Highway Thirteen to Manhattan

Available from Amazon and Barnes and Noble

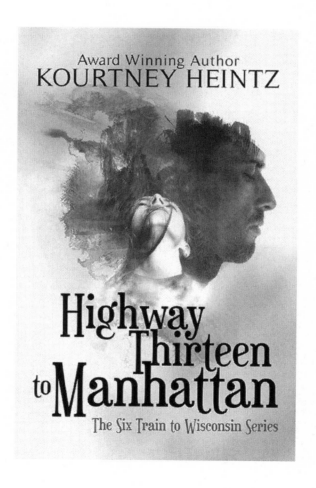

HIGHWAY THIRTEEN TO MANHATTAN

CHAPTER 1

Kai

Like most daughters, I loved my parents, but right now, I wanted them anywhere but here. Hospitals are always hard, but my parents managed to make it harder. My head was already pounding from all the thoughts and emotions coming at me. Not just from the patients and their families and the doctors and the nurses, but also from my mother and father. Instead of shielding their thoughts and trying to make it better for me, they let their emotions crash into me.

My mind wasn't strong enough for all this. Neither was my body. Tubes eviscerated my right hand. A giant bruise blossomed beside the newest IV line. A cast wrapped around my left wrist. My broken pinky finger had been set and taped to my ring finger. The back of my head was held together with stitches. Beneath the blanket, my body was covered in bruises.

I didn't feel any physical pain because of the medications the doctors pumped into me. They said I needed it to recover, but it made my body feel like it wasn't mine. And the steady drip of opiates didn't just steal my physical pain; it left me unable to form the psychic shield I needed to protect myself from the misery swirling around me.

Mom sat in the chair closest to my bed. She wore one of her flowing peasant blouses and faded jeans. Her hair was pulled back in a messy bun, and light brown strands slipped loose to hang around her face. The corners of her hazel eyes were pinched with worry.

Her hand hovered over my arm, unsure where to touch me—if she should touch me. Finally, she laid her hand gently on my thigh. "You just need to rest here for a few more days."

She was wrong. I needed to get out of here. Away from all these thoughts as soon as possible. "I want to go home."

Mom shook her head. "You need to let the doctors help you." *Like they did last time.*

Her thoughts slammed into my brain. She thought hospitalization was the solution to everything.

"Please. Look at what's happened to you. You can't go home until you're better," she said. *I can't lose you. I won't let that happen.*

I didn't know how to reassure her. Yes, I'd almost died, but being here was hurting me more than it was healing me. I swallowed all the words I wanted to say and hoped for Caleb to come back soon. My brother would know how to talk to Mom, how to make her understand.

The doctor came in to check on me and Mom's agonizing fear rose up. *Don't let her have brain damage.*

Dad patted Mom's shoulder. He looked like an older, surfer version of Caleb. Both were tall and muscular with curly blond hair. Dad's hair was a darker blond streaked with platinum from decades in the sun and salt water. His eyes were greener than Caleb's, but like Caleb's, they were rimmed with purple bruises. When Dad smiled, sun lines radiated from his eyes and cut across his cheeks. But I hadn't seen those lines since he'd arrived at my bedside. Instead, waves of exhaustion rolled off him and rippled over me, right before I heard his thoughts.

I can't go through this again, watching you slip away.

My younger sister Naomi lounged in the chair in the corner as far from me as she could get. She had Mom's light brown hair and thin frame and Dad's green eyes and height. She looked nothing like me and only distantly related to Caleb. Her long legs looped over the armrest as she flipped through a magazine. *Thanks for ruining Christmas break. I'd rather be anywhere but here.*

I felt the same way.

At least Oliver was gone for the moment. Mom had convinced him to go home, take a shower, maybe even sleep. I couldn't bear his guilt; it was so thick it choked me.

Oliver. My husband. God. I'd never loved and hated someone so much at the same time. I still couldn't believe he'd called my parents. He knew how bad they were at handling me. How could he have thought that having my family here would be good for me?

Bitterness frosted my thoughts. I was in a hospital, bruised and battered. I'd almost died. That's what Caleb had said. He was the only one willing to tell me the truth. Oliver had said it was bad, but he wouldn't say *how* bad. He couldn't bear to admit what happened to me.

"Who's hungry?" Caleb pulled me out of my thoughts with his question.

He came into my room with a tray of coffee and bagels from a nearby coffee shop. His hair had curled into ringlets. He looked like an angel. Seeing him made everything more bearable. He perched on the side of my bed. As always, he was shielding his thoughts so there would be one less mind invading mine.

I looked up into his eyes. He dropped his shield for a moment, so that his thoughts were clear. *Give them another half hour; then I'll get them to leave.*

He reached over and tucked a lock of red hair behind my ear. I felt a trickle of relief.

I was finally alone and waiting for my brother to return when Oliver appeared in the doorway. His tall frame filled the space. His expression was uncertain, like he was afraid I'd send him away. I hadn't done it yet. I couldn't.

He looked around. "Where's Caleb?"

"He went to get me some ice cream." It was the one thing that tasted right with all the pain medications in my system.

Oliver hesitated. It reminded me of how a vampire waits for an invitation to enter. I would have laughed if it weren't so sad.

"You can come in."

He came over to the bed and sat gingerly beside me. "Kai..." He rubbed his hand over his mouth. "How can I help?"

"I want to go home."

"The doctors want to keep you here a few more days. Just to make sure there are no complications. "

"They don't know what's best for me." How could he agree with the doctors? He knew what hospitals did to me. He was supposed to be on my side.

"As soon as it's safe, I'll bring you home, I promise."

I didn't believe him. He'd keep me here and my parents would encourage it. I'd be stuck inside this hospital room for as long as they could convince the doctors to keep me. My chest tightened. A rush of anger drove away my exhaustion.

"Why did you call my parents? Why did you bring them here?" I demanded.

"They were planning to come for the holidays already. You know that. I had to let them know what happened to you."

"But you could have just told them to reschedule their trip. You could have made up something that would have kept them away. You should have known that they couldn't handle this. They're just making everything worse!"

"I had to tell them. What if…"

You died were the words he couldn't bring himself to say. Saying them would be the same as admitting how close he had brought me to death.

I sighed and let my head rest against the stiff hospital pillow. All my rage dissipated, leaving me exhausted again.

"They don't know what I need, Oliver."

He reached for my hand, touched an IV tube, and dropped his hand back to the bed. "I thought that, after everything you'd been through, you'd want to see them."

"I never want my family to see me like this." It conjured up too many memories of the last time I was broken. They couldn't separate then from now. And I didn't want them having a say in what happened to me because they would try to keep me hospitalized again. Oliver should have known this.

Guilt swarmed me—his guilt. It filled my throat and cut off most of my air. I couldn't escape it. I could barely breathe around it.

His voice was a strained whisper. "I only wanted to make it better."

"I know." And I did. I knew how much he wanted to fix everything he'd broken. I knew he was trying. And it was tearing me apart. Because I wanted him to fix it and I wasn't sure he could.

It was almost 1 a.m. when Caleb fell asleep in the chair by my bed. I couldn't wake him. Not again. He's stayed up with me for too many nights.

I was so tired. I wanted to join him, but I didn't dare. I couldn't take another nightmare. They were twisted versions of what had happened. And they always ended in my death.

Not that staying awake was much easier. Emotions cluttered my room. Fear, pain, anger, hopelessness. These feelings weren't mine. They belonged to other patients. They were overwhelming, but they were just an inkling of what I would face when my own emotions started coming for me. And they always came for me.

The clock on the wall blurred. I was falling asleep. I tried to fight it, but my eyes felt so heavy. I couldn't keep them open.

I slipped into a dream.

I was right back there in that cave again. The smell of pennies and damp earth assaulted my nose. The clammy coldness of being underground clung to my skin. Lukas wasn't there this time. I was all alone. Somehow, that made it worse.

But I wasn't just in the cave. This time, I was locked inside a gilded cage. I could only take six steps in any direction. I was at Nathan's mercy. Again.

My arms were wings, covered in a songbird's feathers.

A shadowy figure circled my cage. I couldn't make out who it was, but I knew. His name filled my mouth. "Nathan."

He reached through the bars and touched my wing. I felt a spark. I jerked away. But it was too late. He'd done something to me. Twisted something inside me. His powers intertwined with mine.

Shadows filled the cave, and I wasn't sure if it was his darkness or mine. The shadows separated and took form. Hundreds of shadow people converged on me, slipping through the bars of my cage and reaching for me. I couldn't escape them. Everything went black.

Then I was on a bicycle, pedaling into the moonless night. Cold air stung my cheeks and pushed against my legs. But I had to get away. I had to escape Oliver's betrayal. Images played inside my mind of my husband kissing Mickey.

Headlights blinded me. A car smashed into my bike. I flew through the air and slammed into the ground. Each breath I took felt like it was pulled through a broken straw. I wheezed and gasped. Suddenly, I was choking on something hot and liquid. Metallic. I tried to cough it up, but

I couldn't. My own blood filled my throat. I knew that my broken bones would never mend because I was dying.

Then I heard Caleb's voice calling to me, "Kai, you're okay. It's just a dream."

The night sky dissolved into daylight. Silver and gold flecks glinted on the tan and black sand. Sun warmed my skin. A gentle breeze tickled my neck. I was at Torrey Pines Beach in San Diego, one of the places where Caleb and I liked to meet in our dreams.

I glanced around, looking for him. Then I saw him moving toward me from the water's horizon. His feet glided over the water.

He was here. I was safe. My heart slowed in my chest. I could breathe again.

As he hugged me, he said, "I'm not sure how long I can keep you here. You need to wake up now."

Caleb's words reverberated in my head and in my hospital room.

My eyes blinked open. I was back in my hospital bed. Caleb was there. Just like when I had awoken from a coma days earlier.

I gasped for air. "Was I screaming?"

He nodded.

"I tried to stay awake."

He brushed the hair off my forehead. "It's okay. I'll do everything I can to get you out of the nightmares when they come for you."

"But you need to rest sometimes."

He gave me a tired smile. "I can survive on a few hours of sleep. You're the one I'm worried about."

"I'm here. I'm okay." Even as I said it, I knew that it wasn't completely true.

Photo by: Brett D. Helgren

ABOUT THE AUTHOR

Kourtney Heintz writes award-winning cross genre fiction that melds paranormal, suspense, and literary into an unforgettable love story. For her characters, love is a journey never a destination. Her debut novel, *The Six Train to Wisconsin* has been on the Amazon Bestseller lists for Psychic Mysteries and Paranormal & Urban Fantasy. She also writes bestselling young adult novels under the pseudonym K.C. Tansley.

She resides in Connecticut with her warrior lapdog, Emerson, and three quirky golden retrievers. Years of working on Wall Street provided the perfect backdrop for her imagination to run amuck at night, imagining a world where out-of-control telepathy and buried secrets collide.

She has given writing workshops and author talks at libraries, wineries, museums, universities, high schools, conventions, non-profit organizations, and writing conferences. She has been featured in the *Republican American*, on WTNH's *CT Style*, and *Everything Internet* on the radio.

You can find out more about Kourtney and her books at: http://kourtneyheintz.com